I0604325

DEMON CORE
2

DEMON CORE

2

D. M. RHODES

AKA RAZZMATAZZ

Podium

All rights reserved. No part of this publication may be reproduced, stored in a retrieval system, or transmitted in any form or by any means electronic, mechanical, photocopying, recording, or otherwise without prior written permission from Podium Publishing.

This is a work of fiction. Names, characters, places, and incidents are either products of the author's imagination or used fictitiously. Any resemblance to actual events, locales, or persons, living, dead, or undead, is entirely coincidental.

Copyright © 2024 by D. M. Rhodes

Cover design by Husa

ISBN: 978-1-0394-4283-2

Published in 2024 by Podium Publishing, ULC
www.podiumaudio.com

DEMON CORE
2

HIDE-AND-SEEK

~ [Grand Crusader Vilheim] ~
Human | ♀ | Crusader
Location: The Demon King's Castle, Floor One
Level: 100

To live to see tomorrow is not relevant.

For those who exist in pure, devoted sacrifice to their faith, the concepts that enamor the minds of the others who live in this world—home, family, creature comforts—they are simply not relevant. It is not relevant whether you have one arm or two, ten fingers or none. Nor is it relevant to count the number of steps one takes during their day, as long as these steps are not taken in pursuit of the heavens.

A sword presses in through the crate that she is inside, piercing her body. But she does not scream and instead continues her prayers.

Pain is not relevant when one lives in the graceful presence of the shadow of the holy world, always present just beyond human perceptions.

Blood leaks out of her body.

Another sword is pressed in through the crate from the outside, cutting through her bicep. Then another, then another; dozens of swords and blades push in through the wood of the crate from all angles and through her body, severing, cutting, and piercing.

Her lips continue to move in prayer.

The pain is not relevant.

All that matters is that her words are heard by her god and that the proof of her faith never stops. For even when she cannot walk, she will still move toward the light of the cherished bounty of divinity.

Anything else is simply not relevant.

Another sword moves in, cutting into her closed eye.

~ [The Demon King] ~

Level Up!
~ [The Demon King] ~
You are now level {83}!

Level: 83 ↗	Experience: 402/657,550
Attribute: DARK	
Soul Points: 178/178 ↗	
Presence: 16.3 km ↗	Obols: 0
Souls Collected: 178,150/1,000,000	

You have {30} free Ability Points to spend!

~ [Dungeon] ~
The Demon King's Castle
Current Number of Floors: 30

Section One - Lust (Floors 1–10)
1: {The Gate to the Underworld} < (RAID {2})
2: {The Precipice of Hope}
3: {The Call of Home}
4: {A Writhing Comfort}
5: {The Mimic Chamber}
6: {The Promise of Power}
7: {The Grasslands with Strange Names}
8: {A Wholesome Promise}
9: {The Lusting Den}
10: {The Pinnacle of Ecstasy}

Section Two - Envy (Floors 11–20)
11: {A Memory That Isn't Mine}
11B: {Safe Room} < (RAID {1})
12: {The Mirroring Pool}
13: {Mystical Mirage}
14: {The Wall of Ink}

15: {A Proof of Heaven}
16: {The Worm's Tail}
17: {The Ocean Challenging River}
18: {Inverse Sunlight}
19: {Total Fragmentation}
20: {The Scale of Souls}

New Area
Section Three - Greed (Floors 21–30)
21: {Empty}
22: {Empty}
23: {Empty}
24: {Empty}
25: {Empty}
26: {Empty}
27: {Empty}
28: {Empty}
29: {Empty}
30: {The Graveyard}
30B: {The Demon King's Throne Room} (💀)(DEMON CORE)
30C: (Demon Quarters)
30D: (Washroom)
30E: (Kitchen)

Estimated Difficulty: EXTREMELY DEADLY	Estimated Intruder Level: 100
Estimated Defender Level: 83	Monster Count: 5,898
Bosses: 4	Traps: 27
Chests: 0	Dungeon Territory: 16.3 km
Rank: SSS	

Swain nods, content with the progress being made regarding the fortifications of the castle. "Excellent work, Byblos," he says, nodding to the spirit cook, who had just successfully completed her task of making the next ten floors. He's sure that she would have rather been cooking, but it's important that everyone lend a hand in this grand project of theirs. After all, they might be artists of a separate nature, but this dungeon, this castle, this is a collaboration between souls of incredible diversity.

The cook bows her head and then vanishes, warping away and returning to her kitchen so that she might continue her own never-ending hunt.

"New intruders have arrived," says Abydos, the painter. "They appear to be much more organized than the last group."

The Demon King turns his head, looking at him. "As expected," replies Swain, his many eyes focusing their vision on the sight of the new wave of human bodies. "They have been coming our way for days now," he explains. "The others so far were just an improvised reaction to us. These are our first real contenders, Abydos," he says, leaning his head down on his massive fist. "I am still a little drained from the assault on the human fortress, but they will need some time to move through the floors."

"My lord," replies Abydos. "Floors one to eleven have already been cleared by the first group." The painter looks at him. "The dungeon can't reset until the first group is fully destroyed. But now it's too late because the new intruders are already here."

"They were," remarks Swain. He shakes his head. "In normal circumstances, you would be right, Abydos," explains the Demon King, looking at his doubtful subject. He turns his head to the side, waiting for a window to appear. "But we find ourselves in anything other than normal circumstances."

A window appears in midair, hovering there on clear display.

~ [Achievement Unlocked] ~
"Fistful of Worms {3}"
Unlocked By: Summoning ten thousand monsters.
Reward: All monsters within the dungeon will RESPAWN within 24 hours of being killed.
(Due to the effects of [The Screaming Harrow], this time further lowered by 75%)

~ [Ruhr, the River Sorceress] ~
Half Elf | ♀ | Sorceress
Rank: SSS
Location: The Demon King's Castle, Floor 11B
Level: 96

"Every second that we wait, hundreds of innocent souls are dying," says Zacarias.

Ruhr, lying upside down on the bed and twirling her hair, looks at him. "Wow, Zeezee, baby, way to kill the mood. That is *so* not my problem," says the river sorceress, looking at the man across the room. "What do you want me to do about it?" she asks. The woman, upside down, points at him. "We're stuck in here until, one, help comes, and two, we get your leg sorted out."

"It's doing better," replies Zacarias, lifting it. "Thank you. The holy water helped a lot."

Ruhr pulls her hand back to her mouth, blowing him a kiss. "Well, you're welcome. Your Ruhr knows how to make all of those aches and pains go away," she says coyly, patting the bed next to her.

Zacarias sighs. "You have no sense of healthy social boundaries, do you?" He shakes his head. "I'll stay here with the holy water," he replies, setting his leg back into the tub. The wound has healed closed, but the area is heavily scarred and bruised, and the bone is still somewhat nicked.

"Healthy?" asks Ruhr incredulously. "Zac, I'm flipping bored out of my skull."

"It's been a day," replies Zacarias, looking at her. "Are you telling me that the world-renowned Ruhr, the river sorceress, can't sit still in a room by herself for one day without getting cabin fever?"

Ruhr shakes her head but smiles, planting a finger on her cheek. "I appreciate that you finally figured out how to properly title me, Zac." She taps her cheek, lifting a leg to kick it up against the wall that the bed is adjacent to. "But I can't even count how many times I almost died this week. Besides, what else are we going to do?"

"We'll sit here quietly, patiently, and wait," says Zacarias.

Ruhr sighs. "I'll get you one day," she remarks, rolling over and planting her face into the sheets. She does think it's probably for the best not to tease Zacarias too much, though. She doesn't know exactly what he lost during the Demon King's ascension. What if he had a wife? It's only been a few days. The man is clearly still in mourning—if he's even begun to do so at all, that is.

"We're friends," replies Zacarias. "As odd as it is for me to say. Let's not ruin that."

Ruhr lifts her head, shocked. Not so much because he said they're friends but because he had just done the unthinkable. "What a load of fiddle-faddle," she says, offended. "Did you really just friendzone me, Zac? I don't think you understand how our market values compare to one another. You can't do that."

"Our what?" asks Zacarias, lifting an eyebrow. "Look, I don't understand you half of the time. I get the nature of our complicated human circumstances here," he explains, shaking his head. "But I just don't believe in having physical relations before marriage. Even at traumatic times like this."

The two of them stare at one another for a time. It's quiet.

And, in a rather sudden escalation, Ruhr purses her lips, tilting her head back before violently stuffing it into the bedsheets and abruptly crying. She doesn't do so because of the rejection but because she's never had someone who just wanted to be her friend for the sake of being her friend before. People have always used her one way or another, so this denial is, in a way, something she is very happy about. It proves that Zacarias is just being nice to her because he's nice and because they're friends, and not because he wants something.

She's never had someone like that around her before.

"Ah, hell, really?" asks Zacarias from across the room. "Why do you cry so much? I thought you were supposed to be some tough, gritty adventurer?"

"Shut up, Zac!" yells Ruhr, her face muffled by the blanket. She wants to tell him to go die outside, preferably while continually fucking himself for making her feel bad about feeling good, but as she lifts her head to tell him to do exactly that—only with a few more flavorful words—the words that come out of her mouth are definitely not the ones she wanted to say. "Then I guess we should just get married then, you frog hopper!" blasts Ruhr, her fists clenched.

The room is as awkwardly silent as it was before, although perhaps a tick more so now as she hears her own words, realizing that this is definitely not what she was planning on saying. Her eyes go wide in terror for a multitude of reasons.

The sound of a horn blowing breaks the silence.

Ruhr immediately jumps out of the bed and runs to the opening crevice, sticking her head out to listen while wiping her face dry. She lifts her gaze, looking up toward the top of the dark pit in great relief as she sees the bright, shining glow come from the top—from floor one—as spells bound out—human spells, holy spells. The others are here. They're saved!

Most importantly, she's saved from what just happened. Seriously, what the hell was that? She must be wigging out because of the constant, never-ending stress and horror.

"Zac!" exclaims Ruhr. "There's a new group on floor one! We're saved! You were right!" she says excitedly, looking behind herself at the man and then back up toward the glowing lights blasting out in all directions with intensity.

Ruhr narrows her eyes. Something is up.

"Those are combat spells," remarks Zacarias, looking out behind her at the light from above.

"Combat . . ." mutters Ruhr. "Zac, we killed everything up there. We cleared that floor. Floor one had those weird ghosts, remember? The ones that tried to get us to eat that poison fruit? There's no need for them to be casting combat spells, unless . . ." Ruhr stops, looking back up at the lights exploding out in a violent cascade, her heart falling into her chest.

Zacarias nods. "Unless the monsters came back. The floors might have reset, too. They'll have to do them with everything restored. From zero."

". . . They can't do that . . ." mutters Ruhr. She spins around, looking at him. "Zac! They can't do that! Monsters can't respawn in a dungeon when someone is inside!" she yells. "That's not how dungeons work!"

Zacarias looks down at her and shakes his head. "Sorry," he says. "I can only guess that they did. Why else would they be fighting up there?"

Her face falls, distraught, and she stares for a while. ". . . You mean it was all for nothing?" asks Ruhr, turning to look back up the pit. "All of that stuff we had to go through, and it was just . . . it didn't mean anything? We didn't even . . . we didn't even clear the way?"

"We have to go back up," explains Zacarias, looking up the shaft together with her.

"No." Ruhr shakes her head. "Zac. No. I am not doing that a second time. I can't."

"You have to," he replies. "If we don't, who knows how many of them will die on their way down? We know floors one to eleven; we can tell them what to look out for."

Ruhr shakes her head, turns around, and grabs the man's breastplate so he looks at her while she makes her point. "Zac. I will literally sit in this room by myself while hundreds of them die if it means I don't have to go through that again." She looks at him. "I don't want to. I won't."

"Then stay here," he says, shrugging. "Use your water spells to get me up to them. I'll guide them down by myself. We'll meet back up here."

Ruhr stares at him. It's a very rational plan, actually. There's nothing reasonable she can say to object to that. If Zacarias goes alone, the newcomers will have a guide who can show them through the first few floors so they don't take any losses, and she can get her wish to stay here and not have to redo everything they have suffered so much to go through.

"Zac . . ." Ruhr's lips quiver as she lets her head fall forward, *thunk*ing against his armor.

"I know," he replies, putting an arm around her and rubbing her back.

Ruhr starts to cry again. "I really hate the Demon King, Zac," she says, hitting his armor with a fist without moving her head. "I hate him *so* much."

"I know," answers Zacarias, dryly. "I think that's fair."

Ruhr has her moment for a while, getting as much out of it as she can while the world above them explodes. Then, after she has time to collect herself, she rubs her face dry and turns around, walking toward the ledge with water channeling around her hands. The river sorceress purses her lips, looking up to floor one.

It's not like she's going to have to do it all from scratch, right? They don't have to go through all of that stuff again because she knows what's coming. They can just power through with no real obstructions. What took them days to do last time will take maybe an afternoon this time around. It won't be so bad, right?

Zacarias hobbles next to her. "Just get me up there to floor one. I'll get them down here to you. I promise."

Ruhr swipes a strand of blue hair out of her face with her shoulder. "*Please*, Zac," she says. "As if I trust you alone in a chamber full of succubi. You clearly need a chaperone."

She lifts her hands, water surging out of her palms to form a great azure dragon which coils itself around and around at the ledge with an upward streaming torrent.

"Listen," starts Zacarias, placing a hand on her shoulder. "About what you said."

"Huh?" She looks at him in confusion, realizing after a tense second what he means.

Zacarias places a foot on the tidal serpent. "We'll forget it ever happened. This is all very frightening, I know. You're just confused. You don't have a clear head," he says, nodding to her and then stepping onto the surging riptide in the shape of a dragon. The water carries him off, shooting him up toward the upper floor in an instant.

Ruhr blinks, staring after him as he goes, her mind processing.

"*What?!* As if I meant it, jerkwad!" she yells after him, jumping into the water and shooting up toward floor one after Zacarias.

~ [The Demon King] ~

"We're stuck," says Cartouche, looking up at him as he sits on his throne. She explains the situation.

The carriage has been constrained and locked in place by the assailants, who have not only killed all of the undead outside but have also physically blocked the carriage from moving any further.

It is a problem.

These newcomers are indeed more resourceful than the first group, perhaps also because their sense of haste has been dampened. After all, it has been a few days now.

Swain sits there, thinking. How annoying.

While he is grateful that they would deliver themselves to him so that their souls might become a drop of ink in the well used to write his great masterpiece, it is quite a burden for them to be hindering the carriage from progressing like this.

Life and art are about progress. To be stuck in one place in either subject is to wither away and die. Life, the short treasure that it is, requires constant motion in order for it to be full of the rich, vibrant experiences that will allow one to create something beautiful to begin with. If one stays in one place for too long, be it a physical or mental place, the refreshing breeze of experience will slowly stop reaching one's face, starkly limiting the well of ideas.

As such, so too is art capable of being limited if one exists in a state too dense and too confined to be able to stretch out the feelers of the soul to try and carefully touch the surrounding nourishment. Like a flower with its roots unable to move because of dirt that is too tightly compacted, it will wither away without the ability to extend itself outward.

Swain sighs, leaning back against his throne, his fist clenching itself shut in annoyance.

Stuck.

He feels like he was stuck for a long time, wasn't he? Back in his old life. The Demon King narrows his eyes, thinking. He was stuck in a place he hated, surrounded by people he hated. He was there, in there, in that quagmire, for so long . . . why?

Why did he resign himself to exist in that place if he has such clear memories of hating it?

The sound of a laughing child disrupts his thoughts as a very real ghost, a girl with a sheet over her, flies across the ceiling, chasing souls around the air. Swain tilts his head, watching her as she laughs while having the time of her life, a squishy, blood-soaked doll in her hand as her other tries to catch the tails of the many wisplike presences around her.

Ah.

That's right.

He stayed in that place, in that home he hated, because of her . . . The creature, the woman with no name. She, too, is like a ghost, dancing forever on the edge of his heart and mind.

There's no need to be upset.

Sometimes, an unfortunate circumstance or a little pressure from the outside is just what one needs to really unfold, both in one's life and in art. He doesn't have enough soul points left to do anything meaningful after summoning the creature inside the human fortress, but that doesn't mean he's out of the game just yet. He just needs to adapt a little more. He needs to become less rigid if he wants to thrive. So far, he has always been proactive in his efforts.

But maybe he can afford to just wait a little.

Not too long, but a little.

Perhaps, with some time, fresh insights will come his way. Muse is a fickle thing which may often not bestow its favor on one for seemingly no reason at all. The only thing to do is to wait and try again tomorrow with a clear mind.

"Kirsch," says Swain. The girl flying in the air stops and looks his way. "Would you like to play a game?" asks the Demon King.

"A game?!" yells Kirsch excitedly, flying down and toward him in an instant, the sheet draped over her fluttering, magical blood dripping down to the stones. "Nobody ever wanted to play games with me!"

Swain nods.

A game seems like just what is needed.

He looks down at Cartouche. "Cartouche. Get the other two," orders Swain, rising from his throne. "We're going to play hide-and-seek," commands the terrible Demon King.

"Yay!" cheers the ghost, flying around him in a circle as he steps down from his throne.

Outside, from the graveyard, comes the sound of cracking bones as unfortunate souls fall down the pit to their deaths, having fallen for one of the easier traps in the dungeon.

~ [High King Mercator] ~
Half Elf | ♂ | King
Location: The Capital City in the Distant North
Level: 100

"The grand crusade has arrived, my lord," says a scryer. "The Demon King has been locked in place for now."

High King Mercator sighs, rubbing the bridge of his nose as he looks back at the map with eyes that have yet to find any sleep at all. The small carriage on the map with the ring around it sits just outside of the leading magical research facility, with which they've lost contact. His food and drink are brought here to him, but he hardly partakes. "What about the Vildt armada?" he asks, looking at his military advisor.

"Reports indicate success," says the man. "A large chunk of their ships have sunk."

"It looked like an accident?" he asks.

The man runs his fingers through his beard, nodding back. "It did."

"Good," says King Mercator. "The last thing we need after this is a war. And the Vildt ambassador?"

The advisor shakes his head. "There was an unfortunate accident. He was on his balcony when it gave way because of the storm."

"Tragic," speaks the king, shaking his head. "But this is the world we live in." He points at the map. "Continue the evacuations; move everyone in every city along the way to the north," he orders. The king taps the map. "Execute every person who declines or is too infirm to leave immediately. Better we take their souls than the Demon King."

"Yes, my lord," replies the advisor, nodding to one of his own men, who runs off to pass the orders along the chain of command.

The king stares down at the map, watching the figurine of the carriage.

He knows that it won't move by itself, as it is always pushed along by the court artist while tracking the Demon King's position.

But as he stares at the carnival on the map with tired, weary eyes, he can't help but feel like it will just . . . scoot forward by itself any second now.

~ [The Demon King] ~

Swain stomps around his castle, the horrific Demon King's ten thousand eyes staring in all directions as he takes heavy strides through the darkness, the shadows of total lightlessness receding in his wake as if they themselves were terrified of his presence.

He marches through the demon quarters, a new part of the castle that he himself has never seen before. It is a long corridor next to the throne room with a series of doors. As per the rules of the game, the private rooms are out of bounds, as are any active floors the enemy is on.

The Demon King turns his head, looking at the rows and rows of paintings that line the hallway.

Since it was his idea to play this game of theirs, it was his responsibility to be *it*. Heavy lies the crown of responsibility upon the king's head.

This game is familiar.

He used to play it with her. He remembers. When he was a boy and she was a girl, they would chase each other in the park like a pair of stalkers in a spiral, one always looking for the other.

Swain stops, looking at one of the paintings, inside of which is a familiar person.

He'd think that the man had painted himself, but as he looks at the painting, the man in it turns to look back at him, betraying his liveliness.

Swain lifts a hand, pressing a massive, sharp finger against the canvas.

"Found you," he says. "Abydos."

Abydos turns his head. "Maybe it was too obvious," he remarks, getting up and climbing out of the painting.

~ [Zacarias] ~
Human | ♂ | Royal Guardsman
Location: The Demon King's Castle, Floor One
Level: 91

"That's the situation," finishes Zacarias, having explained the developments so far to the raid leader.

He turns his head, looking at Ruhr, who, because of her perceived divine favor and given her rare Purity specialization, seems to have fallen into favor with the many faces around them, and she seems to be intent on making full use of that to help her *brand*, whatever that means. Everything from before seems to have been completely erased from the world as she returns to being the person she always was.

Or maybe that's just who she is in public.

Zacarias looks back at the crusader.

"Thank you, Brother Zacarias," replies the crusader. "Your fight was not in vain," he says, nodding. "We will quench the fires of the Demon King, drowning him in our faith."

Zacarias shakes his head. "You don't understand. This place isn't some normal dungeon," he remarks, leaning in toward the man. His harrowed eyes are wide and clearly filled with honesty about what he has to say. "This place?" he asks, gesturing around them. "It's hell."

~ [The Demon King] ~

Maybe there really is something to this game idea.

The terrible Demon King stands in his throne room, looking around the area with his many eyes as he walks past the hundreds of statues, all of them locked once more into place, the last waltz having come to an end.

Hundreds of faces sit all around him, contorted in incredible horror, the air above him full of souls that he has yet to consume. He finds that he quite likes the look of them simply drifting around the throne room. Like fireflies in a romantic night, they are quaintly inspiring to observe.

He walks on, his footsteps thundering through the chamber as he goes.

The one statue near the front row, with a living eye that Abydos once painted, looks across the room.

He turns his head, following its gaze, to look at a statue that has one shadow too many behind it.

The Demon King turns, striding through the mess of sculptures, looking at the petite woman, who does her best to always hide behind the statue, adjusting her position to match his viewing angle.

"Found you," says the Demon King, reaching around to grab her. "Cartouche."

"Aw, dang." Cartouche leans out from behind the statue. "I thought this was a good spot," she says, sighing.

"It was," replies Swain, patting her on the shoulder as she walks over to the throne, where Abydos already is.

The Demon King looks around the area, making sure nobody else is here. He can't let anyone who is still hiding get to them, or they'll get to go free again.

~ [Zacarias] ~
Human | ♂ | Royal Guardsman
Location: The Demon King's Castle, Floor Two
Level: 91

Men walk in horror among the piles of corpses. Dozens of bodies from the first assault lie stacked up on all sides of the structure, having killed each other because of disputes over toys and things of little meaning. Blood still soaks the floor, the wet being stamped into the wood of the house they move through as thousands of boots march down the hallway. The odd hand or leg that is in the way is crushed into a paste by the continued stomping of hundreds of feet as they move onward.

Thankfully, there are no monsters on these earlier floors, and it looks like the challenges haven't reset.

A small reward for their efforts.

He nudges Ruhr with his elbow. She looks at him and nods with a pursed, weak smile.

That's something, right?

Among all of the untold horrors and nightmarish terrors of this world, that, at least, is something.

~ [The Demon King] ~

Two down, two to go.

The Demon King looks around the graveyard, which is filled to the brim with corpses. New bodies have just fallen from above, wetting the ground as if they were fresh raindrops, and the Corpse Collector, eager in its work, brings more and more by the minute. The number of imps and shadow people is exploding, and he can feel the creatures swarming across the landscape within his territory.

Hundreds of them, roaming in packs, hunt down and mutilate any survivors of the demon sickness.

He lifts a massive hand, grabbing the top of the labyrinth wall, and then pulls himself up to look around the graveyard. The wall cracks, crumbling halfway beneath his weight. Within the walls of the labyrinth are thousands and thousands of fresh graves.

The otherworldly Demon King looks around, intent on finding the last two—or die trying.

~ [Zacarias] ~
Human | ♂ | Royal Guardsman
Location: The Demon King's Castle, Floor Seven
Level: 91

"It's down below the ground," explains Zacarias, pointing at the floor. "We have to blast our way through with magic." As soon as he says so, a few casters move to the front of the line and begin blasting away the grass with a barrage of spells, cutting through thousands of squirming bodies beneath the ground. "And don't give any money to the wishing well on the next floor," he explains.

The message is repeated, passed on from crusader to crusader, and makes its way down the line of fighters.

Zacarias looks to the side at the large crate they're carrying. Red, thick blood leaks out of the wood, dripping to the ground.

But he decides it's best not to ask.

~ [The Demon King] ~

Swain stares down at a freshly dug grave and then back up at the gravestone, reading it.

It's a recipe for what looks like a stew.

The Demon King reaches down, a hand digging into the ground as he grabs hold of a leg and tears the creature out of the soil.

"I found you, Byblos," says the Demon King, looking at the cook.

"I couldn't help myself," she explains, sighing as she hangs upside down in his grasp. Her apron flops down over her face.

~ [Zacarias] ~
Human | ♂ | Royal Guardsman
Location: The Demon King's Castle, Floor Eight
Level: 91

"I'm gonna be strong, Zac," says Ruhr, reaffirming her statement. "No matter how badly some demon tries to jump my bones, I'm not going to give in."

He looks at her. "Are you just trying to look cool in front of the crusaders?" he asks. "Because that's not what I expect to happen in a second," explains the man, looking at the door to floor nine—the succubus floor. Everyone has been warned about what is to come. Even if the floor challenges haven't been reset, the few sparse monsters involved in the first ten floors certainly have, and that will include the succubi and incubi too.

She grabs hold of his arm with both arms, wrapping them around him tightly as if she were about to fall off the edge of the world. "Don't you dare let me look bad in front of this many people, Zac."

He nods, stepping forward into the door, the heavy smell of perfume and what can only be described as bodily musk filling the air. Zacarias squeezes his arm in a little, trapping her hands against his side. "I wouldn't."

~ [Manfred Wurzelstam] ~
Human | ♂ | Farmer
Location: A Farm, Some Fifteen Kilometers Away
Level: 70

The man howls with incredible animal terror, blocking the door with his body as he looks around the small farmhouse. Clawed, hungry hands strike against it, trying to break it down so they can enter the room that smells of cooked meat.

The bodies of his wife and children lie strewn around the small room; their skin is bubbled and blistered, and their eyes are cooked out of their sockets. Steaming blood, fecal matter, and viscera coat the floor, spanning across from the small collection of beds all the way to the only table in the single-room household.

The windows next to him break, with dozens of rotting, undead hands pressing through the glass and reaching for him.

His screaming never stops as he inhales the vapors of his family's corpses lying before him.

~ [The Demon King] ~

Now, where could she be?

The monstrous Demon King looks around the area. He had logically worked his way through the quarters, the throne room, and then the graveyard. He's found everybody except for Kirsch.

The entity looks behind itself. It's imperative that she doesn't slip past him and reach the throne. If she does, the others will be free again, and he'll have to start all over.

But where is there left to look?

He lifts his gaze up the shaft. The girl can fly, so she could technically be anywhere. However, given her age and the fact that she is very new to his group of interesting souls, he doubts she would stretch her comfort zone so far. In all likelihood, she is hiding somewhere very close to the throne room.

The Demon King climbs back up onto the wall of the labyrinth, scouring the area like a hungry predator, his thousands of eyes darting this way and that way in an effort to find a hint of where she might be.

But Kirsch is nowhere to be seen.

He thinks, lowering his head as he tries to get into her head.

Where would a young girl hide? Where would a young girl who was entirely sheltered from the outside world hide? He would guess in her room, under her blanket, but the rooms are off-limits.

Wait . . .

No . . .

No.

The Demon King lifts his head, staring back down the corridor toward the throne room.

No!

In rage at himself, he jumps off the wall, the stones beneath his massive presence cracking as he lands, a minor quake spreading through the world.

He's made a horrific miscalculation; one most unbefitting of his noble title.

The Demon King runs back toward the throne room, realizing his mistake.

Where would a girl her age hide?

Why, under her blanket, of course.

A blanket that can make her invisible.

~ [Zacarias] ~
Human | ♂ | Royal Guardsman
Location: The Demon King's Castle, Floor Ten
Level: 91

Ruhr ugly cries, still glued to his arm.

"It's going to be okay." Zacarias rubs her back as they walk, being the first to leave floor nine and enter the boss arena on floor ten.

"It's never going to be okay, Zac!" howls Ruhr.

"We're out now," says Zacarias. "The spell is over. Take a second. Breathe," he instructs, turning to her. "Breathe. The crusaders are going to be here soon. You don't want them to see you like this, do you?"

"*N-no . . .*" relents Ruhr, wiping off her face.

Zacarias nods. He's not sure if he's ever seen a more emotionally unstable person in his life, honestly. Ruhr the river sorceress is entirely deranged when she's out of the public eye. She clearly has a lot to work through to get to a healthy place. "This will just be another one of our secrets," he remarks. "Don't worry. Like I said, you're all mixed up. I get it." He nods his head upward. "After this is all over and you've been back in the sunlight for a week, you won't think twice about me."

Ruhr looks at him, letting go of his arm for the first time since they entered floor nine. "*Shut up*, Zac," she says, pushing him away and walking on ahead by herself. "I'm forgetting about you as we speak."

He shrugs, having expected as much. Those are big words for someone who, under the influence of succubi magic, just said she wouldn't mind if he took what she said before seriously. But she's the clingiest person he's ever met. A drop of normal politeness and social affirmation, and she's wrapped around him like a slime around a rabbit.

He shakes his head.

The world can really be cruel to people sometimes, if it makes them like this, can't it?

~ [The Demon King] ~

He returns to the throne room, knowing as he enters that the game is over.

He's lost.

The Demon King's many eyes stare at the throne, on top of which sits a small ghost kicking her legs.

Kirsch lifts her hand and waves.

He can't even be mad, honestly. It would seem that Kirsch, using her knack for being unseen while hiding under her blanket, was simply hiding in plain sight all along.

The great and terrible Demon King has been beaten, and, as odd as it sounds and as out of place as it might be, he can't help but laugh.

He doesn't think he's ever laughed before in this life.

Not only because of the absurdity of the situation but also because of the thing that he notices as he looks at the throne, surrounded by four people. He notices that he's had some fun.

And this fun, this strange spark of life that should, under normal circumstances, be entirely alien to the concept of the creature that is the Demon King, sparks an idea in him. One that is so absurdly and profoundly simple that it is almost antithetical to the reputation he has established for himself thus far.

The carriage that contains the Demon King's castle is stuck, unable to move forward because of the crusaders stationed on the exterior keeping it locked in place. He is unable to summon a monster because of his lack of soul points, and he is unable to teleport to the top of the dungeon to handle it himself because of the intruders blocking the path upward. By all accounts, the Demon King is locked in place, unable to make a single move.

He claps his massive hands together, striding toward the throne on which a small ghost sits.

"Well done, Kirsch," praises the Demon King. "You've won," he says, and the girl giggles, kicking her legs excitedly. She seems to be having a lot of fun, despite the fact that she was presumably sitting here watching him the entire time.

That sound, that chime of her giggling voice, rings throughout the throne room, and he finds that none of this was a waste. It is a sound which is full of beauty. It is not the beauty of a created work, piece, or experience. Rather, it is the beauty of the voice of a soul coming to fruition, like a flower that has never bloomed in a spring before this one. The girl has likely never had much fun before, and so in the act of her finding this moment of joy now, the Demon King realizes that this, too, has been in the pursuit of beauty.

Sometimes, it's just that abstract, isn't it?

Just like life is sometimes so simple, if one knows how to rid oneself of the filters applied over one's own perception which guide one to complexity and the rigidity of old patterns.

"Kirsch, will you help me?" asks the Demon King, looking at the little ghost on the throne, who tilts her head. Blood leaks down from it as he approaches, and she gets up, letting him have his spot back. "As a friend."

The girl, having never heard anything like this before, obviously has no choice but to say yes.

~ [Crusader Maladina] ~
Dwarf | ♀ | Paladin
Location: The Demon Carnival
Level: 95

Maladina stands watch, as do several dozen others who have been tasked with guarding the entrance of the Demon King's castle and making sure that the carnival doesn't move from here.

Something tugs on her leg.

She looks down, staring at the little doll that looks back up her way.

The woman's screams are muffled by a blanket before she hits the ground.

~ [The Demon King] ~

Swain sits back down on a throne covered in magical blood as he leans back and observes the happenings of the world above the castle through his many eyes. Kirsch is doing a great job, playing the same game that she played back in the human fortress, where he found her.

The Demon King leans his head down onto his massive fist.

It doesn't matter if he can't get past the many intruders, or if he's out of soul points.

After all, he has a friend who can fly straight up the shaft and out the entrance.

He scoffs at himself, watching as the last guardsman falls down, covered in a fabric cocoon from head to toe and melting inside its confines, while Kirsch, doing exactly as she had been asked, flies to the front of the carriage and whips the reins.

The dead undead anqa—its bones crushed and pulverized, its body broken and lying in a heap down on the road—rattles and shakes as it pulls itself together. Piece by piece, the bird rises back up to its feet as shards of bone and old, dry feathers come back together to form a whole entity.

Kirsch whips the reins, and the Demon King's carriage begins to move again as the anqas rear up, screeching, before running on forward down the road. Several bags filled with bodies are tied to the back of the cart.

It's good to have friends.

The Demon King's many maws smile.

It's *beautiful*, even.

~ [High King Mercator] ~
Half Elf | ♂ | King
Location: The Capital City in the Distant North
Level: 100

"My lord, the carriage is on the move again," says the scryer.

Mercator watches as the artist adjusts the little piece which had been sitting peacefully still for a time now, dashing his faint hopes of maybe actually finding some sleep tonight after all.

The exhausted king lifts his head, looking around the room.

For a moment, he's sure he sees some shadowy figure standing in the back corner of the chamber.

But after he blinks and rubs his eyes, the apparition is gone, and he simply attributes it to sheer exhaustion.

~ [Zacarias] ~
Human | ♂ | Royal Guardsman
Location: The Demon King's Castle, Floor 11B
Level: 91

"Home sweet home," says Zacarias, looking back at the safe room where the two of them had been holed up before.

Ruhr looks at him and then at the hole in the wall. "See?" she asks. "I told you we'd make it back just fine."

Zacarias blinks, looking at her. "Excuse me?" he asks. "The way I remember, it was different."

Ruhr waves him off, shaking her head and making a sad face. She turns to look at one of the crusaders. "He's traumatized, you know? It was a rough way down for him. Going twice almost broke him."

The crusader nods.

"...*Really?*" asks Zacarias.

Ruhr nudges him, winking. "Come on, Z-bee boy," says Ruhr, smiling at him. "Floor twelve and the Demon King are waiting for us." She looks at the safe room. "Unless you want to stay here?"

Zacarias rolls his eyes and marches onward as the assault on the Demon King's castle continues, now deeper than ever before with fresh bodies and spirits.

CHAPTER 2

THE QUESTIONABLE HAPPENINGS PRESENT WITHIN THE DEMON KING'S CASTLE

~ [Crusader Manilpin] ~
Dark Elf | ♂ | Grand Crusader
Location: The Demon King's Castle, Floor Twelve
Level: 86

D on't look down!" calls a voice from up ahead, the command being passed down the line of crusaders from front to back.

Following the directive, Manilpin keeps a steady gaze as they walk, marching through the Demon King's castle. He wrings out his wet hair with one hand, balancing the flat, wide thing he is holding above his head with the other for a moment. Floors one to eleven, while disturbing in many ways, posed little challenge to the assault, given the presence of the divinely chosen river sorceress to lead their way. However, from here on out, they've returned to the metaphorical wildlands, with nothing but their faith and spirits to guide them, as well as the warm vapors of their breaths which leak out of their mouths.

Despite the incredible heat present within the rest of the castle, floor twelve is cold. It's bearable without real winter gear for a time, but he wouldn't want to stay here for a long time.

He walks, his hand resting on his belt with his thumb looped through it as he walks, looking around everywhere but down.

Floor twelve of the Demon King's castle is, from what he can see, a strange place. It's a cold, cavernous thing. There seems to be icy water present all around them, and they're walking on some sort of bridge that he isn't able to examine, as it would be breaking orders.

So instead, he simply walks onward.

He has always been a man of faith, but if anyone had told him weeks ago that this is where he'd be, he'd wonder if they weren't pulling his leg.

Life can change so fast, can't it?

A person often finds themselves moving from one phase to the next, and often, when living in this newest phase, those old days are nothing but vague memories that feel like they belong to some other person.

~ [Byblos] ~
Gallu | ♀ | Spirit Cook
Location: The Demon King's Castle, Kitchen
Level: 85

Byblos stands in the kitchen, holding a soul by its tail. The squiggly, wormy thing flops around like a fish trying to escape her grasp, a face pressing itself through the exterior body of the incorporeal entity like a head trying to push through a pillowcase.

She sniffs it and then holds it down against the counter with one hand, fingers spread wide along its body to keep it in place as she reaches over with her other hand and takes a sharp, black knife. She runs it along the length of the soul from top to bottom, cutting it open like a fish she intends to gut.

It rips open like an overstuffed plush, the edge of its head and tail flailing around beneath her grasp as she sets the knife down and reaches inside of it, grabbing a fistful of its core and tearing it out, placing the contents into a bowl.

Cooking with souls is still a very experimental process. She's still in the process of figuring out which pieces are good and which aren't. Can you eat the skin? Or do you eat the insides? Is all of the interior the same, or are there different sections like there would be different cuts of meat on a swine? How does the "meat" of a soul react to heat? To water? How does it react to salting and smoking?

It's still all a great mystery, and it's fantastic that she can just experiment to her heart's content.

She runs the knife over the top of the soul again, slicing off some of its skin as it flops around in her grasp, cutting off a sliver of its soft, blueish-white mass which she drops into her mouth as if she had peeled a piece of flesh off a juicy red apple.

Curiously, she moves it around in her mouth, slowly sliding her tongue around it to try and catch the many different flavors it gives off. The cook works her teeth, chewing very tenderly, to try and get a feel for the density, texture, and mouthfeel of a raw soul. It's warm, sweet. Interestingly, she can feel the same warmth coming from the writhing, squishy thing she is holding beneath her fingers. It's wiggling and pressing against her at the same time as she chews, and she isn't sure if it's responding to her active eating of its body right now, or if it's just trying to escape in general.

Byblos takes the knife, holding the cut-open soul steady, before then chopping down with a firm, strong motion that takes off the fattest, bulbous part of the entity, which she presumes to be the head of the thing.

Interested, she watches as it finally stops moving, now that it has been cut apart.

Fascinatingly enough, the piece of it she has in her mouth changes, crumbling into dust as the soul in her hands dies at the same time. The interior bits that she had set aside just before also crumble away.

Making a disgusted face, Byblos grabs a kitchen towel and holds it against her mouth as she spits out the piece of wet soul into it, looking at the sticky, goopy mess it has become for a moment before discarding the whole thing.

It seems that souls need to be eaten fresh; as fresh as can be. Ideally, they need to be alive for at least the entire process of eating so the meat doesn't spoil in one's mouth.

Very interesting.

She reaches up into the air, grabbing hold of another one, catching it by its tail, and then lowers the whole soul down toward herself, craning her neck back as she moves the squirming, off-white thing down toward her open mouth and extended, spit-covered tongue.

"Byblos?" asks a voice from the side. Byblos looks out the side of her eyes then turns her head as she stares at Cartouche, the dancer.

"He wants to see you," says the dancer.

Byblos nods and lets go of the soul, letting it fly back to the rest of them, darting around the room in a swarm like a panicked school of fish trapped in a basin with nowhere to go.

She'll continue her experiments later.

~ [The Demon King] ~

The Demon King sits upon his throne, leaning back and waiting. A scorched, wilted red flower is in his gigantic hand, brought to him by a spirit at his request. The human onslaught continues against his castle, pressing against him like the waves of the ocean constantly crashing against the shore. While the initial group of encroachers was easily defeated, these newcomers are far more coordinated and are led by the last two survivors of the first party.

This latter problem may be due to his own generosity, but it does not change the fact that it is going to make his life more difficult. But that is the game to be played in life. A raw pragmatic would have simply disposed of them and been done with it, but his heart aches for the soul of the first person who would dare to curse him with such a burdensome title. No. Comedy and tragedy are a duo; they intermingle, weaving in and out of one another like star-crossed lovers.

The heart of the horrific Demon King is that of a romantic who is illogical and full of childish poesy.

Byblos appears before him and kneels down before the throne. Swain lowers his gaze, his dozens of eyes looking at the demon.

"Byblos," calls the Demon King. "Tell me," starts Swain. "I have need of your expertise," says the entity, lifting a massive hand inside of which is held the crumpled flower. "What is it that causes a thing to be nothing like we once remembered it being?" He looks at the dead petals that he holds. "The tastes of youth, the smells of springs past . . . I find that, in my attempts to replicate them, I am always a step further away than I was prior." The Demon King's eyes shift, all of them looking at the flower. He knows this sort. It is the kind she always smelled like.

Byblos lifts her gaze, looking at the flower and then at him. "Tastes change as we get older," explains the cook. "Children enjoy sweet things," she says. "As a person grows, their palate adapts, and they often find stronger affinities toward bitterness."

Swain's many eyes turn toward her. "But why?" he asks. "What happens to make us change like this?" The Demon King closes his fingers, crushing the flower with a strong grip. Smoke drifts out the gaps between his fingers.

"Sweetness is sickening after a while," says Byblos. "Young or old, it will inevitably lead to a sense of revulsion in some form."

She rises to her feet and holds out a hand. Swain looks at her before lifting his fist, letting the ashy powder from the blossom fall down into her cupped palm. The demon takes her other hand, sticks her thumb fully into her mouth, and then presses the wet digit into the heap of powder in her open palm, clumping it all together into a flat ball of flower ash and spittle. Byblos presses the lump flat into a disc and then holds it in the hot, quivering air that fills the core chamber, allowing it to bake on her skin.

"So, as we age, in our hunt for stimulation, we find ourselves chasing curious tastes that, in our younger years, we would have found . . ." She looks at him. A smell of blackened rose and char fills the air around him, painting the air with a smell which causes his many eyes to go wide and the dance of souls up in the superheated air to slow, all of them moving toward the source that she holds—a token which somehow captures not the memory of that old spring but rather the true feeling that he, now, in this moment, holds of it. "Questionable."

A mouth opens on the side of his body, and she moves her hand forward past the many rows of teeth to place it inside, pulling her hand back out as it starts to seal around her. The demon looks up, toward his many eyes.

Questionable indeed.

~ [Ruhr, the River Sorceress] ~
Half Elf | ♀ | Sorceress
Rank: SSS
Location: The Demon King's Castle, Floor Twelve
Level: 96

Ruhr walks onward, leading the charge next to Zacarias. This is all really strange for her. She's never felt as open to anyone as she has to him. But then again, being a second away from death for a straight week on end will do that to you. One's life clock seems to tick much faster than usual when the striking of the hands sounds like a set of gnashing teeth closing with every passing second.

Putting all that to the side for a moment, however, Ruhr can't help but notice something weird about herself.

"Fiddle-whacker," mutters Ruhr beneath her breath, staring absolutely straight-ahead as she walks. Looking down or up on this floor is a very

bad idea. She learned as much from the first man who fell into the water. "Foofoo-fluffer," says the half elf.

"You good?" asks Zacarias.

Ruhr looks at him from the corners of her eyes. "Biddle-bopper."

Zacarias doesn't turn his head, but she can see him lift an eyebrow. "Pardon?"

"Something's wrong with me, Zac," says Ruhr. "It sounds dumb but . . . I can't, you know."

"No, what?" he asks.

"I can't swear anymore," replies Ruhr. "Kitty-clapper."

"Cute," says Zacarias, shrugging and getting elbowed in his side for his efforts, which doesn't actually bother him at all given how he's wearing armor. But it's really about the message. "Wait. Really?"

"Really, Zac," admits Ruhr. "I swear, I'm not messing with you. I want to say f—" Ruhr bites her tongue. "Fff—" She winces. "Fanny-flicker." Zacarias grunts, holding down a chuckle. "But I can't get myself to say it."

He shakes his head. "I've seen something like this before."

"You have?"

"Sure," explains Zacarias. "Trauma can do really strange things to the body. It's almost like magic." Ruhr nods, listening. "I was with a troop of soldiers once to help them clear out a goblin camp," says the guardsman. "Things went south for a bit, and one of them had a really, really bad time. After we finished and got out, that guy would literally scream if you wore green clothes around him." He shakes his head. "Even a year later, the last time I saw him. He got it a bit under control, but you could see him start shaking, like he was freezing to death." He taps his head. "Think about all of the swearing you've done here already. Your body probably shut it down."

"You think?" asks Ruhr. That does make sense. While she is hardly a person who would admit to being traumatized, as it would be devastating for her brand, it's certainly a good explanation.

"I'm sure," replies Zacarias. "When this is all over and you've been back in the fresh air for a few weeks, I won't be able to tell you apart from a sailor."

Ruhr sighs in relief, staring straight-ahead, the reflecting water all around her shimmering.

Something behind them splashes as somebody falls in.

"Eyes forward!" barks Zacarias. "Keep moving," he says, giving the order to leave whoever fell into the water.

They can't be saved. It's already over for them.

She's glad he's here. She won't say it, of course. It'll go to his head, and the gods know that Zacarias's ego is big enough, that pompous slime-smoocher, but she really is.

~ [Crusader Manilpin] ~
Dark Elf | ♂ | Grand Crusader
Location: The Demon King's Castle, Floor Twelve
Level: 86

Manilpin walks with his hands above his head.

How long is this weird floor going to go on for?

It feels like they've been walking for hours now, which, sure, is fair enough. The Demon King's castle is probably a big place, but shouldn't they have been at least in the next room by now?

The dark elf rolls his shoulders, holding the thing above his head as he walks.

"Eyes forward!" comes the call from the front of the line, echoing its way down as everyone repeats it, passing the message on down the formation.

"Eyes forward," repeats Manilpin. But he notices something off about his voice. The man clears his throat, repeating the message, blinking in confusion. It's odd. His voice sounds . . . muffled? He clears his throat, trying again.

~ [Ruhr, the River Sorceress] ~
Half Elf | ♀ | Sorceress
Rank: SSS
Location: The Demon King's Castle, Floor Twelve
Level: 96

"So, what do you think happens to them, Zac?" asks Ruhr, nodding her head to the side but not averting her gaze toward the reflective water. If you look at it, you'll fall inside, and then that's a wrap.

"Hell if I know," replies Zacarias. "I don't really want to think about it."

Ruhr nods. ". . . Yeah," agrees the half elf, walking. "Hey, Zac?"

"Yeah?" asks the man.

They walk for a while longer, the platforms under their boots clacking as they step against a bridge of smooth, flat surfaces suspended in the water. "If I get caught in some . . . wibbly-wobbly Demon King magic, promise you'll take care of it," she says. "I'd rather be dead for sure than whatever that ends up being."

"I promise," replies Zacarias. "And then, after I avenge you and get out of here, I'll tell everyone you died heroically in a fight with the Demon King."

Ruhr smiles. "You're a great friend, Zac," says Ruhr. "But it's cute that you think you have a chance to kill the Demon King without me. I'm the star here, don't forget."

"That seems like a lot to say when there are a few hundred people literally right behind you," remarks Zacarias. "You don't think any of them have a shot?"

"Mm-hmm," hums Ruhr. "And if you could pick any of us, who would it be?"

"It seems like an unfair question," replies Zacarias. "I don't know any of them."

Ruhr sighs. "Just trying to get my mind off of things, I guess."

"Yeah . . ." says Zacarias, his metal boots clacking against smooth glass.

~ [Crusader Manilpin] ~
Dark Elf | ♂ | Grand Crusader
Location: The Demon King's Castle, Floor Twelve
Level: 86

The dark elf opens his mouth, trying to talk. Words don't come out. Bubbles do.

He stops, expecting the man in the formation behind him to bump into him. But nobody does. The man in front of him stops, too, and Manilpin, breaking the rule, looks around himself in confusion. He looks up at the thing that he's been holding above his head. Now that he thinks about it, he's not really sure why. He doesn't even know what the hell he's holding.

The crusader stares at the long, rectangular mirror above his head. His own mirror image stares down at him. He looks forward at the man in front of him, placing a hand on his shoulder.

He feels a hand on his own shoulder from behind.

Manilpin screams in surprise, dropping the mirror that he was holding

above his head; the mirror that was acting as a piece of the bridge the people above him were walking over. A man standing above him tries to scream in surprise as he sinks down, falling on top of him.

The reflective mirror that he had been holding drifts down through the water he's in, falling down toward the murk below. He lowers his gaze, looking down beneath himself.

There, down further below him, are an infinite number of reflections of himself, each of them holding a rectangular mirror of their own above their heads to hold the one above them aloft, and, exactly as he did with his own, each of them screams in surprise and throws their own mirror away, causing the tower of copies of himself to collapse, all of them having nothing else left to stand on as the one below them yanks a mirror away.

All around him, hundreds of copies swim and flail in terror, mirrors colliding with one another and with frantic clones, breaking into thousands of shards from the anarchy that fills the water as they all swim and kick and fight, pulling on ankles and yanking each other down in an attempt to swim back toward the surface faster, now that they've realized the situation they're in. However, in the frenzy and the desperation, the water is filled with muffled screams. Broken shards of infinite mirrors drift through the water, entering into eyes and open mouths, cutting skin, gums, and flesh. The copies grab and latch onto each other, stabbing and impaling one another in their desperation to not drown, plunging shards of broken mirror glass into themselves by the fistfuls in their futile struggle.

And in the end, all that is left is a pool full of red water and an expanse of punctured bodies which are more jagged glass than flesh.

A broken image of a man—copied a thousand times over and then a thousand times more, all of them left with nothing to do but sink endlessly in the bloodied water forever, incapable of reaching a surface that seems so close, as none of them ever stop dragging the other back down with every attempt to ascend in their desire to escape themselves—is all that remains, and it is what remains forevermore, trapped, within the abyss.

~ [**Ruhr, the River Sorceress**] ~
Half Elf | ♀ | Sorceress
Rank: SSS
Location: The Demon King's Castle, Floor Twelve
Level: 96

"Pinky-dipper," mutters Ruhr as she walks over the surface of "water" made entirely out of tiny mirrors, ebbing and rising like the body of the ocean. But despite feeling like they should sink into it, they never do.

As long as they don't look.

The first man to enter the room, a dark elf, made the mistake of looking down into his reflection, and he immediately fell through the water.

Gods knows what happened to him.

But she's glad that, whatever it was, if it happened to her, someone would put her out of her misery.

There's a real, inexplicable, spiritual warmth in that fact.

"Bean-bumper," mutters the half elf, trying to get herself to say a real, meaty swear again. But her subconscious mind just doesn't seem to want to comply. There probably really is something to all that junk Zacarias was talking about.

"*Ooh*, I'm sure the Demon King is shaking in his boots right now," jokes Zacarias.

"Shut up, Zac," sighs Ruhr, looking ahead toward what looks like the exit to the floor just ahead and doing her best to ignore the splashing from behind, as some others clearly tried to look into the water. "Eyes forward!" she yells, listening to the satisfying sound of her order being repeated by the others walking behind her, where they belong.

~ [Seaman Minani-ni] ~
Vildt (Feline) | ♂ | Master Sailor
Location: High Seas of the Great Eastern Ocean, the Abigalia
Level: 76

Countless souls have vanished into the brink. Thousands of screams never reached a single ear, as they were drowned beneath the crushing rain and the waves of just as equal pressure. Minani-ni doesn't know how many ships vanished into the waters of the ocean, as the storm obscures his line of sight. But one thing is for sure—the number of lights in the darkness is considerably lower than it was before.

The *Abigalia*, his own ship, is in poor shape, but it is in far better shape than any of those that have been lost to the sea.

He stares out toward the horizon as the ship crests another wave, rising and falling like a sparrow flying through the air in a gale. However, his

eyes fail to find anything in the distance except for a darkness that never seems to come to an end.

~ [Zacarias] ~
Human | ♂ | Royal Guardsman
Location: The Demon King's Castle, Floor Thirteen
Level: 91

"Floor thirteen," says Zacarias, looking around. "An unlucky number," mumbles the man, watching the area as he hobbles onward without much of a complaint, despite his leg hurting a bit. He carries his shield at his side. It's important for the morale of the people marching behind him that he keeps on going with good, strong form.

"Didn't take you for the superstitious type, Ziddle-fiddle," says Ruhr.

He looks at her. "Was that a new nickname for me, or are you trying to swear again?"

The woman swipes a strand of hair out of her face with a theatrical flick. "Take your pick," she replies as she keeps walking.

The room from before was a disaster in its own right, but not as bad as some of the others. Although he isn't quite sure, as he himself didn't really partake in the bad sides of it. He's become very wary of every step there is to take within this castle. He points to the sides.

"Spread out," calls Zacarias. "One left, one right," he says. The order gets passed along, and as the crusaders file into the next chamber, they split apart, filling the room, which is itself plain.

Icy, crystalline formations protrude out of the ground in the shape of many large spires, reaching up toward the ceiling as if they were great, fallen pillars of some old, forgotten temple.

~ [Slime] ~
Location: The Big-Big Green
Level: 3

The slime hops through the Big-Big Green, which is the name of a nearby forest; or at least that's its name in the language of slimes.

It hops onward, hungrily, determined to reach the far west, where it hopes to find the largest butterfly ever to eat. Why does it hope this?

Because that is what a slime has to hope for. It does not understand the context of crises or Demon Kings or such things. It knows only hunger, together with a few other vague concepts.

Something scampers over some dry leaves, the soft vibrations getting the slime's attention. Its one yellow eye, formed together out of a mass of complex biomaterial in its insides, shoots to the side to observe the rabbit.

FOOD!

The little slime hops with feverish killer intent, flying through the air like a soft, wiggly-jiggly arrow, intent to bring death unto its recipient.

(Slime) has begun consuming (Rabbit)

The rabbit screams, as rabbits that are being eaten tend to do. But the slime doesn't hear this; it does not have ears. Rather, it feels the vibrations of the sharp teeth inside of itself, trying to gnaw and chew their way out of its mass. However, this mistake is one that all prey makes.

Little slimes often have difficulty eating through thick hides and heavy furs, but what they are exceptionally good at—soft tissue—is readily made accessible to them whenever they trap a critter.

It presses itself down the rabbit's throat, filling the flopping, flailing creature with acidic goo as it eats it from the inside out, starting with the soft tissue before moving to the bones and the organs, until after a minute, nothing is left on the floor of the forest except for what looks like a perfectly deflated, wet rabbit skin. There isn't a drop of meat, gristle, or tissue left apart from that.

Content, the slime, somewhat larger than before, slips out through the empty eye sockets of the dead rabbit, and then, fully collecting itself back into shape, continues hopping westward on its grand adventure.

~ [Chief Grul] ~
Goblin | ♂ | Fighter
Location: The Southeast
Level: 48

"What is the demon?" asks one of his tribesmen. "How are we going to kill it?"

Grul turns his head, looking at the goblin who had asked the question. "I do not know," replies the goblin chief. They've made camp for a few hours and are resting from the storm beneath an overhang. They've set up several rocks to protect their fire, which the winds seem intent on trying to blow out no matter the impossibility of the angle or the strength of the blaze. He can't help but feel as if it itself were possessed by the demon spirit. "As with any hunt, we will find out when we arrive," explains Grul. He looks toward the northwest. "Goblins do not fear demons."

~ [Zacarias] ~
Human | ♂ | Royal Guardsman
Location: The Demon King's Castle, Floor Thirteen
Level: 91

The crusader screams in terror at the image of the demon that has appeared before him, striking at it with his blade, which the monster blocks with its forearm.

"Ruhr!" calls Zacarias, lifting his shield. But his voice, while resonating all around the glossy chamber, is lost among the sounds of hundreds of screams and the clashing of metal against teeth and bones.

An onslaught of monsters came charging out of the cracks and crevices, lunging toward them from every facade of the room. Hundreds of them. Creatures with long, gangly arms covered in red, leathery skin, with teeth so large their mouths fail to close, and with nails that drag along the ice behind them, leaving deep scars in it as they move.

Zacarias braces his shield forward, feeling something heavy slam against it.

The Demon King doesn't usually field waves of monsters within his own castle, or at least he hasn't until now. Maybe it's time.

The man presses back, knocking whatever is on the other side of his shield away.

Or maybe something's up.

The man looks around himself amidst the fight. The Demon King loves tricks and games, illusions and deceptions.

Something grabs his leg, and he slams the shield down onto the long, gangly arm.

~ [The Demon King] ~

Level Up!
~ [The Demon King] ~
You are now level {86}!

Level: 86 ↗	Experience: 1,899/957,000
Attribute: DARK	
Soul Points: 184/184 ↗	
Presence: 16.9 km ↗	Obols: 0
Souls Collected: 224,978/1,000,000	

You have {32} free Ability Points to spend!

The carnival pushes onward, rolling down the road toward the north, pressing toward the capital city that he knows lies there. There are many other hubs of note and importance in between, but that is his primary goal as of now.

The Demon Core is already one-fifth of the way there.

Pleased, he sits back against his throne. Humans flood his way, desperate to stop him, and in doing so, they feed the furnace. And it isn't just the ones inside the castle, no. There are others, hundreds of them, people of no note or name, pressing through the night, which is filled with gnashing teeth and chattering legs in numbers so dense that their eyes might be mistaken for stars by the fools who stop long enough to look toward the sky.

Soon, the physical realm will experience a collapse after the core ruptures, and then he will fulfill the desires of his deepest heart.

Byblos ties up her apron again, fixes her dress, and does her best to leave, returning to her other experimentations.

A full deconstruction of both physical and spiritual reality and all of the ugly, confusing sensations that come with it.

The Demon King sits on his throne, staring down at the statues. He meets his gaze with the one that has an eye, and he stares at it for a time.

"What?" asks Swain as the two of them look at the achievement window that he swipes away. It's nobody's business.

The statue doesn't respond.

Then again, how could it? It doesn't have a mouth.

~ [Zacarias] ~
Human | ♂ | Royal Guardsman
Location: The Demon King's Castle, Floor Thirteen
Level: 91

Zacarias charges forward, pressing together with several crusaders at his side as they break a dent in the wall of demons. Long, gangly arms reach around his shield, scratching at his armor with sickly yellow claws.

He doesn't know how many he's hurt, killed, or anything else. It's just anarchy. People are fighting everywhere, the entire sense of formation lost, with everyone returning to small groups of a few dozen wherever they can gather themselves. He's lost track of Ruhr.

The room rumbles and shakes.

Zacarias looks up toward the large, glassy pillars that tower over the room, watching as they quake and tremble.

All of the fighting stops immediately as both crusaders and, apparently, demons look up in terror as the gigantic structures, the size of cathedrals, begin crashing down. Standing atop them, like a tiny pinprick, is a woman with blue hair striking a very proud and dramatic pose while the ground beneath her feet literally falls apart.

Zacarias lifts his shield, casting a spell as the castle quakes, projecting a magical wall ahead of them to stop the rush of ice splinters and rubble as the room potentially caves in.

(Zacarias) has used: [Royal Barrier]

And through the chaos that ensues on the other side, he and a few hundred people watch as the river sorceress strikes a pose, her hair billowing behind her as she triumphantly falls, her descent caught halfway by a great dragon made out of water.

The world shakes. The shield is hammered with splinters of jagged ice, and a heavy, vaporous mist rises into the air as cold flakes drift down from above.

The quiet is interrupted by the sound of someone knocking on a window.

Zacarias lowers his tower shield, looking out past his magical barrier at Ruhr, who is standing there with a smug look on her face. A chunk of ice lays beneath her boot, firmly pressed up against it, as she stands there with her hands on her hips. "You can thank RUHR! THE RIVER SOR-CERESS! For saving you once again!" says the woman, holding her hand by her mouth and laughing smugly.

Zacarias looks around himself at the room full of people standing on either side of his tower shield.

There were never any demons.

It was always just a trick of the eye caused by the strangely reflective pillars above their heads.

~ [Shaushka] ~
Elf | ♀ | Classless
Location: The Scorched Forest
Level: 4

A fat bee flies past her face.

Shaushka turns her head, watching the bumbly, buzzy creature that is certainly out of place, not only because of the rain but also because of its delightful yellow color. It flies around before landing on her nose.

"Ah . . ." says the elf, staring at it with crossed eyes.

The bee rises into the air, buzzing with a heavy vibrating hum as it flies over to some burned flowers. Apparently finding little satisfaction there, it buzzes onward to the next.

She blinks, slowly rising to her feet as she chases after it, heading toward whatever it has to show her.

THE CHAIN OF COMMAND

~ [The Demon King] ~

It is within the nature of men to squabble among themselves, no matter the times. When wealth and prosperity are abundant, piling up toward the sky like a mound made out of gold, people will clamber over one another to climb up to the crest so that they themselves might be the ones who have the greatest view from the lofty heights, even if the foundation is enough to provide acceptable sustainability for the lives of every creature there.

Those who remain down below will comfort themselves, praising themselves in vainglory for their asceticism so that they too might be kings of their own hills, down below at the bottom of the material world.

"I'm not like them. I'm not greedy and selfish like those people in the high places," they will say, heads held high in order to garner the adoration of those around them as they don their crowns of modesty. They will mock the higher positioned and wear robes of poverty as if they were those of an emperor, and they will find comfort in their lack of position, not out of sheer acceptance of the situation and humble desires to live small, peaceful lives, but rather as just the tale they weave for those around them, admiring their projected want for naught.

And those around them at the bottom of the hill will admire these lowborn kings rather than those in the high places, as the separation between their states is not as dramatic and is perceived as achievable.

To be king of the wretches is every wretch's dream in secret.

This is simply human nature.

And in the opposite times, in the times when wealth is not abundant, when scarcity ravages the landscape to such a degree that belts become nooses rather than simply being tightened, that is when the ugliness of

humanity reveals itself. That is when they drop their porcelain theater masks and reveal the crooked, broken maws and empty eyes that lie beneath. When the mound of prosperity is flattened, and all men and women are lowered to an equal footing standing next to each other, that is when they will instead pile up the bodies of one another so that they have something to stand atop.

For the chance to proclaim one's righteousness and position over others, for the chance to stand just a single head higher than everyone else, they will each decapitate a thousand of their brothers and sisters so that they might be kings of a mountain of bones and teeth rather than gold.

The Demon King sits on his throne, watching the humans inside his castle. He watches the humans outside of his castle. He watches the humans in all of the lands and places that his touch has managed to reach, both now in this instant and in days prior, and all he sees as he scours the landscape for as far as his hundreds of eyes can peer is depravity.

Now that he has begun to flatten the fake mountain of human prosperity and abundance, now that he has begun to reduce each human to one another's social height—that of a heap of ash—they have begun to drop the charades of their civility and their goodness. Now that the night of ten thousand teeth and claws has come, threatening to never end, they too bare their own fangs. Yet they do so not at the hissing darkness of his creation but rather at one another.

He can feel them.

He can taste the souls lost to the darkness that never stops, killed not by his doing but by the hands of the men and women around them. Swords and knives, fists and stones, hands grip themselves around frail necks, and boots press themselves down over the skulls of those infants that had not been dashed against the stones and the rocks, and they descend upon each other as would a serpent eating itself.

Horrific.

The Demon King watches as humanity proves itself to be exactly what he holds it to be—monstrous, without a drop of *humanity* within their disgusting souls. Without a hint of true love for the beauty of creation. Ugly.

They are demons of a nature truer than anything he could ever hope to create.

And he watches as they praise themselves, claiming themselves to be good and just and noble and clean, praising themselves to be strong, beautiful creatures of nature, when instead, they are nothing but a perpetually leaking cyst on what should have been a beautiful jewel of a garden of paradise—this world.

~ [Derinji] ~
Human | ♂ | Knight
Location: A Town, Some Fifty Kilometers North of the Demon King's Castle
Level: 60

"Get inside!" orders the man, moving the crowd along toward the village church, which the local priest is drawing a protective circle around in the soil. The line of villagers stretches out the door as the few hundred people who live here all move toward shelter. "Come on, hurry!" calls Derinji, gesturing for the people to keep moving in rank and file.

There are hundreds of small villages like this one lining the wildlands between all of the major cities. Their populations vary from the hundreds to the thousands in some towns.

"Bless your heart, young man," says an old woman, holding out a small parcel for him. "Please, take this," she insists. "For you and your friends."

He looks down at the small basket full of breads. "Thank you, ma'am," he replies, taking it and nodding. "Please head inside the church. It's safe in there," he says, gently ushering her along.

The man looks toward the south, watching the sky in the distance. The storm never stops, howling even here around them and soiling the landscape, which is beginning to flood in places from the constant rain. The Demon King isn't here yet, but he will be soon, according to the crisis window which shows the distance drawing closer and closer to their location.

He turns his head, looking at one of his men, and hands him the basket. "Give this to the anqas," he orders. "They'll need the energy."

"Yes, sir," replies the man, taking the basket and going to feed their animals. They have to ride to the next village as soon as this is done.

The crowd files in, overfilling the church as the priest finishes his warding circle around the structure. After a while in the rain, the building is packed, and the protective warding around it is complete.

Derinji looks at the priest. "We need to get to the next village," he explains. "Will you manage from here?"

The priest looks at him and nods. "Bless you, Brother," says the man. "We'll ride out the storm here until the Demon King passes us by. Thanks to the capital's materials, the warding will hold."

Derinji nods, looking at the small warding crystals they had brought by the cartful. Each town gets a few hundred to boost their defenses against the Demon King's corruption.

"Head inside. We're leaving for the next village now," says Derinji.

The priest nods, making his way to the packed church, and looks at Derinji before closing the heavy doors behind himself.

Derinji stands out in the rain, waiting for a moment.

"Seal it," he orders, sure that there are no stragglers left.

A geomancer moves to the front, placing his hands on the muddy soil. An instant later, walls of stone move out of the dirt, surrounding the entire building as if it were in a crater. Muddy runoff runs down the incline, blocking the doors and the windows of the structure. A team of casters moves up the incline, already versed in this practice.

"Burn it," orders the man.

Each of the four fire casters standing on the upper ledge of the new crater—one on each side of the building's cardinal directions—holds their hands out and releases a constant stream of fire over the roof, which begins to smolder and cascade in.

The screams from the inside of the structure are easy to pretend not to hear with the storm howling as it does and the rain always crashing, unable to extinguish the magical flames that consume the building, which is, in itself, placed in what amounts to a natural cauldron.

They've perfected this technique pretty rapidly in the last six villages.

Derinji turns to one of his men. "Collect the crystals; load them up. We're moving," he orders.

"Yes, sir," replies the man, going to collect the same warding crystals they had already given several other priests and warders along the way.

The night is alight, burning brightly orange, as after a few minutes of sustained fire from the magic against the ceiling, cooking the dense mud and hardening it, the human fat inside the structure begins to catch, and it all rises into a superheated fire that continues to burn by itself while the

soldiers pack up their carts, mount their anqas, and ride to the next town over.

The flames and the smoke are held out of the line of sight of those people by the storm, the screams never managing to leave the caldera as the fire consumes them whole.

Derinji kicks an empty basket to the side as he mounts the large bird, looking over his shoulder once back toward the sixth fire of the night.

It's what has to be done so that the Demon King can't take their souls.

It's the right thing to do.

Besides, orders are orders. His hands are tied.

~ [Crusader Ritani] ~
Orc | ♂ | Paladin
Location: The Demon King's Castle, Floor Fourteen
Level: 90

Before them, blocking the way forward, is a great waterfall that stretches to both sides of the room, a black, oozy tar of sorts running down over the edge. He can only assume that the exit lies through it.

However, there is a wariness about getting anywhere near the liquid after what they have seen so far.

It runs in streams, thousands and thousands of gallons of the ink crashing down into what looks like a bottomless crevice in the rock. Given that they're in the Demon King's castle, one can only assume it's some form of horrific poison.

Currently, the plan is to poke through the waterfall with tunnels made out of magical barriers. But this hasn't led to any success, as in the areas they've tried so far, there is just a solid rock surface behind the waterfall. But the room is massive, and there are plenty of spaces left to look at. Just to be sure, though, other groups have been sent around to examine the walls for any secret doors or levers.

One particular group was sent to the top of the waterfall, having made a makeshift platform with the help of some geomancy and a few barriers, but they haven't been heard from yet. So all there is left to do is wait.

He looks around himself nervously.

~ [Cartouche] ~
Gallu | ♀ | Dancer
Location: The Demon Carnival
Level: 86

Cartouche hums to herself, along with the melody played by the ghostly musicians that accompany her, as she stands atop the carriage that hurtles down the road toward the north. Other wagons belonging to the carnival roll down along the muddy, torn roads. The cobblestones and paving have cracked and broken from the heat, and they slide out of place from the flooding starting due to the rain that never stops. What this means is that the road everywhere within the aura of the Demon King is essentially destroyed.

So the carriage, pulled by undead who are indifferent to such things as poor footing and breaking ankles, throws itself around as they charge down the broken streets, the axle squeaking and screaming from the movements that would, under normal conditions, have broken the carriage.

She, too, standing atop its wooden roof, is thrown around by the forces of the yanking movements. However, she incorporates this roughness into her dance, springing to the left as the carriage throws her that way and spinning on the edge before it manages to toss her aside and then back the other way. Like a nightingale lost in the storm, she flies around through the night, swaying in a dance in much the same way as the carriage itself is doing; as the world itself does.

There is a dance to life that most are simply incapable of seeing, as they are not versed in the mindset of a dancer.

In the same way, this force, this dancelike quality that she holds life to have, is also at the same time something which has nothing to do with the art of dance. It is the same energy that the painter, Abydos, admires through his artistry. For him, there is a visual, crisp beauty to life. This energy manifests itself as such for him. For the cook, Byblos, there is a rare inner sensory depth which she might perhaps describe as life having its own profile of flavors.

However, all of these aspects—the dance, the visuality, the profile of life—all base themselves on the single word they each try to achieve through the filters of their individuality.

Beauty.

For her, life is graceful and serene because that is the mindset she has of herself, and so, her toolset is that of the dance, which in turn paints life as a dance. The same is to be said of the others in their own way.

And, as such, the same is to be said of humanity in its own way.

Those who partake in life but do not partake in the attempt to find or create beauty, through what mindset do they perceive the world? If they do not have the tools of beautiful creation, then there can't be any way for them to understand this deeper truth, can there?

She doesn't think so.

The dancer pirouettes as the carriage tries to throw her into the darkness, just as her old life had done to her. She almost fell for it, for the trap that all the others had fallen for too. The traps of survival and of human desire; the traps of the thoughts of vague responsibilities and needs, of existing with the so-called human condition. She had, in that old life of hers, failed to use the true toolset of her heart's deepest depths, and instead opted to progress toward her future with the toolset of a normal human—survival, situational growth, desires.

These are all well and good, but they won't do anything except let you play the pretend game a little longer. They'll allow you to sustain yourself longer in a game you didn't enjoy playing to begin with.

This new thing, this "death" of hers and revival as a servant of the Demon King—while she understands its meaning through the lens of her old human mindset as being something that they would perceive as horrific or perhaps even pitiful—is for her the most beautiful moment in her life, along with this one now.

The thunder claps while she sways, the carriage throwing her around, and she incorporates these negative happenings into her routine of beautiful pursuit.

To be able to find beauty, one has to let go of survival.

Survival is an ugly, simple, base thing.

And real beauty—transcendent, ethereal beauty of a careening depth that can't be grasped within the physical body of a human—cannot be pursued while one is surviving.

It is not a thing of the physical world.

~ [Crusader Ritani] ~
Orc | ♂ | Paladin
Location: The Demon King's Castle, Floor Fourteen
Level: 90

The stone tower that a group had used to reach the upper area at the top of the waterfall collapses.

People scatter away as the magic fails and rocks tumble downward. Screams fill the air, not from those around the site but rather from high, high up above, presumably managing to carry this far down beyond the roar of the falls only due to their horrific shrillness.

They watch as a few small pinpricks form at the top of the falls and careen down over the sides, their bodies painted black from the ink they're soaked in as they tumble over the edge and vanish into the ravine below, being swallowed by the world.

"Well, frig," mutters the river sorceress, standing near the front of the leadership group. She turns her head. "Get another team up in the air," she orders. "This time, stay on the dry side."

The officer she had given the order to nods and grabs a few casters, going to build a new tower.

So far, it doesn't look like there's anything above the falls, though. There's just another ravine from which the water spews before falling into the one below.

Ritani scratches his head before looking down at the ground below as something catches his eyes.

A vein of black liquid spreads through the stones, dripping and flowing unnaturally just before where he stands. He steps back, nudging the man next to him as the ink begins to draw the shape of a person. Black water drips out through the stones below, like sweat from pores, to create the figure.

And then another one, followed by another. One vaguely body-shaped splotch appears flat on the stones for each person that had been swallowed by the falls. But the shape of their bodies, while vaguely human in their making, is disturbed by an off detail. While their heads, torsos, and all such things are in proportion to what one would expect, the puddles on the ground have fingers that never stop growing.

The streaks from their hands reach outward, pressing forward and along the floor in long, crooked lines that make it look as if their fingers

were endlessly broken, from the start of the digit to the end, which appears at the walls of the grand cavern.

Murmurs move through the crusaders.

The puddles don't move. They just stay there, cutting the floor apart with their presence. The many thin streaks of their fingers create small channels that have cut the room into several islands, each only a few inches apart from one another.

"What the hell," mutters Ritani, staring in abject horror, although he can't help but give in to his curious instincts as he picks up a small pebble from the floor and holds it over one of the puddles, letting go of the stone to watch as it splashes into the body.

~ [The Demon King] ~

One of the great weaknesses of the Demon Core is its limited range. The effects of the demon sickness, while beyond devastating, are limited by his own growth to a radius of several kilometers. This is certainly a sufficient tool for his aims, but it does leave a weakness within his system of conquest, namely that he always needs to be within reach of a region in order to cleanse it of the ugliness present within.

His wild monsters, present over the nation, are certainly an effective tool in their own right, but they are being held at bay by the trained adventurers and guardsmen of the cities outside of his domain. Fighting monsters, even his, is the bread and butter of such people, and so they are making little progress outside of the farmsteads and the small towns.

Even the human capital to the north has begun seeing fringe attacks by the unruly monsters of the wildlands, whose behavior has changed since his rising. But it is hardly a concern for them, other than the strain of a few raised eyebrows.

Monsters . . .

Swain appreciates monsters.

Like animals, they exist in a state of existence that could only be considered pure. Yes, beauty is perhaps a concept too abstract for them to comprehend, but in their own way, they incorporate the perfect, natural beauty of the unblemished world.

It seems a shame that they, like himself in his old life, must exist under the crushing, suffocating, and spirit-killing weight of humanity.

Perhaps he should lend them a hand—

The Demon King turns his head, looking at Kirsch the ghost, who is flying around, playing with the souls in the throne room.

—as a friend.

NEW (DEMON KING) ABILITY
[The Night Tide] (Passive)

Gnashing teeth rip through flesh, and sharp claws may break through bones, but the human soul has been something impervious to most monsters—until now.

Effect: All wild monsters of any attribute other than HOLY or ARCANE in the world are inflicted with status: [Rage].

All wild monsters of any attribute other than HOLY or ARCANE in the world will have their rate of breeding and growth doubled.

NEW (DEMON KING) ABILITY
[Distinctive Regurgitation] (Active)
Cost: 10,000 COLLECTED SOULS

The human soul is a soft, malleable thing that is able to be shaped and changed, much like their flesh.

Effect: In ley line–spanning, high-magic zones, where darkness and fear of the Demon King have gathered as the predominant emotions, release a single corrupted soul, pressed together out of the screaming mass of ten thousand souls by incredible crushing darkness, in order to summon a [DEMON GENERAL] who will lead monster swarms in coordinated attacks and efforts against distant human strongholds.

~ [Demon General] ~
A Demon General.

Akin to a golem of sorts, a Demon General is a particularly powerful artificial soul that has been created as an amalgamation of living souls pressed together into one coherent creation that follows the will of the Demon King.

Spread across the landscape, Demon Generals guide wild monsters, collecting together great armies of snatching limbs and endless legs in order to lead them in coordinated assaults against

human bastions, which would otherwise be impervious to simple monster assaults.

The goal of a Demon General is to capture as many members of the common races as possible before bringing them back to the Demon King to be consumed.

Class: OFFICER	Element: DARK
Type: Commander	Category: DEMON*
Rank: SS	
Level: 86	
[General] || [Red Water {5}] || [Wild Hunter] || [Lamashtu]	
HP: 86/86	SOUL: 86/86
*A demon's stats are based on the LEVEL of the Demon King. Its affinities are based on its past life.	
[Noticeable Darkness]: All wild monsters within the radius of the Demon General will flock toward it, collecting together into a wild army. The radius of a general is the same as that of the Demon King's territorial span, generating outward from within its own position. Currently: 16.9 km	
[Officer]: Is able to give direct commands to any monsters under its control.	
[Leader]: All monsters under the general's control gain an increase to all of their stats, equivalent to 10% of the Demon King's level.	

Swain takes a hand and forces it down through one of the mouths on the side of his body, the teeth breaking and the lips ripping as he forces his arm into it, reaching in to grab the many souls that he needs.

All across the nation, wretched people are unifying in a collaborative defensive effort. It will make his life considerably easier if they are kept busy where they are, stuck in place, waiting for him to arrive rather than them mounting a counteroffensive.

(Swain) has used: [Distinctive Regurgitation] x6
COLLECTED SOULS REMAINING: 209,455

A few generals across the landscape, close to the most significant bastions of resistance, would be wise.

~ [Crusader Ritani] ~
Orc | ♂ | Paladin
Location: The Demon King's Castle, Floor Fourteen
Level: 90

His chest heaves in and out as he tries to catch his breath, finding it difficult to do so. There are too many needle-thin holes in his chest, five on either side, as ten impossibly long fingers, made out of inky blackness, hold him aloft in the air. His blurry vision looks down toward the ground, toward the human-shaped puddle which has moved its hands.

The flat painting of a body pressed against the stones now lifts its arms out of its canvas, holding him aloft high, high above in the air.

Ritani wheezes, his legs kicking, as he tries to grab the skewering fingers that move through him. But his hands glide through as if they were just water, despite the stability of them while they hold his entire body aloft. The man slides downward at an angle as gravity pulls him down along the rails.

He slides down further and further along the fingers, nobody else daring to make a sudden move lest they disturb any of the other pools. And he slides slowly, his blood greasing the array of needles as he descends back down toward the ground at an angle, moving straight toward the human-shaped puddle.

His face is above its face, and his legs are where its legs are. His shoulders, his chest, all of it is aligned with the puddle in the stones from which the ten long shafts of ink had emerged.

And he slides straight down into the puddle, not having enough air left to scream.

It's a perfect fit.

He vanishes.

A new puddle appears on the floor a moment later, spreading its hands out wide with ten long fingers that cut through the entire room, creating a thousand crisscrossing tiny channels waiting for anybody to disturb them.

~ [The Demon King] ~

Swain watches through his many eyes as all around the countryside, large, horrific abominations of shadows, bone, and eyes rise from the shadows beneath dead trees and behind gravestones, becoming whole, significant things of corporeal form rising up to their feet to stand.

Eyes, scattered in the darkness of the night, peer their way as thousands of sharp legs and twisting bodies begin to collect in the wilds.

Good.

Swain looks back to his castle, having some more immediate problems to handle. Being a king does not allow for all too many moments of pure leisure, apparently. There is always more work to do.

Plus, he hasn't written a poem in a while.

Swain looks around his throne room.

Perhaps work and play can be combined once again?

There are so many things to write about. Speed would be good; he could create some sort of force to help the carnival. Or perhaps something to help dispose of these latest intruders in his castle, though they seem to be stuck on floor fourteen at the moment. Or maybe something to help aid the outside effort against humanity, like his new generals? Or maybe . . .

Hmm . . .

"Paper," orders the Demon King, reaching out and taking a stack from a horrified ghost that arrives just in time.

~ [Zacarias] ~
Human | ♂ | Royal Guardsman
Location: The Demon King's Castle, Floor Fourteen
Level: 91

"Grim. What's the plan, Zac-man?" asks Ruhr, watching the last bubble vanish in the man-shaped puddle.

Zacarias looks at her and then around the room, shaking his head. "Hell if I know," he says. "We'll wait for them to keep searching the falls."

Ruhr rubs her head. "I dunno, that seems too easy," explains the half elf. He nods. It does. It wouldn't be like the Demon King to just give them a door behind the waterfall.

Troublesome.

He looks over his shoulder, looking at a crate that the crusaders carry with them.

It doesn't seem to be bleeding anymore.

He can't say if that's a good thing or not.

~ [Derinji] ~
Human | ♂ | Knight
Location: A Town, Some Forty-Six Kilometers North of the Demon King's Castle
Level: 60

Something smells like oil.

Weird.

He watches the sky. They're losing ground. One or two more of these villages, and then they're going to have to evacuate from the region before the Demon King arrives.

"Keep it moving," says Derinji. "Everybody get inside," orders the man, yelling over the storm as the people of the town take collective shelter in the city hall. "Get those crystals set up!" he barks at his men, who are running around and setting up the warding crystals around the place.

It's just for show, of course, so the people of the town will cooperate and get where they need to be. They'll pick them back up once they leave, and then stash them somewhere. When this blows over, they can resell them on the market. For the military, they're write-offs as is, so nobody will care.

He watches as the people all file along, corralled into their pen like animals to the slaughter.

Somebody screams in the distance.

Derinji and the crowd turn to look, watching as some person falls to the ground, a pack of shambling undead having torn them down to the ground, where they now eat them alive. The villager screams, their voice drowning out in the new cries that come from the crowd as everyone surges toward the shelter.

"MONSTERS!" screams a voice, and the crowd panics, people pushing past each other to get inside the warding circle.

The soldier looks around the small town square, watching as undead leak into the city like manifested by the night itself; hundreds of them

pour out from behind houses and out of alleyways from all directions. People are torn in the night, their horrified screams quickly silenced as they are added to the horde.

"Sir!" calls one of his soldiers. Derinji tsks, looking around. There are too many. He looks to the side, down the way toward their route out of the city. The darkness there is filled with thousands of glowing orbs—eyes—and just as many shambling silhouettes.

"Get inside the ward!" yells Derinji, ordering all of his soldiers to enter into the protective circle. "We'll fight off the undead from there!" he commands while he and his men all retreat into the circle outside of the city hall. All of the townspeople have finished taking shelter and are watching from the windows in horror as the undead swarm toward the building, surrounding the warding circle entirely.

It's a good thing they set this damn thing up, even if it was just for show.

Derinji looks around, certainly not relieved, though. The acrid smell of lantern oil still fills the air, never seeming to dissipate despite the storm.

"Casters!" he calls as his geomancers and wizards line up. It's been a long night. They only have so many soul points left, so they have to be smart about their spellcasting. "Wait for a break in their numbers. We'll make our move then."

The undead can't get into the circle, but they can certainly shoot out of it.

It's a problem, but they'll just burn their way out and then finish the job. Derinji stands at the edge of the circle, looking at a mangled face that stops a few feet before him, not able to come closer. It's just a zombie. These all look like low-level undead. It's not a real issue for them to handle.

His eyes wander the night as he looks at the undead horde. They got here unusually fast, but they must have been scouring the landscape when they just flooded over the town by chance. It's bad luck, but that's life.

The man's vision stops, and he looks back behind the shuffling horde trying unsuccessfully to push its way past the magic circle toward them. He narrows his eyes, trying to bring what he sees in the distance into focus.

"The hell is that?" he asks. Derinji takes a step back then climbs up onto a pedestal to get a better view over the horde.

There, standing at the edge of the night, is a gestalt far more composed and coherent than the howling zombies. It is the shape of a man, yet twice the size of one, with a cloak made out of nightfall, and poise composed of the rigidity of a frozen corpse.

The shadow lifts a hand, gesturing with the wave of a single finger toward the side. The undead horde splits, wandering around the edge of the circle as if under its direct control.

It flicks another finger.

The undead stop. They stop howling and gnashing their teeth. They stop reaching and clawing for the magic that they can't break despite their desperate attempts to do so.

It flicks a third finger, and the hundreds of zombies that surround the city hall all take a step back.

And then a fourth.

A hundred-some bodies drop to the ground, and then, with the rain cascading down over them, they begin to burrow, ripping away stones and breaking their fingers, nails, and teeth as they tear away at the roads and the cobblestones. The undead horde begins digging a perfectly coordinated circle around the city hall, exactly along the edge of the barrier.

"The hell . . ." Derinji looks around in confusion. He grabs a wizard. "Hey. Kill that fucking thing back there," he orders.

"Yes, sir," replies the wizard, gathering a fireball around his hands and arcing his arm back to throw it over the distance.

The creature, the large shadow, flicks a fifth finger, and the undead all around them fall down into the channels they've freshly dug.

Derinji looks down at the zombie lying at his feet, staring at its bloated stomach and glass-filled mouth, at the thick, black liquid that leaks out of its face.

He sniffs the air.

Lantern oil.

His eyes going wide, he looks around at the circle lined with bloated, oil-filled corpses from which heavy vapors rise up into the air. In the glint of the fireball, he notices the shine of the broken lanterns stuck to their bodies; the zombies had ransacked the town, covering themselves with anything and everything that is easily flammable.

"WAIT! ST—" yells Derinji, diving for the wizard just as he yanks his arm forward, lobbing the fire through the night.

The vapors catch fire, and a few bloated, fatty corpses explode at once, breaking the protective circle from the force of the explosion.

Derinji tumbles to the side, his back cracking as he is flung against a pillar of the city hall's exterior.

Undead swarm in, the wave of burning zombies pouring down over his men and eating them with burning faces. The horde pushes past him, breaking through the doors to the city hall.

With raspy breath, he lays there, watching as he is entirely ignored by hundreds of zombies.

A set of heavy, thudding steps move toward him, and he looks up, staring at the shadow of a horrific demon that towers over him.

It bends down, looking at him in the eyes for a moment, before nodding its head to the side.

Undead hands grab him. But rather than eating him, they tear him off into the night, along with the hundreds of townspeople in the city hall, ripping them through the ruins and into the darkness, toward the ever-approaching aura of the Demon King.

~ [Zacarias] ~
Human | ♂ | Royal Guardsman
Location: The Demon King's Castle, Floor Fourteen
Level: 91

"I have an idea, but it's stupid," he says.

Ruhr looks at him. "I'm listening."

Zacarias looks around the room. "Let me borrow this," he tells a crusader, taking his spear from him. Zacarias turns the polearm around, reaching over the ravine and into the waterfall.

"Be careful, Zac!" warns Ruhr, grabbing him. "Don't touch the ink!"

"No," he says, shaking his head. "The waterfall is fine. It's the body puddles you can't touch," explains the man. He pulls the spear back toward himself, black, thick ink dripping from the wood.

He lowers it down to the stones at their feet, finding a spot where there is enough room, and then draws a circle with it.

A hole appears.

The door to the next floor.

Zacarias and Ruhr look at each other.

~ [High King Mercator] ~
Half Elf | ♂ | King
Location: The Capital City in the Distant North
Level: 100

"Is the trap in place?" he asks, pointing at the map.

One of his advisors nods. "It is, my lord," replies the man, looking down at the road to the north that the carriage is moving down. A great river with a ravine spans the landscape there. "We're waiting for him to arrive now," he says, pointing at the location on the map. "He'll be stuck there for a while."

"Good." Mercator rubs his eyes and looks around the room. He's so tired. It's been days since he's slept. Blurs and blobs move past him, and he honestly can't tell which people in the room are real and which ones are just his double vision.

Their shadows are odd, too, shifting and blurring and sometimes becoming separate from the bodies they're connected to until he blinks again.

"Good . . ." repeats the man, looking down at the map, toward the trap they've set for the Demon King.

CHAPTER 4

THE DARKNESS WITHIN

~ [Demon General Sieben] ~
Terror | ♂ | Demon General
Location: Kobold Coast, on the Far Eastern Edge of the Demon King's Continent

Ocean winds hammer down onto the coast, together with the crashing pressure of countless waves of the black ocean which surge against the slowly eroding coast. The land itself is being swallowed by the black water of the night that never ends.

He stands beneath the dead apple tree on the edge of a plantation reaching close to the cliffside by the ocean. Screams ring out around him as monsters claw through the darkness, cutting down the humans who run this farm he's been born on—a spirit arising from the soil, from a blackened, rotting apple seed. They don't kill them. They just cut their legs, their hamstrings. They eat their knees and break their shins. They gouge their eyes and stick long, jagged claws into their ears, robbing them of their senses so that they can't escape.

The master wants them alive.

The entity, tall and slender, with robes of rotting leaves that flow down past his legs falling just short of the ground, looks down at his hand, which materializes into existence, taking the whole shape in the lightlessness of the night. For those humans who might remain alive, he isn't distinguishable from the darkness. His long, broken silhouette with seven arms, each with seven fingers, is not discernible from that of an apple tree.

The fingers are long and slender, numbering seven on all hands, with nails as long as the leaves of the dying tree that lie scattered all around his feet, soaking into a broken slurry as the heavy rain tears into them.

He lifts his gaze, staring out over the dark ocean.

Others come. The master can sense them, sailing on their ships and boats across the great sea, a competing force to the people of this nation, yet they arrive in the spirit of mortal cooperation, determined to help destroy the great works of the Demon King.

Something thumps into him from the side and falls down to the soil, scrambling and screaming.

A human.

In terror, she spins around, staring up at him in the darkness of the night with eyes as wide as the obscured moon hidden behind the thick clouds, just as hers are muddied by terror. Her glistening, freshly oiled blonde hair, soaked to her skin, clings to her neck.

His seven eyes examine her as she crawls backward, her legs failing her because of the weakness of her own spirit and flesh.

A voice rings through his head, seeing what he sees.

"Yes . . . master . . ." replies the demon general to the whispering voice of the Demon King, looking at the miserable creature down below, her form obscured behind the forty-nine black, jagged nails of his hands that separate her from his clear vision.

An apple falls from the tree, thudding against the soil.

~ [Seaman Minani-ni] ~
Vildt (Feline) | ♂ | Master Sailor
Location: High Seas of the Great Eastern Ocean, the Abigalia
Level: 76

Seaman Minani-ni plucks an apple out of a barrel of preserving oil, wiping the greasy fruit off on his clothes as he maintains his balance, the rain pelting his face as he takes a thick bite of the fruit. Somehow, the old *Abigalia* has managed to weather the storm. He has no idea how. The primary mast is broken, and they had to throw most of it overboard. They just got incredibly lucky that the secondary sails survived and the hull remained intact after the chain of explosions.

"Land, ho!" cries a voice out over the storm. A bell cuts through the night.

Minani-ni turns his head, running to the front of the ship together with many others to look off into the distance at the land of the distant continent that slowly comes into sight.

No lights burn in the lighthouses. No fires burn in the windows of the towns along the coastline. No ships sail through what is usually a busy stretch of water, full of merchant vessels moving between the continents.

Murmurs move through the sailors as they stare at the black, lifeless continent. There are no birds and no movements. All that lies in the distance is a colorless, vague splotch that is hardly separate from the ocean as masses of water from the rains that never end stream down the cliffsides in new falls that have never existed before, washing away unsecured houses and buildings which hang off of cliffsides, some lost to the ocean, others having gotten tangled and snagged on old roots and each other, now simply hanging from the side of the landmass as if the continent itself had tipped over sideways.

There is nothing to see except for a single glowing red pinprick of light far, far, *far* off on the horizon. It is the light of a star that has fallen down to the world, killing and destroying everything in its path. The ruby-red glow, so very faint, paints the sky far off beyond the coastline.

It is the light of the Demon King.

Minani-ni takes a bite of his apple, the grease-infused juice running down the sides of his soaked face washed away immediately by the rain that has never left his fur and features since they left port on the other side of the ocean.

"Signals!" calls the lookout.

A moment later, a series of lights come to life on the coastline. Torches and lanterns lit up one after the other, illuminating the landing zone.

They're expected, after all.

He takes another bite of his fruit, making a disgusted face and looking down at the apple, inside of which half a black worm crawls around, having somehow survived all of this time.

The man makes a disgusted face, throwing the apple over his shoulder, overboard.

~ [Knight Captain Filanze] ~
Elf | ♂ | Knight Errant
Location: The Eastern Coast, Point Nordost
Level: 90

Point Nordost is a cape on the rural eastern shore of the continent. It has steep cliffsides all around it, high above the ocean, with a single natural point of entry, which is a single path that leads down to a cove with the only beach that can be landed on for days.

"Barriers!" calls the man, marching along the coastline, not too bothered by the thousands of eyes that wander the darkness outside of his grouping of soldiers.

A series of prismatic, magical shields light up the night, establishing a barrier from the outside world. It's an ingenious system, maintained at specific points of interest throughout the country. Usually, a magical wall would need several men to maintain each section. However, at some key ley line nodes, a rather simple construction has been erected, such as here at Point Nordost, the designated landing zone for intercontinental arrivals.

The elf looks over at a slightly elevated stone platform, only about the width and length of a few strides. Inside of it is carved a detailed sigil, and running out of it is a series of stone channels that almost look like rain gutters on the sides of city streets.

In the center of the node sits a single priest, holding onto the sigil with his hands. The man's energy channels through the stonework and runs through the thin channels, out of which arise tall, prismatic walls of holy energy.

Knight Captain Filanze lifts a hand as he walks, idly waving a finger. "Send them back to the Demon King," he orders, turning his head to a group of ten wizards and sorcerers, who salute and form a line, lifting their hands into the air.

Glows of fire and ice surround their fingers, and an instant later, thousands of tiny crystalline projectiles of both sorts of magic are volleyed up into the air against the storm and the heavy winds, calculated by the professional casters so the magic drops down exactly on the other side of the wall, on top of the monsters of various shapes, sizes, and breeds.

He can't be bothered to identify them all, as there are just monsters of every type.

Knight Captain Filanze stops for a moment, turning his head to look through the wall that hundreds of hands and claws press against, inches from his face. Undead with horrifically mangled faces, goblins of many tribes and breeds, slimes and ogres, trolls from the distant hills, and great

vipers from the swamplands lash against the walls, smashing their bodies, hands, and faces against it.

He's never seen anything like it before.

Monsters never cooperate like this. Even inside the dungeons of the world, monsters of violently different species will often engage in their natural instincts and eat one another if it comes down to it.

The wall of raining shards that pellets down from above cuts through the swarm he's looking at, the spells aimed perfectly by the line of casters that slowly rotates from left to right along the wall. Dozens of the monsters die instantly; others become horrifically mutilated. But rather than run in fear, they continue to howl, frothing at the mouth and striking against the wall. In seconds, more pour from the endless night to take the place of those that have died, simply stepping over the corpses and crushing those beneath their legs who have fallen, unable to get up in their frenzy.

He shakes his head, continuing onward. "Get those docks ready!" he calls out at the team of carpenters and military engineers who are already at work, establishing the landing zone and medical centers with the carts of materials they had brought with them. A team of medical assistants runs after them, putting up dozens of tents per minute with the help of crafting magic.

He points to the side of a team surveying the cliffside to check its stability. "Get that cannon ready," he says. "The Demon King's knocking," explains the captain, pointing over his shoulder at the wall. "Knock back."

"Sir!" replies the head engineer, rising to his feet as they run off to set up the experimental weapon they've brought from the capital.

Knight Captain Filanze stands where they stood, hands behind his back, as he stares out over the ocean, watching the ships come to the horizon. The Vildt.

It pains him to let their kind step foot on his continent, but the orders from the capital are absolute, and they need as many bodies as possible to push the Demon King back to hell.

~ [The Demon King] ~

"It's beginning," says Cartouche. "The generals are securing the continent."

Swain nods, looking at her. "Cartouche. What does our route look like from here?" he asks.

The dancer lifts her head. "Now that we've passed the western city and the magical research center, we have to make a choice. The road diverges here into a fork," says Cartouche. "We'll have to choose our path." She lifts her left hand. "The western fork leads us to the edge of the continent. It's an extremely mountainous area," explains the gallu as she looks at a statue. "There is a massive fortress along the mountainside, spanning several towers and ancient bridges that are interconnected. There isn't a big population, but it's home to the old orders of paladins." She looks back at him. "If we turn our backs to them and take the other road, they might become a problem."

Swain nods. "And the eastern way?"

"That's where the scary witch swamp is!" interjects a voice. He turns his head to look at the ghost, Kirsch, who flies in holding her stuffed toy. "We can't go there," says the ghost, shaking her head. "Witches are scary! They'll eat me!"

Swain lifts a massive hand which the ghost looks at and then lands on. "They'll do no such thing while I am here," promises the Demon King. "Cartouche."

"The witches are a problem of their own," explains the dancer as he looks back at her. "They're old and distant from human society. They might leave us alone if we take the other road," she says. "But they might not, and honestly, I'd be afraid of them and their strange magic before I'd worry about the paladins."

"How so?" asks Swain.

Cartouche shakes her head. "Witches don't use normal magic like other casters. They're far, far worse. They adhere to the old rules of the world and work beyond the normal confines of the system. Humans hate them."

The Demon King leans on his throne, the ghost crawling up his arm toward his shoulder.

So there's the choice between a guaranteed threat of modest proportion, or a possible threat of major proportion.

He lifts his gaze, thinking.

~ [Demon General Sieben] ~
Terror | ♂ | Demon General
**Location: Kobold Coast, on the Far Eastern Edge of the Demon
King's Continent**

The Demon King whispers to him, his words overflowing in his mind and dripping down his senses like a thick ooze that coats over them, drowning them in his will.

He looks out through the night, his seven arms tirelessly working out of his line of sight as he plucks the long golden hairs off the woman's head one after the other, tying the strands together into tight cords. She screams incoherently, her state of coherence having long left, as he works, tying her limbs to the many boughs of the apple tree.

The humans have begun their defense of the coast, where the intruders from the distant lands are set to arrive, as foretold by the Demon King.

The general turns his head around, looking at her.

An apple tree doesn't grow perfectly straight, well-aligned branches. They are knotted and twisted, moving up and down and from side to side. It's very difficult to perfectly align a human body with the winding boughs of the tree.

One of his hands grabs her wrist, lifting it up to place it flat on the bottom of a branch. She screams, froth leaving her mouth, as her forearm breaks in half while one of his other hands ties the rope of her own hair around her wrist, fastening the end of the limb with many broken places to the tree, just as her legs, her torso, and all the rest of her have been secured to it.

He tilts his head.

It was very troublesome work.

He stares at the woman, blood dripping from her hairless red crown, dripping down to the muddied soil below the juice of an apple. Her limbs are twisted and mangled, splaying out left and right as they follow the branches of the tree, the same as her torso and waist.

The demon general lifts a hand toward the distant darkness, down toward the coast.

~ [Knight Captain Filanze] ~
Elf | ♂ | Knight Errant
Location: The Eastern Coast, Point Nordost
Level: 90

"Captain!" calls a sorcerer. The man turns his head to look, watching as the night immediately turns quiet.

The air, which only a second ago had been filled with screams in the same number as the songs of larks in spring, now carries nothing with it except for the crashing of the waves against the shoreline and the splashing of the rain down at their feet.

Hundreds of monsters turn away from the wall, vanishing back into the night in total silence. Even the mangled, half-dead monsters at the foot of the wall crawl and claw their way away, back into the darkness.

The hairs on the back of his neck stand on end as he approaches the fortifications, watching the now silent night.

Something is wrong.

"Ships on the coast!" calls a voice. He turns his head around, looking back to see the masts arriving on the shoreline, just down below their basecamp. He lifts a hand. "Send a group to the boats. Collect the wounded and bring them to the tents." He looks back at the wall and then at the casters. "Continue the bombardments. Lower your intensity and aim further into the darkness." He looks back out through the wall. "They're still out there."

"Sir," replies the head wizard.

Knight Captain Filanze rubs his chin, narrowing his eyes.

This is very unusual behavior for monsters. Obviously, he knows these are very unusual circumstances. Something is up. He's loath to attribute intelligence to them, but if he didn't know better, he'd say they're up to something.

Who knows what the Demon King can make possible in the night that never ends?

"Fortify the walls," he orders. The man turns his head, looking at a high-ranking priestess. "Check everybody in the camp for signs of corruption or possession," he indicates. "Once you've finished, start over and do it again. Don't stop until we leave." He thinks for a moment, looking up to the sky. "Throw out any food and drink that has been touched by the rain. Just to be safe."

"Sir!" She salutes and takes her team to start looking for any internal signs of demonic influence.

He's been informed of the Demon King's penchant for trickery. He's not going to take any chances.

Something howls in the night.

The man turns his head, looking at all the other soldiers around him who have come to a stop, all of them staring through the glowing wall. A single voice carries through the darkness. It's wretched and broken, screaming with a shrillness to it that is . . . otherworldly.

"Watch the cliffs," he orders, passing by two soldiers as he walks off. "Make sure everything is locked down tight."

"Sir."

He's not going to let whatever is out there ruin his mission.

The scream carries through the air; like the wail of a banshee, it cuts through the heavy rain and the crashing of the tide.

~ [Demon General Sieben] ~
Terror | ♂ | Demon General
Location: Kobold Coast, on the Far Eastern Edge of the Demon King's Continent

His long fingernail runs along the base of the human's stomach, cutting her open from the bottom of her ribs to the base of her hipline with one long, slow drag of his hand.

Her intestines fall straight down out of herself.

The Demon King has ordered him and the other generals to only take prisoners so that their souls can be claimed for the power of the Demon Core. But in some cases, you need to break a few humans to catch a few more.

She screams like an animal, her body hanging loose as her steaming insides plop right out of her body. Her stomach, her entrails, sag out of her like bloated, gorged, dead worms, sagging and filled warm with the contents of her meals prior. Human waste and blood pool all around below the limbs of the tree, together with her blood and spit.

The nature of the Demon King's magic is one of beauty and the conniving trickery that life itself often embodies. It is a playfulness, almost, that one encounters during their days in this world when confronted with the universe in its happier moments. For those who know only suffering, this fact of life sounds absurd and perhaps almost esoteric, but for those who have glimpsed a twinkle in the glowing light of the sun, as if it were the mischievously shining eye of God, they know that there is a gamelike quality to life.

He picks up an old apple from the ground with one of his hands, looking at it.

With another hand, he pulls back her head and shoves it into her mouth, breaking several teeth, then forces her to chew with his other hands, which ends up breaking several more. He watches as the apple slides down her gullet and into her stomach, which drapes out of her open torso, hanging beneath her and being washed over with rain.

She screams, but she isn't in a state of awareness. It is simply the animal state that lies dormant behind the facade of humanity.

Bending down, he picks up her still attached stomach, feeling it in his hands, feeling the apple inside of it.

Life may be a game in many ways. But games can turn ugly, fast.

But if you're in it to win it, you need to be a little ugly yourself. Especially if you want to use that special magic that life has for those willing to dig deep enough into the rules.

He pulls on her stomach, pulling down her head, and then shoves it into her own mouth as the cycle continues.

Her wails carry through the air.

Playful worms, dancing in the rain, rise out of the soil and play around in entrails that remain down on the grass.

~ [Seaman Minani-ni] ~
Vildt (Feline) | ♂ | Master Sailor
Location: The Eastern Coast, Point Nordost
Level: 76

The *Abigalia* strikes the shoreline, beaching itself almost too vigorously, as if the wind were intent on helping them arrive as fast as possible.

The other less damaged ships of the armada remain out a ways, anchored, and their crew come to the shoreline on small boats. But the *Abigalia* and several other ships are lost causes for the home journey.

Minani-ni looks down over the edge as people begin to disembark.

Ropes and ladders are thrown off the front of the ship, and people begin to climb down, eager to touch soil, even if it is only the soaked, wet sand of the beach.

Guardsmen and priests come down the hang of the cove where they've beached and where the smaller boats are starting to land.

He sighs in relief and then grabs a rope, sliding down himself.

There's work to do. Supplies need to be unloaded, the wounded need to be brought to medics, and a full meeting of all of the surviving ships needs to happen so they can see what their numbers are like.

His boots touch wet sand, and despite the fact that the world isn't moving, he still feels like it is. His head wobbles from side to side, as if he had too much to drink, and the Vildt falls over, turning and landing on his back as he stares up at the sky.

A great sense of relief comes to him.

They made it.

He's spent his life at sea. But he's never experienced anything like this before. This was different.

The other men around him all collapse, too, in their own way.

It's not bad. It's just that a lot of them have a bad case of seaman's legs and severe sleep deprivation. It'll take a little while for them to get back on track.

A priestess leans over him, looking down.

"Are you well?" she asks, her tightly bundled black hair dangling in one knot over him. She smells like work and fear.

He looks up at her. "Never been better," replies the man as the water of the ocean rises up to his feet and then pulls back down away without him again. "We've come to help fight the Demon King," says Minani-ni.

"Water!" she calls over her shoulder to a team of attendants who are doing their best to get to everybody.

He closes his eyes, sighing in relief once again, just because it feels so good to do it. With his darkened vision, the wobbling of the world intensifies even more. But he just lays there and enjoys the sensation.

Something grazes his hand.

The Vildt opens his eyes and lifts his head, looking down at the half-eaten apple that has washed up on shore.

The worm seems to have gone for a swim.

~ [Knight Captain Filanze] ~
Elf | ♂ | Knight Errant
Location: The Eastern Coast, Point Nordost
Level: 90

He takes the admiral's hand, shaking it and nodding his head. "We'll see to your wounded," says the captain. "Point Nordost is currently being besieged, so we're trapped here," explains the elf. "Once it's done, you and your men will be escorted to the demon frontier."

"I see. Thank you, captain," replies the admiral, shaking his hand, a long, scarred set of ears hanging down below his hat. "Is it the Demon King?"

"Something of the sort," answers the captain.

"We have men to spare for lookouts and guards."

He shakes his head. "That won't be necessary. Thank you." He gestures up the cliffside of the cove. "You'll find the camp up there. You and your men have accommodations waiting."

The admiral looks at him and then nods.

Knight Captain Filanze turns his head, watching as the Vildt admiral and his group of officers are escorted up to the lodgings above.

As if he'd let some Vildt soldiers mingle in with his own men on the wall. He might as well throw the key over the wall into the Demon King's hands himself. The elf turns his head, spitting on the ground, before walking off to continue his duties. Now that the Vildt have arrived, they have to break the siege so they can get them to the Demon King as fast as possible, where they can make themselves useful as meat for the slaughter.

For every day longer that a Vildt stands on his continent, the world becomes just a little less worth living in.

Filth.

"What's that sound?" asks a sailor, referring to the wail in the air that belongs to some dying wretch.

"Just the wind," replies a soldier, escorting him to the camp.

~ [Demon General Sieben] ~
Terror | ♂ | Demon General
Location: Kobold Coast, on the Far Eastern Edge of the Demon King's Continent

The serpent eats its own tail.

In alchemical practice, the Ouroboros, the depiction of a serpent doing exactly this, refers to a great many things—the cycle of rebirth and recreation, the endless pursuit of the forbidden knowledge of the world hidden from mortal eyes by the gods.

The transformation of one object into another.

The woman has gorged on her own entrails, which loop down around below her chin before being pressed back into her face.

Her fingers twitch, and her eyes roll back into her head.

He watches the process continue, cycling over and over through herself until seven loops have been completed.

And for the first time, the woman stops screaming.

Her body, tied upside down to the bottom of the branches of the tree, falls limp. Her hands drape downward, and together with her head, her neck presses against the rope of her own hair that had tied her to the branch.

The demon general reaches into the mass of her confused, knotted entrails to find her stomach once again. Grasping it, he rips it fully free from her dead body, clutching it in his hands, and then cuts it open with a black nail.

A fetid, oozy mass runs out over his hand as the stomach, sliced open from side to side, flops open and drapes over his hand like a wet rag.

Inside the mess are several beautiful little apple seeds.

Magic is indeed a curious thing.

And forbidden magic is even more interesting.

He does as the Demon King instructs, heading to the prisoners. They lie, shackled in a bundled heap of screaming meat. He picks them up, one at a time, forcing the seeds down their spasming, screaming throats.

~ [Knight Captain Filanze] ~
Elf | ♂ | Knight Errant
Location: The Eastern Coast, Point Nordost
Level: 90

"The cannon is ready, sir," informs the head engineer. He looks over at the device. It's an interesting, if not limited, prototype weapon.

It's a long tube placed on a platform that can be rotated from side to side. It is mounted on one of the ley line nodes, the same kind the priest is using to amplify his magic in order to empower the Point's walls. With only normal casters around, it isn't worth using the device, as they could just spellcast themselves. But by hooking it into the ley line, it's essentially a free source of magical attacks, as one can channel violent bursts of the world's natural energy through it.

The theory is that it's an excellent coastal defense weapon, which is moot at the moment.

He looks back up toward the horizon.

But it will be important when the order comes to sink the Vildt ships. With its range and power, the device, which is the size of two men, will easily be able to accurately hit even those ships anchored out in the waters off the coast.

"Good work," he says. "Aim for the sky above the orchard," he orders. "I want some light."

"Yes, sir," replies the head engineer as he and his team rotate the gun toward the orchard, lifting its barrel up to the sky. It's, in essence, just a big tube. But the inside is lined with an intricate series of refracting crystals that take the magic and bounce it off a series of perfectly aligned fragments in just the right order to collect them together into one coherent blast.

"Charging." He watches as the ring of gemstones embedded in the platform around the device begins to light up in order, the glow traveling around the circle until it makes a full pass. "Salvo is ready, sir."

"Fire," says Filanze, turning back to look at the wall.

In an instant, the night changes. The wet, heavy hairs on his head rise up into the night, as if grasped by a witch's fingers. The air smells oddly clean all of a sudden, as if he were standing within a lightning strike. A resonant hum fills his ears, and then, the world turns bright.

An arc of light shoots out over the wall and into the night, cutting through the sky like a flying star launched into the air by the hands of men, as if they were throwing one of the god's own lights back at them. The streaking orb flies, hanging heavy in the sky and leaving a glow in its wake that lights up the landscape all around them, as if the sun had chosen to shine only on this particular spot.

"Sir!" calls a voice from the wall. He looks, seeing what the guardsmen see too.

There aren't any monsters left in the orchard. The gaps between the fallow trees are empty. All of the claws and teeth are gone, leaving only a few mangled limbs here and there. But what is of note is that there, off in the distance, are a group of humans and elves chained together and being led off into the night by a group of armored undead.

He narrows his eyes, watching them march on the back edge of the tree line. One of them stops to look up at the light and is pushed forward by the armored creature behind them.

"Should we send out a rescue party?" asks the soldier.

He thinks, staring and watching the people slowly vanish. It's his duty as a knight to keep as many people in his country safe and from falling into the clutches of the Demon King, but . . . "No," replies Knight Captain Filanze.

He doesn't trust this.

Sure, there's no way the enemy could have known they would illuminate the night and reveal their prisoner transport, but he's not taking any chances. If the stories of the Demon King's wiles are true, then this could easily be some sort of trap. What if they're undead pretending to be people? What if they're possessed and are just waiting to be ushered into the walls, where they can knock them down from within?

He's not falling for it.

"They're dead. Leave them," replies the captain.

"Barbarism," says a voice to the side. His eyes twitch as he gets ready to order lashings for one of his soldiers. But his eyes see the Vildt admiral, surrounded by his officers. "You would leave civilians that you could save to die?" he asks.

"It's my job to ensure the safety of this camp and of your men, admiral," replies Filanze, doing his best to suppress his disgust at being talked back to by such a creature. He has to take the high road here. "You don't understand the nature of the Demon King. This is *clearly* a trap."

The rabbit Vildt steps forward, adjusting his hat and waving over his shoulder for his men to gather together. "Knight captain," says the admiral, shaking his head in dismay. "I would fear that in your craze to protect your country, you have lost your humanity."

Filanze's eyes go wide as he clenches his fists. He does his best to calm himself before he engages in an act of war. "Where are you going?!" he barks. "You can't leave the camp!"

The Vildt admiral looks over his shoulder. "My men and I are going to fight the Demon King here, knight captain. Now." He looks back forward. "And not just when we arrive at his castle."

The man's thick accent digs through his head, along with the presumptuousness of his statement. It's a mockery of his rank, title, and position.

"Admiral," he barks. "You and your men are guests on our continent. I am the ranking officer here. You *will* do as I say!" commands the man.

The Vildt ignores him, walking away and lifting a hand. "I believe that as an admiral, I outrank you, captain," replies the Vildt, jokingly. His men laugh as they walk toward the wall.

"You won't be let back inside!" yells the captain.

The Vildt seem unfazed and simply walk through the magical wall, exiting its safety as the night begins to fall down again, the salvo launched into the air from the magical cannon beginning to die out.

The man clenches his teeth, froth practically forming on his lips as he spins around. "LOAD THE FUCKING CANNON!" he orders, screaming at the engineers, who don't dare make eye contact with him. "FIRE AGAIN!"

He wants them to die out there, being torn apart limb by limb. He wants the monsters that are still out there, clearly, to crawl over them as darkness falls and eat them alive.

But it would be a pure diplomatic disaster and a critical failure of the mission that he himself was tasked with; that is, to keep the Vildt safe and bring them to the Demon King's castle.

So as much as he hates them and wants them to die, he's just going to have to be patient and wait for the Demon King to handle it personally.

"FIRE!" he orders.

Another blast from the cannon launches into the air, illuminating the darkness with a fresh star in the sky.

~ [Demon General Sieben] ~
Terror | ♂ | Demon General
Location: Kobold Coast, on the Far Eastern Edge of the Demon King's Continent

He looks at the many monsters that lurk in the shadows, hiding where they may from the brightness of the human's illumination.

The humans saw his bait a little early, but that's fine. He managed to do what he needed to do while their eyes were all focused on the front wall of their little fortification.

The demon general turns his head and watches the waters of the ocean, which just need to do their part now in fulfilling the grand will of the Demon King.

~ [Knight Captain Filanze] ~
Elf | ♂ | Knight Errant
Location: The Eastern Coast, Point Nordost
Level: 90

It is half an hour later.

He stands there, impatiently staring off into the glowing night with a team of guardsmen and priests at the ready, just as a sound fills the air.

His ears perk up; he perceives them to be screams at first, but then, to his confused dismay, he notices that it's a song. They're singing sea shanties.

Those bastards.

Knight Captain Filanze watches with his emergency crew as the Vildt admiral and his men return, weapons and prisoners in hand; the wounded humans and elves they're carrying over toward the wall. It doesn't look like they lost a single man.

"Knight captain," says the admiral, holding a wounded and shackled elf in his arms. "We have returned from our most perilous journey." The Vildt smirks, tilting his head, his annoying, stupid, oversize hat tilting with it and his floppy ears. "It was quite the task, but me and my men managed to beat all five level-nine skeletons." He lifts his eyebrows. "Just barely," adds the man, mockingly.

"Let them in," orders Filanze. "Quarantine them here immediately. Nobody goes into the main camp." He looks at the priestesses. "Check them from head to toe, inside and out."

"Sir," replies the head priestess, walking over to the wall with several of the knights.

He looks back at the engineers and the coastal cannon. "Cease fire," he orders, before looking back at the men coming into the camp.

Knight Captain Filanze rubs his chin, thinking.

He's trying to view everything that happens through the lens of the question, "How could the Demon King use this?" Infiltrating their defenses is the obvious answer, but maybe that's not the case? It seems too easy.

Maybe the provocation insinuated between their factions is the goal? Maybe getting him angry and making mistakes is what the Demon King is planning.

Maybe his overthinking is the exact weapon being wielded against him.

Knight Captain Filanze narrows his eyes, running through every single possibility in his head. The wall goes back up, the priestesses look everyone over with their magic, and then give him a thumbs-up, clearing all of the survivors. They're real people, untouched and uncorrupted. Maybe they really were just prisoners?

"Sir," speaks one of his men. "Bodies are starting to wash up on the shore."

He looks at him. "It's probably just the dead Vildt," he says. "Throw them in a heap and let them be claimed by their own."

"Please!" cries a desperate, frantic woman. "You have to save my husband!" she pleads, grasping onto the admiral's arm.

He looks at her in confusion for a moment. "Ma'am," starts the admiral. "We only saw your group out there," replies the Vildt, lowering himself down onto a knee and placing his hand gently onto hers, which clasps his sleeve with dirty, bloody fingers.

She shakes her head. "No, the cliffs," she explains. "It took him and the others to the cliffs on the coastline!" yells the woman.

"It?" asks the admiral, looking at her.

The woman doesn't reply, the question of the identity of whatever she saw causing her to break down as she falls over and clutches her face, screaming as the priestesses rush over to her.

Knight Captain Filanze stands there, looking at them.

The coast.

That drop from the cliffs all around this region is high enough to kill anything, even the strongest of monsters. Point Nordost is the only place anything can set foot on here for miles on end.

"Sir," speaks the soldier from a moment ago, leaning in. "They're human bodies," whispers the man.

Filanze's eyes go wide. He spins around. *Shit. SHIT.*

"ALARM!" yells the captain. A bell starts ringing in the camp, followed by another one and then another one. "Guards, get to the cape!" he orders. "MOVE!" yells captain Filanze, running off in a full sprint through the rain through the camp, running through the rows of huts and tents as they make their way to the only path atop the cliffs that leads down toward the ocean.

Lanterns and torches light up the beachhead below, which is littered with corpses that have washed ashore. Yes, most of them belong to water-logged Vildt, but many fresher-looking ones lie there, too, and they are clearly human.

The corpses bulge and twist as something moves around inside of them, squirming and twisting as if great worms were pressing through their entrails.

Their stomachs bloat and burst, the living around them running away in panic as, from the seven human and elf corpses, twisted, gnarled trees press up unnaturally toward the sky, their roots digging into the blood- and salt-soaked sand of the corpse-littered beach as they grow with sickening speed, looking like clusters of veins.

Red, thick apples drop readily from their branches and regrow over and over, falling to the water.

Shit.

"CASTERS!" calls Filanze. "Bombard the beach!" he orders. "Destroy those trees!"

"Sir, there are still Vildt there," says a man.

The apples that have fallen begin to break apart, the sickly fruit rotting, and from the mush emerges a claw and then a tooth and then an eye. An instant later, a red, screaming monstrosity pulls itself out of the apple, a creature of impossible size compared to the egg it came from, as if it were simply pulling itself straight out of a hole in hell.

"It's a monster spawner!" barks Filanze. "FIRE!"

The casters lift their hands, firing salvos down into the beach at the trees that drop dozens, *hundreds* of fruits which continuously regrow over and over. A swarm of nameless, faceless creatures—demons from another era, born of unnatural, horrific magics—begins to swarm the area, climbing up the beached ships and raiding them, pressing their way toward the few fighters who manage to hold the line down below.

He knew it.

The Demon King really is always up to something, but he's ahead of the game. He caught it early; they can still control this. Stopping invading forces from rising up the beach is the entire point of this entire location.

"Ready the cannon!" he orders, lifting a hand, listening to the energetic hum fill the air.

The Demon King might think he's clever, but he's lost the element of surprise now. The game is over.

~ [Demon General Sieben] ~
Terror | ♂ | Demon General
Location: Kobold Coast, on the Far Eastern Edge of the Demon King's Continent

He lifts up a worm from the soil down below the bloodied apple tree to his mouth, whispering to it.

The worm wiggles and jiggles in his overabundance of fingers.

~ [Knight Captain Filanze] ~
Elf | ♂ | Knight Errant
Location: The Eastern Coast, Point Nordost
Level: 90

"FIRE!" orders Knight Captain Filanze.

The world shakes, the night glowing alight far too brightly.

He turns his head just in time to watch the explosion of the cannon blast impact into the center of the camp, into the ward-powering sigil, evaporating it and the priest entirely. Stones and shrapnel fill the air.

The wall around the fortification fades, faltering immediately. The heavy darkness from beyond encroaches on the camps, snuffing out flames and lanterns as it crawls toward them.

No . . .

NO.

It turns dark, and he doesn't see to whom the hands that drag him into the night belong, only that there are too many of them.

The beach was also a distraction.

~ [Seaman Minani-ni] ~
Vildt (Feline) | ♂ | Master Sailor |
Thrall to the Demon General
Location: The Eastern Coast, Point Nordost
Level: 76

Seaman Minani-ni and his group stand at the shore cannon they have commandeered on the orders of the great general as the camp falls fully dark, monsters parading through the screaming harrow, clawing into tents and huts, dragging out the sleeping and the injured, and tearing them alive off into the night.

The half of the apple worm he had eaten earlier wiggles around inside his brain.

Minani-ni turns around, lifting a hand and saluting the demon general.

The worm whispers words of praise to him, and he helps, taking apples full of worms and feeding them to the others so that they too can obey the orders of the great general, servant to his majesty the Demon King.

May his night never end.

The last light shining during that night, being within the eyes of a man, dies out as a worm crawls past it.

THE DOOR TO HEAVEN

~ [Ruhr, the River Sorceress] ~
Half Elf | ♀ | Sorceress
Rank: SSS
Location: The Demon King's Castle, Floor Fifteen
Level: 96

Just kill yourself," says the woman, looking at her. She blinks, leaning in toward the half elf and pressing a finger to her neck. "If you make a cut here, it'll go fast."

Ruhr looks at the ghost of a woman and then away from it, her eyes rising up to the thing dangling in the center of the room. It is a giant creature of sorts, easily the height of two men. It dangles from the ceiling by chains that bind its wrists together. Its legs are locked to pillars of broken ebony glass that cut into its body. Its head and face are covered with an iron mask. From its plucked, broken wings dangle no feathers but instead, only old, raw flesh, giving it the appearance of a sickly bat.

In the old depictions of lore, such an entity might have been referred to as an angel.

However, she doubts that such a thing would really be down here inside of the Demon King's castle.

"If you die on your own, before the Demon King gets you, your soul can move on to the afterlife in peace," continues the ghost, leaning in and whispering into Ruhr's ear. "You can be reborn somewhere else, anywhere else, in a time after all of this is over," it says, sounding oddly giddy at the prospect. The ghost shakes its head. "But if you don't, and you die here because of something else . . . well . . ." It shrugs. "The Demon King is very possessive of what is his."

(Montamonari) has used: [Exorcism]

The ghost screams with a shriek as she is blasted away by a priest of the crusade. The soul vanishes, crumbling into an ethereal ash that blows away in currents unfelt by physical senses.

"Thanks," says Ruhr, nodding to the man.

"Don't listen to ghosts," he warns. "These here, they're likely bound to the Demon King. Everything they say is a lie for his benefit."

She shakes her head and walks on. "Wasn't planning on it anyway."

Ruhr looks back behind herself. There are hundreds of ghosts in the chamber, drifting out of the body that hangs suspended from the ceiling, out of the gash that runs through its torso from top to bottom, out of which spirits claw, one after the other, ripping themselves out of its open torso like parasites fleeing a dying host.

"See anyone you know?" asks Zacarias.

She looks at him and shakes her head, watching more and more ghosts fly down from the ceiling. "I guess I never knew that many people, now that I think about it," she replies. "At least ones I'd recognize as a ghost. You?"

"Hey, guys!" interrupts an excited voice. The two of them turn their heads, looking at a spirit hovering next to them. It holds out a knife. "Did you ever think about dying?" it asks, excitedly.

"All the time," replies Ruhr, waving it off. "Get bent." She sighs and shakes her head as they walk beneath the dripping carcass of the angel. "Zac, do you ever think that the Demon King is a little . . ." She thinks for a moment. "I dunno. Childish?"

"Don't let it fool you," says Zacarias, narrowing his eyes. "It's a ploy to get past our defenses." He looks over at her. "Think about everything we've seen; everything childish that the Demon King fields to stop us has been some sort of trap or twisting of our own inner desires and wants." He shakes his head. "No. This is a carefully laid out, monstrous den of impossible horrors. If anything, this disgusting childishness of his is a mockery of the good life that all of us strive to hope for." Zacarias looks back ahead. "Don't let him fool you."

Ruhr looks at him and nods, looking at the door ahead of them.

It's closed.

An ornate sigil winds around the frame of the thing, marking it with

ancient imagery and letters from old languages no longer spoken by the people of the world.

A monster.

A true, old, ancient monster that knows how to manipulate the inner sensations of the hearts of men and women, playing with them as a child would with a doll it intends to break.

A chill runs down her spine as she thinks about what their final confrontation with the horrific entity will be like when they reach him, when they finally arrive to snuff out his terrible flames from this world and return him and his castle to the deep darkness of true sleep in the void between worlds.

~ [The Demon King] ~

The Demon King roars, his thousands of eyes opening in rage and devastation, his many contorted maws screaming a horrible roar, thick, mucusy saliva dangling between the gaps of countless jagged teeth. Pillars crumble, stones fall from the ceiling and crush statues and souls, some of which try to wiggle themselves out from the debris.

The Demon King is many things—powerful beyond imagination, cunning beyond the scales of both man, fox, and god, wicked in measures that demons and ancient monstrosities fail to comprehend. However, he is unfortunately terrible at hide-and-seek.

"You're it!" says the ghost, Kirsch, excitedly as she tags him. She flies off, giggling, as Swain looks around himself now that he has been tagged by her.

Swain looks down at his massive arms, the size of old tree trunks, with fists the size of boulders.

There aren't many good hiding spots for someone of his stature. Perhaps he should make some? It's his castle, after all.

But the point of the game is to inspire creativity and get away from work. A person, even the Demon King, who does nothing but work will never unfold the true creativity that they need in their other fields of life. Experiencing the unusual, putting oneself in odd situations, and not being too prideful to do so is where one comes to learn of the little quirks that are a part of existence.

Variety is indeed the spice of life, but more than that, it is the core ingredient of its more exotic dishes, as he's learned from Byblos, the cook.

Besides, this game . . . it reminds him of his old life, of old sensations, and even more thrilling than that, it fills him with the excitement of the hunt.

Stampeding through the darkness, the terrible Demon King finds those who are weak, those who are not as cunning or intelligent, and those who try to hide in the darkness of the world from the master of all things dark and wretched.

NEW (DEMON KING) ABILITY
[Spies in the Shadows] (Passive)
While one may think that winter nights are often full of wind and crisp air, it might trouble some to know that they are not always actually feeling a gale on their skins during the cool seasonal darkness, but rather that it is the breath of a thousand invisible whisperers who surround them.
Effect: Allows communication with the [Shadow People] under your control. They will report to you.

He snaps his fingers.

The throne room immediately fills with shadows, with hundreds of featureless, vaguely human entities standing before him and lowering themselves in a bow. He looks at one with a wide-brimmed hat that raises its gaze to meet his.

"Find my gallu," orders the Demon King. "Report to me where they are."

The man tips his hat.

The shadow people vanish, teleporting around the castle.

He may lack in the defensive, but the offensive is his strength.

~ [Shaushka] ~
Elf | ♀ | Classless
Location: The Edge of the Scorched Forest
Level: 4

The bee buzzes up and buzzes down.

Shaushka stands on the side of the road, watching it. It doesn't guide her anymore; rather, they've just been standing here for a while.

Her eyes rise up. Her eyes lower down.

Her head rises up. Her head falls down.

The bee rises up. The bee sinks down.

And so goes the song and dance as the two of them stand there for a while longer.

It flies toward her, finally changing pace, and then stings her in the hand.

"AH!" yells Shaushka. She lifts her arm, looking at the fat, bumbly bee attached to the top of her reddening hand.

The ground rumbles.

Shaushka looks at the bee that pulls itself free, leaving its stinger behind, and then bumbles off in a daze through the air before it plummets downward into the middle of the road.

Quietly, with wet eyes, she stares at the bee, her arm still outstretched.

The elf slowly turns her head to the left, looking at the carriages that charge down the main street, dozens of them, with hundreds of soldiers and people.

She slowly blinks.

Before she knows it, they reach her, and her outstretched arm grabs hold of one of the carriage's fronts, and she is yanked along after it.

Confused, the elf pulls herself in and looks at the coachman, who pays her no mind, and then looks back ahead.

She looks down at her hand, looking at the throbbing stinger still stuck in it.

Head empty. Eyes full.

The carriages move down the street, but she doesn't really pay that any mind, as her vision is focused on the stinger.

". . . Ah . . ." mumbles Shaushka.

~ [Ruhr, the River Sorceress] ~
Half Elf | ♀ | Sorceress
Rank: SSS
Location: The Demon King's Castle, Floor Fifteen
Level: 96

"Just jump. Get it over with," says the ghost floating next to her. Rushing waters fill the world around her. Ruhr leans forward, standing on the

head of a great serpent made out of her magic, as she fiddles around with the mask covering the angel's head.

Four other serpents rise from the core of the sphere she had created, each of them acting as a platform for one other person each, all of who are trying to free the limbs of the creature.

The door couldn't be opened, but a scholar of the crusade was able to read and translate the old language, revealing only a simple sentence.

It will lead you to heaven.

One can only assume this means the angel, bound and tied in this room to the ceiling. The entity squirms as they try to free it from its chains.

"Don't you want to see your family again?" it asks. "They're waiting for you, you know."

She looks down at the ground, whistling sharply.

The priest down on the floor below lifts his hands, casting another spell. The ghost next to her explodes.

They're not harmful; they're just . . . annoying and kind of mean, honestly.

She shakes her head.

She supposes that it would be more surprising if the Demon King had nice ghosts. He must really think very little of them, though, if he thinks that some rude ghosts are going to get them to quite literally kill themselves with some mean words after they've come all this way.

She fiddles with the mechanism, finding a piece to pull loose. A small rod shifts, falling down and clinking to the ground. "I think I got something!" she calls down and returns to her work as the others seem to be loosening up the binds around its limbs.

More ghosts crawl out of the hole in its core. "Hey, long ears," says a voice next to her. "I'd just positively die if I had an ugly nose like that."

Ruhr lifts an eyebrow.

How . . . snarky. It's like being a little girl in class all over again. The woman sighs, shaking her head as she unlocks the next mechanism.

"Between you and me," continues the ghost. "You should just go. Just run away and give everyone the thrill of having something to look at before you vanish forever." The ghost flies toward her. "The only good way to look at a person as ugly as you is from behind."

Ruhr whistles.

The ghost explodes as the priest blasts it away.

Another one crawls out of the angel's gaping chest and looks at her. "Hey, asshole. Don't fucking do that."

"Fudge you," replies Ruhr, pulling the rod free from the lock and throwing it at the ghost. It flies through the entity, clattering down on the distant stones below. The mask clicks, the lock having been opened.

"It's your funeral, you reject," says the ghost. "Between you and me, I don't know why you'd fiddle with anything locked up in the Demon King's castle." It shrugs. "I guess all of your growth went to your ass instead of your brain."

Ruhr whistles.

The ghost explodes.

The angel's mask swings open on a hinge, the face covering attached to the cagelike construction wrapped around its neck revealing what lies behind itself. She turns to look at it as the locks around its legs and arms come free.

There is no face.

The space inside the cage where the head ought to be is nothing except a jumble of ten thousand eyes that twitch, spasm, and then turn her way.

Chains rattle as it lurches, pulling itself free from its binds. It has bloody, tattered legs that have been cut into ribbons which hang loosely from the bone, dangling, as its featherless, mangled wings take flight. Its arms, freed from the binds above its head, drop down.

The angel screams, a shrill, piercing sound filling the air and breaking through the soft barriers of their ears to poke and scratch at the sides of their minds, like an animal trying to burrow its way inside.

Ruhr holds her head, yelling in pain as hundreds of eyes focus on her.

A giant hand reaches out, grabbing hold of her whole body.

She has no time to react before the screaming angel plunges her into its gaping, bloody chest, swallowing her whole.

"Dumbass," says a ghost in her ear as she vanishes into the guts of the monstrosity.

~ [Zacarias] ~

Human | ♂ | Royal Guardsman

Location: The Demon King's Castle, Floor Fifteen

Level: 91

"RUHR!" screams Zacarias, looking up at the entity as Ruhr dies. The urge to vomit fights its way up to his neck just as a man from the crusade tears him back as the angel lashes its arms out, swiping away the four others who were up in the air, and sending them hurtling violently across the room. Three of them are caught by priests with feather magic, but the unlucky fourth hits the ceiling, smashing his head against the wall and plummeting to the floor, leaving half of his skull up on the ceiling.

The angel lands, dropping down gracelessly, the floor rumbling as it makes impact. It spreads its wings out like a dragon on the charge as it lumbers down to all fours, screaming an otherworldly scream, blood dripping from all over its broken body.

Water cascades down around them from a failed spell, evaporating from the incredible ambient heat of the Demon Core, creating an immediate wall of mist which the great silhouette of a broken thing lumbers through, screams filling the air like a chorus from another plane.

(Zacarias) has used: [Royal Barrier]

A wall appears between them as Zacarias gets his shield ready. However, he's too slow.

The angel is entirely unbothered by his projection of holy magic and simply charges straight through it like a sickly, rabid dog. A taloned arm swipes his way, and he flies across the room, together with a dozen others, as another arm smashes down, crushing a few priestesses into a bloody paste on the stones.

He tumbles to a stop, lifting his spinning vision, as the angel—its talons digging into a screaming man's legs and neck—tears him in two pieces above its own head, blood, viscera, and urine raining down over its broken, warped gestalt, christening it in sanguine bile.

"Oooh, that's rough, bud," speaks a voice in his ear. "Guess you missed your shot, huh?" asks the ghost, nudging him. "Don't worry, I'll go back to the spirit world and take over," says the entity, winking. "I'll be sure to let her know you sent me."

It explodes as a priest targets it.

Zacarias screams, getting back up and running back into the fight as blood rains down around the room.

~ [The Demon King] ~

The shadow person whispers in a twisted language. Its faceless, mouthless head emits noises toward him that creep and crawl through the darkness like smoke, like the chittering of a spider's legs.

Swain looks to the right, reaching into a giant cauldron in the kitchen. He pulls out the cook, Byblos.

"You're good at this," she says, sighing.

Swain drops her, marching off. "None hide from the gaze of the Demon King." He turns his head, looking at a ghost. "Paper."

It howls in terror, flying off as fast as it can.

~ [Zacarias] ~
Human | ♂ | Royal Guardsman
Location: The Demon King's Castle, Floor Fifteen
Level: 91

The man slides back, staying on his feet as his tower shield takes the brunt of the impact. Dust and stones fly back from behind his boots as he leaves a scar on the floor. Tightening his knees, he presses back forward toward the lashing angel.

It screams, its wings flapping, pressing a violent gale all around itself. Hundreds of spells launched its way are immediately flung back toward the assailants below from the force of the channeling wind.

Many defensive barriers pop up, successfully blocking most of the spells, but not all of them. People scream as explosions ring out and friendly fire goes wild.

A group of archers fires a timed volley, pelting the creature with a line of arrows that runs along its left side from top to bottom. The angel screams again, turning its head toward them.

(Zacarias) has used: [Royal Decree {Halt.}]

Chains shoot up out of the ground, tethering themselves around the entity's legs, wrapping and binding themselves around it.

It simply moves through them as if they were nothing and barrels into the team of archers, sending half of them flying, and eating the other half.

He made the same mistake again.

From the distance, through the mist, he sees the hunched over, gaunt, bony form turning its head. The open door on the cage squeaks as it looks back toward the group of soldiers.

"Sir, should we release the grand crusade?" asks an unsteady man, looking at a superior officer and then at a collection of crates they had brought with them.

The paladin looks back at him and shakes his head. "No. We need to save them for when it counts. They're trusting us not to let their efforts be in vain." He lifts a hand. "Formation!"

The crusaders gather themselves together again, getting ready for another skirmish.

There is a clicking in the distance. The angel twitches. Its bulging eyes are visible through the fog because of their haunting, predatory glow, shining with unnatural fervor.

Zacarias readies himself, gritting his teeth—trying to get the visions of blue out of his eyes and heart—as his boot touches something.

There is a quiet tinkling of metal.

He looks down at an old, metal bolt that someone had thrown down from above.

~ [Slime] ~
Location: The Biggest Green
Level: 4

As it travels toward the west, the slime hops and hops, its goopy body bouncing and jiggling as it goes along what simply has to be titled as the Biggest Green. The Big Green was the meadow it had spent most of its life in. Then the Big-Big Green was a nice woodland. Now here, the landscape has changed, the forest tightening into a dense, deep nest of darkness that little slimes like itself would usually never dare to hop.

Three areas. There are three areas in the world where it has been. Perhaps this is all of the world there is?

It's hard to say. The little slime has only ever known such places. It supposes, in its rudimentary logic, that there must be at least one or two more places between it and the big meal it can feel itself being pulled toward. It still feels like it is very far away.

Still, it's running out of *bigs* and *greens*, so it hopes the next area is neither of these things.

Puddles splash as it lands in them, throwing water out in all directions. It has no idea why it is heading this way, exactly, other than some primal urge to satiate a deep hunger. It, as a very simple creature, possesses a simple feeling that tells it that it is supposed to be progressing in this direction.

As the slime jumps, it leaves behind a trail of goo that is quickly washed away by the pouring heavy rains. As slimes do during their lives, the slime faces a variety of problems and obstructions of all kinds. It has to jump across raging, overflowing streams that have turned into dangerous wild waters, and go through dense woodlands full of monsters that are, quite arguably, far more dangerous than a slime. Luckily for it, most monsters do not enjoy eating slimes, as there is simply not much meat on them, honestly, and they all seem preoccupied with hunts in other directions and areas.

It lifts its one eye toward the sky, looking through the dense tree line, wondering when the sun is going to come back out.

All of this rain is a little bothersome.

There is too much rain, so the soil is soggy, and the worms now refuse to come out, instead staying deep down below the world where it can't get them. But at least the rabbits are being flushed out of their holes and forced to tread water. That makes them easy to find and catch.

The little slime hops onward, toward destinations unknown.

~ [Commander Trinitatio] ~
Orc | ♂ | Oathsworn
Location: The Palisade
Level: 100

The man stands out in the rain, his old beard soaked through to his face with befouled rain, the stink of death and decay drawing ever closer toward them, unable to be suppressed by the constant downpour.

He stands there, staring out from the top of the old, ancient tower, one of seven, that sit high up on the distant mountains. The old fortress here has existed since ancient times, having been founded in far distant, far darker days by the men and women of that age to repel the malignancy of their time.

That tradition, that order of paladins, has existed to this very day, and now the Demon King has once again reared his foul head and dared to besmirch the gracious beauty of their world.

"Commander," says the man next to him. "What are your orders?" he asks, the storm howling with banshee winds.

Trinitatio looks at him and then back out over the cliffsides.

The fortress is in a deeply unique geographical location. The mountain region here is extremely jagged. Nature has created several plateaus and sharp cliffsides, elevated far off the ground with sharp drops. Nine bridges connect the many stone islands. Seven towers are each manned by a champion of an order of paladins, all seven schools of which had come together to form the whole legion that holds the Palisade as one unified force against darkness.

Now, the Demon King is on his way.

They do not know which road he is going to take; if he will diverge to the west, toward them, or to the east, toward the foul swamplands that they have failed to purge to this day because of the strange, twisted magics of witchcraft that govern over them. However, it remains clear that, either way, their orders are to buy as much time as possible.

The word is that there are additional forces on the way from around the world, the first of which should have already arrived on the eastern shores of the continent, coming from the domain of the Vildt.

"What's the news from the capital?" he asks.

The other man shakes his head. "Nothing new."

He sighs, having feared as much. "Prepare the bridges for demolition," he orders, looking back out into the night at the ancient stonework bridge that connects the entrance of the main road to the capital to the first vista. "We'll lock the beast down here."

"Yes, commander," replies the man, running off down the tower to make preparations.

It would be a shame, as these constructs have existed since the dawn of the order itself. However, they are just stonework, material things. Stopping the Demon King in his tracks goes far beyond some old monuments.

The Palisade exists to protect people, not itself.

He watches the storm and the horizon, waiting for the distant, crimson light to finally crest it.

~ [Witch Krokant] ~
??? | ♀ | Witch of the Odd Toadstool
Location: The Eastern Swamplands
Level: ???

Witch Krokant sits on her giant toadstool—which rests inside a strange, crooked house in the swamp—and yawns. The structure is not really what one would, using classical terms, define as being a house. Its walls are made up of roots, and mushrooms sprout from the floors. The doors are made of coffin wood, and the handles are made out of old harpy beaks. Goblins and humans and all manner of creatures and critters scamper and crawl around in their urgency. Puddles of glowing, moonlit water fill the area, shining with a light that can't be sourced from any heavenly body but rather from the magical fungal spores floating around inside them.

A lizard crawls up the wall, flicking its tongue at her, before vanishing. How rude.

Lizards really never have a good mind for sociality. They're always a little deranged. She tries not to take it personally; it's just what nature made them. Now, frogs, on the other hand, are a whole package unto themselves.

"He's almost here," says a voice from down below.

Krokant blinks, looking down at the man standing there. He's from the Witches' Sect, an organization of mortal beings who really, *really* like witches and go far out of their way to be useful to them. She doesn't quite understand them either, but she is grateful for their energy and help. Without them, she might just always sit around and snooze on her toadstool, never getting anything done.

The witch rubs her tired eyes, lying down sideways on her toadstool and resting her head on her arms as she looks at the robed man with sleepy eyes. "Do you think he's mean?" she asks.

The scholar puzzles for a moment. "He . . ." The man clears his throat, rethinking his phrasing. "Yes. I believe that the Demon King is mean, Witch Krokant," replies the man, taking care to maintain his professionalism.

They're all like that. They always seem to be treading on their tiptoes around her. Sometimes, she wished they'd just take a nap too instead.

"Should we be mean?" she asks, blinking with her springtide eyes.

"It would be advisable, should we be given cause," replies the scholar, looking at her.

She sighs, closing her tired eyes and squishing her cheek into her elbow. "Can't we be friends with him?" she continues, looking at the darkness inside her closed eyes.

"It would not be advisable," answers the scholar. "Even assuming that the Demon King would show us favor, given our distance from the rest of the common races, it would be assumed that he, as a mean person, would want you to be mean too in order to be his friend."

Witch Krokant thinks for a time. This makes sense.

She yawns, rubbing her tired face.

"Then I guess we can't be friends," she concludes. It's quiet for a while. The witch opens a single eye, looking at the man. "What's his opinion on horses?"

"Hor . . . ses . . . ?" The man shakes his head, clearly not knowing the word. "I am unable to say," puzzles the scholar. "However, I would assume the worst."

"Good," replies Witch Krokant, closing her eye again.

If one thinks lizards and frogs are real characters, well, horses were a real problem for a while. They were super mean. It's a good thing they're extinct, and that anqas took their place in the world. She doesn't think that the Demon King has anything to do with that—not this one or the last one, whom she only barely remembers. She didn't really have anything much to do with him. He was mean, too, and she doesn't care for mean people.

Witch Krokant falls to sleep atop her toadstool, letting the people down below do whatever it is that they like doing. They always seem to know best. She'll just stay out of the way and sleep in the meantime, hoping that the Demon King isn't mean, and definitely isn't some weird animal.

~ [The Demon King] ~

The Demon King roars in triumph, hoisting Cartouche into the air, who flails in annoyance at her, objectively, very good hiding spot having been found out.

The shadow people whisper into his ears before vanishing back out of the castle and spreading out into the world, haunting all of those people

who would dare try to close an eye within the realm of the terrible Demon King.

~ [Zacarias] ~
Human | ♂ | Royal Guardsman
Location: The Demon King's Castle, Floor Fifteen
Level: 91

Zacarias screams, blood splashing into his face as he slams the bottom of his shield down into the open cage, crushing a dozen eyes with the dull, heavy edge of the metal implement. The angel writhes, trying to lash and flail in vain, while dozens of men hold it down, pinning its legs, arms, and wings with their bodies and equipment after a brutal struggle that killed countless crusaders.

The eyes all look his way, bulging as he slams the metal down again into them, over and over, crushing, breaking, and smashing his way down through its head with a scream that never stops, coming from his core soul. Its wet insides spray out over him, staining his legs and torso, splashing against his face, and soaking him to the bone.

He's lost in the frenzy, his eyes wide.

Somebody places a hand on his shoulder as the shield lifts up into the air.

Zacarias looks at the man as he gasps and pants. The crusader nods his head to the giant body below. "It's over."

He stares at the man for a while, feeling his eyes burn, then he looks back down at the mess that he's standing in. The inside of the helmet is full of viscera. He's standing in a puzzle of smashed eyes and inner matter belonging to a corpse that no longer moves.

It's over.

Zacarias holds the shield up in the air, unable to let it down again. His shoulders feel like they've locked into place.

He screams, forcing his body to move, slamming the metal down one last time.

It's over.

The door off to the side of the room opens, revealing what seems to be the way to the next floor.

With blank eyes, Zacarias sits there, staring at the floor as the crusade collects itself back together, tending to the wounded and immediately burning the dead before they can be used against them by the Demon King.

It happened so fast.

She was just . . .

He turns his head, looking at the corpse of the angel lying there. The man stares at it as everyone begins to move again, heading toward the door. He can't stop looking at it.

"Brother Zacarias," says a voice. He looks to the side, staring at an officer from the crusade. "It's time for us to keep moving," informs the man, placing a hand on his shoulder. "I'm sorry. We'll see her again when we get to the heavens ourselves."

Zacarias watches them march, trying to figure out why he should get up again. It sounds dumb. He came here on a mission, after all. He had a goal long before he met her, right? He came here to kill the Demon King.

He just finds it very hard to get up right now.

Heaven . . . Zacarias shakes his head to himself, not sure if he can believe in something like that right now. His weary gaze moves back to the angel.

Its arms are laid together over its chest, its hands pointed together.

Did somebody move its corpse? When they killed it, its arms were spread wide, given that they were pinned down. Maybe the crusaders did out of respect for the corrupted entity?

Zacarias puzzles for a moment.

It will lead you to heaven.

The sentence that was etched into the door runs through his head. Something about it feels off. Something . . . No. Maybe he's just mixed up.

Zacarias closes his eyes, trying to think about anything at all, but he can't get the picture of Ruhr out of his head.

Hell. This place is literally hell.

His eyes open wide.

Zacarias jumps to his feet. "STOP!" screams the man, lifting his hands.

(Zacarias) has used: [Royal Barrier]

A shield spans across the open doorway, cutting off the members of the crusade who had already ventured inside from the rest of them.

A glimmer of light makes itself visible from behind the mass of bodies, down at the end of the tunnel. Then, a second later, his barrier shatters as a massive wave of vibrantly blue fire presses its way out of the freshly opened door, incinerating all of those who are inside immediately, while others run away, screaming, as the blue fires cover their bodies, eating away at their fats and skins.

It will lead you to heaven.

Zacarias spins to the side, running.

Why the hell would a door in the Demon King's castle lead one to heaven? It doesn't make any sense. It's a threat, a literal promise of death.

He climbs onto the corpse of the angel, tearing into its guts, visible through its eviscerated chest. Ever since its death, the ghosts have stopped pouring out into the world. But where would wicked ghosts come from?

Hell.

Where is the Demon King going to be?

Zacarias tears out an old organ, looking at the void he sees down inside the angel's twitching corpse. The man looks at its hands, which lie on the sides of its chest. Its crooked, taloned fingers point inward toward itself.

"It's here!" yells Zacarias into the crowd. "It's over here!" he shouts before jumping inside the corpse and falling through an impossibly placed hole until he comes to a graceless, unceremonious landing, sliding down an incline and taking a violent tumble over himself, his heavy armor making him far from graceful.

Desperate, the man looks around himself in the darkness of this new place, his eyes rising up to look at the bored face staring down at him.

"About flippity-flopping time, Zac," snaps Ruhr, the river sorceress. He grabs hold of her leg. "What? What the heck?" she asks as he rests his forehead on her thigh. "Get off, Zac! You frog-hopper, you're getting goo all over me! I'm fine, sheesh." It's awkwardly quiet for a time, but he just stays like that. Ruhr sighs, and he feels a hand falling down on top of his matted, blood-caked hair. "I missed you too, big guy," says Ruhr. "For all fifteen minutes."

"I thought you were dead," admits Zacarias.

"Aww . . . Zeezee *baby*," coos Ruhr. "I'm actually sad now, too. That's so cute." He looks up at her. The half elf tilts her head, scratching one of her long ears. "But if you cry, it's really going to ruin the clean, stoic image I have of you in my mind, though," she says. "Which is super hot in a way.

So don't." She thinks for a while. "Actually, it might be pretty attractive if you cry, at least for the first ten minutes. But then, after that, it's going to really kill the vibe we have going, you know?" Ruhr points at herself. "It's going to tarnish my brand if I keep a softy around."

Zacarias sighs, closing his eyes and just letting his head rest there for a time, at least until the others start arriving.

~ [The Demon King] ~

"What are your orders?" asks Cartouche, looking up at the Demon King on his throne now that the game has ended. It's time for them to choose a fork in the road ahead. Either they must go west, toward the old order of paladins who reside in the mountains, or east, to the swamplands in which the witches and their ilk hide from humanity.

Swain looks at her, lifting his gaze from his paper, and then down at the sheet.

"West," he orders.

"Are you sure, your majesty?" asks Cartouche. "The paladins will offer formidable resistance, and the terrain is against us. The witches are distant from humanity. We may be able to recruit them for our ambitions."

The Demon King shakes his head. "If they are distant from humanity, then we have no quarrel," explains the beast. "I do not care for foxes or birds, and so then, just the same, I do not care for them." He leans back against his horrific throne, thousands of souls filling the air around them. His many eyes narrow themselves in disgust, his many mouths curling and biting themselves in agitation from the thoughts of such people—*paladins.*

To devote oneself to the protection of not only this physical world but also its connections to the spiritual one, to stand guard for the ugliness that plagues the domains of the living, man or beast, fills him with an anger he can't begin to describe.

"West," orders the Demon King.

Cartouche nods and teleports away.

Paladins . . . Hundreds such creatures have already died within his castle, hundreds more outside of it. Perhaps it would be good to rid the world of this vermin nest, once and for all.

His many eyes look down at his poem.

He has already made preparations.

The Habiliment
In the darkness beyond us resides not but the grace,
Of the presence of an entity, which has just one face,
The Habiliment has no smile, no frown nor a grimace,
It merely has proportions, that are stretched without
limits,
Its arms are as long as the mountains are high,
Its legs are as wrong as the dead stars in the sky,
With gangly, creeping fingers, it will amble and climb,
Toward the dens of the humans, who it has in eye,
Through their windows it will reach with fingers as thin
as weak threads,
With nails as soft and as light, as dead infants' beds,
It will peel back their skin, to wrap itself warm,
In its seeking of trappings, to its long fingers adorn,
Yet these fingers are endless, with a span quite untold,
So it must collect a lot of skin to quite messily unfold,
It does this for joy, not for the thrill of the hunt,
As the Habiliment treats as toys,
The men of the mount.

CHAPTER 6

KNOCK KNOCK

~ [Schlinge] ~
Elf | ♀ | Initiate {Crossbowman}
Location: The Palisade, Tower One
Level: 5

The tower shakes, a thumping moving through it as something strikes against the wall outside.

Schlinge sits on the ground, her back pressed against the overturned table, her chest heaving as she tries to catch her breath. The woman turns her head, looking to the right at the others. A cold wind presses into the room atop the tower from outside, entering through the jaggedly broken glass facade.

"Ready?" asks a voice next to her. Paladin Abrishka, a colleague from the Order of the Lance.

Schlinge looks at him, her gaze moving over the smear of blood that runs from where they hide out toward the window. The smears are thin and four pronged, the shape of bloodied fingers that had been trying to hold onto the stones, nails breaking off as they clawed on for life while they were pulled away into the night. Schlinge shakes her head, holding her crossbow tightly against her chest. She's not ready. She's not ready at all.

Abrishka nods and jumps to his feet. "GO!" yells the man. Screams fill the room as dozens of people move at once.

SHE'S NOT FUCKING READY!

The Palisade is the old, ancient fortress of the many different paladin orders, all come together under one unified banner and roof generations ago to fight an old, great evil of the world. Since then, they have housed together, grown together. Training takes place between the many houses

of paladins, as do sessions of prayer and reverence, allowing them to become stronger as a unified force.

Each of the seven houses of paladins lives and trains within its own tower, one of seven, each of which is atop its own mesa connected with two bridges. One bridge goes to the prior tower, and one bridge goes to the next tower in the line. The Palisade as a whole is a long, snaky construction that spans the length of the cliffy, rocky region here. At the entrance to the fortress, there is one bridge in—by Tower One, where they are—and one bridge out, by Tower Seven, where she really wishes she was right now.

The entrance bridge to Tower One has been destroyed.

The Demon King and his carnival stand there on the other side of the ruin, their road having come to an end.

At first, volleys of arrows flew from the tower down onto his convoy, destroying and piercing hundreds of undead and ghoulish creatures of the night. This was all well and good, everything seemed to be going well enough, and there were even some jokes being told about how easy it was to stop the Demon King with some bad infrastructure.

Until *it* saw them.

Schlinge screams, jumping to her feet together with all of the others. It felt like an eternity had passed between the instant Abrishka gave the order to move and now, but it wasn't even a second. Her body is pumped full of adrenaline, and her mind is racing like it never has before.

Dozens of boots run off, making a break for their lives. They have to get out of here; they have to make it to Tower Seven and Commander Trinitatio—that's where it'll be the safest, the furthest from the Demon King.

Glass crumbles as something moves through the already broken, jagged edges of the windows and reaches inside. She dives down, hiding beneath another table for a second as a scream cuts through the air, the man next to her having been grabbed and torn out into the darkness. They hear him screaming outside the windows, which is a feat in and of itself, given how high up they are, but nobody stops to go toward him as they all make a break for the doorway, shuffling through into the stairwell.

The paladins shuffle down the spiral staircase. "Let's just go into the quarters," suggests a man as they move. "No windows there."

"Yeah, and one door," replies someone else.

Abrishka turns his head around. "Sounds like a death trap to me. We're going out. We have to get to Tower Seven," says the man. "The commander's there."

They move, the thin windows of the tower stairwell on their right sides aglow with the faint shine of moonlight. Schlinge wipes her face, looking at the glass as they go.

It's outside.

The thing, the lurker, the monster. She doesn't know how it's even possible, but it's out there. It's watching through the windows of the tower, waiting for anyone to come too close, to come out of hiding.

The next window doesn't glow. Something is blocking the moonlight.

She doesn't have time to scream a warning before her instincts kick in and she drops down. Schlinge falls. Glass shatters, and she looks, watching as a set of long, pale, white fingers with too many joints wrap themselves around Abrishka.

It yanks its hand back outside, but it's too wide with the man in its grasp to fit back through the hole, as he is too large as is. Angrily, something pounds on the tower from outside, screams filling the room as it tries again and again to pull its hand back out, refusing to let go of its catch, and, in doing so, repeatedly crushes the man against the narrowing window. His chest compresses in its grasp. His head and neck, too long to fit sideways, break and hang at a full right angle, as do his legs, before he vanishes into the night.

"THIS WAY!" yells the man from a moment ago, grabbing hold of some people and tearing through a door to the left, to the central inner area of the tower. There are no windows there.

Schlinge, lying down on the stairwell, watches them go, running to the side. Something screams outside of the tower, a banshee wail filling the night, as a ghostly, long limb enters back inside the tower, reaching for the door where they're all vanishing.

It feels around, trying to grab hold of anyone, but failing to do so.

Horrified, she watches as they vanish, leaving her alone down on the stairwell. The arm above her flails around as the tower shakes, a fist hitting it from the outside. Schlinge cries, her chest heaving as she crawls forward on her stomach, moving down the staircase, pressing herself as flat as she can to not touch the arm hanging above her.

She's all by herself now.

The woman crawls over the smear of blood left by Abrishka as she escapes. The tower shakes behind her, the long arm still trying to grab hold of anything.

~ [The Demon King] ~

"The bridge is destroyed, your majesty," says Cartouche.

Swain sits on his throne, his head resting on his massive fist as he looks down at the dancer. "All is well, Cartouche," speaks the man. "We're playing a little game today," he explains. "We'll be on the move again soon."

She looks up at him. "You seem to have a penchant for games these days."

The Demon King shakes his head, laughing. "Life is meant for living, Cartouche."

~ [Achievement Unlocked] ~
"Daddy Went to Grab Some Milk"
Unlocked By: Killing a father with six or more children.
Reward: The [Demon Sickness] now applies stacking status
[Tremors] to all orphans, widows, and widowers afflicted by it.

~ [Schlinge] ~
Elf | ♀ | Initiate {Crossbowman}
Location: The Palisade, Tower One
Level: 5

She holds her breath, keeping her eyes as open as possible. One hand presses itself back against the wall; the other clutches the crossbow against her chest.

She made it down the stairwell to the gate house. The bridge to Tower Two is just beyond.

They were prepared for many things. They were prepared for an onslaught of undead hordes, for demons to storm the towers, and for flying horrors that filled the night. They were prepared for soldiers and legions of darkness. But whatever this thing is, they weren't prepared for it.

She's not even a paladin; she's just an initiate. She came here to study the ways so she could decide if it was something for her. Schlinge curses herself. She knew she should have tried the wizard's academy first. Being a wizard is more fun. Paladins are so strict and uptight—not as bad as priests, but she wouldn't want to become a priestess anyways. They're not allowed to do anything and are barely paid at all. But her parents encouraged her to come here. Too many wizards on the market already, they said. Poor pay, poor conditions. Paladins, as partial healers and partial combatants, are always wanted, no matter where they go. Sure, you have to make some vows here and there, but it's a decent gig. Kill some monsters, preach a few sermons.

It all made sense.

But right now, she really wishes she would have done literally anything else.

Something groans in the darkness. A creaky, wordless voice that sounds like it belongs to an old hag fills the air, causing the hairs on the back of her neck to stand on end as she watches the long arm quietly move around the room.

Its fingers, each as long as the tallest men she knows stacked together, crawl and walk like a spider, like a bored child moving its hand over an empty table. The fingers with too many joints bend and curl unnaturally as they flick around, touching, feeling, and sensing for anything that it can grab.

Sometimes, it will find something it thinks is a person, like an old tapestry or a torch that burns it, and it will yank those things away.

Schlinge slides along the wall. She's on the opposite side of the room, but she isn't taking a chance. The arm moves her way. The woman, her heart thudding in her chest, silently slides down the wall onto her bottom and then falls over.

The fingers crawl toward her as she tightens herself into a ball. A large digit lands next to her, her vision filled with the off-white of its skin, as another finger lands behind her and then another. Old, dried blood and gore cakes them, filling her lungs with the nauseating smell of rotting meat that enters into her senses, even if she isn't breathing at all. It smells of dank, musky death. It smells like the unwashed body of a demented senior, rotting during a late phase of their still living presence.

She silently prays, her chest burning from holding her breath for so long.

The fingers step over her, continuing to crawl around the room. She slowly exhales, moving forward toward the exit, toward the very hole the arm is coming through—the open gate to the bridge to Tower Two.

Something lurches.

She lets out a yelp, sure that it's over, that she's been sensed. But the arm glides straight back past her and then pulls itself out of the gatehouse, its owner apparently either giving up or having found something more interesting.

Schlinge breathes, jumping to her feet and running to the gate, carefully leaning against the wall as she looks out into the night, trying to see if she can detect anything there at all.

But she can't.

The storm is too heavy and thick, and even if there is anything out there to see, she simply can't identify it.

A glint of metal catches her eye.

She looks to the side, across the bridge. A man is standing there inside of Tower Two, waving to her to run. He looks to the side, out toward the side of her tower, and changes his gesture, signaling for her to stop and wait. Her fingers grip the edge of the tower. He waits for a moment and then nods, looking back her way with a more hurried motion now that signals for her to run.

The elf takes a deep breath, not sure exactly how she manages to make her own hand let go of the corner wall, as her boots splash through the puddles. Water streams from the bridges, high up in the air above the canyon below, which, while dry only weeks prior, is now full of water with a raging river, the numbing roar of which can be heard even all the way up here.

The woman squeezes her crossbow against her chest as she runs toward the man.

She isn't brave enough to look back, to look at Tower One or at what might be around it. She isn't brave enough to lift her gaze, to make sure that there is nothing looming above her head—greedy fingers, ready to yank her into the darkness. All she does is run. She runs and she listens to the little, hissing voice in her head.

Schlinge isn't particularly good at anything, honestly. She knows it. While some people are clearly called to be tailors or smiths, archers or great wizards, given their obvious natural talents and gifts, she's

always just sort of existed in the middle of things. She's not terrible at much of anything, but she's also not really good at anything either. She's not smart or wise; she's not beautiful or strong. She's just sort of perfectly, acceptably normal in every way possible. Not so much so that people would describe her as boring, but more so that, if they ever actually saw her, they would be surprised that she was in the room at all with them. She's unnoticeable. This is why the crossbow is her favorite weapon. It requires significantly less expertise than other forms of fighting.

However, one thing she's always had is a very strong and well-defined inner feeling. That particular internal voice that is, for men, commonly referred to as a gut feeling, and for women as a woman's intuition, which is actually the same exact thing. She's not sure why this is split up into two ways, not that it matters. What matters is that this sense of hers has always been particularly strong, and right now, it's telling her that something is wrong.

Despite all the logic and reasoning in the world saying that she shouldn't stop, she does, her boots slowly thudding to the end of their pace as she stands three-quarters of the way across the bridge. Schlinge stands in the rain, looking at Tower Two. Her eyes, following the voice in her gut, wander up the exterior walls of the tower, staring at the broken, hammered-on facade and shattered windows.

Lightning flashes on the distant horizon, illuminating a long, meaty tube that presses in through an upper window of Tower Two at a downward angle, which she follows all the way to the man standing in the doorway, waving for her to hurry up.

She lifts her crossbow, aiming at his chest, and fires.

The man doesn't stop waving.

The hairs on her neck stand on end as she hears a voice in the night around her, an excited, giddy moaning. She can practically feel its breath on her neck, waiting for her to do something.

Slowly, the woman reaches down to her belt quiver, pulling out another bolt, not daring to make any surprise movements.

It's right behind her.

The game ends. It knows that she knows.

The man in the doorway stops moving. Five long fingers, pressed into his flesh—one for each limb plus his head—flop down to the ground. The

long-dead corpse used as a doll flops down to the stones as the long arm slithers back out up the stairwell of Tower Two, toward the window.

It was just pretending, playing a game, to lure her out into the open. Tower Two was already compromised from the start.

She sets the bolt into the crossbow, quietly reloading the spring through use of the cranking mechanism. The crossbow shakes violently, as if the wind howling over the bridge were yanking it around, its cool touch intermingling with the warmth of its gleeful breath.

Her hand shaking, the crossbow rattling, Schlinge exhales.

Her plan is to spin around. If she spins around very quickly, before it can react, she can . . . she can shoot it in the eye or the face or whatever it is and make a break for it, right?

The crossbow shakes.

She's such an idiot. Why didn't she just stay inside the tower?

Schlinge's hand shakes.

Now!

. . . She doesn't move, her body not having the willpower to follow the command that her mind gave. Slowly lifting the crossbow, she angles it upward.

She just has to pull the trigger. It'll hurt less. Gods know what will happen to her if it grabs her, right? She saw what happened to the others, sort of. She doesn't want to go out like that.

NOW!

Her body still doesn't move, but her arm does, slowly angling it up just a little higher, moving her elbow just an inch higher, so that the bolt is closer to her own head.

The rain stops falling on her. It continues falling literally everywhere else. One could only assume that this means that something is hanging over her, blocking it.

Her finger twitches on the trigger, her legs shaking.

"*NOW!*" screams the woman, pulling the trigger.

~ [High King Mercator] ~
Half Elf | ♂ | King
Location: The Capital City in the Distant North
Level: 100

"GUARDS!" screams the king, smashing his fists against the table. His eyes—wide, red, and bloodshot like a ruby moon in the sky—stare with terrifying intensity at the court artist. "STOP THIS MAN!" he screams, froth building at the corners of his mouth as he points at the artist. The man has moved the little game piece over the large map again, signifying the movements of the Demon King.

Why would he do this? He's making the Demon King move.

"My lord . . ." starts his advisor. "Please. You need to rest," says the man in concern. King Mercator's eyes, wide and still not blinking, look around the room full of so many people. Most of them have faces, but a lot of them don't.

A shadow hangs over his shoulder, whispering and pointing at the artist too. He's making the Demon King move by touching that damn piece on the map. He's the problem. The shadow whispers to him and tells him this. It makes sense. A traitor. A traitor in his own court—that's how the Demon King has managed to come so far. Of course. He should have seen it sooner.

But the fool artist made the mistake of moving the game piece to the Palisade. The Demon King is going to be stuck there. The paladin orders are ready for him. If there's anyone in the world who can stop him, it's them.

"Where are the Vildt?!" he screams, turning to look at his advisor for affairs of war.

The man stares, lifting a hand and then slowly lowering it. "My . . . my lord. Because we reduced their numbers by your order, the Vildt were unable to repel the Demon King's counterinvasion forces upon landing." He shakes his head. "They're gone. We're alone."

King Mercator screams, grabbing a knife from the table and his advisor with the other hand.

ANOTHER TRAITOR.

"YOU DARE MOCK ME IN MY OWN COURT?!" screams the king, his eyes bulging. The shadows whisper in his ears. *Look at the man's eyes. Look at the glint in them. He's trying to make you look bad; he's trying to insert the sparks of rebellion. Everyone at the table . . . the artist, the advisor . . . they're all working for him; they're all agents of the Demon King.*

"GUARDS!" screams King Mercator, spittle flying everywhere. The whispering intensifies. They're mocking him. They're all against him. They're trying to help the Demon King. They're—

(Royal Guardsman Vandalo) has used: [Sleep]

His eyes grow heavy, and his head droops.

The shadows dance all around him, whispering into his ears, trying to fill his mind with dire warnings and promises.

But the magic is too strong, and he falls to sleep, being caught before he falls to the floors.

~ [Schlinge] ~
Elf | ♀ | Initiate {Crossbowman}
Location: The Palisade, Between Towers One and Two
Level: 5

She screams, falling forward. The bolt flies off at an angle, whistling as it vanishes into the night while explosions ring out all around behind her. Scrambling, she runs, looking over her shoulder just in time to see a long, gangly silhouette vanish into the mist. Magical explosions strike against it as spells are blasted out from her tower. She moves, her heart racing as she makes it across the bridge, looking back as an appendage, long and tendril-like, wraps itself around the entire middle of Tower One, as if the long arm had more joints inside its middle. The stones crack.

The people inside, her group whom she had separated from before, had distracted the creature, attacking it with their arrows and magic.

The tower cracks as a whole as the creature squeezes, stone pressing inward, parts of the structure failing, falling over and off, creating large gaps where bricks and woodwork are missing. Chunks of ancient stone, carved generations ago, fall down into the dark ravine below.

She can't see the creature.

It's off too far in the distance, reaching over with impossibly long arms, standing on impossibly long legs that must reach all the way down to the bottom of the canyon. With those long, gangly arms of its, it reaches into the broken tower, grabbing the people who no longer have any cover.

Schlinge slams the door to Tower Two behind herself, not watching. She jumps over the corpse of the waving man, doing her best not to look

at his skinned, hollowed-out body which had been used like a plaything, while she runs through the rooms toward the exit.

They're supposed to be stopping him, but it sure doesn't feel like that's what they're doing.

Towers One and Two have fallen. She has to get to Seven—that's where everyone is going to be; everyone who's made it. She has to warn Tower Three about what's coming.

She stops, entering the main hall at the base of Tower Two, between both gatehouses.

Red flaps hang everywhere, blood dripping down the odd things draped over the walls, over the banisters, and on the backs of chairs.

Lifting a hand, she grabs a lantern on the nearby wall and lowers it down to look at the flat, draped thing there.

A pair of hollow eyes, lips, and a nose look back her way. They belong to Abrishka.

It's skin.

A human's skinned face, still attached to the rest of their exterior, hangs there like a doll's clothes.

She covers her mouth, dropping the lantern as she runs as fast as she can toward the next gate.

Rubble blocks the doorway, and she comes to a stop, looking around for a way forward. The window. She clambers over to it, looking outside and across to Tower Three.

A horn blows in the distance.

She listens, recognizing the tone. It's the sound of the gathering horn, signaling for everyone to regroup. It's coming from Tower Seven, all the way in the back. Schlinge wipes her eyes on her elbow, feeling herself crying. People are still alive. They're still there.

The sky lights up, glowing as it would during a spring festival, as barrages of holy spells shoot through the air from the back tower. Hundreds of them, colliding and exploding in the night as they either hit the creature or one another in flight.

A scream fills the air, and she takes it as a sign that this is her chance. Jumping out of the window, she lands on the bridge below and runs as fast as she can toward the ajar door, her soaked hair clinging to her neck.

~ [Military Advisor Blumen] ~
Human | ♂ | Royal Knight
Location: The Capital City in the Distant North
Level: 100

He looks down at the king. "Bring His Majesty to his chambers. Call the royal physician to attend to him. Make sure he sleeps through the night," orders the advisor, being next in line, as he sighs and rubs the bridge of his nose.

It must have been too much stress for His Majesty. The man hasn't slept a wink, which after this many days, would destroy anyone.

With his own tired eyes, he looks back at the board.

The Demon King hasn't moved yet; his carriage is still parked at the broken bridge leading into the Palisade.

Maybe it really has worked. Maybe the paladin orders really are holding him off.

Gods bless them.

He can only hope that the crusade—and all of the stragglers still on their way—pressed into the belly of the Demon King's castle can defuse the menace before it finds a way to go on.

All they can hope to do in the meantime is buy more time.

His eyes wander up the road, looking at what would come next, assuming the Demon King proceeds from where he is.

"Send a messenger out," he orders, pointing at the spot on the road ahead marked with a skull.

". . . Sir," replies the guardsman, looking at the map. "That's a dungeon. Nobody lives there."

Advisor Blumen shakes his head, tapping against the map as he looks at the guardsman. "Send it to the dungeon."

"S . . . sir?"

The man looks back at the overview of the world. All of humanity is interested in stopping the Demon King and the reign of monsters.

But he isn't the only thing with dominion over the creatures of tooth and claw. Surely the dungeons of the world, uncommunicative as they are, have a few varying opinions on the matter themselves.

They can't afford to leave any stones unturned.

"Jot this down," he orders, coming up with a plan as he looks at the

skull on the map, one of the forty-nine dungeons spread across the world.

~ [Schlinge] ~
Elf | ♀ | Initiate {Crossbowman}
Location: The Palisade, Tower Three
Level: 5

"GET OUT OF HERE!" screams the old man at her, cowering in the corner. "GET THE HELL AWAY FROM ME!" he howls, swiping through the air with his knife. She backs off, holding her hands in the air.

Schlinge looks around herself. Tower Three is empty. There isn't any blood. There aren't any broken windows or walls. It's just empty. It's like everyone just got up and left, except for this man here, all by himself.

"We need to get to Tower Seven!" she says.

The man looks at her, holding the knife out with wide eyes and a shaking hand. He starts laughing, looking at her with a demented, wild look in his eyes all the while.

A second later, he draws the knife across his own throat and falls down, blood streaming out of his neck as he gurgles and chokes, gasping for air, laughing. All the while, he looks at her, the insignia of his order, a rod and ring, vanishing in the pool of red.

Schlinge runs.

She reaches the bridge to Tower Four and waits for her chance.

The night is quiet.

The elf leans against the gatehouse, doing her best to keep down the nausea in her gut as she listens carefully to the noises of the outside world.

It's just . . . quiet.

The storm howls on like always, but there aren't any horns, there isn't a blasting of spells, or the screams of terrified people. It's just entirely silent. The woman stares for a while, watching and listening.

The rain sounds like it should. It doesn't sound like there's anything here, stopping it from landing nearby.

Taking a deep breath, she checks her crossbow and then runs across the bridge, the only thing that makes noise in the night, crossing over to Tower Four, which is burning with wildfires that aren't quenched by the rain. Tower Four's order is the Order of the Flask—they're alchemists,

brewers, and all manner of spellweavers. Their home is full of incredibly volatile reagents, which seem to have all caught fire.

Schlinge makes it across, despite her bad feeling about the matter, and quietly closes the door behind herself, looking around the area.

Smoke drifts through the tower, which is also devoid of bodies, but for some reason, there are boots everywhere.

The elf's eyes wander as she looks down at the rows and rows of neatly arranged, sorted boots. Small boots and big boots, metal boots and leather boots. All sorts of shoes and slippers are lined up by the hundreds. They're stacked neatly onto tables and on chairs. They're patterned across the room in zigzag lines. There are pairs of boots neatly placed on the chandeliers above.

She gulps, walking across the room past barrels of explosive materials that haven't caught fire yet.

Her eyes stare at them for a moment as the idea comes to her. The woman grabs some of her crossbow bolts, dipping their heads into the alchemical solutions. A little extra firepower can't hurt, right?

Carefully, she stows them away, sorting them apart from one another—as combining the liquids will result in an explosion—and then makes her way to the exit before looking around and running across as before to Tower Five.

The horn sounds again, from up atop Tower Seven, when she's halfway across, and she quickly vanishes into the tower, her heart racing.

Everybody must have already evacuated and regrouped at Tower Seven. She's probably the last one trying to get across.

The elf steps inside, leaning back against a wall to catch her breath, the warm vapors of which rise up in the air, drifting past idols and altars of Tower Five, belonging to the Order of the Salve, priests and priestess who devote their lives to praying, healing, and mending wounds.

Her eyes follow her own breath rising up to the stained-glass windows that fill the room's upper area, past the full moon which is behind a central image of religious iconography.

The moon vanishes for a moment as something draws over it, and then rises back up again.

Her body shakes with strong but slow, janky shakes as the terror comes in a new form, with the elf starting to cry again, her chest lurching, and her throat aching as warm urine runs down her leg and down into her

boot, pooling beneath her foot, and dripping down to the stones as she stares at the window and the moon behind it, which is actually an eye. It stares back at her through the glass.

The span of a large, gangly smile with many sharp, wildly spaced conical teeth is visible only in part through the many, many windows that it spans. Dozens of small visions of its face come together into a collage.

Its eye is purely white and unnaturally round. It is surrounded on all sides by misshapen, uneven black squiggles, as if it were a poor drawing of a face. Streaks of black hair, as long as the night itself, drape down around its angles, wet and greasy. The red splotches covering its face, born of the stained glass, look like endless streaks of blood.

It's like a child looking down into a dollhouse.

Playing.

It moves away, leaving her standing there against the wall, the bolts in her quiver rattling as the wooden poles strike against one another.

~ [The Demon King] ~

~ [Achievement Unlocked] ~
"It's Not a Thing, I Swear!"
Unlocked By: Causing a hundred people to urinate themselves in public.
Reward: All flowing bodies of water within your territory are now corrupted, increasing the spawning rate of wild WATER and POISON monsters by 100%

Swain holds back a laugh, the grunt scratching in the back of his throat as he looks at the window that has appeared.

"OH *NO!*" yells a voice to the side. He turns his head, looking at Kirsch the ghost. She looks at him. "I just remembered that I have to tell my mom that I need new bedsheets!" she says, looking down at herself, at the blood-soaked cloth wrapped around her body. She looks at him. ". . . She's gonna yell at me . . ." finishes the ghost, sadly.

The Demon King looks at her. "Don't worry about it," he says. The Demon King looks to the side, grabbing a terrified ghost out of the air. "Bedsheets," he orders, his voice growling and shaking the rocks, his dozens of eyes bulging. The ghost flies off in terror, coming back a moment

later with a set of fresh, white linens, the source of which is not wise to be questioned within the confines of the Demon King's castle.

He hands it to the ghost. "Just replace them with these and hide your old ones," he says.

She tilts her head, looking at her doll and then at him as she takes the sheets. ". . . Isn't that lying, though?"

Swain leans back on his throne. "Sometimes, lying is the best thing you can do," explains the Demon King.

"But isn't lying wrong?" asks Kirsch.

Swain looks at her with his dozens of eyes. "Your mom is going to be mad if she finds out, right?" he asks. The ghost nods. "So by not telling her, she won't get mad. It's the best thing, isn't it?" continues the Demon King. "Don't you want her to not be mad?"

Kirsch thinks for a moment and then nods. "That makes sense!" she says, clutching the bedsheets to herself and immediately staining them with the blood streaming through her own sheet. "Thank you!"

Swain nods, waving her away with a swipe of his fingers as he leans back on his throne.

~ [Achievement Unlocked] ~
"It Wasn't Me!"
Unlocked By: Teaching a child to lie.
Reward: You are now keenly aware that all children are demons who can never be trusted.

Truly, the immorality of the Demon King knows no bounds.

~ [Schlinge] ~
Elf | ♀ | Initiate {Crossbowman}
Location: The Palisade, Tower Six
Level: 5

She doesn't know how she did it, but she made it. Ignoring all sense of shame, Schlinge keeps on walking as she reaches the gate to the bridge leading to the last tower.

She's almost there. Just a little further.

A horn blows atop Tower Seven.

The barrage of spells comes again, dozens of them flying out of the tower and into the night behind her, where she assumes the creature to be.

This is it.

Schlinge gulps, breathing in heavily as fast as she can, her mind and heart rushing with energy. She screams, running across the bridge and toward the door to Tower Seven, which is closed.

She reaches it, hammering against it to get it to open, which it does.

The elf steps inside, her chest heaving as she looks around herself.

She made it.

She made it to Tower Seven.

This is the only place that's safe. She's just an initiate, so she can't leave the sanctuary that is the Palisade. Her level is too low, so she wouldn't survive within the territory of the Demon King. The fortress's protective warding keeps her safe from the Demon King's magic.

She listens to the cracking of spells in the night coming from upstairs and runs to the staircase, heading upward toward the top of the tower. Tower Seven belongs to the Order of Command and is home to the Grand Oathkeeper, the leader of the Palisade, and the father of all orders of paladins.

They're staging the defense here. The woman runs up the stairs, patting her crossbow that she managed to lug all the way with her. She can make herself useful here. She wouldn't mind pelting out a few arrows into the darkness now that she's not alone anymore.

Schlinge runs past many open doors and many people standing by windows, hurling spells out into the night.

She reaches the top, hoping to find some officer there to report to, looking at the insignia on the back of a rod and ring.

Commander Trinitatio himself, the leader of Tower Seven and of the orders, the commander.

The spellcasting stops.

The commander's bare feet leave the ground as the fingers pressed through his torso lift him up into the air, together with many other limp bodies that are pulled out through windows and doors. None of them have shoes on.

She falls down, back onto her bottom, and crawls back against the wall, kicking an old horn to the side inadvertently as she lifts her gaze,

looking up toward the sky, following a long, long, slender thing that rises up for as far as she can see, vanishing into the mist.

Only a large, toothy, gapped smile is visible, together with two perfectly round white eyes that glow like a pair of moons in the night.

It was just playing with her.

Everyone is dead.

Everyone has been dead this entire time.

Crying, she holds her crossbow aimed up at the giant in the sky—larger than any of the towers, larger than all of the towers put together.

Schlinge grabs her explosive bolts, firing them off and screaming between each shot. The bolts don't even come close to reaching its face. Even with the power of a crossbow, they just fly somewhat up and then are taken away by the wind, striking uselessly against the landscape below or just against its torso, which doesn't bother the creature at all.

She grabs her last bolt with a shaking hand, loads it into the crossbow, and cranks it back up.

A shadow moves over her head as an arm reaches across the darkness. It's long, so impossibly long, that it reaches all the way through the night, kilometers back to Tower One, past Tower One, where it grabs something and lifts it into the air.

Schlinge aims the crossbow at her own head for a second time this night.

Joints crack as the giant arm moves and then stops before the tower, holding a carriage in its open palm kilometers up in the air. Its other hand carefully plucks a handle on the side of the wagon, unfolding a stage that opens up like a walkway across the abyss. A heat, a steam, escapes from the open carriage like the hot breath of an open mouth.

Terrified, Schlinge looks at the creature.

In one hand, it holds the carriage for her to enter.

In the other, it holds aloft dresses and clothes made of skin and meat for her to wear as they play some more.

She's just a plaything for it. A toy. A puppet. She has been this whole time. It has been playing with her, like an excited child moving a doll through a little house. Now, the game has come to an end, and it's time to play something new.

It smiles.

Schlinge pulls the trigger.

There's a loud snap, the thing in her hand jolting. Crying, heaving, she looks out the side of her eyes at the broken crossbow. The string has given way, snapping apart, rendering the weapon useless.

The last bolt clambers uselessly to the stones, rolling against the wall.

The shaking elf cries as the choice is made for her.

~ [Military Advisor Blumen] ~
Human | ♂ | Royal Knight
Location: The Capital City in the Distant North
Level: 100

His heart thumps with dread as the artist purses his lips, looking at him as he grabs the game piece on the map of a carriage and moves it onward, just a little further past the canyon.

THE MESSAGE

~ [Dungeon Core Inmir] ~
??? | ♂ | Dungeon Core
Location: The Hollow Core, Floor 100
Level: 100

There's nobody there.

The young man floats, bathing in the totality of the true darkness of the core of the old dungeon, staring with wide eyes that receive only flickers of dim light at the blank surface of the wall he's sitting down in front of now, as he has been doing for . . . well, for a while. His knees are held in his arms, which are wrapped tightly around them. His short, well-cut, and trimmed hair, which has become a mess over an indeterminate period of time, adorns his head above his sharp ears, and his half-buttoned, dirty, but expensive clothes give him the appearance of being some well-off elf's child who wandered astray in the dungeon.

With a twitchy, nervous glance, he turns to look to the side of the room.

There's nobody there.

The only thing that would betray his appearance of belonging to something akin to humanity or any of their ilk is the fact that he has no skin of any discernible tone except an unnatural alabaster white, which almost glows with a passive shine, and that his eyes, within their normal sockets, are pupilless and large, like an insect's.

He floats overhead, levitating in the total void of the Hollow Core, perplexingly giving its interior some content.

The boy closes his eyes, as he always does, bringing on a darkness that is deeper still than the emptiness of the core chamber.

And there, within the confines of his deep imagination, he is above a world of golden wheat and chaff, aglow with sunlight rays that are the color of warm marigold honey. He looks around himself in that place, feeling the wind coming to him, hinting in its sweetness at the coming of spring soon, and bringing with its flow the shine of the bright morning light.

His eyes scan the pleasant world, lingering for a time on the waves of wind upon the fields that come to a crescendo beneath him as he looks around a place that must surely be paradise.

Except that there's nobody there.

He opens his eyes, breaking the imagination, and screams, his fingers violently clawing at his head, face, and hair, tearing at them, ripping at them. His nails break as they dig into his gums, fracturing on the sharp edges of his teeth and on the ridges of his skull as he burrows down to the bone beneath his flesh.

The boy screams and self-mutilates, and it doesn't really matter what happens during that process because at the end of it, his body regenerates through the powerful magics of the void in which he is immersed, and his feral cries are all swallowed by the Hollow Core, which may never satiate itself on the voices of those near to the edge of hell.

Panting, he floats alone, his wide eyes scanning through the darkness as he slowly puts himself back together, adjusting his hair as best he can with his hands, and closing up his shirt as best he can, but it has one less button now than it did before.

The boy pulls up his knees, tucks down his head, and resumes.

With a twitchy, nervous glance, he turns to look to the side of the room.

There's nobody there.

Nobody saw him.

Nobody ever sees him.

Sure, there are things in the dungeon. There are monsters and creatures; there are things that crawl and creep and chitter and chatter, but they are just base, simple things that wouldn't be able to understand the abstract dreams and visions he has. They're not there.

As of late, there has been an increase in the number of humans in his dungeon, too. Before, it used to just be adventurers. They'd come here and push into his refuge, pressing with their blades and boots into unwelcome

territory against his wishes as the master of this domain. They flooded into him like parasitic worms, looking to drain him dry. They were only here for material gain, for their own survival at best, and for their pursuit of wealth in the worst.

They're also just base, simple things that aren't compatible with what he wants.

Now, however, there are more people—many, *many* more people. People who aren't adventurers have come into his dungeon, and they dwell here; they have set up shelter on the first floor of their own instance, not even having the politeness of a usual adventuring party to leave once they're done defiling the temple of his body. Instead, they've burrowed themselves into his flesh and now reside here.

He wishes they'd just go away.

They don't get it.

They're empty. Even if he looks at them, those strange creatures, even if he stares into their eyes, they're just not . . . there's just nothing in them that resembles what is in his own.

All they ever do is scream if they see him.

The entity closes his eyes again, beginning to try to escape to a realm of imagination once more, as it has done thousands of times before and will do many thousands of times more.

This is his full existence, and it has been ever since the dungeon was completed hundreds of years ago.

There's nothing left. There's nobody left. Now, it just floats in a place that nobody, no living soul, has ever reached.

The deepest pits of the Hollow Core dung—

"Excuse me! I have mail!" says a voice abruptly from the side.

Inmir screams, flailing and spinning around like a fish that has suddenly gained ten fingers, as the first voice of a dozen generations breaks the sanctity of its hermitage.

There, standing upright in the void she has broken into, is a human woman jogging in place and holding out an envelope. The light bag on her back bounces up and down, as does her short hair, while she seems to be unable to stand still. Her outfit—a puffy pair of off-white pants tucked into thin brown boots and a sleeveless, dark top—seems out of place for the usual adventuring fair. There aren't enough belts and buckles. Wrapped

around her waist is a light jacket of the same gray tone as the pants, its sleeves tied off.

"*WHO ARE YOU?!*" screams Inmir, covering its face and baring its teeth and clawed fingers all at the same time as it confusingly turns around. All of its body language is entirely out of sync.

"Got mail," she repeats plainly, making a clicking noise in her mouth. Inmir looks over his shoulder, staring at the intruder. "I'm a courier."

"Get out! GET *OUT!*" screams the dungeon core.

"Sure thing, boss," she replies, waving the letter around. "But you've gotta take the letter before I can go."

Inmir's eyes go wide. What the hell is going on?! A letter? How did a human get down to the core of the dungeon? It's a hundred floors of its most deadly and dangerous monsters. Terrible beasts, the likes of which the children of men never even dare to dream of during their most horrible nights, scour these dark recesses of the world. "How did you get down here?!"

"Took the stairs, boss," says the courier, plain as day, holding a finger to her upside-down wrist for a moment as she continues to jog in place. "I tried to get you to respond up on floor one, but I guess you were busy."

Inmir looks at her. ". . . What are you doing?" asks the dungeon core curiously. It would ask if all humans were like this, but it knows they aren't.

"Gotta watch your pulse in this kind of work," she explains, slowing her jog. But instead of coming to a stop, she just sort of springs up and down with her entire body, her feet, now firmly planted, never leaving the ground. "Too much and you get winded, too little and your body gets cold." She looks at it. "Can you take this letter now? I really gotta get going," she says, looking behind herself.

"What's in it?" asks Inmir, its curiosity now having gotten the best of it. All questions aside—including how a single human had managed to do what thousands of adventurers haven't even come close to managing—who would send it a letter? Inmir has obviously never gotten a letter before, ever, and it doesn't exactly have any contacts, given that it has been living in desperately quiet isolation forever.

"Mail," she replies, shaking the envelope as she bounces up and down on her knees. "So? How about it? I really gotta go if I want to outrun the Demon King."

"Demon-what?" asks Inmir, shaking his head and slowly lowering his arms.

The woman doesn't scream as she sees its strange body and features; instead, she just keeps bouncing up and down, focusing on her tightly timed breathing. "Got some water?"

"What?"

"Never mind. Look, boss, I really need to leave," she says, pressing the letter toward Inmir.

The dungeon core looks down at the letter bobbing in its face, and then up at the woman, who stands in contrast to the total void by the simple merit of being someone, anyone, who is there to fill it.

Inmir reaches out, its clawed fingers twitching as they come close to grazing the bobbing paper envelope.

"You can't leave until I take the letter?" he asks.

She groans, rolling her eyes. "I have to ensure delivery," she explains. "But don't be a weirdo about it, or I'm allowed to use force to defend myself. Every creepy guy tries that one."

"Do you deliver many letters?" asks Inmir.

"I'm a courier; it's my job, boss," she says, pushing the envelope forward and pressing it against his face.

Inmir turns his head sideways, not even angry. This is the first time something else has touched it in a thousand years and more. "To dungeon cores?" he inquires curiously. He has no contact with its species, as he lives in full isolation here.

"You're the first and the last, if I don't leave soon. I'm really gonna be in trouble, okay?" says the courier. "Take the letter. Please," she pleads in annoyance, pressing it forward a few times, the envelope wrinkling as it folds against his cheek.

Inmir looks around the void, not sure what's happening. Why is this happening? Is it imagining something again? Sometimes, it loops back and forth between reality and imagination so often that it gets stuck in one or the other and forgets where it actually is. He's had dreams like this before.

The envelope squishes against its face, the woman's fingers practically touching him. "Come *oooon!* Look, there's this whole thing going on out-side, and I will literally die if I get out of here too slow."

Inmir looks at her from the corners of its eyes. "That's not really some-thing you should be telling a dungeon core," it comments.

The courier pulls the letter back, slapping it across his face. "I'm not an

adventurer. I don't have skin in the game. So don't be a dick and take the damn letter so I can leave, and you can be alone again."

Leave?

Inmir looks at the spot where she's standing; a spot that is full. He doesn't want it to be empty again, even if it is a human, and even if he hates them. This one seems fine; besides, he hasn't had anyone to talk to him in a long time.

Besides . . . there might be a mix-up here on her part.

She sighs. "Fine. Okay. I'm just going to drop this here and cancel the contract. I'm not dying for this," says the woman, turning around and throwing the letter up into the air.

"*WAIT!*" yells Inmir.

She catches the falling letter between her fingers, bouncing in place as she looks over her shoulder. "What?"

Inmir covers his face while thinking. This is all too much. He hasn't talked to anyone in so long. He hasn't been looked at in so long, or had anyone or anything to look at. He doesn't want the stranger to go just yet. But he . . . he . . .

"How long did you need to get down here?" asks Inmir, looking through the cracks between his fingers.

"What? Look, I don't—"

Inmir leans in, excitement growing in his bug eyes. "A deal!" he exclaims. "I'll make you a deal!" it offers. "How long? You planned that time in to go back up too, right?"

". . . Sure . . ." she replies uncertainly. "But that's why I have to go now. I'm really pushing it," says the courier. "One and a half hours down and one and a half up. One twenty-nine now."

"One hour," replies Inmir, lifting up a finger. "Stay here for one hour, and I'll let you use the shortcut up to the exit," he offers. "You'll be ahead of schedule by almost half an hour then!"

She lifts an eyebrow, starting to jog again. "Can't you just take the letter and let me use the shortcut right now?" she asks. "It would really be a huge help."

Inmir stares quietly for a time at the jogging woman, trying to piece this all together. "Just one hour!" he reemphasizes, entirely ignoring her question. "And I'll open the door for you myself. Hand on my heart," promises the dungeon core.

The courier thinks for a moment. "How do I know you aren't lying?"

"Why would I?" asks Inmir, shaking his head. "If I wanted to kill you, you'd already be dead—"

"As if," she throws in.

"—and I'm not a liar!" finishes the dungeon core. "Besides. You're already down two minutes now."

She makes a clicking noise in her mouth, looking to the side for a moment before nodding. "Fine. We have a deal," she agrees.

"WATER!" screams Inmir excitedly.

"Huh?"

Inmir gestures for her to stay there, looking around the total void. "You're thirsty, right?" he asks. "Hold on, I'll get you some water!" says the creature excitedly, running off into the full darkness in search of some.

It hasn't had any guests in so long. It hates humans, but still, this is rather exciting, isn't it?

The entity looks around himself in the darkness, trying to remember where he put the water. Humans like fresh water, right? The dungeon core scratches his head, his fingers running through his messy hair as he thinks.

. . . His hair.

The dungeon core screams, clawing at its face and falling to its knees before flopping over to the side and sobbing as it realizes that it had looked unpresentable during its first contact in so long.

"You good?" asks a voice from the distance.

Inmir takes a deep breath and stays quiet for a while. "I forgot where the water is . . ."

~ [**Ruhr, the River Sorceress**] ~
Half Elf | ♀ | Sorceress
Rank: SSS
Location: The Demon King's Castle, Floor Sixteen
Level: 96

The crusade rests.

It is truly a rare sight to behold, but even the grand crusade, as full of zeal and fervor as it is, is made up of mortal bodies with mortal needs, wounds, and requirements. Floor sixteen is currently entered, but there doesn't seem to be any immediate sign of danger or any obvious traps.

"Well, Zac," starts Ruhr, looking around the area. She's standing next to the man, who is sitting down on a big rock.

"Don't," says Zacarias, sighing.

Ruhr turns to him, nodding. "We've both cried now," notes the river sorceress. "That makes us best friends forever."

"I didn't cry," replies Zacarias. "I was resting my head."

Ruhr lifts a leg, planting her boot on Zacarias's good leg, and points at herself. Zacarias clears his throat. "Didn't make my own pants wet, Zig-gly-wiggly," she says. "Ruhr! The River Sorceress!" begins the woman, with particular emphasis on her title as she looks at the crusaders next to them, before lowering her voice again to return to the conversation. "Hasn't wet the bed since she was . . . uh . . . never mind, actually."

". . . What?" Zacarias looks up at her.

"Nothing. Shut up, Zac," replies Ruhr, taking her boot off of him, but making the drag of her walked-on boot sole over his pants and armor particularly slow.

Zacarias wipes off the grime. "Huh? No, really. What?" he asks, looking back up her way. "You telling me that the world-famous—"

"I said shut up, Zac!" she hisses, looking around, having said too much. "I used to have a real drinking problem, okay?" she says, leaning in. "It helped me get through the nights."

"I see," he replies. The man nods to her in approval. "I'm glad you stopped. What did you do to make your nights better instead?"

". . . Better?" Ruhr blinks. "It never got better, Zac," she says. "I just cried by myself instead, and look at where the hell I am now." The half elf shakes her head. "I should've kept drinking."

Zacarias rises to his feet.

"What, and deprive present me of the joy of your company?" he asks, standing on his bad leg and wincing a little.

The question may be sarcastic, or it may be serious; she can't tell anymore, honestly. This is a very weird, strange thing that the two of them have going on. Is this what friendship is?

Ruhr frowns, finding that her hand is playing with the tip of her ear as she stares at him.

Zacarias elbows her. "Come on. Let's get our spot set up before they steal all of the good ones," he says, nodding his head lightly to the crusaders.

"Yeah," replies Ruhr, rolling her eyes. "Wouldn't want to miss out on the best experiences the Demon King's castle has to offer," she says snarkily, but as Zacarias goes, forgetting his bag, she picks it up for him together with her own, quietly thankful that it is implicit for him that the two of them would set up together at the same spot.

As friends would do.

She runs after him. "So, you have to tell me something embarrassing now," prompts Ruhr.

"Pardon?" He looks at her. "Oh, sorry. Thanks, I forgot," says the man, reaching out to take his bag. Ruhr spins to the side, walking sideways and holding the bags out of his reach.

She lifts her nose. "I told you something embarrassing by mistake," she continues. "Now, you have to tell me something too," argues the river sorceress. "Otherwise, there's an imbalance in our relationship."

"Uh . . ." Zacarias looks ahead of himself, thinking for a while. "I don't really have anything."

"Oh, come on, Zac," remarks Ruhr. "No dirty underwear? No broken hearts and third marriages?" She leans in, raising her eyebrows a few times. "I'll also accept scandals."

Zacarias and she find themselves in a corner, near a pile of rocks. "Oh hey, look," says Ruhr. "Some loser wrote poetry on the wall here." The elf narrows her eyes, leaning in and trying to read it.

"I guess I used to write poetry too," says Zacarias, finally catching her off guard and snatching the bag from her. Ruhr yelps, reacting too late to stop him from stealing it back.

"You?" she asks, looking away from the scrawls.

"Yeah," replies Zacarias. "Remember how I told you we had a whole course on decorum for when we guardsmen are around nobility?" he asks. Ruhr nods. "Well, as an add-on to that, we have a whole bit on chivalry." The man rubs the back of his head. "It turns out that a larger part of that than you'd think is just writing poems," he says, looking back up her way sheepishly. "Very flowery poems."

"*Aww.*" Ruhr clasps her hands together by her face, blinking as slowly as she can, trying to make doe eyes. "Will you write me one, Zac?"

"Sorry," replies Zacarias. "They were only intended for women of proper status," he explains. "Not some nob—"

He winces as her boot kicks against the side of his bad leg, bracing himself against his shield, but still falling down despite that.

"I didn't deserve that," says Zacarias, letting out a slightly pained gasp as he moves his leg, lying on his back.

Ruhr drops her bag and sits down on his chest plate, pinning him there and crossing her arms. "You're right, Zac. I went too far," she admits. "But what do you expect from some improper creature like myself?" she asks, opening an eye to look down at him.

"Good question," replies Zacarias, sighing. "Better question." He looks at her and then rolls his head over to look at the wall. "If we were the first ones here, who the hell wrote that?" he asks, looking at the scratches on the wall.

"Some nobody from the crusade, or . . . ?" She trails off, eyeing the poem. "Wow. It's so lame."

Spooky ghosts and scary things crawl around the dark!
With whispering fits and twisting limbs—their claws
leave big mean marks!
Funny faces and long, sharp hands, march like creeping
ants!
So they can steal your laces, and then your frilly
underpants!

~ [Achievement Unlocked] ~
Ruhr, the River Sorceress
"Don't Make Me Get the Belt"
Unlocked By: Making a child cry.
Reward: You get to know what you did.

The two of them stare at the window and then look around themselves.

"I'm surprised you didn't get that one before."

"Shut up, Zac," says Ruhr, looking around at the crusade for signs of anyone sniffling.

~ [The Demon King] ~

Kirsch the ghost howls, crying.

"There, there," consoles Swain, patting her on the back with a massive hand that is as large as she is. "Don't listen to them," says the Demon King, shaking his head. The ghost continues to violently cry, stuffing her face into her stuffed bear and hiding it. "They're animals. They don't appreciate true art."

"I—I wanted to write great poems like you!" she cries.

Swain looks over to Cartouche, who shrugs.

Monsters, the lot of them.

"Cartouche," starts the Demon King. "Get my paper."

"Yes, my lord," she says, teleporting away.

He'll show them. Humans are ugly, wretched things that mock the efforts of a child because of their own distorted, warped, sick perceptions of reality.

His many eyes narrow themselves; others gaze in frothing rage.

They'll pay for this ugliness that they have brought into the world.

~ [Dungeon Core Inmir] ~
??? | ♂ | Dungeon Core
Location: The Hollow Core, Floor 100
Level: 100

"So, water, huh?" he says excitedly. "Not bad, right?" asks the dungeon core, sitting excitedly with crossed legs while looking at her.

The courier has finally come to a standstill, staring at the large urn she's "holding." It's massive, in fact, standing up to her chest and entirely filled to the brim with water.

". . . Is this cursed?" she asks, looking at the ancient pottery embellished with hundreds of twisted, screaming faces.

"Cursed? What? That old thing?" Inmir laughs before falling silent for a moment as he thinks. Was that the cursed urn? He had one of those somewhere.

The dungeon core lifts his gaze, looking at the urn's many horrified, screaming faces, some of which leak water from the inside, giving them the appearance that they're weeping.

"No, no . . ." he finally says, shaking his head. "This is my good urn. The cursed one is up on floor thirty; I almost forgot."

"Oh, great," says the courier. "Thank you for the water."

"You're welcome!" replies Inmir excitedly, leaning forward and watching her with wide eyes as she takes a smaller flask from her waist and dips it in to fill it. She caps it off and shakes the little container before opening it again and sniffing it. Seemingly satisfied with whatever comes back to her, she takes a sip and then empties it entirely before filling it up again a second time and sitting down. "How is it?" asks Inmir.

"Ah, thank you," says the courier. "Very refreshing."

"What does it taste like?" continues Inmir, leaning in forward so far that he loses his balance despite sitting cross-legged, his eyes going wide.

"Tastes like water, boss," she answers, pointing at him with a finger. "So, what's up?"

Inmir stares at her for a while.

What's up?

The dungeon core looks down at the stones, his heart beginning to race as he tries to understand what's happening here. She's asking him what is up. Obviously, she's asking about the dungeon above them.

Duh.

Inmir looks back up excitedly. "Floor ninety-nine above us has an undead hydra!" he exclaims, twisting his hands together. "But instead of dragon heads, I attached heads from five different monsters!" The dungeon core nods proudly. "Their tongues are made out of human skin."

"What? No," she says. "Ew."

"Ew?" Inmir's heart is racing faster now. Did he say something wrong? It was the human skin thing, wasn't it? It was probably the human skin thing.

She points at him with a finger from her flask. "No, I mean, what's up with you, boss?" asks the courier.

". . . Ah?" Inmir stares for a while, processing the question. What is up with him?

Up . . . What is up with him . . . His body is down here, where he is. The entity lifts his gaze, staring into the void above. A strand of hair catches his eye.

A strand of hair from above. *Up.*

She's asking about his messed-up hair?!

Inmir screams, burying his face in his knees, and quickly tries to fix his hair. However, his screams never stop in the meantime, as is proper behavior in such a situation.

Cold water hits him, and he jolts together, looking through his clawed fingers at the woman still sitting across from him, who had swung out her flask to splash him with his own water.

She gets up, refills the flask, and sits back down again. "I'm asking you what this is," she says.

"It's not my cursed urn," replies Inmir, water dripping down his head.

"No, I mean . . ." She gestures to everything around them, which is actually nothing, since they're sitting inside the void. "This."

"This is the Hollow Core," he explains, matter-of-factly.

"Sure, but . . . what's your deal?" asks the courier. "Why do you want me to stay here for . . . thirty-seven more minutes?"

Inmir looks at her and then down at the letter sitting between them.

"I wanted somebody to talk to," admits Inmir, understanding now. His eyes go wide. "Do you want to imagine wheat fields together?!"

"Uhh . . . that's gonna be a no from me, boss," she says. Inmir frowns. But maybe it's for the best. He can imagine wheat fields when she's gone. Still, it would have been nice to imagine something together with someone. "If that's all you want, why not talk to the people up on floor one?" she asks, pointing upward. "A few hundred villagers set up shop there," she explains. "They're running from the Demon King."

"NO!" argues Inmir. He can't talk to them. They're . . . they're too far away.

He quietly stares at the ground and then back up at her. What do humans like? What do they like talking about? Gold? Humans like gold, right? They like engaging in their animal behavior, and they like . . . uh . . .

". . . What?" asks the courier, after a full minute of totally silent observation.

"Do you like frogs?" asks Inmir

"Frogs?" she says. "I mean . . . they're alright, I guess."

Inmir nods. Good. This is good. This is progress.

The conversation is moving along excellently.

"Do you like rabbits?" he continues.

"Sure," replies the courier. "I like them more than frogs, I think."

EXCELLENT.

Inmir smiles with pride. He's cracked the puzzle.

Humans like things that hop. They sort of like frogs, and they like rabbits more. Both of them are things that hop . . . *Okay. Think.* He needs more things that hop so he can keep this conversation rolling.

Uh . . .

Inmir stares at the ground for a while.

But he can't think of anything else that hops.

He's blowing it. This is all going wrong.

The dungeon core shakes, his hands digging into his chest as he grinds his teeth. What other animals hop . . .

"WHAT OTHER ANIMALS HOP?!" screams the dungeon core in exasperation, his harrowed voice swallowed by the void.

Did he scare her by screaming? Humans are usually scared of screaming.

Nervously, Inmir looks up through his arms wrapped around his head and torso.

She sits where she sat, an eyebrow raised, her arm back, looking as if she was ready to throw the water at him again.

"Grasshoppers," she says, lifting a finger from her arched-back arm.

GRASSHOPPERS!

"Of course!" exclaims Inmir, losing all of the tension in his body at once and hitting his fist into his open palm.

Saved.

This is going well.

At the rate this is going, maybe he can even ask her to come back again some time . . . That would be nice, right?

Inmir closes his eyes, thinking about it.

"Whoa, weird," says the courier.

Inmir opens his eyes. Weird? What's weird? Is he weird? "AM I WEIRD?!" cries the dungeon core desperately, falling forward and crawling over on all fours toward her like a scampering critter. She presses him back with her dirty boot, sticking it on his face.

This is a good sign in human culture.

He recalls once seeing a man actually pay his adventuring colleague his share of their dungeon treasure to do this to him in their tent. That poor fellow must've been a real wreck if he had to pay. Here he is, getting it for free, and he isn't even human.

Inmir flops onto his back, smiling. What a good day. He's having some trouble, but he never thought he'd be so good at this. Communication is nice. He's not weird. What a relief.

Frogs are nice.

"No, that," she replies. Inmir looks up behind him, seeing the void shift and wobble. A second courier, with a frog on her head, dissipates and vanishes.

"Oh, that? That's what happens when I imagine something in here," he explains. "The core makes it manifest." Inmir taps his head. "That's how I'll make your shortcut."

"In twenty-four minutes," she says.

Inmir nods, pleased. She must be counting the minutes too because she's also worried about it ending. Wow. He was so scared of being alone because of his fear of rejection and of doing something different after so long, and all this time he had been a master at talking and making friends.

He should correct her on her time thing, but . . .

Wait, she was impressed by that, right?

"Let me show you!" says Inmir excitedly, closing his eyes.

The chamber turns to the color of auburn, summer's gold, as the scene around them shifts to one of a vast landscape in which he flies, the woman hovering there.

"Wow . . ." she says, clearly impressed as she looks around at the sights. "It feels so real."

"It *is* real," replies Inmir. "The Hollow Core swallows things, people, places, screams, whatever, and then whenever I imagine something, it remakes that image as best as it can out of the things it has collected," explains the dungeon core, glad to be able to talk about his work for a moment instead. It's an easy topic, and she doesn't seem bored by it right now. "Some places look bad because it doesn't have everything I need it to have. But other places like this one are done. They're perfect. I have wheat. I have grass, rocks, dirt, and a sky," says the dungeon core. "I come here a lot."

"Must suck being alone down at the bottom of a dungeon forever, boss."

Inmir opens its eyes. The spell vanishes immediately, returning them to total darkness.

"I guess I get it now," she says. "I'd want to talk to someone too if I was cooped up forever." The courier pauses. "Twenty-two."

~ [Zacarias] ~
Human | ♂ | Royal Guardsman
Location: The Demon King's Castle, Floor Sixteen
Level: 91

Ruhr snores into his ear.

Zacarias lays there, staring at the ceiling, as a low grumbling makes itself heard next to his head, followed by a soft whistling that blows into his ear.

He turns his head, looking at her face, only to receive her breath in his eyes instead of his ear for his trouble. Zacarias turns his head back, looking at the ceiling again. He and the rest of the wounded are exempt from guard duty, but he can't sleep anyway. Something is bothering him.

The man just doesn't know what it is, honestly.

Something rustles in his other ear.

Zacarias turns to look at their two packs, leaning against the rocks that seem to be . . . moving? "The hell . . ." mutters Zacarias, narrowing his eyes. A rat?

The bags don't open. There isn't a rat, but something slides out through the partially opened flap. Zacarias reaches out, yanking it and sitting upright.

He knew something wasn't right here!

The man gets ready to scream the alarm, holding on to a pair of frilly underpants that he stares at in marked confusion.

Ruhr mumbles quietly next to him, rolling and stretching as she wakes up. The man quietly throws his underwear back to the side before allowing himself to be wrapped up in a new social disaster.

"Zac?" mumbles the woman, looking out of one eye at him.

Is he losing it?

Zacarias looks around the room and then back down at the bags. It was probably just loose inside the bag and finally fell out by itself, right?

"All good," says Zacarias. "Go back to—"

Someone screams an alarm on the other side of the camp. Bells start ringing, and everyone rouses, coming out of small tents and out of the clusters of bodies they've made, grabbing their weapons in a panic as the room then falls into a silence.

"What? What is it?" whispers Ruhr, looking around but not seeing anything.

The room rumbles as a long, jagged scar runs through the stone-work floors, tearing up the foundation as if a dragon's talon were ripping through it. Then more. Dozens of them appear as unseen creatures move through the lantern light. People shout and try to attack them, but their weapons don't hit anything.

Whispers fill the air, coming not from the people of the crusade but from haunting specters looming in their midst, speaking in tongues unspoken in the modern age.

Confused cries fill the room as people are torn off their feet, flopping down to the sides as they're knocked over. Screams of terror fill the camp while the crusaders try to hang on to those taken to little avail. They are torn away or ripped into the air, where . . .

Their boots are removed, unlaced, and put back on.

A few dozen crusaders flop down to the ground again. Others, having been released, crawl back to the crowd, who quickly pull them back to safety.

". . . The fuzz?" asks Ruhr. "AH! *ZAC!*" yells the woman, pushing past him to snatch at the pair of undergarments from before, which have begun levitating into the air, held by an unseen force.

Zac grabs her and they fight against it, but both of them are beaten, and they fall down together, watching as that piece and hundreds of others, stolen together with hundreds of boot laces, hover up into the air before slowly flying away, dozens of questionably desperate crusaders trying to get their possessions back. Others, given the unsanctimonious nature of some of the confiscated garments, do not make any public attempts to claim some very specific articles that fly away.

"Those were my favorite ones . . ." mumbles Ruhr, dropping her hand.

Zacarias sighs. "We truly suffered a terrible loss today."

She looks back at him. "Zac, do you ever wonder if the Demon King is a little mixed up in the head?"

Zacarias nods.

The two of them turn to look back at the poem on the wall of their camp.

But it's been scratched away by a heavy claw.

~ [The Demon King] ~

"My lord," speaks Abydos, the painter. "We're coming up to a dungeon on the side of the road. What should we do?"

Swain thinks for a while. A dungeon isn't exactly a human ally. Dens of monsters and animals aren't his concern.

"Leave it be," he says, riding past.

"There are likely humans hiding inside from the nearby region," explains Abydos.

"A pittance," replies the Demon King. "I want the beating heart of their society—their capital."

~ [Dungeon Core Inmir] ~
??? | ♂ | Dungeon Core
Location: The Hollow Core, Floor 100
Level: 100

"It's time, boss," says the courier, rising to her feet. She starts stretching herself out.

"No . . . I . . ." Inmir lifts a hand and then drops it, lowering its head. "You're right," he relents, looking over to the next curiosity that life has to offer. The woman picks up the letter, holding it out to him.

Inmir looks at it then at her, taking it before ripping it open with a claw. His eyes scan the page from top to bottom, and then he looks back up at her.

"Do you have a response?" she asks, standing on one leg and stretching the other one upward at an impressive angle before switching to the other.

Inmir scratches his cheek, holding out the letter for her to see. ". . . I can't read human," explains the dungeon core. "Could you, uh . . . please?"

She drops her foot back down to the stones and takes the letter, clearing her throat. "To whom it may concern: We are requesting your immediate assistance in stopping the approaching caravan of the Demon King through use of your monsters," reads the courier. "It is in the interest of our own mutual survival that this threat be stopped. In return, we will happily provide you with anything you require in the future, from resources to additional land." She folds the letter back together and hands it over to him. "Signed, His Majesty, blah blah."

"So what the hell is this Demon King thing?" asks Inmir. "What's the problem?"

"He's expected to drive past here not long from now," she explains. "Please use your monsters to stop him," she asks, touching her toes.

Inmir thinks for a moment. How odd.

The humans are asking something of him. But . . . why? What purpose would this serve? He supposes they don't like this Demon King creature. But it also seems like sort of a *them* problem, doesn't it? They've never asked him for anything before, ever. In fact, she's the first person to ever talk to him down here. Why should he care if they're getting a bonk on the noggin up there?

He's sad that she's going now, though. They had such a fun conversation.

"Your response, boss?" she prompts, starting to bounce again. "And my shortcut, please. We're wasting time."

"Do you want to stay here and imagine hopping things together?" he asks, mimicking her bouncing.

Of course. He really should have figured the frog thing out sooner. She came down here like this, after all. This is fun.

She shakes her head. "I have to go. This is really important."

Inmir sighs, closing his eyes.

"A promise is a promise," he says, imagining a way out to the top of the dungeon. He can hear her filling up her water one last time and then starting to warm up again to jog next to him.

Anything he wants?

Honestly, he isn't sure if humanity has anything to offer him in exchange. All of his monsters is a big ask. Sure, they respawn by themselves. But they're still his monsters. He made them to protect his dungeon. Just sending them all out to fight some creature is . . .

Hmm . . .

"I'll send them out," says Inmir, bouncing on his heels.

"Really? Thank you," she replies. "I'll be on my way, then."

Inmir smiles, listening to her go. "Goodbye," says the entity, listening to her jog away.

The creature opens his eyes again, floating alone in the total void of the Hollow Core once more.

His eyes wander the darkness, staring off into the emptiness around him, in which nobody stands.

Closing his eyes, he imagines his favorite place. He imagines golden wheat and ruby sunlight shining over the horizon, painting his prized piece with a nostalgic glow. The dungeon core flies up in the air like always in this dream, but now, he stares down at the world below, at the single woman who jogs down the path, running toward a destination she'll never get to.

The Hollow Core keeps what it swallows. There isn't a way out. That's why he can't talk to the people on the first floor.

But he isn't a liar.

He himself knows that this is imaginary, this fake place. That is why he can only ever stay here for so long before the spell breaks and he is driven back into solitude and madness.

Inmir reaches out from a distance, its hand obscuring its friend as she moves.

However, she doesn't know that.

As far as she knows, she's back outside.

Inmir smiles, watching her go as the illusion fades, feeling good about itself.

He did well today.

It made a friend. Humans are complicated, weird things. But maybe they aren't all bad? Maybe one or two of them are okay.

Okay.

He'll do it.

But . . . well . . . there may be another problem.

(Inmir) has used: [Dungeon Breach]

The dungeon rumbles, quaking and shaking as things are set into motion. During a dungeon breach, all of the monsters contained inside of a dungeon will all storm the exit, leaving into the world to wreak havoc.

It hasn't had to use this ability that often, as it's sort of a mess to organize everything again afterward. The hydra needs to be brought back down to floor ninety-nine, and the urns need to be refilled with souls, and all sorts of stuff like that.

Inmir opens a door next to himself, steps through it, and then steps out of the dungeon gate.

At least in his imagination.

Thousands of monsters, ghoulish fiends, and shrieking harrows escape into the night that never stops, and then . . . simply do nothing.

He looks down at the ground, at the track marks in the mud where dozens of caravans have already driven past hours ago. The Demon King was already here and has already left.

Inmir scratches his cheek and opens his eyes again, finding himself standing in the full, black void of a chamber that he never left.

One, he or anything else it swallows can't ever leave the Hollow Core. And two, well . . . when one is lost in daydreams, time does seem to flow at a somewhat different speed, doesn't it? The minutes the courier had been counting weren't the real amount of time that had really passed.

Oh well.

He closes his eyes, deciding to visit her again in his imagination, and finds joy in just flying there in silence, watching her run and sometimes even hop forever, as free as can be.

CHAPTER 8

THE WORLD BEYOND THE CHAOS

~ [Crusader Valtos] ~
Orc | ♂ | Crusade Legionnaire
Location: The Demon King's Castle, Floor Sixteen
Level: 83

The crusader's heavy armor drags him down like an anchor as he makes his way through the dimly lit, musty corridors of the underground castle belonging to the terrible Demon King. In spite of the power and resolve he had when he initially started out on this quest, a creeping sense of hopelessness has begun to take hold of his heart in recent days as they plunge deeper and deeper toward the true heart of darkness.

His comrades in arms, his fellow crusaders, advance beside him with what appears to still be deadly resolve etched over their features. However, the orc just can't escape the notion that they are all heading in the direction of their certain deaths.

The fact that he is currently suffering from chafing beneath his armor is not helpful in the least. They have discovered some of the stolen undergarments that were left behind by the spirits along one of the many corridors. However, his belongings have not been found yet.

He can't speak for the others, but he certainly is becoming more and more exhausted as they continue to move through room after room inhabited by ugly monsters and other vile, corrupted things. His feet hurt, his armor is irritating on his flesh, and the arm that holds his sword is heavy and numb. He can't help but worry about how much longer he will be able to keep going, as well as what would happen to him and his comrades if they were unable to complete their mission. In a sense, his acknowledgment of his own discomfort and his distaste for it make him feel almost ashamed.

In spite of his misgivings, Valtos continues to march, not that there is anything else to do. He is compelled to do so by the strong feeling of duty that remains, and by the remembrance of all those who have been harmed at the hands of the wretched Demon King—a vile plague on this world. But as time passes and they get no closer to reaching the end of the castle, he can't help but worry whether everything he's been through will have been for nothing in the end.

What if he dies?

What if he dies due to some stupid trick or mechanism, like so many others have already? It's not like his death will have been some noble sacrifice, then. It'll just be dumb. It'll be pointless.

The crusader stands back and watches the others as they proceed up the path, led by the divinely chosen half elf. Their expressions are carved with resolve and intent. However, the more he looks at them, the more he gets the impression that they are nothing more than a group of naive idealists heading in the direction of their own ends. He begins to doubt his own intentions for joining this campaign, and wonders whether he made a mistake by leaving behind his comfortable life to fight in this futile struggle. He also begins to question the motivations of everyone around him for joining this crusade.

The man looks down, rubbing his face, wondering what's gotten over him. He's certainly not the most zealous person, but he's not some whiny quitter either.

However, the longer he stands here, stuck in place as it were while the crowd moves on around him, the more the once impregnable warrior gradually loses his bravery and self-assurance. Immediately, he starts to picture himself as a failure; a coward who is unable to press forward, if not even a full-on failure at life in general. He reflects on the people he cared about, including his family and his close friends, and how he would never see them again if he died down here. He has this nagging feeling that he should have just remained in his hometown and had a quiet life there.

Shouldn't he have?

What difference does he make here? He's just one man.

The crusader's thoughts become entangled in this web of self-doubt and despondency, and he begins to fall farther and farther behind the other members of the gang. He can't shake the sense that he is holding

them back, and he begins to question whether it wouldn't be better for everyone if he just turned around and went back right now.

"You need to keep walking," says a voice from next to him. The orc turns his head, looking at the heavily armored, sticklike woman wearing a helmet with slits in its visor, allowing her to peer through. She nods her head to the side. "It makes it go away."

"Pardon?" asks the man, looking at her as she turns to walk along with the rest of the crusade, leaving him standing there still.

"You need to keep walking," she repeats, lifting a hand to wave it over her shoulder as best she can in her heavy armor. "Makes it go away," finishes the woman as she vanishes into the crowd.

The crusader stares after her, trying to decipher her message for a moment, as obvious as it is. He watches the crowd move, realizing that he isn't the only one who harbors these sorts of doubts as he watches them, observing uneasy steps, clusters of people moving in groups to stay safe with their friends, and paranoid glances out into all directions. They're all having the same exact thoughts that he's having.

But the difference is that they're still walking.

He gulps, steeling himself as he moves his foot forward again, breaking it free from the spiritual ice that had bound him in place. And then, as if by magic, the next step that follows is so much easier. Then, another and then another, and pretty soon, he is moving together with the rest of the tide.

Valtos exhales, releasing a little of the fear he had inside of himself, but not all of it.

He's a man of faith. He isn't afraid of the darkness in the world, is he? No. This peculiar sensation must be coming from the terrible Demon King's miasma, which is contaminating both his thoughts and his body, and nothing else could be the cause.

Is what he tells himself, and it works.

~ [The Demon King] ~

"What do all of these things have in common?" he asks, his grizzly voice rumbling through the throne room as he finishes showing them his visions of several people around the world.

His followers, all gathered, look either at one another or around the room as they ponder, none of them having an answer to his question.

"... They're all humans?" asks Kirsch. He shakes his head.

Cartouche lifts a hand. "They're all afraid of you, my lord?"

"Yes, but that is not what I am after," replies the Demon King. "That is only a part of it."

Abydos the painter and Byblos the cook both shrug, not having an answer either. "Let me show you more," he says, lifting his massive hand to cover his sight of them, while his hundreds of eyes glow with magical power, bulging out of their sockets all over his body.

Their frail bodies tremble as his powerful magic covers them.

~ [Vava Malti] ~
Elf | ♀ | Seamstress
Location: The Human Capital, a Cozy House
Level: 13

The elven woman is sitting in her modest home in the nation's capital all by herself at the table, peering out the window. She is beyond exhausted. As the freshly relit lantern light emerges out in the streets, an eerie orange glow spreads across the city in pulses, as if a failing heart were trying to beat fresh blood through a body one more time. Long shadows stretch out across the cobblestone roads, creeping through the light-untouched crevices. She is able to make out in the distance the sound of horns and drums as the national army runs drills and preparations.

Malti wonders about her children, who are blissfully ignorant of the impending threat, not only because of their age but also because they are fast asleep in their beds. Knowing that she brought children into this world just to see it fall apart causes a sense of remorse to sweep over her in a way that she has never really felt before. She desperately wants to defend them and keep them safe from the unspeakable atrocities that are ravaging across the land, but . . . who is she? She's just some woman. She's a tailor. There's nothing she can do. Her entire future and that of her children lies in the hands of other people, and that thought is . . .

Malti thinks of her husband, who is said to have been killed by the demon sickness rampaging in the south. He was a traveling merchant. She really wants him to be with her right now, to comfort her, hold her hand, and reassure her that everything will be well. However, he has left

this world, from what she has been told by others who fled the region, and now she is alone with her children.

Unlike them, she finds no sleep.

The full brunt of the burdens of the worlds of two children are resting upon her shoulders, and she is overcome with a sensation of helplessness and despair at the thought of having to do this alone. She hasn't even had time to mourn her husband yet. She's just . . . she's just been sitting here and staring for a while. She hopes that one day this will all be over, and that the endless fighting and suffering will come to an end. But she is well aware that this is not the end; rather, it is merely the start of a new nightmare for her.

If they survive, what then? How is she supposed to just . . . be normal again?

There really is nothing she can do to stop the Demon King's army from coming closer, and it *is* getting closer. At this point, there is nothing left for her to do but cross her fingers and say a prayer that her children will pull through this.

The woman—who is quite exhausted, since she has been able to get so little sleep over the previous several days—looks about the room as she feels a sensation of dread sneaking up on her, as it does from time to time; as it does so frequently lately, ever since she stopped sleeping. How many days has it been? She rubs her tired eyes, but she can't shut them. She doesn't want to sleep.

And this is despite the presence of shadows appearing to move around on the periphery of her vision. But if she looks directly at them, the shadows disappear, leaving her uncertain as to whether or not they were ever genuine to begin with. Her mind is falling apart from stress and lack of sleep. She can't shake the sensation that someone is watching her, so she rubs her eyes.

The elf gets to her feet and shakes her head, her recently cut brown hair shaking past her face as she attempts to redirect her attention to anything else—anything else—in an effort to divert her attention away from the shadows.

She turns her head and stares at her children, who are lying asleep in their beds in this humble home of theirs. As nature and the warmth of good souls both intend, she feels a flood of love and protectiveness wash over her as she stares at her children, safely sleeping quietly in their beds in the

corner of the little house that is really just one room large. They are protected here at the moment, not because of her but because of other people.

It makes her feel so powerless.

The exhausted woman's eyelids begin to droop, and her head begins to slump as she continues to lose more and more of her energy. She makes an effort to resist it, to remain awake and maintain watch, but her body is too exhausted to comply with her will. Since the passing of her spouse, she has just been . . . She can't seem to fall or stay asleep. When she is asleep, she is able to see him.

As she begins to nod off, she becomes aware of whispers in her ears that are gentle but persistent, much like the sound of leaves rustling in the breeze. At first, she believes that her mind is playing tricks on her, but the murmurs continue to get louder and more intense as time passes.

Malti jumps, startled back into consciousness in an instant, the rapid beating of her heart audible in her sternum. She casts her paranoid gaze all across the room, but there appears to be nobody there . . . as always. It's just the three of them now.

The whispers keep going, getting louder and more frenzied, and she can't help but feel a mounting sense of dread and impending doom in her chest. It feels so heavy, it's like there's a weight in her gut. The elf can't really help but get the feeling that she's going crazy. She really needs to sleep, but she, well, she just doesn't want to. She can't bear to. The elf instead tries to clear her mind and concentrate on what is happening in the here and now by closing her eyes and taking a deep breath.

She is aware that she will need to go to sleep at some point. It's just that . . .

Later. It's okay if she sleeps later. She does not need to do so now, right? She is simply not prepared to face him again at this time. It's better to stay awake so she doesn't fall apart in front of the children. They need calm and stability right now, most of all.

Nevertheless, the whispers keep coming, and she can't escape the sense that something is watching her, as evidenced by the fact that the hair on the back of her neck is standing on end.

~ [Arsurni] ~
Human | ♂ | Hunter
Location: A Hunter's Lodge in the Remote Southeast
Level: 37

The contents of metal tankards quietly slosh around as the men sit quietly, drinking and eating over the spoils of their work here in the remote regions of the world. A dark shadow has fallen over the world, and this seems like a safe place to be. However, even this far away, nature has become . . . difficult. The animals have become strange, and the trees have become strange.

Arsurni lifts his gaze, looking at his compatriots in the lodge with him; fellow hunters.

The people have become strange.

As a result of the Demon King's march over the world, the wild animals have been in a panic, and the hunts have grown far more deadly and unpredictable.

The hunter is currently surviving at an old lodge deep in the woods, surrounded by other hunters. It's best to stay out of the cities right now. However, the mood is strained as is. Hunters who venture out this deep into the woods are already strange types to begin with, often those who don't do well with others.

The hunter casts his gaze over his fellow adventurers, all of whom are grizzled veterans of the art. Each and every one of them is a man or woman of action who is motivated by the excitement of the pursuit and the surge of adrenaline that comes with the finality of the kill. However, even they are beginning to see the gravity of the threat that is all around them, even if it is so far away. If he were to describe it, he would say that he feels as if he were on the opposite end of a rabbit hunt. It's like he's here, hiding in a burrow, and some large, thumping monstrosity is just above, waiting . . .

The man recalls the most recent hunt, when he and the others were surprised by a pack of feral wolves while they were out looking for game. The animals' eyes were wild, far more than usual, and their yellow, gnarled teeth smelt of death. Now that the sun never rises, the nocturnal hunters of the world never stop hunting. Wolves, large cats, and all manner of monsters prowl the world, never coming to rest as they partake in a time of great feasting and gorging.

It is the hour of the hunt for everything that has been hunted up until now.

Which is very unfortunate for the hunters of the human and other species, as they are somewhat outmatched.

It took everything they had to withstand the wolves' attacks and make it back to the lodge in one piece.

Arsurni mulls over the current predicament of the planet, how everything is deteriorating as a direct result of the Demon King's befoulment. He is aware that things are only going to grow worse. Survival is the name of the game at the moment, and hunting for sport is going to go on a very long pause until this is all over.

He straightens up, sitting upright in his chair, as he takes another sip from his tankard and another bite of his bread and venison. He's going to have to hold out here for a while, at the lodge. With any luck, in a week or two, this will all blow over, and they'll just all go their separate ways. He's probably going to take a break from the south for a while.

Something scratches at the front door.

"The hell?" asks a man sitting across from him.

The other men stop eating, and everyone sits quietly and listens as something continues to scratch on the thick wood. The noise isn't very, very loud, but it is always present, scratching. The men, despite their reputation, can't quite seem to hide their concern as they cast nervous looks at one another and unconsciously go for their knives and crossbows.

"The wolves?" whispers a man, only to get shushed for his trouble by his neighbor.

The sound of scratching continues, and it gets both louder and more persistent as whatever is on the other end of the wood begins to try harder. The hunters can see the door begin to wobble once whatever is on the other side of it starts to push against it—lightly but noticeably. Arsurni can feel his heart thumping in his chest, and his tongue drying out.

"Hey, go check it out," says a man, knocking him on the shoulder.

Arsurni blinks, looking at him and then around the room. Somehow, everyone is looking at him all of a sudden.

He looks back toward the door and grabs his knife, slowly rising to his feet as it continues to wobble.

The man takes slow, measured steps as if he's stalking prey and approaches the door, placing his hand on the latch as he moves closer to the entrance. When he glances back at the others, they give him a nod, indicating they are prepared to confront whatever is out there—of course, not as the first men up front. But they're there and ready in the second row.

After taking a deep breath, the hunter unlocks the door to the room and tears it open at once, his knife held ready.

~ [Trall] ~
Orc | ♀ | Fighter
Location: The Wildlands, Just South of the Human Capital
Level: 23

The party of adventurers runs for their lives, storming through the howling night that never ends as they escape from hordes of wild monsters who are pursuing them from the shadows, practically nipping at their heels as they flee for their lives out of the wilderness toward the north.

They had been examining an ancient ruin in the middle of the wilderness for wealth and any notable treasures when . . . well, when something just changed in the air. A man screamed. Then the next man had screamed, and before they knew it, everyone was running for their lives.

Trall pants, sweating as she sprints. The ruin they had been exploring was an ancient one. They had only just gotten away with their lives, and now they are fleeing toward the north in the hope of finding some kind of refuge from the unrelenting pursuit. The city isn't far from here. In retrospect, maybe it was dumb to try and loot a place so close to the capital. Surely, it's been combed over a thousand times by now.

She looks out of the sides of her eyes as they run. The group of adventurers consists of a rather misfit crew, each member possessing their own set of special talents and capabilities. The troop is being led by a brave individual who is brandishing a hulking greatsword—that would be her. Notable is that she actually had to leave her greatsword behind, though. It was too heavy to run away with.

There is a rogue who moves stealthily through the shadows while keeping a vigilant eye out for any ambushes or traps, in theory. He is also running away. A mage who is performing spells to slow down the pursuers as he runs away, casting all sorts of magic into the darkness, and a priest who is tending to those who have been injured—himself—as he runs away. In essence, they are a perfectly normal adventuring party like any other.

She grits her teeth, clenching her eyes as they run as quickly as they can, but the monsters are getting closer to them, and their roars and screeches are getting louder and more frenzied—she can practically hear them and feel them on her skin.

Trall's terrified mind entertains the possibility that she won't make it, that the monsters will capture her and eat her alive. But then her thoughts turn to her comrades, the relationships that they have developed over the course of their fights together, and the ways in which they have battled together.

It's not much further. The city isn't far.

Just a little more.

They can make it.

~ [The Demon King] ~

"They're . . . uh . . ." Byblos the cook stops, thinking for a moment. "They're all moved to action in some way by your presence."

He shakes his head, wanting them to find the way on their own. "Think as artists," instructs the Demon King. "You are watching with your eyes when you should be watching from further away than that. Look again."

~ [Vava Malti] ~
Elf | ♀ | Seamstress
Location: The Human Capital, a Cozy House
Level: 13

The tired mother is hunched over her children's beds, glaring at them intensely with her eyes wide open as she watches them sleep. Their chests rise up. Their chests fall down. Breath goes in. Breath goes out. Perfect.

She smiles, staring at them with dry, red eyes.

Everything is perfect.

Her previously serene countenance is now etched with concern, marking the edges of her eyes, and her body trembles from tiredness, which she dutifully ignores in her state. Her thoughts and memories are all over the place, and her mind is a complete mess as a result. Shadows whisper into her ears, telling her how imperfect everything is. Her husband and love are dead. Her children are going to die. She's going to die—a failure, a nothing, screaming.

But she pays the shadows no mind as she stares at her children, her smile growing wider as they breathe, like good children should.

She observes as they sleep, their serene and pure features providing a striking contrast to the atrocities that are occurring outside in her mind's eye, which she pays no mind to. She has an overwhelming feeling of love and protection for them, as well as a resolute resolve to keep them safe no matter what. So, she has to stay here and make sure they behave, that they sleep, and that they don't die like their father.

She recalls the many things she has given up for her children, including sleep when they were babies, as well as the many hours she has spent fretting and worrying since those many years ago. She goes back to the moments when she had the desire to give up, when it seemed as though the burden of the world was too much for her to carry. However, she never stopped fighting for her children.

Malti smiles, the corners of her dry mouth cracking as she watches them turn over to their sides.

She wishes that she had the power to allay all of their concerns and apprehensions and protect them from the calamities of the world. However, she is aware that this is not possible, and so she remains where she is, keeping watch over them with a heart that is heavy with both love and grief. Her eyes are wide open, and her skin is as dry as she looks.

She leans down lower, hovering over them, her face inches from theirs as they sleep.

~ [Arsurni] ~
Human | ♂ | Hunter
Location: A Hunter's Lodge in the Remote Southeast
Level: 37

The hunter stands with his knife at the ready.

But there is nothing there.

Confused, the man blinks, looking around, and then steps to the side, showing the others the emptiness. "Nothing there," he says, shrugging and closing the door again. They murmur as he walks back to his chair, looking over his shoulder toward the door. "Must've been the wind."

"It's never the fucking wind!" yells a man from across the room. Arsurni shrugs.

He picks up his mug again, returning to his meal. But the others don't seem so content. They look around at one another, clearly still paranoid. It's not wrong to feel this way. These men are seasoned, old hunters. Their gut feelings are what have kept them alive so long to begin with.

Arsurni takes a bite of his venison, looking back around the room.

Somehow, everyone is still staring at him.

"What?" asks the man, chewing as he looks at the many faces showing the telltale signs of paranoia. If he didn't know better, he would start to get the sneaking suspicion that there is something nefarious going on in their minds.

"You didn't smell anything?" asks another man, looking at him.

Arsurni swallows. "Smell . . . ?" he repeats. "No, just the usual."

"Nothing touched you?" continues the man.

Arsurni narrows his eyes. "What are you getting at?" asks the hunter.

"Something was at that door," says the questioning man. "That wasn't the damn wind!"

The others murmur in vague agreement, looking over at him. "What? What the hell?" asks Arsurni. "You all watched me open the door; what the hell is supposed to have happened?"

"Witchcraft," replies the seasoned man next to him, scooting his chair back a little."

"Wit—what?!" exclaims Arsurni incredulously. "Didn't no goddamned witch touch me," he remarks, pointing at the man with his piece of meat. "It was three seconds."

". . . That's enough for a witch," replies the old hunter, eyeing the piece of meat being pointed at him.

Arsurni looks around the room, his trained eyes picking up on subtle cues such as a twitch of the eye in one man or a shift in the manner in which another one whispers, looking his way, his friend nodding. They start murmuring to one another in low tones and lower registers of their voices.

This might be a problem.

The hunters begin to infect one another with their paranoia, which quickly becomes contagious. Nobody says anything to his face, but given their looks and glances, he can tell that something has spooked them, like animals. They maintain their distance as though his very existence posed a new danger to them, as if the very air from outside the lodge had somehow tainted him.

"You guys are kidding, right?" asks Arsurni. "This is absurd. I opened the door because you asked me too. There's no witch outside. What the hell?" he says, looking at the paranoid men.

Somehow, his trivializing of their nonsensical paranoia doesn't really help, but he can't understand what's gotten into them all of a sudden. These are rational, calm men under most circumstances.

His fingers graze the edge of his knife.

~ [Trall] ~
Orc | ♀ | Fighter
Location: The Wildlands, Just South of the Human Capital
Level: 23

The group of adventurers, still desperately fleeing toward the north, are overshadowed by the looming dread of imminent death. They have exhausted all of their reserves, including their spells, weapons, and energy. Equipment has been dropped, potions drank, curses flung, and tears cried—all so they can run faster still.

In fact, they are so desperate that they have begun to shove each other away into the darkness in an effort to distract the monsters long enough for the rest of the group to make their escape.

The first person to fall away from the group is the priest, who had been leading the others with a magical glow in his hands. He puts up a fight, but the thief was determined to get him into the shadows before he himself was taken by them. The next one to go, however, was that very same cloak-wearing thief. He tries to fight back, but one quick, strong shove from the orc sends him off-balance and flying into the darkness, where he screams in terror.

Surely this must have bought them some more time.

Trall gnashes her teeth, listening to the screams in the darkness as they run. The light on the horizon grows brighter and brighter as they get closer to the city. It's so close. It's right there. She doesn't have to die out here. It's right there!

"SORRY!" yells Trall, her heart smashing against the inside of her chest as she swings out, hammering the party wizard right in her gut and sending her crumpling down to the ground.

She's going to make it.

~ [The Demon King] ~

"My lord . . ." speaks Cartouche, the dancer. "These are just . . . people, aren't they?" she asks, shaking her head. "They're deranged. Beasts," she says. "They're falling into panic and delirium and descending onto one another because of that."

"Yes, and no," remarks Swain, looking up toward the ceiling of the cavernous throne room. "This is what's happening; you are correct. But look a layer above that," he instructs. "You are observing what is happening as would any person," points out the Demon King. "But as an artist, I want you to tell me what is happening," he indicates, as the visions continue one last time.

~ [Vava Malti] ~
Elf | ♀ | Seamstress
Location: The Human Capital, a Cozy House
Level: 13

Her children are awake.

She is still there, standing unmoving and staring at them. Her eyes are entirely open, yet she has no emotion on her face, and her body is totally still. The youngsters stare up at her with a mixture of confusion and fear on their faces as they lie within reach of her breath.

Her girl, the older one, opens her mouth. ". . . Vava?" she asks uncertainly. However, Vava Malti doesn't react to her question. The child's worry quickly escalates into a deeper panic as she attempts to shake her to rouse a response from her, but she continues to be unresponsive to her efforts. "Vava!" yells the girl, who is already crying, as she is too terrified of the wide, hovering eyes pressing down on her, bloodshot and deeply red.

The smaller child begins sobbing and clinging to his older sister, as he is still too young to understand the nature of the situation and comprehend what is taking place. The older child makes an effort to soothe the anxiety of the smaller youngster, holding him as they crawl back over the bed, pressing their backs against the wall to look at her.

She stands there, where she stood, and slowly cranes her head to look at the two children, frozen in fear as they look at her.

Such good children. Look at them breathing. Those are fine, strong breaths.

They start crying in terror, both of them now, and she smiles, looking at how wet their eyes are, not like hers. Hers are so very dry.

Such good children.

~ [Arsurni] ~
Human | ♂ | Hunter
Location: A Hunter's Lodge in the Remote Southeast
Level: 37

Arsurni kicks his chair back, knocking it over while he sits on it—the crossbow bolt shoots past his face, sticking into the wall as men begin to scream.

It's devolved.

He rolls, jumping up to his feet and lashing out with the knife, immediately cutting the arm of the man trying to grab him, who stumbles back and snarls in pain. Arsurni swipes the blade through the air to keep them away, kicking over an old table to dive behind as crossbow bolts shoot through the room.

An instant later, he's on the move again. When being hunted, one has to stay on the move. He jumps out. A man tries to tackle him. With a twist, he ducks down halfway, cutting him in the gut, and then making a break for the door.

Their eyes are like those of wolves. They're no different from the animals they themselves had fled from before.

Arsurni realizes that the Demon King doesn't just make monsters and animals strange and dire; he does the same to people too. The man grabs hold of the door, yanking it open a second time to flee into the night—even with the wolves, it's better out there than in here, where he is guaranteed to die.

The door crashes against him, something barging in from the outside and knocking him down against the wall.

His vision spinning, Arsurni watches as snarling beasts storm in through the open door, as if they had been waiting for their chance. It doesn't make any sense. Wolves are smart bastards for sure, but not like this. They don't have this kind of planning.

Hunters scream in terror as a full pack of them tears toward them, ripping the armed but unprepared men to the ground with violently gnashing teeth. Panting in terror, pressing his back against the wall in fear, something clicks in his head, and Arsurni jumps to his feet before, ironically enough, he runs out of the door, slamming it shut behind him, sealing both of his problems and their screams and howls inside the lodge.

Rain pelts down all around him as he runs into the night, separating himself from whatever the hell that was, only coming to a stop as he sees the other thing out there with him in the night.

The hunter's senses scream to him that something is off. He reaches for his knife, but he has lost it in the prior fray.

Instead, he stands there, grasping around on his belt and stepping back as a looming, towering shadow turns his way. A strange, twisted husk with a long, lanky frame, its presence mimicking the tall pines, stares at him.

It bends down toward the hunter, wearing the fur of wolves on its skeletal body.

Its face is hollow and empty, like dried skin pulled back over an old skull. It purses its lips as its face hovers before Arsurni, his heart freezing him in terror, and it lets out a long, soft howl that carries through the night.

Many dozen howls come in return from behind him.

Terrified, he looks over his shoulder as the wolves violently drag the hunters from inside, their ankles and tendons having been chewed through so they can't run as they are dragged into the darkness.

". . . What . . ." He looks back at the thing, finally being able to take a step away. "What are you?"

It smiles, the yellow of its teeth matching the faded tone of its dead skin. "A hunter," says the demon general as the man is pounced on from behind, animals chewing through the back of his knees.

~ [Trall] ~
Orc | ♀ | Fighter
Location: The Wildlands, Just South of the Human Capital
Level: 23

Trall is an uncoordinated mess, screaming and flailing as she finally manages to reach the light of the city, falling down to her knees and then

crawling as she emerges out of the darkness of the wild for the very first time since the panic began. Snot and tears run down her face, her heart aching so badly from the exertion, and her head spinning so wildly that she's sure she's about to just die right here and now anyway.

She's the only one who made it.

She sits on her knees, catching her breath and looking back over her shoulder toward the darkness in which her party had vanished.

Nothing.

After a few minutes of recuperation, she rises to her trembling legs, moving toward the gates of the city.

Laughter.

"Huh?" mutters Trall, looking back behind herself at her party members—all of them. They are very much uneaten, unmangled, and unkilled.

They walk toward the city, talking to one another and making jokes like nothing ever happened as they reach the light and look toward her. "Guys?" she asks.

"There weren't any monsters, asshole," says the wizard, looking at her and holding her gut. "Turns out that some wimp just screamed for no reason," she explains, rolling her eyes. "We may have gotten caught up in the whole thing a little." She narrows her eyes. "Fuck you, by the way."

"No . . . monsters?" mutters the orc, going through her visions of what just happened.

It's true. She never saw a single monster, did she? Somebody screamed, and then somebody else screamed, and the panic after that was just kind of what happened. It took over the group as a whole. In essence, they made themselves afraid of nothing.

She sighs, lowering her head, and then starts laughing, understanding now why they were laughing when they got here after her.

"So, this is going to be awkward now, huh?" she asks.

"I'm quitting the party," replies the priest.

"Me too," remarks the wizard. "Fuck you guys, seriously. What the hell? Should report this to the adventurer's guild, actually. Betrayal is grounds for exclusion," she threatens.

"Whoa, whoa," says Trall, lifting her hands and walking back toward them. "Let's take it easy here. We all got a little overexcited. There's no need to make this a big incident."

"You literally threw me off to die," hisses the wizard, narrowing her eyes.

Trall points at the thief. "And he gut punched the good brother priest," she says. "Look at them now. They seem fine to me."

The two men look at one another.

The wizard crosses her arms, lifting her nose. "For the next week—no, the next month. I want all of your drops. Every single one. Or I'm out, and I'm reporting this," she threatens.

"That's not *fair!*" argues Trall. "It was life or death!"

"Take it or leave it," says the wizard, holding out a hand to strike their deal with. Trall grimaces, her face going through a very wide variety of expressions.

Fuck.

"Fine!" she relents, seeing no other way out. If she loses her membership in the adventurer's guild, she's going to be screwed, with or without the whole Demon King thing. It's her only lifeline. She grabs the wizard's hand, shaking it. "We have a deal. One month, and then this is all going to be forgotten."

"Give or take a few days," replies the wizard, her voice lowering, sounding like gravel running down an incline. She turns her head to look at the orc. Now that she's close, she can see the flesh-covered rod breaking in through the back of her skull, hidden by her long hair. "The castle is about three-and-a-half weeks away by foot as of now."

Trall doesn't have time to scream before she is yanked into the darkness by the thing that caught not only all of her "friends" but now her too, to complete the set.

The demon general of the north scurries away, having picked off more stragglers from the human capital for the Demon King's benefit.

May his darkness cover this realm forever.

~ [The Demon King] ~

"Inevitability," says Abydos as the vision ends.

Swain looks toward the painter, pleased. He has found the magic word. "Each story carries a narrative with a sense of hope in some way," he explains to the others. "However, each is just an attempt to avoid the inevitable.

"You are correct, Abydos," says the Demon King as the others look his way, clearly unsure as to what this all is. "The reason I show you this is to remind you of the inevitability of this existence." He looks down at his massive hand, clenching it slowly shut as he imagines what it would feel like to have the neck of the person who had once betrayed him within its grasp. "No matter which life you live, human, gallu, or demon, the end comes one way or another." His many eyes look at his artists. "Will you have finished your masterpiece by then?" asks the Demon King. "Or will you go screaming into the night, lying to yourself that you didn't have enough time?"

~ [Vava Malti] ~
Elf | ♀ | Seamstress
Location: The Human Capital, a Cozy House
Level: 13

A voice whispers from the right. "You need to kill them."

"Put them to sleep. Take the pillow," suggests a helpful man from the left.

"Press it to their faces," instructs a woman behind her.

Vava Malti listens to the whispering shadows as she stares at her very good children—very, very good children. She has such good children. They're breathing. If only they were asleep, like good children should be.

A shadow leans into her ear. "They'll be bad if you don't make them sleep."

"Good children sleep."

"They're awake. Make them sleep. Bad children."

Her hands shake as she continues to stare at her young, who have howled themselves empty and now sit in distant terror, their backs pressed against the corner of the bed and the wall. She grabs the pillow from her and her husband's bed, which is right next to theirs, and slowly lifts it, doing as the shadows instruct. They know what they're doing. She should listen to them.

The woman lifts the pillow, having never blinked once.

As it passes by her face, the old sheet that she hasn't changed ever since he left smells like he did. Her husband.

It's not a good smell, like a perfume. It's the smell that a body pressed against fabric leaves. It's the perfectly normal, everyday smell of a man

who sweats a little now and then, who has regular hygiene habits, and nothing more exotic than that. It just smells like him, that's all.

And that's all it takes.

Malti collapses, her head falling against her children's bed as she howls, crying in desperate anguish for the first time in days. Her eyes sting like wildfire from the moisture. She sits there on the floor and screams into the pillow, screaming until the voices and the shadows go away, and then she screams some more, until familiar hands touch her from the bed.

It couldn't have been put off forever.

She didn't want them to see this. She didn't want them to realize how broken their last parent was. But with all of the pressure, with all that's going on, well . . .

It was inevitable.

~ **[Crusader Valtos]** ~
Orc | ♂ | Crusade Legionnaire
Location: The Demon King's Castle, Floor Sixteen
Level: 83

Valtos readies himself for whatever is coming next.

This place is a hellhole.

But he came down here to fight, and by the gods, he's going to put his soul into it, even if he is afraid. If everyone around him can do it, then so can he.

"Pardon me," says a voice from his side. "Excuse me?"

Valtos looks at a woman who shambles just alongside him; her leg is clearly hurt from some incident. She closes one eye playfully as she tries to keep pace, clasping her hands together in a slight asking gesture. "Sorry. Could you help me, please?" she asks. "Just for a minute!" she quietly promises.

He looks down at her leg, which, given her pacing, must be brutally hurt beneath that armor. Yet here she is, walking on together with the rest of them. Someone with a real fighting spirit and a desire to keep going; someone who hasn't given up the ghost just yet.

"Of course," he replies, letting her lean on his shoulder and slowing down just enough so they can keep walking together.

Something tickles inside of his ear.

THE PRETENDING GAME

~ [Erschein] ~
Human | ♂ | Initiate
Location: The Triumvirate Academy for the Magical Arts
Level: 6

She's right next to him. The game isn't over yet.

The young man sits at his desk in the classroom, his folded hands held as stiff as his straight back, which practically aches from the unusual rigidity. He doesn't move an inch, staring straight forward toward the lector's board at the front of the lecture hall.

Life is often quite challenging in ways that are simply not easily understood until a person is finally confronted with them, having thought they were prepared for this situation beforehand. However, often when this situation does then arrive, the variables are different than the ones said person initially considered in the back of their minds. The smells are different, the textures, the presence of it are all simply different, and despite the fact that the rest of the plan lines up with what was considered prior, that little bit of difference is often far more than enough in order to fully disrupt and destroy the best laid plans.

His trembling lip holds firm, never opening. His shaking eyes never leave from their firm lock on the board, all of this as her breath presses against the side of his face. The warm dew wicks against his open eye, which he doesn't dare to blink. The smell of metal moves in through his nostrils as he listens to the soft *tap, tap, tap*ping in his ear, coming closer and closer by the second.

He was prepared for her, in theory. But then, when theory came to practice and he found himself in the room together with everyone else—and her—well, the theory went to shit.

Wetness wicks against his shoe, soaking through the thin leather and wicking into his sock. It's blood, from the pool of it puddling around his feet. The desk to the left of him is tossed over, his classmate, Babel, lying headless, blood streaming out of her stump. The desk ahead of him is flipped over, having been used to violently bludgeon Cardigee to death.

They lost the game.

But he can't look at them. If he does, he'll lose the game too.

Erschein stares, his eyes burning as he focuses on the blackboard, only on the blackboard, despite the smell in his nose, despite the clicking and tapping in his ear, and despite the wetness of a long, slimy tongue pressing its tip against the side of his neck. His eyes are locked onto the words carved, not written, on the chalkboard by an unimaginable horror.

The rules of today's game:
You must look at this board.
You must never look away from this board.
If you do, you lose!
If you last until class is over, you win!

Water doesn't form around his eyes anymore. That's all done with already. It's been hours now, and he is the only one left. He's the only one who hasn't lost the game. He's the last man standing.

There's just him and . . . her.

This isn't his first game. This is his fourth. He's . . . he's pretty good at the games. But that's because he's a good thinker. He's able to keep himself busy in his own head, enough so that he won't get any dumb ideas, like losing the game by trying to take a peek at the woman, who is breathing in his ear.

The opponent.

Her face is long and slender, like that of a gaunt woman, as if someone had shoved their fingers into her mouth and ripped her jaw down low, letting it heal that way. Her mouth is full of rows of blunt, flat teeth. Her hair is black like seaweed rotting in a dead tide.

And she is very good at the game.

A finger creeps up toward his face, his mouth. It is long and round and knobby, its joints bulging out like orbs between the rail-thin sections

of bone that connect them. Slowly, it slides past his cheek and toward his lips. The skin of her hand feels cold and damp, like one's hands would after having been underwater for a time, and he can feel her pressing against his face—the soft layer of meat between the skin of her finger and the end of her fingerbone compressing too easily as she applies pressure to his face, as if the meat below were old and softened by decay.

Slowly, she slides it toward his sealed lips as he intently stares at the board, not wavering as she grazes over his mouth, lightly flicking his lips around as she swirls her finger over the area. The smell of death comes up to his nose from her hand—not only from her but from the gore, viscera, and bile of his classmates who lost the game that she wipes onto him, before slowly working her way into his closed mouth, running her finger along the inside of his cheek, over the outside of his teeth.

But he doesn't look away from the board.

A crystal chimes in the air, suspended above the door, as it absorbs a timed magical frequency that signals the end of exactly another hour, making eight total.

She slides her hand out of his mouth and gets up, staring at him as she returns to the front of the classroom. The monster—akin to a spider masquerading in an old corpse, given the way it moves—moves, grabs a cloth, and wipes over the chalkboard, to little effect.

The rag gets snagged on the scratched-in rules she left on the surface and rips apart. A moment later, she drops it to the ground and picks up the chalk, entirely nonsensically as she turns around to look at him again, her arm moving straight back behind herself as her eyes never leave his.

Class Three: IIII
Me: -

She drops the chalk to the ground and simply walks out of the room.

Erschein breaks, immediately vomiting all over the floor, his body shaking as he finally gives in to it, now that he has the luxury of doing so.

Heaving, the young man looks around himself at his classmates—his horrified Dranta, who was strung to a noose made from his own intestines, or Miri, who was impaled on the rector's pointing stick all the way through and simply left there, propped against the wall.

They lost the game.

Shaking, he gets up to his feet, the last one left from his class, as he looks at the tally on the board.

How many more?

How many more does he have to win?

He has to get out of here.

The windows are barred.

The doors are chained with massive, broad chains that could restrain a giant.

It doesn't matter which dormitory of the academy he checks; it doesn't matter if he goes to the dean's office, the classrooms, the bathrooms, or even any of the hundreds of corridors in between.

The entire academy has been turned into a prison overnight.

It was a normal day like any other, barring the evacuations in the days prior given the presence of the Demon King. But not everyone was evacuated. Evacuation implies there is a place to go after fleeing, and for many of them, there is no place to go. The Triumvirate Academy is a boarding school mixed in with an orphanage at the same time. They all live here, sleep here, eat here, and grow up here from adolescence until adulthood. There's nowhere for them to go and, so, rather than letting them run off into the wilds where they might have a chance of escaping, the dean of the school simply locked all of them, who had no other family or money, inside, saying that the academy was perfectly safe to weather the storm in.

Of course, he said this as his servants carried away his bags to his carriage before he locked the doors and then rode up north to the capital.

It was fine at first, if not a little haunting. The students who remained banded together and made do. It's not like they turned into violent animals overnight. They continued to make their beds, they organized cooking and cleaning duties that were rigorously followed, and they studied, though not as much as they should, in all honesty. They were surviving pretty well, all things considered.

Then, a few days ago, somebody pinned notes around the school— fliers—that advised them to prepare for the games to come.

Every class assumed it was a student group from another class trying to organize something to lift everyone's spirits.

They were mistaken.

Erschein quietly closes the door to classroom three behind himself, standing out in the hall as the other doors open too, once the other games come to an end. He is the only one who made it out of five today. Three days ago, his class had forty people. Everyone he's gotten to know for the last few years since they moved into the advanced classes—his friends, the cute girl he had a crush on—they're dead.

They lost the game.

He looks to the side, staring at classroom one, from which three people come out. This morning, nine went in. His gaze turns toward classroom two's door, which quietly opens, revealing a single, small girl stepping outside and then vomiting. He recognizes her as the quiet girl from their class. The typical short-haired bookworm type. He waits for more to come out after her. Classroom two still had ten people this morning.

Nobody else comes out.

Finally, classroom four.

Six people went in this morning.

Nobody comes out.

The woman, the creature, the monster—she plays games with everyone. Every game has a different set of rules and conditions each day. The price for winning is being allowed to leave, only to come back to play tomorrow's game. The price of losing is obvious.

"I CAN'T!" screams one of the three from classroom one, pushing the other two away. "GET OFF OF ME!" she yells, grabbing hold of her hair and falling down, slumping against the wall. He recognizes her as one of the more extroverted girls in class one, not that he knows her. But she's one of those people whom you know of, just because you see them every day, since you're in the same space but not the same circle. Her classmates don't bother trying to console her, which he understands.

He just stands there, too, with nobody to console him. Traditionally, as the rector would say, it is not the place of a man to be the one who needs consoling; a man is the one who consoles. The validity of such a social theory is, at least by the old ways of this institution, unquestionable. The academy is extremely socially conservative.

And so, Erschein consoles himself.

"Sorry, I'll help you," speaks a voice from the side, interrupting his thoughts. He blinks, looking at the lone survivor from class two.

"What?" asks Erschein.

"You're Erschein from class three, right?" she asks. He nods, somewhat confused. She points over her shoulder, past her ear-length, poorly cut hair. "I threw up," she says, as if that would give it all some context. He looks at her puddle of vomit and then back at her, replying not with words but with a questioning expression. "You're on hallway mopping duty today," she explains, plainly.

"Oh . . ." replies Erschein, staring at her for a moment as the girl from the other class descends into violent sobbing, together with her friends, who also join in. "I, uh . . . I think . . ." he starts, wanting to tell her that that just isn't really a priority right now, in all honesty. Before the games started, it made sense for them to keep up with their chores. It kept them and their minds busy. But now . . . well, it doesn't really matter if there is vomit in the hallway or not, does it?

One of the others nearby screams something incoherently, running off down the corridor, likely looking for a way out.

He watches them go, wishing them luck, but knowing that they'll be back tomorrow. He's already looked everywhere too. He checked every window and door in every room he could, and none of them, not a single one, was available to be opened.

The young man turns back to look at the girl from classroom two, who is still standing there before him.

What the hell else does he have to do?

"Sure," replies Erschein. "I'll go grab the mop," he says. She nods, going off to get some water in a pail. The two of them clean the hallway and mark the chore done off of the list, the only one that has been completed today out of the entire collection.

He stares at the list of names for a moment, and then picks up the chalk again, striking through the names of everyone in his class.

"This one too," remarks the girl, pointing at a name and then at another and another, until they've marked off everyone from their classes except themselves; Erschein, and the quiet girl, Verschwind.

He follows her name, noticing that her chore for the day isn't done yet either. She spent her free time helping him clean up. Erschein taps against the box with the chalk, looking at her. She has to clean the fireplaces out today. "Come on, I'll help you," he offers.

The junior classmen lowers her gaze. Each of the classes is sorted according to its time here, with the fourth class being the oldest and the

first class being the youngest. All of them are adults at this point, but still have a couple more years to finish their education. "That's okay . . ." she says, shaking her head. "I can manage. You didn't make the chimneys extra dirty," explains Verschwind.

He sets the chalk down. "I don't have anything else to do," he admits. The last few nights he has spent talking with his classmates and trying to find ways out. But now, he has no classmates left, and there is no way out, so he's stuck in a very deep sense. "Let me help you."

Verschwind stares down quietly at the floor for a time before quietly mumbling her approval and walking away.

Chimneys are the worst chore of them all; you always get filthy from it, and somehow, the work always seems to take longer than you think it will, even if you expect it to take forever.

He, of course, takes the opportunity to look up the chimney shaft for a way out.

But it is too tight to crawl out of after a few meters.

The day ends too fast, the two of them not really talking too much but still hanging out together as they work. She's not really a talker, and even when he finds something to talk about, she somehow manages to craft replies that are a few words long at best and never leaves an opening to continue the conversations. It's difficult.

Then, after work, they simply sit there.

You can't be late to class.

On the first day, there were people who were late. They weren't there by the second day.

Erschein, with a shaking hand, grabs hold of the door handle to classroom three, taking a deep breath as he tries to build up the nerve to open it. He doesn't want to. Everything in his body tells him that he doesn't want to, from the sweat that collects in his damp socks to the feeling of nausea welling in his gut, to the ice in his veins.

But he has to.

Being late means that you lose the game.

He takes a deep breath and opens the door with a quick, sharp tug before he has the ability to think about it anymore than that.

It, she, is standing there, by the teacher's desk. Her head slowly turns to look at him with a wide smile, as if to welcome him in for a new morning.

His heart falls into his gut as he looks at her long face. She stretches her arm out, beckoning him inside and telling him to sit.

Terrified, as he ought to be, the young man steps into the classroom and closes the door behind himself, staring in confusion at the others. There is deeply tense silence except for the one girl from class one who can't stop crying. Crying isn't against the rules. There is also the quiet girl, Verschwind, and one more from class one. The corpses of his class have been "cleaned" into a pile in the back of the room, where their limp, mangled bodies are simply stacked over one another in a gruesome, rotting display.

The room smells as you would expect.

There is a shrill, sharp scratching in the chalkboard as the creature writes on it with her long, curved nails, cutting deeply into the stone, the noise of which causes him to deeply wince.

For the sake of efficiency, classes one through four have been merged.
The rules of today's game:
You must eat.
Everyone must eat all the meat before the bell rings.
If you manage, you all win!
If you do not, you all lose.
Vomiting is permitted, but you or someone else must re-eat.

The creature smiles, staring at them as the crystal chimes, signaling the start of a new day in class, and the new game. She stares at them, her recessed eyes pulling back into her skull as if something were sucking them in, giving her the look of a pulsating insect as she stretches her mouth open and hangs her head downward. A bulge forms in her throat, her abdomen distending and her jaw unhinging, as the left half of a naked human torso simply drops out of her mouth, covered in a slimy concoction of stomach acid, saliva, and blood.

The head is missing, but on the flappy half of the neck that remains, there are clear noose marks to be seen where the skin was freshly burnt from a rope.

This would be the missing member of class one, who had likely assumed she had found an exit of her own. But you can't try to kill yourself.

It's against the rules of the game.

The crying girl intensifies her howls; the boy next to her covers his mouth. The teacher smiles broadly, a long strand of saliva connecting the monster to the chunk of corpse. Her long fingers *tap, tap, tap* against the desk, signifying the passage of time.

The boy from class one is muttering incoherently to himself, his finger stuck on the top of his head as he stares down at the desk.

Verschwind leans over. "Siblings," she explains, summarizing the story in one word as she points over her shoulder to the boy from class one who is having a breakdown, which is perfectly allowed today. But it's costing them time.

Erschein blinks, looking down at his desk too. *Costing them time? What the hell kind of thought is that? As if the boy were in the wrong here.*

But what else are they supposed to do?

After days one and two, he was a bit stretched, and day three was rough in its own way. But this . . . With every passing day, the games are becoming sicker and more twisted.

Tap. Tap. Tap, taps the knobby finger against the desk, the woman watching them, her eyes having returned to "normal."

"I don't want to die," admits Erschein, looking at Verschwind, as if this statement were some great secret that nobody else was meant to hear. She looks toward him, staring at him for a time without replying, and then simply scoots her chair back, rising to her feet.

He watches her walk over the deep, large bloodstains on the floor while she moves toward the teacher's desk as the first. The teacher seems very pleased, smiling broadly as Verschwind approaches. Erschein looks over his shoulder at the other two, who are still in the middle of their thing.

The young man scoots his chair back, rising to his feet as the second one. Even this . . . Even this, he's willing to do. The drive for survival is stronger in some than in others, and in him, it is particularly strong. There's no real reason for it. It's not like he has any family waiting on him on the outside, or any lofty dreams or particular goals. He's just interested in living for the sake of living. He wants to live for no other reason than the fact that he wants to live.

And that's perfectly fine.

He stands next to Verschwind, looking down at the mutilated torso covered in scratches, claws, and tears. Flaps of meat hang from the flayed ribs, the organs already removed—or digested. A small human's torso, minus organs, for a young woman of this size weighs thirty to forty kilos? He's not really sure at all. This is half of that, and no organs.

This train of thought stops him for a moment as he catches up with it and lifts his gaze to look at the teacher, who is just silently standing there and watching them.

With four people, it should be doable. It's disgusting. But they have just less than eight hours to do it.

But that's assuming they all . . .

His own reality catches up with his thoughts and drive for survival as he stares at the piece of human meat again. This was a person yesterday. He saw her.

Before he can spiral too deeply into anything like that, Verschwind drops down and sinks her teeth straight into the flesh of the torso. He watches her go, half shocked and half lost in horror as old blood drips out of the meat and stains her face. A moment later, following her example, he begins to tear at the soft flesh of the stomach before he has any more time to think about it and stop himself.

He bites through the skin, which makes an odd, light popping noise in his mouth as his teeth break through. Fluid presses into his throat as the meat only slightly gives way, requiring him to bite down harder to rip through the flesh.

The contents of his stomach press up against him immediately, as soon as he has something in his mouth. He covers it with his hand, wincing and forcing it back down, together with a sliver of unchewed meat.

"You need to chew," speaks a voice from his side. Gasping for air, he turns to look at Verschwind, who turns to face him, old blood streaking down her face. "If you don't, you won't manage all five," explains the girl, before biting back down.

He's silently grateful to her right now, as he watches her tear into the human body like a monster.

It eases his conscience as he continues his work.

He doesn't want to lose the game.

After an hour of this—which becomes easier as time goes on, once he simply decides to stop thinking about it in the middle of the process—one

of the others from class one arrives, the girl, and looks down at the corpse of her classmate and friend, which has now been gnawed on by three creatures, who step aside and make room for her as she, crying, joins in.

Erschein looks at the teacher, who diligently watches them from the other side of the desk.

On the first day, people tried to attack her.

Those people lost the game.

The only way to survive is to play along, but for how long? There's no end in sight, as far as he can tell.

Blood squirts past his face, splashing onto Verschwind with a red streak that runs as a cut would across her skin when he bites into an old, clogged artery that bursts.

The dead girl's brother cannot be convinced to join the game.

Not joining the game means that they would all lose the game.

They force him to join the game. Verschwind and Erschein hold him down as the other girl shoves pieces of his sister into his mouth, practically jamming them down his throat with her fingers.

By the time all is said and done and the crystal chimes, there are only bones left on the table.

The teacher looks pleased.

She turns around, standing to face the chalkboard, and lifts a clawed hand.

Class Three: V
Me: -

The haunting woman then just walks to the door and leaves, leaving four animals behind her in a room full of carcasses.

They won today's game.

Erschein stands before the list of chores, staring at it.

Today's chore for him is to hang the laundry out to dry.

This is obviously impossible to do, given that one, there is no laundry being done, and two, they can't go outside to dry it.

"The classroom hallway," says a voice next to him. He turns to look at Verschwind, who has just been silently following him this whole time, ever since the afternoon. Neither of them has talked about what happened; not

to one another or to the other two. He's not sure what they're doing or if they're talking about it. He doesn't exactly intend to talk about it, either. It is what it is. They did what they had to do to survive.

He still feels nauseous from the sheer volume of raw meat sloshing around in his gut, ignoring its source.

"We can hang it up in the classroom hallway," explains Verschwind, referring to the laundry.

He looks at her and then back at the board. She is free of chores today. There's no reason for her to be helping him with his. Well, other than the reason he himself has already gone through.

It's better than being alone.

"There isn't any washed laundry to hang up," replies Erschein.

She looks at him, staring for a time, before she then simply starts unbuttoning her shirt right in front of him. He watches her for a moment, and then, realizing this, turns around. "We will have to wash ours," she says.

"Did you have to start doing that here?" he asks, clearing his throat. A shirt lands at his feet, having been thrown there by her. He looks down at the bloodied rag, staring at it as a hand touches his back.

"We're going to die," speaks the voice from behind him, echoing around the room. The two of them stand there for a while like that as he thinks about that statement. They're going to die? Really? No. No, he doesn't think so. He doesn't want to die. Erschein turns around, looking at her. "We'll wash our clothes," she says. "Then, we'll have something to dry."

Erschein undoes his shirt, covered in the gore of today's game, and drops it to the ground. The two of them just quietly stare at one another.

"We're not going to die," says Erschein, looking at her. "We made it this far."

She shakes her head. "All games end eventually."

"What if we beat her?" he asks, leaning in. "What if we beat every game until she runs out?!" His voice echoes around them, drifting past her unchanging, mostly blank expression which never really seems to change. "Why would she kill us if we win?"

"Asked the mice, as they spoke of the cat," finishes Verschwind for him with a sentence that really illuminates their situation in a clearer context.

He stops, his mouth slowly closing as her words sink in and silence his hopes. "Then why are we even playing the games to begin with?" asks the young man, his question receiving no answer.

She bends down and picks up the shirts, walking away. "Why are we doing the laundry?" she asks in return as she quietly walks off. He watches her go, mulling over the question.

He doesn't find an answer and shakes his head, walking after her in silence.

They wash their shirts, together with the meager amount of laundry the survivors of the last days had deposited, throwing them into the basin of spinning water powered by the resonance of an enchanted mechanism. The washing pit is essentially a hole in the ground with a clean, cylindrical shape. In the middle of it is the mechanism, and the interior is filled with sloshing water that they occasionally pour soap into.

The two of them stand there as the laundry spins beneath them.

A pair of pants fly into the mix from above, and he turns to look at her, not even surprised. They're going to die anyway. Might as well have clean pants. He shrugs, taking off his own and kicking them in too.

"I like doing the laundry," she says, sort of out of the blue.

He watches the water spin around and around. Laundry is one of the better chores. You just have to throw in all of the laundry, make sure the mechanism is on, and then you're done. It's essentially the same as having a day off. Hanging laundry is, however, the worst chore to have, as it requires a lot of bending, moving, carrying, and walking. It's a full few hours of work just for one's daily chores, making it a real nuisance, especially during winter when clothes still have to be hung up outside, too.

"Yeah," replies Erschein.

The two of them stand there in silence for a time, just watching the water. It isn't really awkward; it's an expected silence, rather. The two of them just stare at the hypnotizing spell of the water swirling around in an endless circle, streaks of blood washing out of many pieces of fabric and vanishing in thin stripes, little by little.

They're going to die.

It doesn't matter if they win the game or lose it. They're going to die.

He turns to look at her, and she turns to look at him, and both of them, without needing any words, use the opportunity and one another to cross one more thing off their lists before the games finally come to an end.

When all is said and done, the night is half over. They get up again to finally hang up the now washed clothes in the main corridor. Once that pointless task is done, and they check off the chore on the chart, the two

of them return to his dorm and continue with one another as before until they fall asleep together.

It feels nice to have someone fall asleep with you. The other stuff too, but mostly this. It's quiet.

He wishes he had done this sooner.

Groggily, Erschein opens his eyes and then quietly rolls his head, looking at Verschwind as she lies there, her arm and leg draped over him.

Quietly, he slides out of the bed, doing his best not to wake her. She just mumbles in her sleep as her arm flops against the pillow and her leg against the mattress, and he slowly rises to his feet.

The young man wanders out of the room, silently closing the door behind him before he heads into the hallway.

He's not really sure where he's going, honestly. Instinctively, he bends off toward the bathroom, taking a moment to relieve himself.

There is a distant sobbing coming from one of the stalls in the back. He turns his head, listening. It's the boy's voice; the other survivor from class one.

Erschein stands there, listening for a moment as he dries himself off, and then walks back out of the bathroom.

Crying isn't against the rules of the game, and he's hardly in a position to try and console the boy whose sister he helped eat. She was dead already, of course. But the moral line here is obviously dubious at best, so he decides to just step over it entirely and let the boy cry. They're going to die, after all.

Why not cry.

He should cry his heart and soul out, if that's what he wants to do.

Erschein looks around, deciding to put away the hung-up laundry by himself. It should be dry by now. He walks through the school in his underwear, passing by the other surviving girl, who is sitting in the library, feverishly reading through obscure books on demonology and the like.

If that's how she wants to spend one of her last nights, more power to her. They're all going to die, so if she wants to read, she should read until her eyes turn dry.

She lifts her gaze, watching him shuffle by like the undead in all of his indifference.

Erschein grabs the hung-up clothes and begins folding them before stacking them neatly on the cart that he pushes along the hallway past the classrooms.

He stops, looking at the doors, and then, without knowing what he's doing, wanders out of sheer, idle curiosity to the other classrooms. This is how he wants to spend one of his last nights.

The hinges creak as he looks inside at the rooms, reading the last games that the prior denizens had gotten to play.

Three, he knows, as he was there. But for classes one, two, and four, he has no idea.

Class one, the class with currently two survivors, had to sustain a scream from three people for eight hours. He's not going to make assumptions about how they did this, but it would explain a few things.

Class four, across the hall with zero survivors, had to, as their last challenge, complete a perfectly sized replica of a human using pieces of their own skin. Half-flayed and bled-out bodies lie all around the room.

Class three was his challenge.

And class two, which has Verschwind as its sole survivor—

He opens the door, looking inside.

The rules of the special game!
You must betray one person who trusts you in another game to win!
This special game can only be played by one person.
This special game has a duration of three days.

Erschein looks at the room, at the two other students sitting at their desks, bound, their heads having been violently bludgeoned with something blunt as he processes what he has just read.

He takes a deep, slow breath, quietly closing the door again before standing there in the hallway in silence for a time, something aching in his gut.

Quietly, after a moment more, he pushes the laundry cart back to its spot and takes fresh clothes for the two of them, heading upstairs again and back into his room, where she is still lying. He sets the shirts down. Disturbed from her rest, Verschwind opens an eye and looks at him in a daze.

"Bathroom," explains Erschein, lying back down in bed next to, then over her as he thinks about what he read down below in her classroom.

The night ends soon enough, and a new, very fun game begins.

The rules of the game:
You must point at somebody.
You must point at the same time.
You must be pointed at.
If you are pointed at, but not pointed at the most, you win!
If you are pointed at the most, you lose.

The four of them stand there in the room, from which everything has been cleared except four desks. The teacher stands there with a bright smile on her face as she looks at them all.

They all look at one another, trying to figure this one out. There's not really a way out this time, though; it might really be it.

Or?

Four people, each pointing once at someone else.

"If we all point at our neighbor," says the girl from class one, "we'll have fulfilled the criteria," she explains, her haggard face revealing the lack of sleep she got and, given the fact that she's here with them, it doesn't look like she found any answers about demons in her books last night. "If everyone is pointed at once, nobody is pointed at the most. It'll be a draw."

In pure theory, this is true.

The game is very easy. This solution is so simple that anyone could think of it. Everyone gets pointed at once. In and out, the game is over in less than a minute in total.

But it's not that simple, is it?

Erschein looks around at them. At the boy whose sister they ate to survive. He might hold a grudge for that. Plus, he's emotionally unstable; he could do anything. The girl herself from class one seems like a reasonable, logical person. He'll guess she'll stick true to her own plan and point to Verschwind, who is next to her. Verschwind should then, in theory, point to the other boy, who is her other neighbor.

But that's not so simple either, is it?

Given her special game, she has to betray him. He's the only one with whom she has established trust, thereby qualifying him as a candidate to be betrayed. She can't betray the other two because they expect nothing from her. He's already quietly accepted that. He's going to die anyway, so what

does it matter if she betrays him or not? Still. There's a game to be played. So, in theory, she is going to point at him out of order, making him the person with the most votes, assuming the other boy follows his assigned role.

It's impossible to say for sure, but this is the most likely thing.

So, for his own survival and for him to win the game, he should point at her.

The crystal chimes, signaling the start, and four arms slowly start to rise into the air.

The girl from class one points at Verschwind.

Verschwind points at him, breaking the defined order as expected.

The boy from class one also points at Verschwind, when he should have been pointing at him instead. But of course he is. Verschwind is the one who first started eating his sister, and he and the other girl are in the same class, even if she did force him to join in.

The teacher grins a large grin, her flat, wide teeth showing as she looks at them, her mouth held wide open as her eyes, together with everyone else's, look at him.

His hand is held out, his thumb pointing back at himself.

There was never a rule about the person needing to be somebody else.

This brings him to two votes: his own and Verschwind's. The other two have no votes.

". . . Why?" asks Verschwind, looking at him, despite that maybe being his question to ask, given the finger pointed at him.

He shrugs, looking at her. "What else am I going to do?" he asks. "The rules don't say anything about choosing yourself. It's a tie," he says, looking at the teacher. "The rules say only the single most pointed-at person counts."

"Wait!" yells the girl from class one. "You can't do that! It's CHEAAH—" The teacher grabs her head, slamming it back against the desk, and rips her mouth open with her other hand so forcefully that her jaw audibly cracks. She reaches down, grabbing hold of her lips, and tears them off in long strips with violent yanks, blood pouring down into the girl's mouth.

Turning around, the teacher holds her up, pressing her face against the chalkboard. Her body below kicks and flails as she screams, trying to escape, as the monster arches her half-broken head back and writes on the chalkboard with the girl's teeth still in her mouth.

Erschein looks at Verschwind, who had just freshly tried to deliver him to this exact fate. He reaches down, and she reaches over, grabbing

a hold of his hand in hers as they watch in silent horror as the score is updated in grim fashion.

Class Three: VI
Me: -

She turns around, dropping the girl to the ground. She isn't dead; her face is simply shattered, and her teeth have been filed down and broken. Desperately gurgling, she tries to crawl away, but the teacher plants a foot on her back and gestures to the door.

Today's game is over.

Not needing to be told twice, Erschein yanks Verschwind out after him. The other boy tries to run away too, but Verschwind shoves him back, and Erschein plants the sole of his boot against his chest, kicking him away and toward the monster before tightly slamming the door shut.

Adrenaline courses through his veins in a way he can't explain, having never come this close to death before. Horrific screams come from the other side of the door as the two last members of class one are brutalized. The two of them fall against the hallway wall and one another, lost to an animal senselessness of their own as they listen to the noises, fueled by the thought that they themselves were this close to being the ones making them tonight.

Games are exciting.

Tomorrow is the last game.

It has to be. There are only the two of them left.

He lies in bed, staring up at the ceiling.

Then he sits upright, the blanket falling from his chest as he gets an idea. It's a strange idea; one that doesn't make much sense in any logical context. He looks down at the woman who almost murdered him today, his hand running over her back. But the best games aren't logical.

They're fun.

Games have to be fun. If they're not fun, they're bad games.

"I have an idea," he says, looking down at the sleepy eye that looks up at him from the pillow.

The crystal chimes, signaling the start of a new day and the final game.

The door opens, and the teacher comes in and looks at Verschwind,

who is sitting at her desk, and at him. He's standing at the chalkboard, tapping against it with the chalk.

Erschein looks at the creature and then holds out his arm, gesturing for her to sit down as she has so often done to them.

He watches her observe him, and then, without much else, she walks over to the students' desks and sits down there.

As are the rules of the game.

See, the thing that he realized is that they're just playing pretend. She's pretending to be the teacher—this is her game; this is fun for her.

But today, he got here early. Today, he has the chalk, and today, he is the teacher.

The rules are easy, once you manage to understand them.

Erschein writes on the board.

The rules of the game:
You must count to five.
Everyone must count aloud, vocally.
If you count to five, you win.
If you do not count to five, you lose.

It's simple, really. But fun—for him. Just as the other games were fun for her.

Erschein taps against the chalkboard, signaling for them to start.

"One . . . two . . . three . . . four . . . five," counts Verschwind.

He looks at the creature, which opens its long, stretched-out mouth. However, it does not know how to speak, and even if it did, the shape of its tongue and mouth would not allow it to enunciate the words properly.

Its smile turns into a frown as he taps against the chalkboard, counting out the time, and then, soon enough, the game comes to an end.

The two of them turn to look at her, the loser, who is well familiar with what comes next.

~ [The Demon King] ~

The Demon King sits on his throne, the carriage rolling on toward the north, toward which they draw ever closer. The old poem in his hand burns into ash.

I look from afar and see the crack of your smile,
Which makes me realize the lack that is mine,
My face is wrinkled, so old, and decrepit,
And I as a person remain fully neglected,
I am and unwanted for stakes of scholarly mind, or for
my still beating heart,
For my outer exterior, is too far apart,
From that which you hold to be . . .
Normal.
So I pretend to be smart, so that you'll stay attentive,
I pretend to be pretty, so that I am fully respected,
I will lash with stern hand, my students repented,
And I do these things, so we can play games, pretending!

~ The Thing That Pretends ~
- Summoned Entity -

The Thing That Pretends is a strange, humanoid creature that takes the shape of something akin to a woman. However, it is not quite successful in its abilities to transform and is quite upset by this failing of its character.

The Thing That Pretends will assume the role of a person who people respect and like, such as popular authority figures, and take over their position to the best of its ability.

It loves to play fun games in the hopes that they will make it new friends!

Class: MONSTER	Element: DARK
Type: Nightmare	Category: TERROR*
Rank: SSS	
Level: 60	

***Terror is a classification term used for all monster types that do not fall into traditional monster categories such as UNDEAD, GOLEM, GHOST, etc. Terrors tend to have unique makeups and behavior patterns, and lean toward hyperviolent tendencies.**

"My lord . . ." says Cartouche as they watch his Terror entity succumb to a grim, violent death at the hands of the two humans, who tear it apart like crazed animals before tearing into one another atop the fresh carcass, as one would expect of frenzied beasts.

"Sometimes, Cartouche," starts the Demon King, watching the two of them with a raised eyebrow. "In a game, we must sacrifice in order to gain." The Demon King looks at the two of them as they fully forsake their humanity for the gift of depravity, bathing in and plunging the demon blood into one another through method of tongue and body. He watches their bodies start to break, their bones start to crack, their limbs start to stretch, and their skin start to tinge.

~ Demon Knight ~
- Corrupted Entity -
A Demon Knight is a formidable creature of true darkness, born out of a fully corrupted and warped human soul, its physical body becoming a monument to its spiritual depravity. Highly versatile, adaptable, and loyal, Demon Knights serve as an in-between, midtier soldier in the ranks between the Demon King and his ever-distant generals.
They would be comparable to succubi, if not for the fact that their desires deepen far further than just into the realms of lust, treading into the agonies of life.

Class: MONSTER	Element: DARK
Type: Nightmare	**Category: CORRUPTION***
Rank: SS	
Level: 99	
***Corruptions are deformed souls belonging to members of the common races. As such, their values are highly individual, based on the nature of their corruptions and the aspect they most embody.**	

CHAPTER 10

CROSSING OVER

~ [Shaushka] ~
Elf | ♀ | Classless
Location: The Scorched Forest
Level: 4

The elf stares with wide eyes at the wreckage.

Broken wood, twisted metal struts, and other destroyed constructions of the like jut out in all directions, as if she were amidst a wasteland.

Screams fill the air; the caravan has come to a sudden stop in the ambush. The crashing of the carriages, tripped up by debris thrown into the way, had flung her out of her seat and straight across a clearing, where she rolled and flopped over a few times before coming to a stop in the grass, covered in scratches and marks.

"... Ah ..." mumbles Shaushka, her head spinning with dizziness and nausea as she sits upright holding her forehead, strands of loose, matted hair falling down past her face while she watches with blurred vision as people fight. Humans and monsters of the darkness engage in frenzied combat, which is being won by the latter.

The elf blinks heavily once, tightly pressing her eyes closed for a moment in order to let her vision reorient itself by the time she opens them again a second time.

By then, the fighting has mostly stopped. The animals that pulled the caravan along have been put to silence, and the people aboard it are being dragged off into the dark forest around them, screaming as they claw into the dirt.

Shaushka sits there in the dead grass of the forest, looking at the trail she left behind herself where she rolled over after impact.

Her vision of the spot is blocked when something large and imposing moves. Beads, strung together on chains of bone, click and clack in the

night like a baby's rattle as the giant moves—moving, gliding, more like a ghost than like a person or a beast, which is bound by steps and strides.

The elf tilts her head, staring quietly as she sits there.

Is this the next thing?

Minute by minute, the night loses its voice as the last people are wrenched out of their hiding spots and torn into the darkness by so many monsters, all of which simply ignore her, together with the odd survivor who tries to run away past her and past the giant too.

Then, after a time, it is done, and all that is left is the voice of crackling fire spreading from broken lanterns and lost torches.

The entity, the giant mockery of the shape of a man adorned in the regalia of the old kings of the deep forests, turns its head away from the destruction to look over its shoulder and then down toward her.

Shaushka blinks.

"Ah?" she asks.

The monster silently turns its head away, looking back into the darkness before moving, gliding away toward the north.

She rubs the back of her head, then her sore back and bottom as she gets up, her hand covered in the same ash and mud that paints her body as she rises to her feet, watching the demon general vanish into the ashen, scorched woods.

The elf looks around herself, not seeing anything else. She shrugs and runs after the levitating spirit and the screams, wondering where they're going to bring her next.

~ [The Demon King] ~

Level Up!
~ [The Demon King] ~
You are now level {100}!

Level: 100 ↗	Experience: -
Attribute: DARK	
Soul Points: 2,000/2,000 ↗	
Presence: 20.0 km ↗	Obols: 0
Souls Collected: 478,001/1,000,000	

You have {38} free Ability Points to spend!

~ [Achievement Unlocked] ~
"The Apex of the World"
Unlocked By: Reaching level 100!
Reward: The rich get richer. Your stats and values have been rounded upward and significantly increased.

~ [Achievement Unlocked] ~
"I Am the Master of All Dominion"
Unlocked By: Becoming the highest-leveled living DEMON in the world.
Reward: All DEMON entities across the physical and the spirit worlds will now hear your call and will undergo great efforts to reach you, no matter what barrier lies in between.

~ [Dungeon] ~
The Demon King's Castle
Current Number of Floors: 30

Section One - Lust (Floors 1–10)
1: {The Gate to the Underworld}
2: {The Precipice of Hope}
3: {The Call of Home}
4: {A Writhing Comfort}
5: {The Mimic Chamber}
6: {The Promise of Power}
7: {The Grasslands with Strange Names}
8: {A Wholesome Promise}
9: {The Lusting Den}
10: {The Pinnacle of Ecstasy}

Section Two - Envy (Floors 11–20)
11: {A Memory That Isn't Mine}
11B: {Safe Room}
12: {The Mirroring Pool}
13: {Mystical Mirage}
14: {The Wall of Ink}
15: {A Proof of Heaven}

16: {The Worm's Tail}
17: {The Ocean Challenging River}
18: {Inverse Sunlight}
19: {Total Fragmentation}
20: {The Scale of Souls} < (RAID {1})

Section Three - Greed (Floors 21–30)
21: {Crush}
22: {Smother}
23: {Press}
24: {Rage}
25: {Drown}
26: {Kill}
27: {Ruin}
28: {Decimate}
29: {Destroy}
30: {The Graveyard}
30B: {The Demon King's Throne Room} (☠)(DEMON CORE)
30C: (Demon Quarters)
30D: (Washroom)
30E: (Kitchen)

Estimated Difficulty: EXTREMELY DEADLY	Estimated Intruder Level: 100
Estimated Defender Level: 100	**Monster Count: 16,876**
Bosses: 4	**Traps: 50**
Chests: 0	**Dungeon Territory: 20.0 km**
Rank: SSS	

Swain sits, his hand resting on his massive fist as he stares at the windows that have appeared through his great and terrible efforts of . . . sitting quietly on his throne.

The man looks back out over his throne room, at the gallu who stand there and clap. The spirits hovering all around them fly, recoiling in their ever-present terror.

"Save your praise," says Swain, watching as their bodies grow to match his strength, tied to his level as his loyal servants. "This power means

little," he finishes, staring back down at the paper on his lap, the edges of the sheets crumbling and smoldering from the heat of his body, tufts of smoke rising into the air.

"The humans are progressing well, my lord," speaks Cartouche. "They've reached floor twenty. Only ten floors separate them from us now," remarks the dancer. Swain looks back up at her. "Should we construct more floors? It would be trivial," says the demon as magic condenses around the tips of her fingers, already starting to sway in a dance meant to flow into her body.

He lifts a hand, stopping her. "No," replies the Demon King, interrupting her.

"My lord?" she asks.

The Demon King looks down at his writing. "The greater work is a sum of many parts, Cartouche," explains the horrific monstrosity. "Each piece belongs to one of us. It is important that no voice reaches dominance over the others," says the Demon King, his fingers tapping against the throne as he thinks. "Each of you has contributed one section of the whole."

"I haven't!" interjects Kirsch, the ghost.

He looks at her. She is indeed one of his servants, but she is not a gallu. She is something entirely different. "Thank you, Kirsch," speaks the Demon King. "But this is not something you can contribute to, I am afraid," he explains, looking at the ghost.

She lacks an artist's soul. She is merely a being that exists, joyous and carefree and capable of escaping the ugliness of humanity, yes, but incapable of producing a piece upon the canvas, as she lacks the drive, the passion, and the desire to create at all costs.

She frowns as he looks back down at his poems.

One castle per king. One section per gallu.

These rules are perhaps arbitrary, but they are his. The Demon King plays fair. To utterly crush humanity, to simply wipe them out as he could very well do, isn't something beautiful. What's beautiful is the story, the attempt, and the act of their climbing and fighting toward the spire of his cruelty with every drop of blood and sweat in their body, only to then be crushed at the precipice—or not.

This is what is beautiful about the act in the play that is happening here on the stage he has set. It's not about the act of winning or losing, as he is going to win anyway, that much is certain.

It's about the act of doing so beautifully.

Swain's eyes on his body shift, sensing something in the distance. The Demon King lifts his head, staring off to the side for a time, looking at and through a wall.

~ [Ruhr, the River Sorceress] ~
Half Elf | ♀ | Sorceress
Rank: SSS
Location: The Demon King's Castle, Floor Twenty
Level: 96

The floor shakes beneath her feet, the gilded metal of the great bowl creaking as it moves, hanging downward with the weight of the thousands of people who stand in it. Violent energies press past her face, whipping the strands of her azure hair back behind her as she holds her hands out ahead of herself, shooting a torrent of water across the chasm toward the beast on the other side—a serpentine monstrosity with no scales of its own. Rather, in the place of each scale is a face, a porcelain mask.

It writhes, lashing and whipping out as the faces all along its body change, moving from expressions that carry smiles to those that carry screams in some places, while other masks carry the smirks of clever children and others the harrowed faces of mothers who have lost their young. Thousands of faces, masks, turn and move to face them from the other side of the scales, from the other bowl.

Floor twenty of the Demon King's castle lies in a great chasm, in the middle of which stands a statue of the spirit of justice, larger and grander than any monument ever hewn by man, and standing taller than mountains with its impossible height.

Hanging from her hand is a two-bowled scale which acts as a bridge between the two floors, above and below. On one side of the scale is them, the crusade, and on the other is the beast with one million faces.

"COUNTER!" yells a voice in the crowd as the serpent rises, sending hundreds of its masks flying into the air from the impact of their spells and arrows. The fallen masks, the broken faces that have crumbled off of itself, lie in the scale all around it, revealing a mass of writhing eyes beneath its shell. The revealed orbs pulsate, gyrating sickly in circular

motions, filling the air with a wet squirming, squishing squelching. The mouths on its body, made up of porcelain, move.

Ruhr looks around herself as the air shakes and the mind-influencing magic of the beast flows toward them in its counterattack.

"Ruhr! Ruhr!" calls a voice to her side.

The elf stops, lowering her hands, and looks around herself at the crusade. There they still remain, all present but changed.

All of them are wearing masks of varying expressions, born of the same porcelain as those covering the boss monster's exterior. They look around at one another in confusion, seeing that they're all covered in these things. Ruhr touches her face with her wet fingers, feeling the glass exterior there too, covering her skin in an expression she can't know, as she can't see it.

Whose voice was that?

It wasn't Zac's.

Ruhr blinks, looking around herself then toward the other scale where the boss was a moment ago; a titan. It's gone now.

The scales, unbalanced, begin to realign, theirs lowering itself into the abyss below.

"Get this fucking thing off me!" yells someone to the side, panicking as they claw at their face, their panic spreading to those around them as people fall into chaos.

"Ruhr," says a familiar voice.

"Zac!" calls Ruhr, looking at the man. "How did you recognize me?" she asks. The man reaches over, lifting up a strand of her long hair.

He shakes his head, a strong, plain face of humble neutrality adorning his head. "Your weird hair is hard to miss in a crowd," says Zacarias.

"Wow. You're such a romantic, Zac," replies Ruhr snarkily, pulling her hair back out of his fingers. "That face suits you, by the way."

"I should say the same," replies Zacarias, turning to look at the scale opposite theirs, where the boss is missing. The other scale is rising up into the air, whereas theirs is sinking, presumably to a place that is very bad, if she knows the Demon King. And honestly, she thinks she's sort of pinned him down a bit at this point.

She blinks.

"Wait, what's mine?" she asks, feeling her face.

"Don't worry about that," says Zacarias. "What the hell is this?" he asks, receiving a very well thought-out shrug in return.

The scales separate further.

"We're too heavy," notes Ruhr. "Should we throw some people off?" she asks, pointing over her shoulder.

Zacarias grabs her wrist, pulling her pointing hand back down. "We will not."

"Ooh, do that again, Big Daddy Zac," says Ruhr, moving her wrist that he's gripping tightly.

"Get a grip, Ruhr," replies the man, letting go of her and shaking his head. "We're about to die."

"Exactly," she replies as he looks around for a solution while they descend lower and further toward the darkness below, in which an eternal gnashing of teeth can be heard coming ever closer and closer. The void is like water full of hungry monsters, and their bowl is dropping toward it, ready to be filled to the brim with screams and claws. "This might be my last chance, Z—"

Ruhr stops as Zacarias's hand now suddenly rests softly on the side of her face, which he is shamelessly touching. "Z . . . Zac . . ." mumbles the elf, her ears softly drooping as he looks down at her from up close. Something warm squirms in her gut. The two of them stare for a moment.

Was his hand always this big? It feels like it's covering her whole face. It's . . . He's . . .

His fingers grab the edge of the mask, ripping it off her face with ease. It comes off as if nothing had ever held it in place.

Indifferently, Zacarias looks at the mask, which is very clearly painted in the expression of a spoiled, crying child throwing a tantrum, and then simply tosses it over his shoulder and into the void, shrugging.

The others of the crusade, seeing this or having figured the trick out themselves, do the same. The masks can't be removed by oneself; it always requires someone else, someone with a different expression than the one any individual is wearing.

"It's a metaphor," explains Guardsman Zacarias, looking up as the great scales slowly rebalance themselves once hundreds of heavy masks are torn off faces and cast into the darkness. "You know the Demon King loves this kind of pagean—Will you knock it off?!" he barks, looking down at Ruhr, who is hammering against his armor with her fists and kicking at his bad leg at the same time, her mouth chewing on his hand like an animal as she glares up at him.

The scales wobble as they come to equilibrium, and the masks, which they had cast into the void, float back up as if they were disembodied heads, returning to the great, roaring beast on the other side before the fight continues now that they're on even footing.

~ [Peribsen] ~
Human | ♂ | Craftsman {Engineer}
Location: The Northern Pass
Level: 29

The wizards run around behind him, preparing their grim work.

Amazing!

Look at it. It's not giving an inch.

Hot, scorching winds roll past him, rising up out of the massive ravine that he stands on the edge of. The hot air crawls up from below, as if the spirits of demons from the pits of hell were reaching around his legs as they come unto the continent. The drop before him is long and substantial, being far more than enough to kill any man or beast. Down in the distant valley below, there is a river that runs through it. Peribsen watches as the long, corded suspension bridge sways back and forth across the valley. It's not just a simple rope bridge, like you'd find in any old hick town with a few bumps and hills.

No. This here is the sum total of his life's work.

He's spent years planning this construction out, years begging for funding and crawling around noble estates, trying to convince them of the economic promise this bridge would bring them.

This chasm has always been a large problem with the nation's trade routes. There's simply no easy way across it, and a conventional bridge, due to the length, would have been far too expensive given the unique geographic constraints of the area. The high winds and the strong pressures involved in a span like this needed special ideas to surmount.

Peribsen holds a hand against the frame, watching it sway in the air.

The Demon King's rise has caused an unusual cascade of biological and climate phenomena. Ignoring the demons and the monsters and everything else, the sheer heat radiated by the monster's presence, together with the perpetual night that covers the world, has led to a massive temperature exchange. Slowly, over the course of these few days,

everything outside has been losing its stored heat, growing cold to the point of almost freezing.

But there is a central generator of heat, which is the Demon Core. Add in to that the heat generated by human settlements and cities, the gatherings of millions of people, and there have been actual shifts in the passive air currents of the world to a notable extent.

Especially here.

The hot air coming from below from the natural hot springs in the lower valley rises up past the bridge in an updraft—past his wide-open eyes which stare in childlike wonder—as it comes to meet the cooling air of the night that falls down back over all of it like a smothering blanket.

Peribsen gets down on his knees, crawling forward to look over the edge.

But not down at the valley; instead, he looks at his bridge. It's a masterpiece. It's his great work, the fruit born of his soul, his gift to the world. This bridge is the reason he was put on this planet.

He observes the fasteners below, wrenched deeply into the rock of the cliffsides, while the suspended body of the bridge sways in the violent currents. His hand rests on a beam, feeling the movements running through its body coursing into his fingers as if they were a living pulse, a rising of a chest full of breath, and as it sways, groaning back the other way, he exhales together with it as if they were both the extension of one another.

It's just . . . It's just . . . so . . .

"Amazing . . ." mutters Peribsen, his strands of sharply clumped, straight woodland-black hair blowing in the heavy winds that steal his words and breath. He turns his head, looking at a man standing there. "You know, conventional ropes couldn't hold this weight." He nods his head to the bridge. The wizard, who hadn't said a thing, looks his way. "We thought about chains first, but they would've been too heavy and too bulky. The metal would have rusted and worn through eventually. Too dangerous and risky to replace," explains the engineer, unprompted, as he looks back at the construction dancing in the air despite the impossibility of it, like a wingless angel adrift atop the sea.

"So we used Vildt hair." Peribsen gestures with his hands. He plucks out a piece of grass, holding the blade between his fingers on both ends. "Human hair, even fashioned into a rope, has a very poor tensile strength,"

continues the engineer, pulling on the blade of grass until it pops in the middle. "But Vildt hair . . ."

"Uh . . ." starts the wizard.

Peribsen ignores him and takes another blade of grass, then rolls it together between his fingers into a cylinder, repeating the motion as he pulls on it. "It has such an unnaturally high tensile strength that it's actually one of the strongest building materials we could have hoped for to make this." The grass doesn't give way at all. "Thousands and thousands of bushels of long hair had to be imported from the east and fashioned into ropes," explains the engineer, rising to his feet. "It was one of the largest trading projects between continents in decades. Bet you never even heard about it, right?" he asks, looking at the wizard.

The other man stands there, looking at him with an off, curious look before waving him away. "Settle down, weirdo," says the caster. "We're blowing it in a minute, so stand back."

The engineer stares at the wizard as he turns away and walks off. The man's shoulders droop, looking down at the blade of grass in his hands, which slowly begins to unfurl now that he has let go of one end.

Peribsen sighs, loosening his fingers. The wind takes the blade of grass, blowing it away and into the ravine, and he watches it sail into the distance, vanishing into the storm, his hand touching the wet strut of the bridge. He runs his fingers up it, feeling the damp material.

"These struts are wood," he explains, feeling them and talking to nobody but himself. "Not just any wood, though." Peribsen smiles, knocking on its painted exterior. The paint is also a special blend, but he'll get into that in a minute. "This wood is from the witch swamp itself," he says. "The high moisture content of the region allows the trees there to grow to become particularly pliable and soft, with a very high fracture point, allowing them to bend and sway naturally with ease," he explains, looking at the beams. "We had to make all sorts of deals with the witches to get some of that wood, but it was worth it." He smiles, knocking on the bridge.

"No other material would've held like this. Just look at it!" he exclaims, holding his hand out in front of himself to gesture at the bridge before planting both of his palms on his hips and staring at it as it sways in the wind.

"Beautiful . . ." whispers the engineer.

They don't see it.

The nobles he had to beg and sell his soul to didn't see it. The people he had to convince to even get this project going didn't see it. The workers, even during construction, didn't see it and called it a waste of their time. Everybody didn't see it. They didn't see what he sees.

The bridge carries the ripples of the wind within itself, with separate sections of it rising up and down in midair as if they were the waves of a crashing tide, suspended aloft in nothingness. It's not just a thing; it's organic. It's a living, breathing entity made out of the principles of construction. It moves. It gives. It takes.

It's not just infrastructure. That's all they see when they look at it. He's dedicated his life to infrastructure. He's built roads and canals, ditches and towers. He's worked on houses and marketplaces, courts and castle walls—those are all things, infrastructure and buildings.

But this here . . .

Peribsen holds the ropes with one hand as he stands on the entryway to the bridge. It's wide enough for two carriages to pass one another easily enough on a calmer day than this one, with a little caution on windier days. There's literally nothing like it anywhere in the world. It's unique. It's not a creation of some blueprint; it's a creation of his muse.

This here is *art*.

The engineer steps out onto the bridge, letting his fingers glide along the ropes of Vildt hair, which have been treated with a heavy mineral oil first to keep them strong and healthy, and then, after a process of drying, coated with an unusually rare resin from the distant northern pines, guarded by dens of spriggans and other wild things.

Every component of this bridge is anything but mundane. Every board has a story; every fiber of hair, coming from a living person, has seen lives come and go, felt experiences of sorrow and joy, and carries with it these tinges. He's sure of it. All of the feelings held by the owners of these materials and by the materials themselves, stemming from such unusual, high-magic areas, come together to form the bones of a golem—his child.

He could talk about it and think about it for hours and hours and hours. There's so much involved. There's so much to tell.

Peribsen hears the voices, but he doesn't pay them any mind as he walks out onto the bridge, feeling it shake beneath him, feeling the boards move, and feeling his body sway around together with it left and right in the heavy winds—but despite that, he never loses his footing.

He smiles, feeling pride in his chest as if he had watched his own first-born son win a championship.

The man stays in the middle of the bridge, hanging over the chasm, explaining the reason for his stability here despite the fact that he should, by all accounts, be flying around as wildly as the bridge is.

"That's because of the double-layered balancing mechanism down below my feet," he says, speaking to the wind. "The bridge has two layers of footing; the upper is balanced on a layer of brick webbing that's filled with neutralized slime jelly." He touches the wood at his feet, his hand resting on it. "So even if the bridge is shaking, this upper platform will always stabilize as a counterforce." He nods. "This not only allows the person atop the bridge to remain stable in their footing, but the counterforce movement of the jelly stabilizes the bridge's sway."

It's perfect.

It's beautiful.

Peribsen clutches his face, letting out a muffled scream, because there's no way to save it.

The nation has ordered the destruction of the bridge to hinder the Demon King, and while he, of course, thought about simply killing the wizards in their sleep on the way here, he knows that wouldn't matter. Even if he stops them . . .

He turns his head, looking at the ropes.

The resin on them, holding the hair fibers, glistens.

The bridge wasn't meant to sustain heat in its center, no more than it would on a summer's day, with a large margin of error. Things like wildfire aren't a threat, given its incredible height. But with the Demon Core coming closer, the resin protecting the ropes will melt. The mineral oil–covered hairs will catch heat and soon flame. The gel pads beneath the wood will cook through, drying out and breaking the stabilizing mechanism, like the knee of an old man with no cartilage left.

Even if he were able to kill the wizards, it wouldn't matter, because the Demon King is going to pass by here, and it's all going to fall apart no matter what.

He takes a deep breath, exhaling and then rising to his feet.

Peribsen looks over his shoulder at the casters, who have readied themselves for the demolition and are, by the looks of it, giving him a brief cautionary period to return to the land.

The engineer turns his head back forward, looking at something he had entirely missed before.

"Ah!" he says excitedly, running forward deeper into the open waters of nothingness. "These slats here," he explains to himself, pointing at the downward-slanted edges of the boards. "This is a really great idea. It's so simple too!" he exclaims with enthusiasm, following a small groove in the wood in which rainwater streams down. "The core concept is that—"

He flies forward, flung onto his face from the pressure of the explosion coming from behind him, the ripple that runs through the wood causing him to roll at first from the pressure and then from the gravity of the movements to come.

Engineer Peribsen holds on to one of the ropes, looking back behind himself at the magic-impacted construction which the group of casters had launched a combined strike into.

It's quiet for a time as the smoke clears and the rain hammers down around them.

Then, after a moment more, it's interrupted by laughter.

Peribsen slaps his leg, pointing at the burned ropes and damaged wood where the strike hit, having completely failed to make the bridge collapse.

A warm smile comes to his face as a tear runs down his cheek, welling with pride. He turns his head, holding a hand against one of the bridge's ropes as he looks at it. "You did good," says the engineer, resting his head against it and closing his eyes. "Real good."

A second blast comes, this time severing the connection, causing the bridge and himself to hurtle down into the abyss.

They probably think he's crazy.

But they don't get it. They can't ever understand what he feels.

This kind of . . . beauty . . . the alignment of man's will with the graces of nature, rather than establishing his dominion over it, is too much for the world to understand. It is too esoteric. For them, he is just a weird guy obsessed with his pet projects. But his vision was that the creations of man need not disrupt nature; they can move with it and grow with it in the same way a clean seed would—fluidly and organically. They could make things that sway, move, and dance and are filled with sunlight, air, and energy.

They could make beautiful places and creations *with* the world—not on it.

But they never saw that.

He dies.

~ [Ruhr, the River Sorceress] ~
Half Elf | ♀ | Sorceress
Rank: SSS
Location: The Demon King's Castle, Floor Twenty
Level: 96

With each change of the phase, the drop of their scale goes faster and faster, until they are almost in free fall, losing their footing as they all, heaping and tumbling over one another, try to tear off the masks and throw them into the void, doing so just in time as blackness begins to peek into the bowl they're in.

The scale stops dropping.

A moment later, it begins rising again, rebalancing itself.

"I'm getting dizzy, Zac," remarks Ruhr.

He nods, using his tower shield to support himself. "This should be the last time," he notes as they come into sight of the snake one more time, its body essentially just a naked worm covered in eyes.

Porcelain masks rise out from the depths, returning to its exterior, but far fewer than before. Only a handful remain, as most have been destroyed.

"Ready!" calls a voice from the crusade as they begin to align their spells and arrows.

The river sorceress rubs her face, getting ready for what should be the last skirmish against the boss of floor twenty. They've actually been doing well. They haven't lost anyone, as far as she knows, which is very unusual for a fight in the Demon King's castle.

Ruhr lifts her hands, water dripping out of her fingers and running down her arms as her magic begins to grow. But something stops her. She's not sure what it is.

The spell trickles down her arm, running down her sleeve, and dripping onto her leg, which causes Zacarias to snort, holding down a laugh. "What's the matter?" he asks. "Get scared?"

"Shut up, Zac," she says, her eyes shifting in suspicion. "I'm thinking."

"Oh boy."

"*Sssht!*" she hisses, her eyes glaring at him as she looks around the arena for a while. "AH!" exclaims the river sorceress, hitting her fist into her open palm. "Zac. Order a retreat."

"What?" he asks. "We're about to—"

"ZAC!" she barks at him.

He groans. "FALL BACK!" calls the man, receiving a barrage of wary, curious looks as they hear the order. "BACK!" yells Zacarias, the order propagating around the arena to much confusion.

Ruhr grabs him, pulling him into the crowd as she hurries toward the entrance. "FALL BACK!" yells the river sorceress.

Most of the crusade listens, though begrudgingly, as it is commonly known that abandoning a boss fight in a dungeon will cause that boss to reset, requiring the fight to be restarted from the beginning.

"What's the problem?" asks Zacarias, trying to keep up with her as she runs, her hand stuck in the collar of his breastplate and yanking on him as they push through the confused crowd. "MOVE!" he yells to the side, pulling on another man who is sort of lost in between places.

"The fact that we're fibble-fabbling dumb-dumb goo-brains is the problem, Zac!" she snaps back at him.

"Wow, really swearing like a sailor these days," he remarks, raising an eyebrow.

"Shut up, Zac. We're on a scale!" she snaps, pointing back at the obvious as they exit the bowl, returning to the walkway at the start of the floor.

"Yeah, so?" he asks, looking back at the emptying arena as people pour out of the fight.

A voice comes from the side. "Brother Zacarias," says the chief crusader. "What is the meaning of this?" he asks, pointing back at the boss monster which was about to be destroyed.

"Well . . . you see . . ." starts Zacarias, looking back at Ruhr.

She looks at the crusader. "What do you think happens when we kill it?" Ruhr points at the scales. "There'll be nothing left to balance the scales out."

". . . We'd plunge down into the abyss," notes Zacarias, understanding now. If they kill the boss, there's no weight left on the other side of the scales. "It was a trap."

The last man leaves the scales. Metal groans, and the balance shifts; the monster, now the only thing of weight left, plummets immediately

downward into the darkness below, into the ocean of eternally gnashing teeth.

A minute later, the scales rebalance, as they now are empty.

They stare. "Now what?" asks Zacarias.

Ruhr smiles, lifting her hands. "Now, my pious Zacarias," starts the river sorceress. "You can fall down and start kissing my feet to worship me," she says, water blasting out of her hands across the arena and into the other bowl on the far side, where the boss had been.

She pours her magic out, filling it for a time, before nodding in satisfaction and jumping into their bowl before Zacarias can stop her, yelping and reaching after her.

"Ta-da!" exclaims Ruhr, holding her hands out at her sides. She smiles, flicking a strand of hair out of her face.

"Huh . . ." says Zacarias, apparently pleasantly surprised, which is actually sort of offensive. His expression of surprise signals that he hadn't expected anything from her to start with.

Ruhr lifts her nose in the air, offended by his being impressed by her actions, turning around and walking across the scale, jumping over into the other one by herself, and then wading through the waist-deep water until she is the first one to cross over to the other side.

Today, they beat the Demon King without losing anybody.

"You see that?" she asks, looking down at the abyss below, narrowing her eyes. "I'm coming for you," promises the river sorceress, sure that he can hear her.

~ [Peribsen] ~
Human | ♂ | Craftsman {Engineer}
Location: ???
Level: 29

It could have been so much more.

Imagine, if you will, a world filled to the brim with the implementation of such ideas. A world made up not only of indiscriminate brickwork and gray facades. Imagine a world made up of dynamic, moving, breathing constructions interwoven with the beauty of organic life, a world in which houses served not only as domiciles but as beautiful artworks in and of themselves. A world in which roads served both the functions of mankind

and those of nature by interconnecting them with migratory pathways through reduced use of construction materials and a deeper integration of innate, natural sensory memory. A world in which people understand where his thoughts are coming from.

Of course, he's always been a little out there. He knows that. He's always been called eccentric, strange, or an oddball—in polite company. His ideas have been vastly discredited as being uselessly pageantific by his colleagues in his field, which values mathematical pragmatism so highly.

It's so hard for him to get them to understand what he understands. It's not about a building costing a thousand Obols more or less. It's about the long-term, global effects on society which could be had by making such apparently eccentric changes. Change a house, and you change the family living inside of it. Change a road, and you change the nature of those who walk it. By changing the architecture of the world itself . . .

They all fail to realize that the world they are building is a tool. Like a book, like a story, like a song, buildings are tools that can be used to leverage the human soul in a specific direction, and not just one by one, but by the hundreds, by the thousands. Beautiful people don't necessarily make beautiful cities. But beautiful cities make people beautiful. He's sure of it.

But . . .

"They'll never understand that," says the voice of God, harsh and rough, with the reassuring tone of a world-weathered father.

Peribsen listens to it echo around himself then sighs, closing his eyes as he accepts its words.

"Why did you make me like this, then?" he asks. "Why did you make me feel these things that nobody else felt?"

The water stirs, trembling as if in a quake. "I did no such thing," replies the voice. "But the answer is because you are cursed." Peribsen reopens his eyes, lifting his gaze to stare at the source that stems from the void he is adrift in. "You are cursed to wander the lands of the dead as the only living being present there," explains the voice. "Cursed to be the only one with eyes in the kingdom of the blind; cursed to be the man with a voice in a house of the deaf."

"Why?" asks Peribsen.

"Because the world is an ugly place," replies the voice, scarring his soul with its harrowing presence.

"I don't believe that." Peribsen shakes his head in spite of it. "I don't believe that," repeats the man, adrift in silence. "It's cruel, hard, and sad," he remarks. "But I don't think it's ugly." He uncurls himself from the ball-like position he was in. "It just . . ." He looks down. "It just needs some work."

"How much?" asks the voice, lowering itself to a whisper which floats through the crevices in his incorporeal form.

"What?"

"How much work?" it asks again, floating in from all directions. "Is there enough paint in the world? Is there enough metal, enough wood?" it asks. "Is there enough drive?" Peribsen floats, not able to answer that. "Even in your perfect vision, if everyone was like you, do you think there would enough of what you need for the world to be what you desire it to be?"

"I . . ." Peribsen looks down, holding his face then rubbing it in frustration as he thinks. He feels something smear over his skin. Confused, the man lowers his hands and looks between his fingers at the sticky goo there—resin. "I . . . don't . . ."

"Or could it be that in this world, imperfect as it is, there is no hope of this true beauty ever existing?" asks the voice. "Could it be that everything you long for," it speaks into his ear, "everything you hope for and strive for"—his hand shakes—"that it's just a dream?"

"Don't," says Peribsen, lifting his gaze and clenching his fist, staring into the darkness. He yells, pointing at it and glaring. "DON'T YOU DARE TAKE THIS FROM ME!" screams the ghost of the man, lashing out through the water with his fist, droplets of resin washing away and drifting into the abyss. "Don't . . ." he repeats, his voice softening as he, as angry as it makes him, knows there's something true about what the entity has said.

"I would never," replies the voice. "I'm here to give, not to take," it assures, the seducer clawing at his soul, pulling him closer and closer toward its source, a great, blinding white light in the distance. "It's real. It exists—that thing you want," it promises. "But it's not here."

". . . Then, where is it?" asks Peribsen as the glowing, blinding light begins to engulf him.

"Just over the bridge," replies the heavy voice, laughing as Peribsen is torn from the waters of death.

CHAPTER 11

THE CRACKING OF JOKES, WOOD, AND BONES

~ [Shivelo] ~
Marionette | ♂ | Crusader
Location: The Demon King's Castle, Floor Twenty-One
Level: 91

Shivelo is a crusader, a brave and noble warrior who has dedicated his life to fighting the forces of darkness. He wears a white cloak over his metal armor, a symbol of his purity and faith. He carries a silver crossbow and a dagger, weapons blessed by the holy light. He follows the lead of his commander, a wise and venerable priest who guides them through the perilous halls of the Demon King's castle.

But Shivelo is also a puppet. Literally. He is a wooden marionette whose strings are controlled by an unseen hand. He has been cursed, along with all his comrades, to lose their humanity and become toys in the Demon King's twisted game. Shivelo does not know this; he does not see this; he does not feel this. He simply walks with stiff and jerky movements, unaware of how his joints creak and squeak with every step. He speaks with a monotone and wooden voice, unaware of how his words sound hollow and empty in the air. He looks with blank and glassy eyes, unaware of how his vision is blurred and distorted by the spell.

He is oblivious to everything around him, except for one thing: his mission. His mission to slay the Demon King, to end his reign of terror, and to save the world from his evil. He, as a crusader, is driven by one thing: his faith. His faith is in the holy ways, the divine plan, and the righteous cause.

The stumpy-legged marionette bounces as he moves.

Until his legs leave the ground, and he, not really realizing it, is lifted up toward the ceiling above all of their heads.

~ [**Ruhr, the River Sorceress**] ~
Marionette | ♀ | Sorceress
Rank: SSS
Location: The Demon King's Castle, Floor Twenty-One
Level: 96

Dust and wood chips rain down over them.

"Say, Zac, old pal!" starts Ruhr, the river sorceress excitedly, her wooden body bobbing up and down with exaggerated movements, causing her strawlike strands of long blue hair to bounce around the air. "What do you think about the Demon King?" asks the river sorceress, holding her hands on her hips as she essentially dances in place, the painted-on mouth on her flat face turning into a smile that is just a single black smear where her lips should be.

Her friend, Zacarias, looks back at her, the strings holding his head aloft from above shimmering in the auroral light of the dungeon. His features, like hers, are all painted on the wooden sphere that acts as his head. Ruhr tilts her head, looking at him; the string holding her noggin aloft moves to the side as the invisible puppeteer above makes this accommodation.

"What?" asks the man dryly.

Ruhr, tapping her wooden chunk of a foot painted in the color of her boots, continues to bounce as she looks his way. "You know, the Demon King!" says Ruhr, leaning in toward him.

"The Demon King!" whispers a voice from the side, from another crusader in the circle.

Another man, also a puppet, lifts a wooden finger, the string holding his arm aloft rising into the air. "I heard he eats babies!" says a man. People gasp all around the crowd.

Another woman chimes in from the side, her head swaying back and forth. "Why, I heard he reuses the same bathwater every day!" Shocked noises come from around the room from the hundreds of puppets. "And then he pours it on cold orphans!"

Ruhr nods, her arms crossed, the painted expression on her face

moving as she talks, as if her features were being continually redrawn every second. "Did you know, Zac?" asks the river sorceress.

"What?" asks the man.

"That the Demon King eats worms three times a day?" She waves her finger with the bobbing of her body.

"Really?" asks Zacarias, raising an eyebrow.

She nods, leaning in. "And then he pukes it all back into baby birds' mouths until they die!"

"I heard he likes to crawl under people's beds at night!" calls a voice from the side. They all turn to look at the other man who said that.

". . . Why?" asks his neighbor, a priestess who, for some reason, has her arms out to the sides and is waving with both her hands as she bobs around.

The man confidently crosses his arms. "To pull away their blankets while they're sleeping and uncover their feet!"

Horrified murmurs move through the crowd.

"That old meanie the Demon King is a real *jerk*, Zac!" says Ruhr as the man turns back to look at her.

". . . Why are you bouncing?" asks Zacarias, raising an eyebrow.

Ruhr waves at him with a finger, smiling. "Because there's a *spring in my step!*" she jokes.

Everyone laughs.

~ [The Demon King] ~

Swain stares blankly at the crusaders through the vision granted to him by his many eyes. The intruders have been turned into wooden marionettes through the magic of floor twenty-one of his castle.

He slowly turns his head, looking at the creator of the section: the spirit cook, Byblos.

The once dark elf turns her head, feeling his gaze, and stares back at him. "What?" she asks.

The horrific monstrosity that is the true horror, the beast of the hopeless wildlands, the king of the damned, and the lord of all that suffer, gestures vaguely toward the distance. Byblos turns around, crossing her arms.

"I like puppets, okay?" she admits.

Swain looks back into the distance. "I just thought it'd be something about cooking, is all," admits the Demon King.

She lifts her nose, turning around again. "I love cooking. But that doesn't mean I can't have other interests." The gallu stares off into the distance for a time before looking back over her shoulder. "It's important to collect a . . . variety of experiences in life," she explains, looking at him as she remembers something that happened. "To help broaden your . . . ah . . . capabilities," remarks the demon, playing with the ties of her apron, which may be covered in what is either copious amounts of blood or strawberry jam, as she walks toward the throne.

It is impossible to say.

The Demon King, not entirely unimpressed, snaps his fingers for a sheet of paper to write on as he gets an idea, which is delivered by a howling ghost that just as quickly flees in horrific terror, though he finds himself otherwise distracted from the noble, artistic pursuit.

~ [Cartouche] ~
Gallu | ♀ | Dancer
Location: The Demon King's Castle, Demon Quarters
Level: 100

"This is where you'll stay," she says as the new gallu walks into the room, looking around himself. He's still dazed from the transformation. She recalls the sensation herself. It takes a little while before the power of the Demon King's blessing is fully absorbed by the living vessel of the body. "When you are ready, come find me," she finishes, closing the doors to leave him there.

The confused man, still covered in afterbirth, his short hair sticking to his face and obscuring his vision, looks her way. "Ready for what?" he asks.

She tilts her head. "That's up to you," replies the dancer, closing the doors and walking away to get back to her practice. Ghosts appear from the walls, orchestrating her movements, even the mundane ones.

The demon narrows her eyes, looking at a trumpeter who has been playing a note for every step she takes. The ghost plays a long, drawn out, falling note as her eyes lock onto its.

~ [Ruhr, the River Sorceress] ~
Marionette | ♀ | Sorceress
Rank: SSS
Location: The Demon King's Castle, Floor Twenty-One
Level: 96

"Take that, you dooby-wooby!" yells the river sorceress, holding her hands out in front of herself. Blocks of blue painted wood fly outward, thudding noisily against the head of a skeleton, bonking against it, and collecting over the ground below in heaps.

The skeleton lifts its hands dramatically, shrieking somehow, as its bones fall apart into a jumble.

"Don't waste all of your magic on trash mobs like these," says Zacarias, looking over at her, his wooden body clattering as he moves.

Ruhr laughs smugly, waving him off. "Don't worry, Zacco," starts the river sorceress. "What's a little magic here and there?" she asks, leaning toward him. "It's—"

"I *will* hit you," he warns.

The two of them stare at one another.

Ruhr opens her mouth. "No—"

"I mean it," interrupts Zacarias.

She closes her mouth, and the two of them look at one another from up close.

She lifts a hand, holding it against his chest. "Say, Zac, you hunk, when did your muscles get this hard?" she asks, her fingers running down his wooden torso.

"I . . . huh?" he asks, confused at the sudden shift of topics.

"IT'S NO SKIN OFF MY BONES!" yells Ruhr as quickly as she can to get the joke out, ducking away from the confused man and laughing as she dives under his arm, which swings over her head, and instead of hitting her, clears her head and catches hold of the marionette's strings, holding her up.

Ruhr, pulled back by the tug on the strings attached to her head and limbs, flies off her feet and lands on her bottom, sliding down onto her back over the stones.

"Oh, hell," says Zacarias. "I'm sorry, Ruhr!" apologizes the man emphatically, looking down to help her up. "I didn't actually mean to hit you."

Ruhr, lying on her back, stares up toward him. Despite lying there, her legs and shoulders pull in and out, as if she were still on her feet, bouncing up and down. "That's okay, Zac!" replies the river sorceress, her painted-on face changing through a variety of expressions on her wooden face. "I guess you—"

He sighs, looking down at her. "You're gonna 'swept me off my feet' me, aren't you?" he asks, interrupting her.

"Really *swept me off my feet!*" finishes Ruhr, entirely ignoring his comment and laughing.

The rest of the crusade laughs too.

Some of them watch as one of the others in the back of the crowd is slowly lifted up into the air, the strings on his body holding him taut as the puppeteer above chooses him to be pulled into the thick darkness above their heads, where light doesn't seem to pierce. But even those who do continue laughing at the spectacle of the two of them.

Chips of colorful wood rain down from above a moment later.

~ [Zacarias] ~
Marionette | ♂ | Royal Guardsman
Location: The Demon King's Castle, Floor Twenty-One
Level: 92

He doesn't trust this one bit.

Zacarias's wooden eyes look around the room, scanning the arena for anything that's wrong or out of place. But so far, they've only been encountering normal monsters, which is extremely strange for this place. There are always traps and tricks of some sort, but . . . everything just seems *normal*, for lack of a better word.

It makes him very suspicious.

But there is nothing wrong at all, anywhere. It's just a dungeon.

"Hey, Zac," speaks Ruhr from ahead of him, her wooden head turning a full one-hundred-and-eighty degrees to look at him. A second later, her body turns to follow the same direction, walking backward. "Why don't you lighten up a little?" she asks, looking at him. The river sorceress gestures to him, then to everyone else. "You're really killing the mood, you know?"

"The . . . mood?" asks Zacarias, looking at her and then at the rest of the crusade who bounce by, some of them dancing and some of them

bobbing around nonsensically. The man looks back toward the half elf. "Ruhr. We're in the Demon King's castle, remember? The only mood here is *bad*; that's it."

She places her hands on her hips, her legs stopping as her body just slides backward as she stares at him. "Oh, Zac," smiles the half elf.

He waits for more to come.

But nothing happens. She just stares at him and smiles, continuing to bounce around.

". . . What?" he asks. "*Oh, Zac* what?"

"That's just like you!" remarks Ruhr, laughing.

"I . . . huh?" Zacarias looks around himself, at some of the other chuckling crusaders who continue their march. "Ruhr," starts Zacarias, looking back at her. He grabs hold of her shoulders, leaning in. "Listen," he whispers. "Something is up," explains the guardsman, looking around the room before looking back at the side of her carved head. "I don't know what it is, but . . . we're walking into something here, don't you think? It's been too quiet. There hasn't been a single trap or anything yet."

Ruhr slowly starts to float up into the air as something pulls on her strings, their eyes not separating from one another. Zacarias, his hands already on her shoulders, pushes her back down to the ground, not really thinking about it. "Maybe," answers Ruhr. "But maybe the Demon King also just has, like . . . one or two floors that aren't butt, you know?" she asks, tapping the side of her head.

"I highly doubt it," replies the man, looking around himself for anything that's wrong.

Ruhr's back leg, attached to a string, starts to lift itself up behind her in an arch as his hands rest on her shoulder. The two of them turn to look at her lifted foot, raised into the air as if they were in a kiss, and then back at one another.

"Why do you always have to do this?" asks Zacarias, sighing. "We can sometimes just have a talk without you making it weird, you know?" He shakes his head. "I get that we're in a bad place, but . . . it's a lot sometimes, you know?"

"I'm sorry, Zac," apologizes Ruhr, lowering her head. Her other leg lifts up in the air too, just the same as the first one. Zacarias rolls his eyes. "I can't help it, I swear!" she says, looking back up at him. "Look . . ." says the river sorceress as her legs fly up into the air behind her, starting to pull

her waist back up with them. "I'm messed up, and this is how I cope, okay? I'm a broken person."

Zacarias shakes his head. "No . . . I'm sorry. I know you're just you," says the man. "We're going to die here one way or the other, so let's die as friends. I shouldn't be nitpicking your personality."

"Gods, you're going to make me cry, Zac." She rolls her eyes. Her body has fully left the ground. She cranes her neck upward to be able to look at him, until her body has risen up so high that he has to lift his gaze now to stare at her. "As if I don't have enough issues, now you're going to make me clingy about you, too."

"As if you aren't already," replies the man, holding his arms up onto her shoulders still, stretching his fingers as she slides toward the ceiling. "Was it your dad?" he asks.

"Isn't it always?" replies the half elf.

Zacarias shakes his head. "No."

Ruhr's eyes open wide. "Oh! *Oh!*" she says excitedly. "Are you going to tell me something about you for once?" His fingers slide off her as she is pulled into the air, moving toward the darkness above them. "Backstory!" calls Ruhr out into the crusade, holding her hand by her mouth. The crusaders all look her way as she hovers in the air, the strings frozen. She points down at him. "Zac's gonna tell us his backstory!"

"What? What the hell? Ruhr!" he snaps. "I was going to tell you!" hisses the man.

"Zacarias? As in Guardsman Zacarias?" asks a voice from the side, one of the crusaders. "I heard he's secretly a villain!" whispers a man.

A priestess bouncing next to him covers her wooden face with her wooden hands, bobbing up and down. "Why, I heard he's a lost lover of the king's dead daughter!" she says, excited murmurs traveling through the crusade as many priestesses, interested by this, start to scoot his way. Ruhr drops down a few feet, batting them all the way from above, yanking on their strings.

"I heard that he's actually . . ." starts a voice, everyone falling quiet as they look at the man, whose body doesn't move but his head bounces in place. "Just kind of a normal guy."

Aghast expressions and voices carry through the crowd, which begins to turn his way.

The ground beneath them begins to shift and change; wooden boards slide in from all around the room, pushing themselves beneath the feet of the thousands of people who pay them no mind as a construct begins to emerge. Walls build themselves up, windows begin to form, and rooms begin to take shape as many people are lifted into the air—the chips that rain down moments later are pressed into the material that makes up the new scene.

Of course.

Zacarias groans as he is lifted and placed in the center of a room, but on his way down, he grabs Ruhr, yanking against the taut strings that were taking her to the darkness.

"Am I in this too?" she asks. "I think this is your scene, Zac."

"I didn't agree to do this," remarks Zacarias as flakes of a dead priestess rain down on him from above. "So you're going to be stuck here with me. It's your fault."

She lifts her hands, grabbing one of his with both of hers as she shakes her head. "I don't know what came over me," she says. "I swear! I'd never tell anyone your secrets." She rubs her face in frustration with her wooden hands. "It must be that fanny-fuddle demon magic. The one that doesn't let me swear either."

"You're just traumatized," replies Zacarias. "It's not demon magic."

"Zac!" she argues, elbowing him. "I don't want to be double trauma-tized!" she snaps. "My childhood was already bad, so what kind of person would I be if my adulthood was traumatic too?"

"A nonfunctional one," he replies.

Ruhr slides across the floor as something pulls on her strings again. She looks at him and then down at her hands, not aware of her sliding away. "Oh . . ." says the river sorceress as her back thuds against a wall that has formed, the strings pulling through an open window behind her, which she is lifted toward. Zacarias absentmindedly walks over, closing it and clamping her strings down against the frame.

Ruhr hangs there, pressed against the wall. "Hey, Zac," she starts, lift-ing an eyebrow mischievously.

"Yeah, yeah. I know, I know," he says. "You're 'hanging out,' right?"

She stares at him as he walks by, inspecting the building that has formed, before looking back over his shoulder at her.

"I'm *hanging out!*" She laughs.

"I just said that!" barks Zacarias, pointing at her.

Something opens the window from the outside, and Ruhr is pulled toward it. The guardsman grabs her arm and pulls her into the house, whatever force is outside its four walls letting go. "So where are we?" asks Ruhr as he sets her down.

"Stop playing around, Ruhr. Please," asks Zacarias, looking around. "This isn't the time."

"Sorry," she replies. "I really . . . I dunno. I feel funny, Zac. Something isn't right," remarks the river sorceress. She looks down at her hands, which are painted wood orbs in essence, with some crude, stacked cylindrical tubes attached for digits. "I feel . . . I dunno." She rolls her shoulders, looking up at him. "Stiff?"

"We've been sleeping on the floor of the Demon King's castle for days now," replies Zacarias, looking at her and then into the next room. "I'd be more surprised if you weren't stiff."

He feels an elbow in his side.

"Do not," warns Zacarias.

"I mean, considering that we're bunk buddies" starts Ruhr.

"Ruhr."

"I'm more surprised that—" A wooden finger shushes her. Zacarias shakes his head. "I'm sorry, Zac!" apologizes Ruhr a third time, pulling his hand away and rubbing her face. "I don't know what's wrong with me. I feel like someone made a caricature of me and put me in it, and it's making me . . . I dunno, double down on who I am for the sake of some sick joke."

"Breathe," says Zacarias, looking up at the open ceiling of the lidless house they're in through where their strings pass, as they should; as is perfectly normal and not really to be questioned. Why would it be? It's as mundane as air. "I need you on board here, Ruhr. You're stronger than I am." He looks at her. "You're probably having some kind of panic attack," explains the man, making an effort to overexaggerate his slow breathing so that she catches on. "Let's take a second, okay? Tone it down a little."

Given that his entire body is made out of inflexible wood, there aren't really any movements to see or mimic other than the expression of blowing lips painted onto his wooden face.

She mimics him, though, and nods after a moment of recomposing. "Okay," affirms Ruhr, nodding. "Thanks, Zac. I think I'm good now." She

looks around herself. "So, where are we?" asks Ruhr, picking up a small ornamental vase from a table next to them.

"My place," replies Zacarias.

Ruhr looks at him, starting to say something, but then catches herself and clears her throat, quietly setting the vase down. "Nice vase," she changes the topic to something more normal.

He waves over his shoulder. "Actually, that's an urn," he says. "Dead people."

Ruhr winces. "Flutes." She looks around the house, likely trying to examine the area to avoid stepping into any more awkward moments. "Your parents?" she asks.

"No," he replies, walking toward a door and grabbing hold of it. "They're in here," explains the man. "It's probably going to be a whole thing." He nods to the room. "You know how the Demon King is."

"Yeah, and also, *aw*, that's so sweet, Zee Bee," she says. "You looked after your folks when they got old?" He nods. "So, who's in the vase? Grandparents?"

"Wife," replies Zacarias, getting ready to open the door, looking at the half elf from the side of his eyes, her strings shifting. "She took her own life because of their bullying," he explains.

A long exhalation of the letter *F* leaves her mouth but never forms a word. Ruhr holds her arms out to her sides. "Just gonna drop that on me, huh? Just like that? No buildup?"

"You asked. Besides, knowing the Demon King"—Zacarias turns the handle slowly—"this is going to be some sort of monstrosity made out of meat and terror in some sick metaphor used to contort my inner failings against us, kind of like back on floor eleven with your dad."

Ruhr nods. "The Demon King is like that, so you're probably right," she relents. "But sh . . . shoebox, Zac. Sheesh." She folds her arms over her chest and looks away. "I thought there was going to be like . . . this whole thing, you know?" She gestures to the stage set around them. "That we'd work through your dark and mysterious past in a sequence of events where we learn more and more about you through a series of horrific experiences together, until ultimately coming out stronger in the end after we've beaten some dire, evil monstrosity."

"Exactly," replies Zacarias, tapping his head knowingly. "That's why I told you the big secret now, right away, so the Demon King doesn't have

anything left to play with." He looks at her. "My parents weren't good people, Ruhr, but I still felt obligated to take care of them." He shakes his head. "I pulled someone else into my obligation, and then neglected her for its sake," explains Zacarias, opening the door.

"And your folks?" asks Ruhr, looking back his way. "Demon King?"

The door swings open, revealing the pulsating, gyrating meat that hangs from the ceiling—a cancerous growth with dozens of long, pale, lanky arms that reach and touch all around the room, feeling for things to grab hold of with their slender, sharp, witchy fingers covered in clawed nails.

The paint all around the room is scraped off. The wood is dug out for as far as the hands could reach, burrowing into the room and consuming it, many others reaching up and catching the shredded flakes of those outside of the house who are torn into the darkness of the ceiling.

"No," replies Zacarias as the mass inside the room shifts. Dozens of arms move through the squelching flesh, coming together at the front to contort themselves onto the growth, forming the image of a hungry face. "People like them never seem to die," says the man as the arms break formation and begin to reach for him. He looks at the drooling monstrosity covered in wiry hairs and a strange gel that oozes down its exterior. "Probably because people like me keep them alive." He shakes his head. "We water the weeds and not the flowers."

He lifts his shield off the ground, which is one and the same, as many of the arms bear on the joints.

"Dang, that's poetic," she notes, putting a hand on his shoulder.

"I'll handle it," he says, walking toward the clawing, hungry tumor. "This is on me."

A hand pulls him back. "No," replies Ruhr, shaking her head as she looks at him. "We're friends, Zac. Friends don't let friends suffer the consequences of their own actions alone," she says, wiping a "strand" of blue hair out of her face, which is actually just a series of blue wooden beads. "We're going to kill your parents *together*."

"Are you sure?" he asks. "I get that this might be weird for you."

Ruhr shrugs. "No. We're good." She knocks against his chest. "I've always wanted to kill a parental figure, so if anything, I owe you for letting me get in on this." There is a loud scratching of nails as blackened, fouled hands dig into the wood at their feet, just barely unable to reach them.

The digits of hundreds of soggy palms try to grab them, only a breath away, scraps of the dead and the constantly dying raining down slowly over them as members of the crusade are slowly, one after the other, pulled into the darkness above.

"So do I kill your mom or your dad?" she asks, looking at the mess beyond them that is hardly separable into such clean-cut categories.

"Don't make it weird," remarks Zacarias, turning to face the thing that can't reach them.

"Okay, well, then I'm gonna kill your dad," says Ruhr. "You seem like a mommy-issues boy."

"Whatever, daddy-issues girl," replies Zacarias. The two of them nod and charge in, pressing the hands back together with the wooden tower shield and the force of wooden water.

~ [The Demon King] ~

"My lord, we are about to reach a new fork in the road," informs Abydos the painter, holding out his hands to the side. "One road moves through a collection of villages that have established some . . . unusual fortifications. It would seem they've managed to use some unconventional methods to capture a wild demon for their benefit."

"A demon?" asks Swain, looking at him and at the half-written poem in his lap now that Byblos has left it and returned to her work elsewhere.

"A wandering creature of the depths that existed before yourself, my lord," explains the painter. He lifts his other hand. "The other road is usually an empty route, but it appears that a large contingent of armored riders is moving to the north there; we would overtake them on the road, though it is unlikely they'll stop, and we'll need to give pursuit." He lowers his hands. "They're likely trying to reach the north to reinforce the capital."

The Demon King lowers his head in thought. He'll have to make a choice on the matter.

"Any news of the witches, whom we've ignored in the past?" asks the beast, considering the last time such a choice had to be made.

"No, my lord," replies Abydos. "They seem content to exist in mutual disinterest."

Swain nods, thinking about it.

It is unlikely that the human forces, if allowed to fester in their interior, will not come back to haunt them later down the road should they be ignored. However, much the same, allowing such a powerful group of additional soldiers to reach the human capital will significantly aid its defenses for the final push.

He must consider it carefully.

~ [Ruhr, the River Sorceress] ~
Marionette | ♀ | Sorceress
Rank: SSS
Location: The Demon King's Castle, Floor Twenty-One
Level: 96

Wood clatters, chipping away in all directions, the beads on her head rattling in the violent winds as magic presses out of her stumpy wooden hands, totally consuming the entity as she screams, letting out a few things. The monster, pelted with sharp, jagged wood, flails and screams, blood and sinew flying all over the place as it is bludgeoned and ripped apart. It's vile innards, consisting of misgrowths such as eyes and teeth, spill onto the floor, connected by strands of sinew and odd veins that connect to useless pieces of a body to feed those parasitic chunks with blood.

A hand reaches out, grabbing hold of all the strings attached to the top of her body at once, causing Ruhr to tightly compress together into a backward bent ball, her joints moving in directions they really shouldn't, but she doesn't notice that.

An instant later, she lurches, her body hanging free again and falling to the ground as a heavy tower shield cracks into the arm, breaking it at the elbow and causing it to let go, flopping uselessly on the stones. Ruhr jumps to her feet, running to the side just in time as another fist comes down where she landed, cracking the ground behind her with a wave of hammering strikes, smashing down like the hammers of a piano as she runs along the edge of the room, holding her hands out toward the creature again. Ruhr sees Zacarias out of the corner of her eyes, both of his hands locked against a pair that grips him from the front, pushing back against him as another fist now raises itself over his head.

She holds her hands up.

(Ruhr) has used: [Aquatic Dragon]

It rushes toward him in the same instant as a great serpent made out of azure rips through a dozen arms which fall to the ground, their severed nerve endings wiggling like worms as they come into contact with the air, the beast catching the fist before it hits Zacarias and smashing it against the wall.

Ruhr grabs a shield, spinning around once and chucking the heavy thing through the air toward him—definitely not with enough force to damage any of the limbs like he had. "Zac!"

The man looks to the side and pulls his hands out, catching the shield and then spinning, cutting through the lower wrists of the two appendages with the bottom of the shield and sending sprays of black blood everywhere through the air, coating the strings above his head with a greasy fluid that drips down toward him, running along their wiry lengths.

The two of them lean against each other, looking at the flailing, oozing monstrosity that hammers the room with its remaining fists more violently than ever, thrashing like a beast in rage.

Ruhr moves behind Zacarias, holding her arms around him and planting her palms on the back of the shield. "Hold it," she instructs. "As long as you can."

The man plants his legs steadily down, placing the shield firmly in the ground and holding on to it as water begins to spray out of her hands, chunks of wood splintering and crashing down around their feet as she applies more pressure, intensifying the spell and then even more still, the metal rattling, splinters flying through the air in all directions like shrapnel.

"RUHR!" he barks as the hands move toward them, lumbering, greedy fingers that always yearn to take more. In the grave, before the grave—it doesn't matter. More. More.

Black hands crawl around the shield, reaching for them.

More.

"NOW!"

Zacarias pulls his arm free of the shield's breaking straps, the sheet of metal shooting straight through the air, filling the room with a loud, sickly cracking noise.

The two of them stand there, looking at the growth in the center of the

room which has a hole going clean through it. The tower shield is bent and embedded deeply in the opposite wall.

The arms stop and begin to fall down to the ground, one after the other, as the monster dies, shuddering in a spasming death that sends viscera and goo everywhere in the throes of a beast that can never scream.

One arm falls down before him where the shield had been, a gently curled index finger running over his cheek with its back side, as if to offer any solace. If mocking or not, she can't tell.

The two of them stand there in silence before looking at one another.

Ruhr purses her lips in a smile of sorts and nods to him once.

Zacarias nods back.

There's not really anything else to say that hasn't been said.

Especially now that the spell has been broken.

Ruhr opens her eyes in her real body, staring down at the room she was just in with Zacarias from above—as if she were hanging from the ceiling. Wooden puppets lie down there limply in the arena, one with blue hair.

The half elf's eyes wander to her own arms, which are adorned with strings and wires that lead down to the marionette below; she follows them, looking at the blue doll, and twitches a finger. The doll twitches a finger.

"The hell . . ." mutters Ruhr, blinking to focus her blurred vision before turning her head back around herself and looking up at where she expects the ceiling to be, given that she assumes her back is pressed tightly against it.

Yet there is no ceiling. There never is, is there?

The whole surface is it. It is much like the thing below, but spread flat all across the entire floor, like a meat paste smeared onto brickwork.

Long, cankerous hands hold her aloft—the very same as the ones they had just fought below. Many of them hold people, like herself, who are only now starting to wake. Many others hold nothing and simply hang there, limply, having already consumed their prizes—the puppet and the person that was holding them.

An eye looks down at her from above, having been waiting for a long time to pull her into the toothless hole that is waiting for her not far away now.

(Ruhr) has used: [Torrent {Holy Water}]

Water explodes out from her, bursting in all directions, tearing the hands off herself and those around her as they fall down in free fall with the wave, mostly roughly crashing into the ground below and looking up at the ceiling that has become visible now that the act is over.

Hundreds of impossibly long, gangrenous arms dangle toward them like vines in a jungle, the puppeteer from above having finished the act but not the show. Ruhr blasts the ceiling, shooting down hundreds of people. They must have gotten caught in a trap when they entered the floor.

What a disgusting thing.

The river sorceress continues the stream of magic, pressing waves of water against the ceiling which immediately rain back down over them and the floor as a whole in her attempt to drown the thing above and free as many others as she can.

"Zac!" yells Ruhr over the roar of the magic as the crusaders come to wakefulness and join in on the counterassault, blasts of radiant magic of all kinds flying up into the holy water that drizzles down around them, intermingled with blackened blood. Her eyes frantically scan the arena, not seeing him. She turns her head around, looking at the puppets.

The strings.

"No. No. No. *No*," mutters the woman, not seeing the doll anywhere, and then looking back up toward the ceiling. "ZAC!"

A long, gangly arm whips through the water. She turns her head just in time for its clawed, rotting fist to smash right against her face. Ruhr flies back, a loud, sickly crack ringing through the room as her head roughly strikes the wall of the fake house, her vision going dark immediately before she has the chance to limply fall over.

Next to her, an urn falls from a table and shatters.

CHAPTER 12

THE DANCING RATTLESNAKES AND THE DEAD BIRD (1/3)

The Pursuer
Of all things of men, and beast, and foul,
Stray few things that could still cause a scowl,
To form on the faces of those souls—now marred,
Who see not life's graces, past their skin, now hard,
The men of old ways, of strength and cruel paths,
Formed in the strongest of days in which nurturing had
lacked,
Yet these ruthless monsters that they have become,
Fear not but one thing,
The Pursuer, among,
For these men fear not death, as the two are familiar in
pace,
But what all these men fear is the thrill of the chase,
When they are not the ones with prey in their eyes,
But instead are themselves on the run from demise,
Hard men are strong, they fight to the last breath,
Yet they are winded too quickly,
By the thing on their left,
Their strength is their weakness, their stubbornness—
their fault,
As men who had never run, can never outrun the haunt.

~ [Barlow] ~
Human | ♂ | Mercenary
Location: The Northern Procession
Level: 100

F asten it down!" yells a squirrely voice, running past him.

Metal screeches. Stones and dirt fly through the air as hundreds of wheels violently rattle, a single file procession of carriages hurtling down the winding mountain road in a tight, gapless formation of dozens of long, strapped-together carts pulled by a full flock of two dozens anqas running in a stampede. The sky is filled with unusually vivid light and heat, a great, cloaking barrier of magically altered air staying above the chain of carriages, keeping the cargo and the passengers safe and dry from the rain above that never ends, illuminating the landscape all around them with a dusty, orange glow.

Unfortunately, the eggheads overtuned it a little, and now it's like they're trapped in an oven that follows them around. The heat has been diverted somewhat after a few quick alterations on the fly, but this just resulted in the majority of the heat now being pushed to the sides of the carriages rather than directly onto them from above. So it's essentially still just as hot here for him and everyone else, but with the added bonus that the air and the ground around them literally burn, turning into a dry, crumbling dust as all of the moisture is sucked away. It's like they're moving through the desert.

That's okay, though. The desert is where he's from.

"Hold it! Hold it steady!" yells the voice again from next to him, having run back again. The mechanics of this operation are a bit wacky, but that's not his problem. He's just being paid to keep the cargo safe.

Sweat drips down Barlow's face, the droplets navigating their way through the thick, black stubble adorning it. The man—leisurely sitting atop the carriages on a stack of strapped-on supply crates, his feet kicked up, his wide-brimmed hat blowing in the hot winds as they ride toward the north—lets out a slow puff of air that escapes past the downward-angled brim of his cattleman. A trail of woody smoke shoots past him, carried into the distance by the rushing, hot winds—thick vapors from

the burning cylinder in his mouth, full of dried herbs from where he was born and raised.

A bell rings loudly from the front carriage, the man sitting on the coach sounding an alarm. "CURVE!" cries a voice along the Procession before then being repeated by another man in a window, who yells the word to the next man, and so it's carried from front to back just in time as the carriages, moving at a terrifying speed, come to a violent bend on the mountain pass, dry sands and crumbled greenery shooting up into the air in a dust cloud as the entire procession takes a tight mountain turn with such speed that half of the chain loses its contact to the ground with all four wheels of each carriage, the middle segments riding on two wheels for a second.

Someone yells in terror next to him.

Barlow reaches out, slowly grabbing hold of some fabric for a moment, never bothering to get up or move as his body sways.

A second later, the construct lets out a loud crashing sound as it returns to the road, having never stopped for a second, several carriages whipping dangerously close toward free fall over the unguarded edge of the mountain way.

He lets go of what he had grabbed a hold of as someone flops down at his feet, having almost flown off to their death. As the work here is very dynamic, nobody is secured. Dozens of people are just running freely around the top of these carriages or moving through them. They're a special design, cut open in the front and back of each unit to allow a long tunnel to exist between them.

Hundreds of mounted soldiers ride behind and ahead of this wild construction, all of this to protect some obscure, special cargo that is needed to reinforce the capital city against the Demon King. The soldiers are just an added bonus.

But that's none of his business. He's just here for the job.

"T-Thank you," says a very relieved voice. There's a slight rattling of metal.

Barlow looks up a few inches, lifting the brim of his hat to look at the pale, sweaty face of what may be the most androgynous, soft person he's ever seen. He thinks that they look like a lake fish and an elf had a kid. The stranger looks up at him, their short, sharply cut hair matted to their soaked forehead, dry dust blowing past them as they move, billowing the

white-and-blue striped collar of their weathered button up shirt past their suspenders.

Around their wrists are a set of dark, ironclad bracelets, the metal stamped with the insignia of the military's logistics branch as a title of ownership—of the person, not the metal. They're an indentured servant, forced into employment by the state, with the alternative being consequences the nature of which are of course undesirable. Military prisoners, political dissidents, criminals, and sometimes even just people who were in the wrong place at the wrong time get moved into this kind of work during *times of need*, as they are called by the laws allowing this sort of thing.

Although, there have never been any times that haven't been deemed as "of need" by the powers that be. Funny how that works.

The bracelets are currently not fastened to anything so the person can do their work. But outside of these times, they have the purpose of being bound to chains for transport or storage. They're apparently with logistics, the wackjobs responsible for this entire death trap.

Barlow blows out a mouthful of smoke at them before lowering his hat and biting down on the cigarette as he talks. "Die out of my sight if you're gonna," says the man, the taste of ash filling his mouth.

"I'm sorry, Mr. Barlow, sir," they reply in an accent from the deep country, getting back up to their feet.

Everyone on this operation knows who he is, which he isn't actually keen about. He's a freelancer—a specialist, if you will—and usually, the nature of his "security" work is simple. He gets paid. He goes in and out. The work gets done. Nobody talks to him, and he doesn't talk to anybody else either. But his reputation got ahead of him, and now he's working for some bigwigs in the noble families. He usually doesn't care for whom he works, as long as they pay. However, because of this and the formality of the operation, he's been presented to everyone as a key figure here.

"I SAID STRAP THAT DOWN!" yells the person, rising to their feet and running off down the carriage chain.

Barlow leans back, folding his hands on his stomach, the leather on his waist creaking amidst the wood and metal carnage of the Procession. He looks over his shoulder, staring at the logistician from behind for a moment. Quietly grunting, the crusty, dusted man shakes his head, grabbing a flask from his hip and taking a swish of it, the burning liquor

mixing with the smoke in his throat as he lowers his head again, the bell signaling another violent curve to come as they veer toward the west.

~ [Swig] ~
Half Elf | ⚥ | Indentured Servant {Logistician}
Location: The Northern Procession
Level: 20

It's a few hours later.

Swig's hair blows wildly in the winds as they climb down the ladder, the soles of their boots slapping the metal rungs as they spare one last glance out of the hatch, toward where the distant sunset ought to be. The sight of freedom. The inside of the Procession is just as loud as the outside, really. The only difference is that you don't have the wind in your ears down here. However, in exchange, you have the road noise just down below your feet.

They walk through the Procession, the inside of which is a tightly packed wooden hallway with many moving segments. The walls are jam-packed with shelves full of crates of weapons, resources, and all manner of alchemical substances. There are small cupboards on either side which are meant to be rooms of sorts, technically to store even more boxes. But they've made themselves at home here. It's a long job, and the Procession has been moving for at least a week now from the distant south at least.

"Swiggy Bird!" calls a voice from the side, whistling sharply. Swig turns their head, lifting a hand just in time to catch an apple thrown their way from one of the old timers. "Heard you tried to leave the nest today," laughs the old man in charge of making food for them. He's in officially for a total of eight years.

This is his fourteenth year now.

The bracelets on his wrists, sitting beneath some fabric padding a lot of them wear to stop them from rubbing against their skin, jangle.

Swig turns as they walk, never stopping as they point at him. "You know me, Four-Four. I'm gonna fly away any day now, you know," replies the half elf, completing their circle to return facing back ahead as they walk through the corridor. The old man laughs, his voice vanishing into the churning of the wheels as Swig squeezes through the tight passages, biting into the apple. It's kind of old, so the skin is a little wrinkly and the

inside is a little grainy, but food is always something to be happy about. They aren't starved, as their owners realize they need enough nutrition to stay productive. However, there's a careful science to it. They get just enough to survive in their work, but never enough that they'd gain enough weight to survive without any food for a long time. It keeps them in line and from getting ideas. On the plus side, the meagerness of Swig's body combined with their lanky features lets them move through these places pretty easily.

"Hey, Swig," clicks another member of the crew from the side. "We're setting up for some dice. You in?" she asks, shaking her hand.

Swig grabs hold of a bar between carriages, the doorway of which is blocked by a large crate that had no better place to be put, and pulls themselves up and over it into the next carriage. "Sorry, Buckle," says Swig, hanging halfway upside down and shaking their head, the strands of their now dried hair hanging low. "I got a long one today. Need those hours."

"We'll be thinking of you!" calls the voice after Swig as the half elf vanishes into the next carriage.

It's a weird situation, socially. Honestly, there's nobody here who doesn't get along with anybody else. You'd think there is always this group and that group in places like this, but somehow, fortune has worked out in their favor. They're all laborers at the end of the day, people just trying to get by. But they're not suffering to death every day, despite their being forced into this situation. This has all led the entire group of them to just sort of . . . quietly coexist. Everyone here is just doing their time and doesn't want any more than that. The years go by easier if there isn't any weird shit going on.

Swig moves through a few more, stopping at a half-drawn curtain as someone hisses on the other side.

"You good?" asks the half elf, peeling back the curtain. "Ah, hell. Cheeky, what in damnation happened to you?" Swig steps inside, pulling the curtain fully closed, and looks down at the old woman sitting with her back to the "door," her shirt off, an old, inflexible arm reaching behind herself to try and dab some fresh marks with a rag.

Swig takes it from her, kneeling down and dabbing the damp cloth against the red, straight bulges crisscrossing across the weak skin that doesn't have much fat left beneath it. Cheeky's an old woman. These are lash marks. She's been caned. It's one of the more common punishments

for them if they make a mistake or disobey. She's been here for twenty years now, even if she only had ten worth of time.

"I messed up in the manifest," explains the woman, hissing.

"Hold still," says Swig. "I got it. Here, have the rest." Swig reaches around, giving her the other half of her apple.

"Bless you, child." Cheeky looks back ahead. "My eyes aren't what they used to be. I missed a line on the manifest," she sighs.

Swig tsks, moistening the cloth by spitting on it, and then dabbing it back against the wounds, trying to wipe the splinters out of her heavily scarred skin. Her back has so many lines and grooves that, from a distance, you'd think she was a reptile. Over two decades, a lot of punishments have taken their toll. The old woman hisses but sits still. "They sticked you for that?" asks Swig. "That's harsh."

"The supervisor is on edge," says the woman, shaking her head and biting into the apple.

"Still . . ."

"Hush," she's reprimands. "Keep your head down and be quiet," scolds Cheeky.

Swig purses her lips and nods, continuing their work.

They can complain about it as much as they want, but complaining is a punishable offense if heard, and right now, punishments are at an all-time high, given the stakes.

Swig looks over the frail woman's shoulders at the bracelets that dangle off her wrists. On some days, the metal is so heavy that she can't even lift her old arms anymore, so she was relegated to paperwork.

"You should go," speaks Cheeky.

"I always have a minute for you, Cheeks," replies Swig, working on the next spot and pulling out a few pieces of wood from her back.

It's true. Swig does have a minute. Swig has two at least, in fact. In reality, they probably have more than that—hundreds, thousands more.

There is a kink in the system.

Yes, Cheeky *only* has to do ten years' time for whatever happened in her past. However, there is a catch to the way this deal works.

Only work hours count.

The time spent sleeping in prisoner quarters, the time spent shackled up when there is no work at all, which can be months in the dry season, the time spent taking their forced lunch breaks which often have far less

food than allotted time, the time spent traveling—all of these things don't count toward their sentence. So to work off ten years of sentenced time, that's ten years of work hours and nothing else.

These "ten years" in reality mean a number far, far higher than that. That's not including the fact that they're not obligated to even get work hours to begin with. If a supervisor finds one of them unlikable for whatever reason whatsoever, well, they might just not happen to have any work anymore for that particular person—ever—and so, no hours are ever tallied away.

There are some people who get out now and then, but by the time they make it, they are so old and broken that there isn't much life left for them anyway.

But nobody outside of this system cares about all of this, and so the military and the government are quite comfortable using it, and the common, everyday people of the world are indifferent to its existence at all. Even if any outliers do raise an eyebrow or two, the mild sentences presented to the public via written records of a few odd years to serve here or there, which aren't different from those handed out by normal public courts, placate most voices, and at the end of the day, they're all still in irons. Normal prisoners go to normal prisons and programs, and ten years are ten years, maybe less with good behavior.

Here, for them, ten years are a lifetime.

The system works fully as intended. They're all people who are wanted to disappear by some power or another, and have been made to do so not by outright killing them but by pressing them dry like a piece of juiced fruit and then discarding the peel that remains at the end.

"You're a sweetie, Swiggy Bird," replies the woman. "It's a shame that you don't pray."

Swig wipes their forehead dry as best as can be done before returning to the work. "Not sure how that will help me, Cheeky," says the half elf.

"The gods will listen to you if you do," explains the old woman as Swig pulls the splinters out of her raw back.

Swig shakes their head. "You know I love you, Cheeks," starts Swig. "But if prayer really worked, then why are you here?"

The old woman looks back over her shoulder. "If it didn't, then why are you here with me now?" She laughs, shaking her head. "Bless your confused heart, child."

Swig purses their lips, smiling with a nod as they finish the work. Everyone here finds their own way to cope. Four-Four found joy in work. Others find it in gambling. Cheeks found religion. And Swig? Swig found it a strange delirium born of the nickname given to them by the others—Swiggy Bird.

None of them use their real names here, although at this point, these *are* their real names. They may even be more real than the names they had before.

Birds fly away, and so that's what Swig thinks about whenever there isn't any work. It doesn't really make sense for anyone who lives a normal life, but in conditions like these, the mind becomes . . . strange. It finds ways to adapt and cope that any normal person would think absurd.

Swig closes the curtain and returns back to the corridor. It's hot in here, like an oven. However, the sorcerers and magical engineers have been given strict orders to ensure stable climatic conditions for the cargo, and they've certainly managed to do that in some fashion.

Swig's forearm runs over their sweaty brow as they enter into the next carriage. Guards stand at the door of the next room. They're not in irons. They're with the military and are here to guard the main cargo, which is the real reason they're moving toward the north.

A bell rings.

The half elf braces themselves with an arm against a wall as the Procession turns.

"I'm here for my shift," says Swig, holding an arm out as the carriages land back on their wheels.

One of the guards looks at a list on the wall and then grabs Swig's wrist without saying anything, examining the stamped mark to make sure it's the correct one. The man nods, wiping his hand off on his leg before pulling out a heavy key ring and opening the door.

Vapors release from the room, together with the smell of metal and smoke.

Swig takes a deep breath, looking out of the window of the carriage for a second at the illusion of an endless sunset beyond before exhaling and stepping into the room.

This job is a big one.

Swig was promised two years commuted off their sentence if they pull this off. That's enough to get them out of here before they turn

thirty, assuming they get the same hours in the future after this, and they don't die.

Thirty is good. Swig can live with thirty. There's still so much life left to live, then. There will still be so many things they can do after that. All of their dreams and hopes are still on the table, not like some of the others here who have much longer than that left.

"Flying away," mutters the half elf quietly as they set to work.

Eventually.

~ [Barlow] ~
Human | ♂ | Mercenary
Location: The Northern Procession
Level: 100

It is much later.

Magical technology has come very far.

There is a ratcheting of metal as a grooved cylinder spins in his hands. The man is playing with the latest toy he's been given. It's not uncommon for these high-profile jobs that the customer outfits him with obscure mechanisms and gear. Most often, he has to give it back in the end. Other times, they try to kill him after the job is done to keep his mouth shut.

But this has happened so often that he'd be more surprised if a customer didn't try to have him murdered at the end of a job than if they just paid him and let it be good. It's not like he'd say anything anyway; he's a professional. However, that's just not how this world works.

Barlow lifts the weapon, an experimental version of the large cannons the nation has been fielding on the coastlines for naval defense on strong ley lines. They're able to collect ambient magic from the world's currents and condense it down into a focused point of energy, which is absolutely devastating for anything like a boat that's hit by it, let alone people.

However, that's an entire cannon, meant to be manned by a team of technicians.

This here is a smaller, weaker version. It's light and only needs one person to use it, only functioning in the hands of high-level casters with a lot of magic to spare. It's a type of weapon that will change the nature of war forever to come. It was already in development long

before the Demon King showed up, with the intent of being used to conquer the Vildt continent as soon as the technology was ready to be mass-produced.

But fate intervened.

He aims the experimental weapon down and off the side of the train, pointing it at the military officer leading the hundred-some riders behind the Procession, closing one eye to stare down the length of the thin, metal tube engraved with a series of numbers and characters meant to serve the weapon's designation.

This weapon is the end of an era.

When it's spread around the world, men like him won't be needed anymore. They'll die out. Strength won't come through age, expertise, and practice—it'll come through the act of possession alone. Levels will be meaningless. A level one commoner with this weapon will be able to aim it at the heart of a level ninety-nine noble-blooded champion and pierce their heart from a distance with the pull of a finger. It will be the end of the age of true heroes, the end of the age of Demon Kings and beasts.

Barlow clicks with his mouth, dropping the arm and holstering it again as he stares back behind them for a while, narrowing his eyes.

Shit.

He whistles loudly, his fingers stuck in his mouth. The officer below looks up, following his pointing hand to look behind them at the sky. Barlow turns to one of the logisticians, yanking him over by his dirty, grease-stained dress shirt. "Boy. Ring the alarm," he orders, nodding his head to the cloud forming behind them in the darkness.

"Mister Barlow?" asks the boy before he stumbles as Barlow pushes him away.

"Get," orders the man, spitting off the side of the carriages and into the valley below as he pulls out another smoke from his pouch, lighting it up and watching as the barrier above them, radiating with heat, begins to flicker and buzz as the now intensifying rain strikes against it.

He takes a draw of the cigarette, the wind blowing the fabric of his poncho toward the oncoming danger he's facing. He exhales a puff of heavy, acrid smoke, and the vapors snake behind them, taking the form of a serpent for only a fraction of a second, if anyone so happened to be looking at it long enough to see it do so.

The death of an era, huh?

His hand rests on the weapon. As the dark clouds draw closer on their trail, hundreds of dead things—rotting things with teeth and claws, things with stretched, warped, leathery skin and fangs like broken knives—hound them on the horizon.

"Demon King's here," mutters the man as the terrified boy runs off to do as told.

The rear guard splits, with half of them breaking off to turn around and intercept the pursuing threat.

Barlow looks ahead of them. Here on the mountain trail, they can't be intercepted. The path just isn't wide enough for more than their single-file construct of carriages. But they're already moving downhill, and there, on the other side, are open plains.

An odd hundred men ride back down the way they came from. The anqas are particularly well suited to moving in masses in this narrow, treacherous environment. After the rear guard splits in half, Barlow looks up at the mountainside to the right, his finger tapping against the iron on his waist as he thinks.

Something moves up on the rocks.

His eyes go wide.

"AMBUSH!" yells the man as shadows drop down from above.

~ [Swig] ~
Half Elf | ♀ | Indentured Servant {Logistician}
Location: The Northern Procession
Level: 20

Iron is the key component.

Swig sits on the chair, their face pressed down into their work as they fiddle around in the inner chamber of a long version of the experimental weapon with a set of precision tools.

It's long been known that fairies hate iron, but it was never really understood why. It was just a natural weakness and accepted as such, in the same manner that undead hate holy magic. However, magical research has recently discovered the real reason for this in the black facilities of the nation. Fairies are living beings, considered to be members of the common races like humans or elves. However, there is a snag, and that is that

fairies aren't born to parents; rather, they are born from the world, from its natural ambient magics.

This was the first hint.

It turns out that it isn't that fairies are averse to iron in and of themselves; it's that the world's ambient magic currents, for whatever undiscovered reason, seem to act differently around iron than around other metals. The reasons for this are still unclear, but it doesn't really matter why. What matters is that the concept, even if not understood, can be harnessed.

By placing iron filaments in precise, delicately decided locations in a cylinder, ambient magic, which is present in the air around oneself at all times, can be moved through a funnel, bouncing away from one disrupting iron filament to the next until it reaches a critical stage of energetics, at which point it finds the only way out—the end of the cylinder.

It's a beautiful technology. It will truly change the world.

Swig has always had an affinity for this sort of work, and after making an offhanded suggestion to the head researcher of the operation in passing, they were immediately requested to be allowed to work on these sorts of devices. It's obviously a very unusual job for an indentured servant to have, but this is an unusual time, and Swig obviously intends to make full use of it. It's sitting work and guaranteed hours.

Bells ring all around the Procession. Shouts and cries fill the air.

Swig lifts their head, wiping their face free from the grease that has smeared it with their sweaty sleeve before looking around. They run to the window, sticking their head out and looking back behind themselves at the dark aura that fills the sky past the glowing light of the spell covering the caravan, dry winds rushing through their hair.

There's a loud crashing sound on the ceiling. Swig looks up and then quickly shuts the window as the doors burst open, guards running in to grab weapons from the racks.

The light from outside flickers as something touches the glow above the Procession.

Claws rip through the roof. Swig screams and falls down, covering their head as a man is impaled with a long talon and dragged through the hole, the other guardsmen trying to pull him back in.

~ [Barlow] ~
Human | ♂ | Mercenary
Location: The Northern Procession
Level: 100

A crack shoots through the night, like the strike of a whip, as he holds his hand outstretched against the wind, smoking metal singing as something drops down dead at his feet, a hole cutting straight through its head.

Barlow looks at it out of the corner of his eye. It's a scaly, leathery thing. It has two legs like a man, but its face is stretched out and contorted like a lizard's. It has long claws like curved knives.

All in the same moment, his hand has been moving over the weapon, cranking the hammer on the back of it into place before his finger presses down a second time, sending another shot straight-ahead into the neck of a second one.

He dives out of the way, rolling across the rattling carriages and aiming where he was just standing as something crashes down into the spot from above, roaring at him until the iron roars back and it falls over, dead.

The day glow of the aura above their heads is cut through with wildfire, concentrated blasts of magic shooting through the air by the hundreds as the mounted soldiers remaining behind the Procession aim up toward the cliffs, firing up at the dropping shadows that fall like rainwater.

Bodies of all kinds, dead and alive, thud down around them.

A hiss fills his ears, and he looks down at a survivor running away from him toward the front of the carriages, toward the coachman at the far end. He quickly aims at it, pulling the trigger.

Something hits him in the back, and he fumbles, the shot missing and cracking into the cliffside as he falls over, rolling just in time to catch the clawed hand pressing down toward his face. Barlow presses his legs against its heavy gut, the muscle-bound animal snarling and swiping at him like a rabid bear as he, with his back pressed against the roof of the carriage, kicks and rolls to the side.

The monster falls off of him, its claws scrambling for the edge of the carriage as it tumbles.

A second later, its grip releases as thunder cracks. Barlow, having grabbed the iron weapon, turns and aims down the carriages, narrowing an eye to make the shot, which is out of the weapon's optimal range at best.

The man bites on his cigarette and pulls the trigger, a flicker of light cutting through the air and through the monster's waist, the projectile having dropped in height as he fired it against the wind.

"Shit!" mutters the mercenary, scrambling to his feet, trying to fire again, but the iron is empty. It needs a recharge after six shots. His palm spins over the cylinder in its core, a rotational device meant to funnel in a stronger flow of ambient magic through its rotation.

However, he's too slow.

The monster reaches the final carriage, roaring as it drips black blood everywhere at the coachman, who looks behind himself.

A streak of yellow cuts through the air, its head splitting in half and sending a spray of black blood and viscera through the air, together with fragments of bones.

The half elf from before is leaned out of a window, holding a longarm. They turn back his way from the distance.

He nods before turning back to look at the area behind them.

The dark cloud hasn't slowed down at all. Whatever the hell that interception team was supposed to do, it sure as hell didn't work.

The ground at his feet wobbles.

Barlow looks down below himself at the carriage he's standing on top of as its momentum changes somehow.

What the . . .

He turns his head, realizing it's been separated from the rest of the Procession. The man runs as they fall behind, gritting his teeth as he jumps across the growing gap. Screams fill the air behind him when something catches in the wheels of the detached carriage, causing it to tumble and crash into the fully speeding riders behind, sending half of them flying off the mountainside, the other half breaking their bodies in a horrific impact.

Barlow catches the edge, kicking his legs down into the head of one of the lizards that had snuck inside, sending it careening down onto the road and breaking its bones as it tumbles.

The man swings his legs for momentum before dropping into the torn-open back segment of the Procession, looking down at the mangled, half-eaten body at his feet of some cook with shackles on his wrists before turning to look back at the wreckage behind them, trails of smoke from his cigarette leaving in the wind as ash crumbles from the edge of it.

They survived the ambush, so they have a pause for now, but it won't take long until they're caught up with.

The cliffsides lessen as they leave the ambush territory; the carriages move through the mountain valleys that they now leave. The road takes a downhill turn.

~ [Swig] ~
Half Elf | ♀ | Indentured Servant {Logistician}
Location: The Northern Procession
Level: 20

"Strip," orders the officer.

It is an hour later. Swig knows better than to argue at this point, and removes their clothes. "Turn around," he orders. "Touch the wall."

The half elf turns around, placing their palms against the wall.

He reaches past them, fastening the chains to the iron bracelets around their wrists.

It's only ten. As long as they don't scream, it's only going to be ten. So it'll be fine. Ten is easy. They've done ten before. Hell, Cheeky had ten today too. If she can handle it, then this is going to be fine. Swig likes to remind themselves of these sorts of things before such sessions begin.

If you scream, you get additional punishment for fostering demoralization among the ranks.

The thing is, good intentioned as it may have been in the prior situation, raising a weapon is never, ever, EVER allowed for an indentured servant to do. In a life-or-death situation, the official military stance is for them to choose death. So given that Swig's life wasn't directly in danger per se, well . . . rules are rules.

Swig slowly exhales, loosening their back.

"Thirty," says the officer.

Swig's eyes open again, staring at the wall in sudden fear. Thirty?!

A deafening crack fills the room.

Spit flies out through Swig's quickly clenched teeth, the foaming of it preventing a sharp yelp from leaving their mouth. A sharp burning moves through their back as the broken skin rips open where the cane strikes, peeling open as if a hot knife were running over their back. Their ears ring.

He hits again, and Swig's fingers curl against the wall they're chained to, their muscles spasming from the pain. Blood begins to form on the red skin.

"I still need it for work," speaks a man from the side, who is watching. Swig doesn't turn their head but recognizes the voice as belonging to the researcher in charge of the weapons.

"Don't worry," says the officer. "It'll work."

A new crack runs through the room. Swig doesn't bite their lip. That's a lesson learned from the old-timers. If you bite your lip, you'll bite through it. Instead, they fill their mouth with air, clenching their teeth. But Swig does cry—quietly. As long as one doesn't scream, urinate, or fight back, it's only the designated amount and not one more than that.

"Twenty-seven."

There is another crack, and the metal bracelets rattle against the wall they're bound to.

Swig tries to think about flying away. But thoughts don't come so easily right now.

"Twenty-six."

Swig makes a mistake and screams after all. It really does hurt a lot.

"Thirty."

~ [Barlow] ~
Human | ♂ | Mercenary
Location: The Northern Procession
Level: 100

Barlow sits inside atop a stack of crates, playing with the weapon in his hands, his feet kicked up as he smokes inside the carriage chain.

A door opens nearby, and he looks as the half elf, holding some fabric in their arms, is thrown out of a room, landing down naked on the floor, blood running everywhere down from a grotesquely mangled back. The heavy shackles on their wrists clatter as they hit the floors.

He draws from his cigarette, blowing some smoke into the air, and watches as they just lay there.

The door behind them slams shut.

And that's it.

Nobody comes to move the creature away. Nobody comes to clean

them up and bandage them. Nobody even comes to tell them they're in the way, lying there bleeding and naked in the middle of the corridor.

"It was a good shot," says Barlow, looking back out of the window. "Guess you're a natural." He puts his weapon away, puffing on the cigarette for a few minutes.

By the time he looks back, they're just sitting there on its knees, holding the stained clothes in its arms and staring at the wall with eyes that don't really blink much.

There's a light splashing sound.

The metal flask in his hand catches the light as he shakes it, choosing to ignore the urine dribbling onto the floor below the half elf. Sometimes there are just days like that. He gets it. "You drink?" he offers.

The half elf turns their eyes toward him, staring for a time, and then looking down at themselves.

A shaking hand reaches out for the metal flask.

"Your friends are dead, probably," continues Barlow. "Lots of uneaten hands back there," he says, nodding behind himself to the back carriages of the Procession. The half elf's fingers touch the metal only lightly, as if it were expected for him to yank it away any second now. He instead lets go, and the half elf lets out a yelp, scrambling and falling forward to catch the dropping flask, having not expected him to do so. "All the bits that were covered in metal. Guess they didn't like that."

The broken half elf sits upright on their knees, leaning back and drinking from the flask without bothering to even sniff-check it.

A second later, they cough, spluttering as the violently strong alcohol claws at their throat, but then just leans back and downs the rest.

Barlow drops his boots down to the ground, rising to his feet and walking through the puddles of spilled liquor, urine, and blood, indifferent to their presence—combined or otherwise. They're common fluids in his field of work.

"When you're done, put on some pants and meet me at the front," he says. "I have a job for you."

~ [The Demon King] ~

Bones churn, cracking and breaking apart, as hundreds of men who had come to intercept them scream in terror as they're ripped off their

mounts and pulled into the vortex of clawing, creeping meat that lumbers hounding after the convoy of carriages they're still chasing down.

"My lord," speaks Cartouche. "They've left the mountain. We'll catch up to them within the hour."

"Good," replies the Demon King, nodding his head. "Cartouche," he says, looking at the dancer. "This dance is yours," he commands, looking back at the vision of the human convoy. "Please me."

She bows out, vanishing.

"It'll be a show you'll never forget," promises the dancer.

THE DANCING RATTLESNAKES AND THE DEAD BIRD (2/3)

~ [Barlow] ~
Human | ♂ | Mercenary
Location: The Northern Procession
Level: 100

The screaming winds of the world outside howl past them as if they were a blade cutting through the neck of a banshee. Radiating, orange heat presses in from all around them, entering into the windows of the procession as an unwelcome guest. The man's overthrown poncho blows past his shoulders as he stares out ahead of them at the distant openness they've arrived at. The tight mountain pass has come to an end. From here on out, there's nothing.

There are some rocks and some shrubs here and there, but all there is from here on out is prairie dust.

This used to be a great, grand meadow once. A flush forest full of life. However, during a prior one-hundred-year crisis, it was entirely obliterated, and it never recovered. Now, all that remains is a barren desert, wholly out of place at the western edge of the heart of the nation, surrounded on all sides by forest and stone.

Metal ratchets into place, thousands of cartridges of finger-sized vials full of alchemical powers rattling around in a container. Barlow turns his head, looking at the half elf who has thrown a shirt over themselves, the fabric sticking to their own back because of the blood covering it causing the material to crust and bind to their skin, staining it deeply brown and red. The half elf hasn't said anything yet; he's just doing what he said.

Well-worked fingers click the small vials into place in a leather

alchemist's bandoleer, the kind usually worn by battle alchemists to store their dozens of potions before a fight.

Barlow looks at the stranger as he reaches down to his belt to pull out a cigarette.

He knows this creature. He's seen this person a thousand times already in his life. A person who has thrown themselves down at the feet of their circumstances; someone who does everything they can do to get by, to survive another day; someone who deludes themselves that tomorrow is going to be better if they just make it through today.

The Procession rumbles, its specially made wide-gauge axles and extra-width wheels churning over. There's a click as he opens the lantern next to him, holding the paper tube to the flame before biting down on it as he watches the half elf work.

Sometimes, this person wears the face of a guardsman moving to the front lines of an insurrection "just until their next station." Sometimes, it's a woman who has to work the streets "only for a few nights." Sometimes, it's a kid who just has to wait "only until their family comes back." But in the end, it doesn't matter who's wearing the face the day that he sees it.

None of them ever make it out. He's never seen a single one do so.

The half elf stops, looking up toward him for a moment—likely because he's staring, smoke puffing out of his lips—before returning their focus to the work.

Today, it's "just until my time is done."

What these people never understand is that they're deluding themselves. It's a survival mechanism of the spirit to lie to oneself to the point of delirium when such absurd statements seem almost realistic.

Nobody gets out alive.

"I was born this way," says the half elf, not looking up from their work, their face burning red from the whiskey they clearly aren't used to drinking, but it seems to be doing a good job on the pain. The smell of the liquor leaves them; the burning cigarette almost glows more intensely from the fumes in the air.

Barlow exhales, a trail of smoke being carried away by the wind. His vacant staring has been misinterpreted.

He saved the half elf from falling once. The half elf saved the coachman with that long-distance shot, thereby saving his own mission, his own money, and his own reputation.

They're even. One for one.

The man turns to look at the weapons lining the wall, smoke and red dust filling the room. These things . . .

They're here in all shapes and sizes. There are small, personal ones like his own. There are longarms, like the kind the half elf used, and between them are mountains of odd, experimental designs he doesn't care much for. Not that he cares much for these things to begin with.

The cigarette moves to the other side of his mouth.

With weapons like these, men like him won't be needed anymore. It'll be the end of his work, his profession. Not that there are many others like him. Most either die or get out of the game before they get to this level. Triple S–ranked mercenaries are few and far between, especially those willing to walk through very gray zones. He's an exception for many reasons.

Normal adventurers who work their way through the ranks tend to be . . . of a very specific personality type.

It's funny.

This job, if successful, is probably what will put him out of work.

Just this one job, rings through his head, his own inner voice not cutting him any slack. He's the man who's making his own coffin, one way or another. Either the delivery is successful and these weapons are propagated throughout the world, which will be his end, or it'll fail, and he'll have failed his mission.

He plays with the metal on his hip before turning around to walk past the half elf. He has something to do. The man stops, looking back over his shoulder once.

"Then how are you gonna die?" asks Barlow in response to what the stranger said, before pulling the sliding door open to leave, the Procession roaring as it moves at full speed.

Wind presses through the now open door, a powerful draft moving through the entire chain of carts as it presses out of the many windows and openings, carrying only a single word his way, mingled with the violently burning tinge of cheap alcohol, which comes with less hesitation than he had expected.

The door slides back shut behind him as his thick, leather boots walk down the creaking corridor, a flock of birds flying alongside the carriages on their own route of escape for a moment before lifting up higher into

the air and away from the clanging metal and spiderwebbed glass, covered in scars and blood.

Free.

~ [Cartouche] ~
Gallu | ♀ | Dancer
Location: The Demon King's Castle
Level: 100

The marrow inside fresh bones churns as the pile of corpses of soldiers and their mounts quivers and shakes. The meat and sinew pop as her demon magic affects them. The Demon King has entrusted her with this task, and she's not going to step down from the challenge. Challenge—most often self-afflicted but sometimes external—is what forces a person to grow. A person who does not face challenges and does not face difficulties that puzzle the mind, body, and spirit will never develop further than what they are now.

The same applies to the art of dance.

The artistic pursuit isn't just the pursuit of the perfection of an act itself. A dancer may perform the same routine a thousand times over in pursuit of the physical perfection of the actual act of the dance, yes. However, this then perfected dance is just another tool of a higher level. Much the same way as a musician will master a piece, only to then learn another, only to then learn another, so, too, does the instrument of the body itself move, following the grace of unheard, ethereal notes of song in pursuit of a perfection of a higher state.

It isn't the perfection that matters.

The perfection is just a side effect, an unintended consequence.

The spirit of the artist is revealed in the very first step taken, the very first stroke of the brush, the very first imperfect, janky note that causes people to wince and recoil—because revealed within the ugly gracelessness of talentlessness is not so much the seed of beauty; rather, there, buried, is beauty itself.

The ugly dance contains as much soul as the practiced, expert movements of a sidewinder. The shaky, weak, and out-of-tune keys of a piano hold within themselves the same level of soul as the master's notes. In such things, the only difference is how those on the outside perceive them.

The talented artist is perceived as better than the nontalented.

The popular musician is perceived as better than the street busker.

In a physical sense of pure skill and objective ability, this is true, yes. However, the level of soul present within these contrasting entities is one and the same. The soulfulness, the purity, the radiance of whatever a person declares to be the artistry of their soul is entirely, fully decoupled from the nature of skillful work in regard to spirituality.

Are the paintings of the world's great ancient masters more soulful than the joyful pictures made by a child? Not better, but more soulful?

No.

They are one and the same, as both entities are simply after a very simple concept.

Freedom.

The full release of the spirit from the body through the tool of their work. This is what art tries to achieve, no matter what form or level of abstraction it takes.

Flesh bubbles, blistering and leaking, as the carriage thunders down the mountainside, together with the dozen others of the demon carnival, led by a horde of undead who stampede down the way in pursuit of their target.

Cartouche spins, her body moving to the song of rot and the magic of the gallu bestowed upon her by the Demon King, adding spectacle to her performance as the bodies all around her begin to take on new shapes— teeth, bones, fingernails, and hair all liquefying.

~ [Swig] ~
Half Elf | ⚥ | Indentured Servant {Logistician}
Location: The Northern Procession
Level: 20

Swig stumbles back through the corridors of the Procession, having finished the job that Mr. Barlow had for them to do. Now that that's over, there's another job which has to be done—that's her normal one.

Being almost killed by the Demon King's monsters, violently lashed to exhaustion, and then becoming drunk are not valid excuses to miss work. Missing work is severely punished.

The half elf braces with an arm against the wall, the ground beneath their boots shaking wildly for a variety of reasons.

A second later, Swig hangs their head out of the window, vomiting their guts out.

It turns out that being a lanky lightweight who is chronically overworked and underfed leads to a terribly low tolerance for alcohol, or whatever the hell was in that flask.

Swig finishes before then hobbling back to the back carriages, or at least what's left of them.

The half elf's ears twitch as they look around at the destruction that is still more than evident.

Any dismembered body parts have been discarded, likely just thrown out of the back rather than collected for anything close to a dignified burial. People like them, they don't get buried. They get dumped.

Dusty short hair covers Swig's eyes for a moment as they turn their head, looking at a blood-and gore-soaked corner that is absolutely torn to shreds. The burlap sacks and crates there, full of wet fruit and caking flour, are covered in blood and shit from an evisceration.

Swig looks down, bending over to pick up something from the ground that's still there.

An old fruit knife. Its short blade is covered in the black blood of a monster.

"Good for you, Four-Four," mutters Swig quietly, looking around the area where the old man had been when she last saw him.

The back of the carriage is open, having been ripped apart, with the world behind it clearly visible—though the sight offers nothing of value. All that's behind them is the same as all around them in all directions on the compass—dust. The only difference is the black encroachment coming up on them faster and faster, as if it were their own shadow trying to catch up after having been left behind.

Who knows? Maybe it is.

Swig turns to get to their shift, their lanky arm reaching up to the hatch above to start clambering onto the roof to make sure the cargo there is still secure, their eyes looking at a pair of dice still lying on top of a crate down here which was used as a table for a game of chance that they had decided to skip.

Snake eyes.

Swig climbs to the roof.

~ [Barlow] ~
Human | ♂ | Mercenary
Location: The Northern Procession
Level: 100

"We'll need to change our route, Reverend," says Barlow, standing before the desk of the man sitting there with folded hands.

"Absolutely not," replies the officer in charge of this operation without a second's hesitation. He's not just a military figure; he's also a ranking member of the Holy Church who has a large presence in the underworld of national magical technology development. His tightly fitting, perfectly tailored uniform sticks to him like glue as he points down to the map on the desk with his right hand. A small experimental weapon of the same manufacture as all the others sits nestled tightly in his right breast pocket, the grip sticking out over his dress shirt as if it were an ornamental piece rather than a functional one. "Mr. Barlow. We're heading straight for the capital, just like before. Especially after this shit show." He clears his throat, making a loud coughing noise.

Barlow stares at him for a moment before pulling the still lit cigarette out of his mouth. The two men stare at one another as he puffs out the smoke and simply puts it right back between his lips.

"Demon King's gonna catch us," replies Barlow, placing both of his hands on the desk and leaning over it, pressing his face and the lit cigarette closer toward the man, ash dropping on his ironed uniform coat, which he quickly dusts off. "When a predator that's faster than you has your scent, you don't run straight," explains the mercenary. "You take some turns."

"Mr. Barlow," speaks the officer. "You are a guest in my operation. I ask that you mind your place."

Smoke leaves through Barlow's teeth. "I'm a guest the same way you're a man of the cloth, Reverend," says the man, looking at the vaguely maybeor-maybe-not offended officer, who is trying to figure him out. "We're both here for the money." Barlow leans back, pointing down at the map. "The Demon King doesn't want us. He wants the capital." His finger trails over the map, over the prairie they're traversing—not to the north but to the west. "If we break off and go west, he'll just ride past us on his way

to the capital," explains Barlow, tapping against the city far to the north. "Demon King's faster than we are. We should just let him pass, wait a day, and then keep going."

"That will not be possible, Mr. Barlow. I didn't take you for a coward," insinuates the man, raising an eyebrow and waiting for a moment to see if he reacts or not. Apart from the cigarette switching to the other side of his mouth, nothing much else happens. "Our route came from the nation's high command," continues the reverend, almost let down by the lack of escalation. "We're not allowed to deviate."

"I think you'll agree that the scribes in some tower didn't write those orders with the Demon King breathing up their asses," remarks Barlow.

It's quiet for a moment as the officer crosses his hands on his desk, staring him down. "Do you drink, Mr. Barlow?"

"Every day."

"You look the part," replies the reverend. "I don't. Ever." The man rises from behind his desk. "You see, Mr. Barlow, I am a functional member of a proper society. I don't need such crutches." He stands there, holding his hands behind his back. "I am, unlike yourself, a capable, self-regulating adult who knows how to groom himself, how to take care of his health, and who—most importantly, Mr. Barlow," says the officer, folding the map together, "knows how to do the work he is being paid to do without overstepping."

He opens a drawer, putting the map inside.

The officer nods to the door. "I suggest you do your job, which you are capable of doing in any room that is not my office."

Barlow draws the last of the cigarette down to its base, the orange cinders encroaching on his stubble like wildfire. "He'll catch us when the moon's out," says Barlow, looking at the window painted by orange light as he takes the stump out of his mouth and flicks it into the air, blowing out the last of the smoke as he turns to leave the room.

There's a fuss as it lands right inside the still open drawer, to which he pays no mind as he closes the door behind himself, walking past a stained whipping cane on the wall.

The difference between the people of formal society and those of informal society is always stark, and the complexities of such interactions are deep in many ways, often. Even within higher-bred families reaching the tiers of nobility, there are formalities that must be regarded in

interactions. The officer, while not a noble, is still a high-ranking member of both the military and the Holy Church, putting him in a tier above the elevated merchant class of lower society, but below the lowest tiers of nobility.

This means power.

But the gaps here are immense. The gap between a low-tier noble and a man such as the officer is overwhelming. Just the same, the gap between the officer and an indentured servant or even himself is, theoretically, overwhelming.

However, he's achieved a reputation that surpasses his blood, creating a status and ranking for himself that is ascendant from the origins of his birth.

In short, he can do whatever the hell he wants. If he's talking to a noble, a high born, a slave, or anyone else, he's free to act as he wants and, in turn, suffer the consequences of those actions accordingly, rather than being bound by tight social laws.

He got out of the system.

Barlow goes to get ready for the hunting night to come.

He's free, in the truest sense of the word, and this is only possible because of the span of his power being far above that of those higher-ranking people around him. With things like these weapons, however . . .

That's threatened.

~ [Swig] ~
Half Elf | ♂ | Indentured Servant {Logistician}
Location: The Northern Procession
Level: 20

The orange streak of magical light blazing above the carriages of the Procession cuts through the darkness that fails to cool in any substantial way. The radiating, cooking heat presses out into the darkness as they shoot across the landscape, giving, perhaps, the appearance for anyone watching from off in the distance that they were a comet cutting through the night—bright and blazing.

That they were flying.

It is many hours later. Swig has since returned to work, drinking the allotment of water that was theirs and then also the allotment that

was meant for the dead. The hot winds cause the air around them to wobble.

"POTIONS!" yells Swig, pointing down the line to the front. Another logistician there yelps, scrambling to secure the crate that had come free and was in the process of sliding off. Swig's boot is pressed against a metal-framed box tied down with a leather strap, which they're holding on to and pulling back to tighten. Given the haphazard logistics of this operation, a lot of this was done on the fly, and it's a wonder they haven't lost much of anything yet.

But that's because they do good work.

The half elf looks at the other worker, Dot-Five, standing just next to themselves, pulling on a strap. The woman has her eyes closed and is breathing heavily to try and survive the heatstroke. But she's wobbling on her legs. "Just a minute longer," says Swig.

There's not really another option. Either you do good work, or you get replaced with someone who does, and you won't get hours anymore. Swig's seen a few people come and go from the team, entering for only a few shifts before then just never getting assigned another one ever again.

The second shirt Swig has put on, unbuttoned, flaps in the wind; the first one is also open but stuck too tightly to their back from crusted blood to be removed without reopening the wounds.

The heat from above is nothing compared to the passive heat in the air, though. The Demon King's presence is something else. It's beyond any summer heat. It's like being in an oven. Add to that the misaligned spell from above, and it's amazing that the carriages—or any of them—haven't all caught fire yet.

But it makes it impossible to work. The heat is too much. They can only ever manage a minute or two before they have to go back down again to recover before then climbing out again. However, this level of exertion is just as unhelpful as just staying in the heat would be.

"Dot! Let's get this down!" orders Swig, looking at Dot-Five next to them.

Who isn't there.

The other strap next to where Swig is standing flaps freely in the wind, with nobody to hold on to it.

For a second, Swig looks back behind them into the darkness, the Procession shaking wildly from its pace over the uneven terrain, and then

back at the straps, grabbing both of them and pulling tightly to secure the load, grunting and wincing as the shirt on their back rips free from the crusting wounds, the popping of the fabric and the skin indistinguishable from one another.

All of these items are secured. However, given the nature of the Procession and the terrain that it crosses, straps, fastenings, and cords all have a way of loosening and becoming undone by themselves. They need to be regularly adjusted.

Someone whistles from the front, the tone being passed down along the line until it reaches Swig, who then essentially drops over, crawling back down into the hatch below, not so much climbing down as flopping into the hole, soaked to the bone from top to bottom with sweat—so much so that it honestly doesn't even feel like it's helping them cool down anymore and is instead making it even harder to breathe, to live. The world spins, as it has been doing for the last few hours of this shift.

It's a little cooler down below.

Swig closes their eyes, just lying on the floor in the wet, and purses their lips to pass the whistle on, even though they're the last in the line, passing it on to those who lie behind the Procession in significant numbers, letting them know they can take a break now too.

"Do you make these?" asks a voice from just next to them.

Swig opens their eyes, rolling their head to look at the stranger, Mr. Barlow, who is looking down at them with his weapon in his hand, but Swig's vision is spinning so much that it looks like there are five of him, each of them holding out an arm in a different direction, coming together into a collage of wings formed of metal and rope.

A bucket of water is poured over their head from above.

Swig coughs and sputters, breathing in a large mouthful of it before spinning around onto their stomach and pressing it back out.

The half elf lifts their gaze, looking at him, diluted blood running down their nape. "No, Mr. Barlow, sir. I just assemble them," explains Swig, trying to figure out what he wants. "The head researcher—he's the one who makes the pieces."

Swig looks down at the water puddled beneath them on the floor, staring at it, and then up at the man without saying anything, as if quietly asking if it was okay to drink it.

Barlow kneels down, squatting at face height, holding his weapon sideways between the two of them.

"What's your name?" he asks, his voice growling like the crushing of rocks beneath the iron-clad wheels of the carriage they're in.

Swig sits upright on their knees, looking at it and then at him. "S-Swig, Mr. Barlow," says the half elf, rebuttoning both of their shirts to cover up again.

He spits to the side on the floor. "Don't give me that shit," barks the man, entirely indifferent. "What's your name?"

The half elf stiffens for a moment, hands stuck to the buttons they were fumbling with. Swig's eyes wander the carriage, soaked in the filth of the bodies of everyone who has ever died in this work, whether today or last month or the years before. There are hundreds of people like Swig. Thousands. And in one way or another, the presence of their death is always present. The half elf is one of them. They're not whoever they were before this.

That person died, too. They also fell off the Procession.

"Swiggy Bird," replies the half elf, looking back at him, their soaked, greasy, short hair stuck to their face, unsure of what he wants.

He grunts, getting up.

"I have another job for you, Swiggy Bird," says Barlow, looking down toward them.

Swig shakes their head. "I can't, Mr. Barlow. I already helped you once, but I can't drop this shift." Swig points to the ceiling and the cargo above it. "Cargo needs to stay secured." They lower their gaze. ". . . I'll get the stick if it falls."

Barlow shakes his head, walking a few steps away toward the door to the carriage leading onward. "Oh, they broke you good, huh?" he asks. Swig lifts their head, looking at the man. "You're a dead bird in an open cage, Swiggy," says Barlow.

"W-What?" asks Swig.

"Your choice," says Barlow. "Take the job, or die here."

He lifts the gun, and Swig flinches, covering their face and falling back onto their hind in terror, only to watch a second later through the gaps in their arms as he lifts it higher still, holding it above his head.

A second later, there's a crack of thunder and a radiating, violent light filling the room as wood and metal splinter in all directions, breaking glass

and the weakened legs of half-broken shelves. The carriage rattles, and Swig falls around, tumbling for a second as there's a disturbance, landing on their hands and knees and looking on ahead as the two carriages in the back begin to separate from one another—the one where the half elf is in falling back into the darkness behind the Procession.

Barlow holsters the gun, tipping his hat as they begin to separate from one another. "Now, would you look at that?" he says, shaking his head. "The carriage just came off by itself." The man shrugs, shaking his head, his poncho blowing in the winds that begin to fill the gap. "Guess all the cargo is fucked. Oh well."

Swig's eyes go wide as they scramble, crawling at first and then clawing and then running as they sprint through the tiny corridor for the few steps available, all in one strangely graceless yet highly efficient motion as they scream, jumping across the gap and flailing, just barely grabbing hold of the other side's connecting door and Barlow, who is standing on the foot-width back platform. The terrified half elf looks back at the darkness behind them, at the carriage that hits a rock, crashing violently over itself before vanishing a second later into the night in a violent wreck.

A moment later, Swig turns back to look back at him. "You smoke?" asks Barlow, raising an eyebrow and reaching into his shirt, past one of Swig's sweaty, terrified, skeletal hands, which is still holding on to his chest for dear life.

"N-No. Mr. Barlow, sir," replies Swig, letting go of him and leaning with their throbbing back against the wall as the two of them watch the darkness behind them, which seems to somehow be closer than it was only moments ago.

There's something there, moving not far in the distance.

The Demon King is almost there. Even down here, below the top of the Procession, the heat is becoming unbearable.

"I think I'd like to start, though," says Swig, looking at him.

"And the bird opens an eye after all," replies Barlow, holding the first cigarette in his mouth to light it before passing it on to Swig and starting a second one for himself.

Swig looks down at the burning thing in their hands. As an indentured servant, they're not allowed to hold weapons, drink, smoke, or partake in any variety of luxury items meant for "real people," as the rules say.

The half elf looks at it, watching it smolder by itself, before looking at him and watching how he does it. Swig copies the motions, drawing in too much at first and coughing, breathing out an uncoordinated exhaust of smoke, wincing. "What do you want me to do?" they ask, looking at the man, who turns his gaze away from the ever-encroaching darkness.

From the distance behind them, two pinpricks of orange light trail off into the night.

It is many hours later, and the night has come.

The moon hangs high in the sky, its white, cool blue glow poisoned by the flickering magic above their heads.

Swig kneels down on the floor of the restricted room, scrubbing it clean with a rag as boots march down the corridor from one side. The door opens, and a dozen soldiers file in from the front carriage, each of them grabbing a rifle from the racks before marching down through toward the back.

Something bumps into them.

Swig looks up. "Apologies," says the half elf, crawling to the side and out of the way as another guardsman files in, grunting as he grabs a rifle and heads after the others. The door toward the front of the Procession slowly swings back closed.

The half elf crawls along, cleaning up quietly and watching, out of the corner of their eyes, as they all leave. With their leg behind them, they quietly push a used rag into the gap between the frame and the door.

"I trust you won't touch anything tonight," says a voice from the side. Swig turns their gaze, looking at the head researcher of the project, and then shakes their head quietly. "Good. You're suited for this work, but I will replace you if I need to."

"I understand," replies Swig, returning to the floor scrubbing. "Thank you."

The man nods. "Big test tonight. Doesn't get bigger than this. Get ready for a long shift when I'm back from the show."

"Yes, sir," replies Swig, not saying anything else as the man gets up, taking several journals with him, and walks out the door toward the back.

The half elf works quietly, not breaking the pattern, looking only once out of the corner of their eyes toward the softly ajar door which leads to the very front of the Procession.

~ [Barlow] ~
Human | ♂ | Mercenary
Location: The Northern Procession
Level: 100

The soldiers line up neatly on the roof in rows of three, kneeling down to make an orderly formation to allow them all to fire. The reverend stands there, his hands behind his back. On the sides of the Procession are several dozen front men, who have moved back a little.

"Mr. Barlow. I'm pleased to finally meet you outdoors rather than inside," says the man, looking his way. "It makes the smell more tolerable."

"That's alright, Reverend," replies Barlow, not looking at him and instead focusing on the distance. "Your perfume is pretty strong," he remarks, then turning around and clapping him on the back, "Not for me."

The reverend clears his throat as Barlow walks off.

"Mr. Barlow. There is work to do. I trust you'll be staying?"

Barlow turns toward him, reaching down and freeing himself before starting to urinate off the side of the Procession. "Gotta take a leak," says the man matter-of-factly, the reverend making a repulsed face and looking away. "Almost thought you wanted to watch, Reverend." Barlow watches out of the side of his eye as the other men and soldiers look back toward the shadows before quietly tossing the key ring he just stole down into the hatch next to him.

A second later, he shakes himself dry, letting the wind do a little work too, and returns to the back.

"So. Ever fight before?" he asks, looking at the reverend.

The man doesn't have a chance to reply before the night is cut short by the screams of ten thousand wailing dead. They turn back to look as the vague shadows of the distant horizon, which have until now contained only faint nightmares and imaginations, come into full formation. The ground shakes, the orange light above their heads flickering wildly as the magic is overpowered by an approaching presence, until the heating spell simply dies out entirely.

"Lights," orders the reverend.

The men behind him aim their rifles to the sky, shooting a barrage of slowly falling, illuminating magic out into the night behind them,

the crashing fake stars painting the monstrosity chasing them with full glow.

Men scream and fire without order.

~ [Swig] ~
Half Elf | ♀ | Indentured Servant {Logistician}
Location: The Northern Procession
Level: 20

Swig quietly scrambles over the floor, looking up at the hatch above which is aglow with the light of violent magic and a thousand cracks of thunder. Out of the sides of the windows, the half elf can see the riders shooting into the distance behind them.

Ignoring that, the half elf fumbles around in the dark, feeling over the wood for the touch of metal. A clinking gets Swig's attention, and they pick up the stolen key ring, hiding it in their trousers as they run through the Procession toward the reverend's office.

"Hey, Swig!" calls a voice from the side. Swig stops, quickly turning to look. "What's going on outside?" asks one of the workers.

"Demon King," replies Swig before running on ahead to the office, sparing little mind to the stained spot on the wood outside the door.

The air is clear, and the half elf pulls out the key ring, fumbling with it and the lock to try and find the right one before managing and barging inside the small office.

Rushing to the desk, Swig pulls on the drawer.

It's locked.

Cursing, the half elf pulls over the key ring again, looking for a small key for the drawer, and manages to find it.

The map.

The half elf pulls it out, spreading it wide open on the desk, and reads it for a moment, following the landmarks with a finger in the dark room to try and figure out where a good spot would be.

There.

That's not far from here now, though. They'll have to hurry.

Swig folds the map together, tucking it away, and runs back out of the office, heading toward the front where they stashed the huge cache of vials in bandoleers that Mr. Barlow had them work on earlier.

"Hey!" calls a voice from behind. Swig freezes, turning to look at the worker from a second ago. "Swig? What the hell are you doing? What you got there?" asks the man, reaching to take the map.

Swig acts before thinking about it any deeper than at the level of immediate instinct, and the man falls over, clenching his gut and letting out a muffled, throaty noise as he falls back and looks at the old fruit knife stuck in his belly.

For a moment, Swig looks back, but then runs on and away, doing what Mr. Barlow said to do.

~ [Barlow] ~
Human | ♂ | Mercenary
Location: The Northern Procession
Level: 100

Gunshots fill the air, cutting through it like the lashing of countless whips. The impact of their shots strikes against flesh, as there is nothing else to hit—not the sky, not the dirt. Behind them stampedes a raging colossus. A sharp face, beaklike, formed from the broken skulls of the endless dead, cuts through the air. Its mouth is open, filled with suspended, soft strands of fine, black hair instead of teeth. Its long, tubular body winds along the sands like a snake on the hunt, displacing entire dunes with each movement of its horrendous mass.

Stuck wedged between its many segments are the carriages of the Demon King's carnival, which have become a part of the meat. They move with it like stiff joints surrounded on both sides by pulsating flesh propelled forward by ten thousand small, sharp feet—each the size of a giant man—which fail to hold the weight above them upright as they sink into the sand, causing the creature to wobble just as much as it sways, giving it the illusion of being a piece of meat held on a string being dangled toward them.

Undead riders mounted on rotting beasts charge ahead of it; just as many of them are trampled by the monstrosity itself as are shot by the gunmen atop the Procession, shooting through the night.

"Told you we should have turned off!" barks Barlow at the reverend, neither of them having drawn their weapons, as the range is too great for these smaller sidearms.

The reverend looks his way, his sense of superiority evident given his smug smile.

"I guess you really are all show, Mr. Barlow," replies the man. "A tough act, but when it comes down to it, there's nothing of substance there." The reverend sharply whistles, sticking his fingers into his mouth. "Not anymore."

Barlow narrows his eyes.

The sliding door at the back of the last carriage opens.

"You see, Mr. Barlow," continues the reverend, crossing his arms behind his back again as gunfire whizzes past their heads toward the demon beast. "We live in a new world now," explains the officer, looking his way. "It's a world that people like the man you are now ought to be terrified of." He narrows his eyes. "A world that the Demon King ought to be terrified of, Mr. Barlow." He smiles. "But that isn't your real name, is it?"

He stomps down twice onto the ceiling above the soldier below, inside the carriage.

There's a sound of cranking gears and winding mechanisms as somebody turns a handle, moving a device into action. A slow progression of clockwork fills the air.

"You see. I do my research. I'm a professional, Mr. Barlow. You're a long way from those glory days now." He shakes his head. "But I'll tell you myself, here and now," continues the man, staring back at the monstrosity hounding them and coming closer and closer by the minute. "In the ear of God, from me to you, one man of station to another—it's over." He shakes his head. "The age of heroes. The age of crises. We're done." Barlow's fingers twitch. "Do it."

"Yes, sir," replies a voice, giving an order to the person below.

A second later, the cranking mechanisms come into play, and he's sure that, for a second, the lights above have been reactivated, given how bright it becomes all of a sudden. But instead, the new light comes not from this old source but from another—hundred or so—sources which materialize like fairy lights. Projectiles launch through the air, fragmenting and ripping apart the monster as if it were nothing. Hundreds of shots are fired off in the span of seconds by a man with a crank gun mounted below inside the carriage, the roar of which overpowers anything he's ever heard before—dragon, demon, or crisis.

"I hear summoned heroes fall far after their missions end and the gods leave them as they found them," says the reverend. "But I never suspected it was this bad. I pity you, Mr. Barlow."

"You don't know what you're talking about," replies Barlow, watching as the greatest creation of evil he has ever seen is broken apart and butchered by volleys of magic. His shaking fingers graze the metal on his hip, twitching as they touch it, before wandering to the flask next to it.

~ [The Demon King] ~

He watches Cartouche move, gracing the night with her presence as the magic of the poem combines with her attribution, having given form to the new Terror that has only just begun.

~ A Thing That Pursues ~
- Summoned Entity -

**It can't be escaped. It can't be fought. It can't be hidden from.
It is the poison that eats at the soul.
The bane of the prideful, A Thing That Pursues isn't only a monster made of flesh and bones, existing also on a spiritual layer below which is connected to people's hearts. It is the monster that hunts those it has already caught, that stalks those it has already found, and eats those who have already been consumed by its influence.
It is the obsession that haunts a person's head, living in it, gnawing away at them until, one day, they are willing to give themselves to it freely.
And when they do, it will never let them go—just as it never has before either. They were always its.
However, it will then be in body as it has always been in spirit.**

Class: MONSTER	**Element: DARK**
Type: Nightmare	**Category: TERROR***
Rank: SSS	
Level: 80	
***_Terror_ is a classification term used for all monster types that do not fall into traditional monster categories such as UNDEAD, GOLEM, GHOST, etc. Terrors tend to have unique makeups and behavior patterns, and lean toward hyperviolent tendencies.**	

CHAPTER 14

THE DANCING RATTLESNAKES AND THE DEAD BIRD (3/3)

~ [Barlow] ~
Human | ♂ | Mercenary
Location: The Northern Procession
Level: 100

What exactly is a man's purpose in this world?

The philosophers have been arguing about this question for as far back as we can trace their profession, and even before the advent of such a defined role, the men of the world have been discussing it among themselves beneath the heavenly starlight which hints toward the existence of divine makers who crafted the lot of them. There, within the glow of campfires and the shadows of tall trees in the night, such discussions make their way round and round the circle, not just once or twice but over and over for generations.

The question is passed on from one to another, and even those who are outside of such tightly knit social circles somehow find that the question manages to make its way to them nonetheless.

What exactly is a man's purpose in this world?

As far as anyone can tell, there isn't really a definitive answer. Everyone lives their own lives bound within their own unique circumstances, and as such, the purposes toward which a person is drawn or toward which they grow, pushed by their unique environments and circles, are different. One man's found purpose is to protect his family and nation with life and limb; another man's purpose is to do the same for his starving kin by taking the resources of another so his own people might survive. Some men find purpose in the peace and toil of gentle labor. Other men find their

peace in restless travel and the never-ending establishment of kinships with the strangers of the world, acting as a binding link of sorts that connects the many circles of society together.

It is very rare that a man is given a purpose full-on out. Every man must find his own; that is the burden of manhood, and those who fail to do so become restless, for their spirit knows they lack something undefinable, yet they fail to recognize and find what this thing could be, causing them to spiral down into a degradation of the body, mind, and soul which they likely fail to see themselves, blaming the lack of their lives on the world as a whole, while the truth is that they simply failed to find a purpose.

It isn't given to anyone. It has to be made up; it's pretend. One has to fake life until they make it through.

Except for a rare circumstance—the summoned heroes of the world. Those great, powerful, rare souls who come in times of dire crisis in order to right the wrongs of the universe. They are beings pulled specifically into this world to stop some great evil or threat. Their purpose is very specifically designed, designated, and accepted.

There is never any question.

However, what happens when it's over?

What happens to the hero when the Demon King is gone, to the knight when the dragon has been slain, and to the beast when it has devoured everything there is to devour?

Their purpose, while having been fulfilled, is now, through this act of conquest, eradicated.

Triumph is for such souls an act of self-mutilation, for when the work is done and the sun sets on the hour of catastrophe, and a man stands there with sword in hand but none against which to swing it, he will have no choice but to turn it against himself. If he does not do so immediately, literally, then he will do so metaphorically over the rest of his now irrelevant existence.

Heroes are quickly forgotten. Their names go into the same history books as the great monstrosities they've killed, and then the book is closed, and both of them are forgotten forever.

Their greatness, their purpose, and their entireties are but shadows that fade in the sunrise they themselves have brought.

Barlow stands there, the wind howling in his ears as the demon beast

is erased from his vision, magic pressing through it, cutting and ripping, metal cranking and churning in his ears as burning liquor slides down his throat.

The reverend looks his way. "We have this under control, Mr. Barlow," says the officer. "Feel free to go back inside." He turns to watch the giant demon scream and lash as it fails its chase, dying more and more by the second, its spindly legs breaking and flying off, black, thick, oozing blood spraying through the air, causing its massive, lumbering, wormlike form to careen, a great dust storm rising into the air from its disturbance. "I just wanted you to see this." He folds his hands behind his back, not looking away as he stands there, straight and tall. "That you and your kind have been replaced."

Barlow empties the flask and turns, walking back toward the hatch. He caps the flask off, pressing it back into his belt, and turns to look over his shoulder.

However, he doesn't really have a witty comeback.

Instead, he looks back down and then climbs back into the Procession, his fingers straddling the gun on his hip.

One hundred years ago, there was a great crisis in this world. A beast, not unlike the one that is on the world now, had risen and spread the horrific malignancy of its presence over the nations of the planet, sinking them into turmoil and fear.

One hundred years ago, he was brought here to this world by whatever powers there happened to be at the time to save it. He was, back then, a true hero, a summoned hero—he was the one who ended the great crisis of that century and, in doing so, ended his own singular claim to fame and life.

When it was done, he was forgotten.

Given the unique magics of his situation, his own power, and some other factors, age and time aren't really a problem for him, physically.

When it was done and his party left him to live their own lives, when society moved on past the need for a hero, he made his living then instead through the act of selling his services as a mercenary to whoever needed him for whatever job.

It was amazing how fast the world started eating itself as soon as the great evil was destroyed. Missions to shut down worker strikes at iron mines. High-paying jobs to kidnap people who said the wrong thing to

the wrong person. Putting down societal rebellions that were fighting for the betterment of their standards—these came pouring in countlessly.

The world itself is more than happy enough to eat its own. They don't need a Demon King or Queen for that.

And so, he found a new purpose in this work. It's not easy to say if the abandonment changed him or if the roughness of the work did, but one of them did, and he became the man he is today.

And now . . .

His hand straddles the weapon.

These things . . . they've come along, and they're going to steal his purpose from him. Raw strength, potency, and a reputation are all he has as a man to keep him moving. Work is all he has to live for. It's all that he has.

There's no way back to the old world.

He's trapped here.

And so, all he has is the job.

But he's not going to have that when this is over. This trip here—this is his last one. When these weapons propagate from one nation to the next, it'll be over. Every person, no matter how weak they are, will be able to defend themselves from the monsters of the world, be they of the body of beasts or of men, and people like him will, once again, become forgotten.

He can't do it a second time.

Barlow stands there, staring at the ground, his fingers running over the metal on his hips as cranking mechanisms and churning clockwork cut through the dense air, laden with the horrific screams of an otherworldly beast.

He lifts his gaze, looking down the line of carriages.

~ [Swig] ~
Half Elf | ♀ | Indentured Servant {Logistician}
Location: The Northern Procession
Level: 20

Swig works, sweat dripping down their forehead to the dusty roads below, fine sands flying toward their squinted eyes as they lean down between the gaps between carriages, wrapping the bandoleer of alchemical flasks around them tightly, securing the construction in place with its own clasps.

The half elf lifts their gaze, looking to make sure the coast is clear, before picking up a series of bandoleers, slinging them over their shoulder, and running with a rifle in hand down to the next doorway in line, dropping everything to set up the next one on the next connection.

The carriages are all held together in a chain by a series of interlocking mechanisms which mimic a joint, allowing it to turn left and right together and even allowing for a slight difference in height between the carriages. It's a relatively simple but ingenious construction which has made the transportation of goods extremely efficient in its test runs. But this design is still rather experimental, the same as everything else on board.

Swig leans down, the spring-loaded sliding door on the back of the carriage pressing into their side as they lie on their stomach and lean down between the open-sided gap, slinging another bandoleer around the squeaking hinge and working to fasten it tightly, squinting their eyes to avoid the crumbling dust flying up toward their face as their hands work a foot above the stampede-marked ground. Swig purses their lips, focused, as they start to clasp together the bandoleer.

Something shimmers in the sand, unusually.

The half elf blinks, watching it for a second as they move, and then Swig's vision is disrupted as something grabs on their shirt, yanking them around.

"The hell are you doing?!" yells the soldier, standing over Swig and looking past them down at the hinge, where the belt is half looped around. Swig's eyes look at the man and then past him, toward their rifle leaning on the crates just next to the soldier. Following their gaze, the guard turns his head, looking at the weapon.

"Flying," replies Swig, pulling back a lanky leg and kicking as hard as possible into his gut. The man wheezes, stumbling back as Swig jumps to their feet, grabs the rifle, and aims it forward at his chest. The soldier grabs the barrel, pushing it up into the air, and the shot blasts through the roof of the carriage, wood splintering over them as he, much stronger, presses Swig back, the two of them fighting over the weapon. The long-arm gets stuck in the doorframe at an angle, separating the two of them as they both yank on it.

A second later, Swig flies back, the world spinning as a fist clocks them in the face. They stumble over the gap, barely grabbing the railing and

falling down on the other side as the guard pulls the rifle free with his other hand. Being a malnourished, lanky, overworked pseudoslave bodes poorly for one's ability to stand their ground in a fight against a trained professional soldier in good health.

He aims the rifle down. Swig's legs dangling freely over the ground between the gaps offer no way to jump back up in time, their hand instinctively covering their face. A second later, there's a crack that cuts the air like thunder.

Swig flinches, scrambling, their back moving no further as they press against something. They lift their gaze to the arm hanging above their head, a smoking gun in its grasp. The half elf looks back at the soldier, who has fallen down where he stood, the longarm jammed between the crates without the person who had been holding it.

The smells of sweat, ash, and liquor come to Swig as he lowers his hand, holstering the weapon and looking down. "What're you doing down there?" asks the man.

Swig sighs in relief, a hand on their chest. He saved the day again. "Looking for something, Mr. Barlow, sir," jokes the half elf, pulling their legs out of the gap and rolling back onto their stomach as he steps over them to the dead man.

"You always got an answer, huh?" he says. "Be careful," warns Barlow, picking up the rifle as Swig clasps the bandoleer lined with potion vials shut. Swig looks back up, rising to their feet as Barlow hands them the gun. "You might just find whatever it is."

The half elf grabs hold of the rifle with their hands while he still holds on to it, the two of them staring at one another, the roar of gunfire still filling the air from the back of the Procession, together with the groaning of the strained hinges and wood. Sweat, dirt, and blood stick to Swig's face as they stare at Barlow.

"Why're you doing this?" asks Swig. "We'll both be killed if we get caught, Mr. Barlow."

Barlow lets go of the rifle, staring at Swig as they clutch it tightly against their chest, their double-layered, blood-caked shirts flapping in the wind, pulled free from the scabbing of their mutilated back. "Lookin' for something," says the man.

Swig looks his way then slowly nods once, pulling the map they stole out from their pocketless clothes and handing it to him. "Think you'll find it?"

"No," replies Barlow, dryly, before taking the map and lighting up another cigarette. "Are you ready?"

"Only one left," replies Swig, pointing to the bandoleer behind him. Barlow looks at it and picks it up, tossing it to them across the small gap. The half elf catches it, slinging it over their shoulder. "What happens after this?" they ask. "When we escape?"

The Procession roars as it rolls through the endless sands, the two of them looking at one another. There's a glint of metal, and Swig catches the half-empty flask thrown their way, looking down at it for a moment before looking back at him.

"That's your problem," says Barlow, turning to walk down the rest of the carriages. "Meet you there, Swiggy Bird."

Swig looks down at the flask, opening it and looking at the wet metal opening for a moment before watching him walk away. The half elf lifts it, pressing it to their lips, and drinks from it.

There's no telling how all of this is going to work out for either of them.

But there's no coming back from this.

Swig winces, pulling themselves free from the flask as the burning filth snakes into their mouth and down their throat, making a slight hiss for a moment. The half elf caps the flask, admiring it for a moment, before pressing it into their belt the same way he wore it.

"I will," replies Swig, the man having already left, a hand weakly fumbling with the fabric over their heart. "I will," repeats Swig, running down the tight passageway to the back, the lanky, awkward creature moving with the longarm and an explosive load.

~ [Reverend Wicker Marvin] ~
Human | ♂ | Officer
Location: The Northern Procession
Level: 85

He stands there, a smug smile on his lips, as the world behind them crumbles to dust.

Monsters, beasts, and such things are nothing in the face of technology. Just like the bow fell to the crossbow, this new weapon will surpass the crossbow and, furthermore, advance society past the era of monsters.

A weapon in every hand, and an army with thousands of such things will ensure an entire continent is free of danger. Every goblin will be routed from its nest, every harpy shot from the sky, every minotaur broken through its heart, until all that is left is a pure land belonging to its rightful owners—humankind.

Once the beasts of fur and claw are dealt with, they can move on to the other beasts of the world—the elves, the Vildt, the orcs, and so on.

It's going to be a glorious new world. A world made as clean and whole as the gods intended for it to be, before such malignancies had the chance to fester on its jewel body.

"Cease fire," orders the officer, and dozens of guns fall silent immediately. The crank gun stops, as do the riflemen, both mounted and on the train, as they watch the destroyed monstrosity fade into the distance behind them.

"Sir," asks a man. "Should we finish the job?"

He and his soldiers are going to be cheered for as heroes when they arrive.

So it would be for the best if their appearance was appropriate.

"Mercur," says the officer, looking at the soldier. "I do believe I had a slip of judgment prior."

"Sir?"

"What is Mr. Barlow's official duty?" he asks.

"To protect us from the Demon King, sir," replies the rifleman.

Reverend Marvin nods, looking back behind them as they roll away through the dead lands. "Find Mr. Barlow again for me and be so kind as to . . . direct him toward the Demon King," orders Reverend Marvin. "Surely, it would be a waste on our part not to send the old hero his way. I'm sure the crusade and the Holy Church will be very grateful."

The riflemen look at him and then at one another, nodding before climbing back down into the Procession.

Reverend Marvin stares off behind them at the nothingness.

It is truly the end of an era.

Just like that, the Demon King was stopped in his tracks. Not by a great champion; not by magical heroes or token feats of greatness—no, just by ordinary, simple men. Humans.

The ground shimmers.

He looks down, staring at it for a time, not sure what he just saw.

But nothing happens, and he heads back inside, patting the crank gunman on the shoulder. "Keep a lookout."

"Sir," replies the soldier, facing back behind them as Reverend Marvin walks down the Procession to clean up a few last ugly details.

~ [Barlow] ~
Human | ♂ | Mercenary
Location: The Northern Procession
Level: 100

Barlow stands up behind the coachman atop the Procession, looking at the world around them.

He stares out over the landscape, which is destroyed and barren. There's nothing left of it; the destruction that happened here generations ago wiped out kilometers upon kilometers of land in a massive impact site, and the ground has never recovered from the heat of the blast that day. It's turned into a mixture of loose sand and solid slabs of glassy rock, causing the Procession to shake violently as it tumbles its way forward, the axles shaking wildly over the uneven terrain. Wind presses against his face, pressing beneath the rim of his hat, wicking away the beading sweat on his sunburned, dry forehead.

This is the spot.

"Mr. Barlow," says a voice from behind. He turns to look at the soldier. "The reverend wants to see you."

Barlow takes a drag from his cigarette, holding it between his teeth. "Don't care."

"It's urgent," explains the soldier.

Barlow grunts, not moving.

The soldier makes a bothered face and turns his head, whistling.

Several other men walk up the side stairwells, aiming their rifles at him. "Mr. Barlow," says the soldier. "I'm afraid you're going to have to get off the Procession," he orders, half a dozen longarms aimed his way. "Reverend's orders."

Barlow reaches up. The men all tighten their stances and aim immediately. He slows his hand, moving it to pull the cigarette out of his mouth, the poncho blowing in the wind toward them as he exhales.

"How old are you, kid?" asks Barlow, holding the cigarette for a second and then flicking it off the side of the carriage.

"Please cooperate, Mr. Barlow," says the soldier. "Out of respect for you being a hero, I'm giving you ten seconds to jump; otherwise, we will shoot," he warns, steadying his balance as the Procession shakes from left to right, moving over the jagged terrain.

"I was your age too, last time I was here," continues Barlow as the soldier counts down from ten. Barlow turns his back to them, staring out at the destroyed landscape and listening to the metal clinking and clanking all around them.

He lowers his head, holding onto the brim of his hat.

"That was a long time ago, Mr. Barlow. Please don't make me shoot you," says the man, having stopped at two.

"I'm not a hero," replies Barlow, looking over his shoulder. "That man died here," says Barlow. "I'm just what's left."

And then it happens.

~ [Swig] ~
Half Elf | ♀ | Indentured Servant {Logistician}
Location: The Northern Procession
Level: 20

Swig splutters for air, thick hands wrapped around the half elf's slim neck, their hands slapping against the face of the reverend, the officer, who hadn't even caught them doing anything suspicious. The last bandoleer was already in place, and Swig was on their way back to Barlow.

The man just started choking them out of nowhere.

There's a gunshot to the side.

Swig, spit pressing out of their mouth, looks as another indentured servant, an orc, falls over with a hole in his head.

"Reverend!" argues a voice from the side as Swig's hands, losing their strength, fail to pry him off. "I need that one!" argues the head researcher, pulling a hand off Swig's neck, the half elf not able to gasp for air as their throat somehow seems to stay tightly closed, even if released.

The officer shoves the researcher back and resumes choking Swig, the half elf's body burning and their vision going black as their legs kick and

spasm. "I'll get you a new one," he says. "One that isn't an abomination," finishes Reverend Wicker, staring into Swig's dying eyes as a weak, skinny hand slaps against the shaking wooden floor one last time.

The dull thud moves through the groaning, creaking floorboards—the tiny vibration adding to the mass of movement coming this way and that from the rough terrain, shaking the creaking joints of the many carriages of the Procession and shaking the small, metal vials wrapped around the majority of them in tightly bound leather wraps.

Swig's body spasms as all of the joints explode at once in a violent chain reaction, tearing the dozens of carriages of the Procession apart at once. People fly everywhere, some out into the desert, others onto one another, as the many carriages, no longer tethered to the lead carriage and the anqas pulling the entire construction along, all shoot off into uncontrolled crashes in the wildlands to the sides, entire segments crashing against rocks, stones, and glassy debris of the violence of a bygone era.

~ [Barlow] ~
Human | ♂ | Mercenary
Location: The Northern Procession
Level: 100

Six shots ring out in the air. Six men, shocked by the explosion behind them, fall off the sides of the lead carriage, clenching their guts as they land in the desert.

Barlow spins the cylinder on his weapon, holstering it before turning around and sitting down next to the coachman, the old man turning to look his way.

"Real shame that the Demon King got the caravan," says Barlow, leaning back, kicking his feet up, and lowering the brim of his hat. "All that fancy technology, lost to the sand."

The coachman quietly whips the reins of the anqas to make them go faster. What's left of the Procession, which is exactly just the front carriage, the two men, and nothing else, shoots off toward the distant horizon in which there is no sunset and no such thing as a good man. He looks back for a moment before lowering his gaze again, adjusting the brim of the hat anew.

But there is a man who will live now longer in a world that hasn't outgrown him.

~ [Swig] ~
Half Elf | ♂ | Indentured Servant {Logistician}
Location: The Northern Procession
Level: 20

The world spins. Swig flops to the side, the carriage finally coming to an end, broken wood and jagged splinters flying everywhere as it strikes against a rock. Through some happenstance of luck, maybe, Swig flies.

The half elf's dazed, confused form tumbles gracelessly through the air—a bird with no feathers—as they come crashing down into the sands, tumbling over stones and rocks. Swig's ears are filled with roaring as they desperately pant and claw into the sand, into which their fingers sink. They crawl away, slowly looking around as they try to orient themselves in the chaos.

What happened?

Swig winces, gritting their teeth and flopping down in pain, wheezing for air as they try to breathe through the crushed throat, inhaling in mouthfuls of fine, upturned desert sand. The half elf tries to get up, managing only a few movements before screaming and falling back down, flopping into the sand and rolling around, looking at the massive splinter of wood jutting straight through their left calf.

The half elf pants for air, trying to orient themselves to the direction of life as they crawl back away from the debris, their back pressing against a rock as they stare out at the desert.

The Procession lies everywhere. Carriages, broken wood, crates, shelving, and bodies lie everywhere in the sand, together with gnarled, twisted metal.

The vials exploded.

Why did they explode?

Mr. Barlow said they wouldn't explode until later, until they got further away, until . . . until . . .

Swig winces, spit and blood leaving their mouth, as they watch something stir in the shadows. People are still alive after the crash—soldiers, the reverend maybe. Swig's unsure.

The rifle is still strapped to their chest, having been dragged along through the sand. Swig reaches down, pulling it up and clutching it against their torso as their raspy breathing tries to catch up with their body and panic.

Someone moves in the smoke.

Swig screams and shoots, a crack breaking the air as the shot hits a man whom Swig can't even identify, only able to watch his silhouette fall down into the sand from behind the growing smoke of fires.

The half elf vomits, leaning over to the side.

Why did it explode?

Something moves.

Swig screams and shoots again, hitting another body and causing it to fall down.

Mr. Barlow said it wouldn't.

Something moves.

Gunfire breaks out in the air like the striking of a hammer against a resistant nail, screaming out over and over to overpower Swig's crying and the yelling of distant voices until there's nothing left but a hollow clicking and the quiet sobbing of a defeated person aiming the gun at a man who comes limping out of the dust.

The reverend.

He lied.

He *lied*. That bastard.

Swig cries, aiming the rifle at the man's heart as he approaches; nothing happens as often as they pull the trigger, apart from a soft ticking sound like that of a dead clock. Barlow lied. He used them. It was a trick. It was all a bunch of SHIT!

Swig throws the rifle at him, missing, and then reaches down to grab the flask from their hip, hurtling it at him too.

It strikes the reverend on the chest and falls down limply to the sand beside their own leg. He walks over it, pulling out a small pistol from his inner shirt and pointing it at Swig's head.

The world shakes, everything going black as a great quake causes him to fall over, his legs sinking into the sand as the Procession is swallowed by a shimmering lake of sand behind them, dozens of men screaming and clawing into the loose silt as they try to escape the sinkhole, out of which then, a second later, come out ten long, black,

impossibly sharp legs which press into the sand on all sides of the trapdoor.

Then come ten more.

And then ten more.

Soon, there are many more, crawling and skittering out of the shimmering sand where it had been all along, the beast with ten thousand legs, the demon that had pursued them, having not been dead at all.

The ground sinks.

Gunfire rings out, the reverend screaming and shooting as he crawls away, the down-sloping sand pulling him and all of the others toward it, together with the wreckage. Swig throws the rifle behind the rock their back is against, holding on to the strap and praying the rock doesn't start moving. A hand grabs Swig's leg, the officer gripping onto their boot and pulling on Swig's hurt leg.

The half elf screams too, or perhaps simply continues screaming, kicking him in the face over and over again, his nose breaking flat, his teeth breaking inward, until eventually, his grip slips and he slides away, trying to crawl and claw against the angle and the riptide sand, but being unable to as he is swallowed by a wall of spindly legs.

Even if they had gotten free; even if this had worked . . . what would have been the point?

In a world this terrible, this horrible, this cruel . . . what would there have been to do anyway?

There's no escape.

It doesn't matter what anyone does or is.

There's no escape from the nightmare that life is.

Swig grabs the small pistol that had fallen, shooting it at the monster until it clicks empty before throwing it as a final act of defiance as a dozen-some legs begin to skitter toward them, obscuring a flock of birds which fly in the sky and obscure the starlight above them all.

There's no such thing as freedom, and there's no such thing as escape, when the world itself is the cage.

Swiggy Bird grabs the dropped flask, arcing their arm back to throw it a second time, now at the monster slowly approaching, leg after leg.

A hand grabs Swig's wrist.

The half elf's eyes go wide, and they turn their head, looking up at Barlow.

"That how you treat a gift?"

Swig's lips tremble as they cry, yelling at him, unable to look at him in the face because of their rage. "WHAT ARE YOU DOING HERE?!" screams the half elf.

"Lookin' for something," replies Barlow, breaking the strap of the rifle, the now useless gun dropping to the sand as two arms pick up Swig, haphazardly tossing them sideways over the single anqa he had ridden back on.

"Mr. Barlow!" yells Swig, looking back at him.

Barlow hits the anqa, barking a command, and the animal shoots off with Swig laid over it. Swig screams as the anqa sprints through the desert in pursuit of the rest of the long since distant carriage, the half elf looking as the single man stands alone in the growing distance between them, facing the great beast that is a hundred times his size, the wind of the desert howling in rage, the fine sands growing into a storm, his poncho blowing in the gale, his hat flying free and off into the wilderness, a single glow of orange light leaving his lips as he draws for his hip.

And there, where there was night only a second before, a new sunset arises for a brief few seconds, together with what sounds like the chiming of a bell which marks the presence of the abilities of a true hero of the world, even an old one, both of which overpower Swig's cries as the dust swallows everything whole while two birds, one with feathers, break off and escape, in the search for such an obscure thing as freedom.

And before the hour is over, the sun sets, and the bell stops ringing.

The Northern Procession has been destroyed. The experimental weapons that could have posed a great threat to the Demon King and to the world as a whole are taken by the sands of the desert, together with the minds who made them, prolonging the era of sword and magic by generations, if not longer still than that.

And as far as the public is concerned, there were no survivors of the event.

But who is really to say?

It's impossible to perfectly follow the strange dance that life is.

A WEIRD REALITY

~ [Revir] ~
Half Elf | ♀ | Priestess
Rank: SSS
Location: The Demon King's Castle, Floor ???
Level: 100

 S omething feels off.

In the midst of a malevolent, undulating sea of darkness, the Demon King's horrific castle looms, its twisted spires piercing the underworld like a thousand obsidian daggers forged in the infernal fires of some monstrous, otherworldly pit. It is here that the very normal and absolutely resolute priestess Revir, an ethereal vision of grace and divine power, accompanies the ragged remnants of the once vaunted crusade, a motley assortment of warriors, rogues, and sorcerers, their hearts steeled against the insidious tendrils of fear that grasp at them, threatening to engulf their very souls.

Or something.

As the brave band of adventurers breaches the latest threshold of this unholy lair, pressing down into a new floor after leaving behind the fresh horrors of the last, a new room awaits them, its walls constructed of mirrored glass of such eerie perfection that the reflections adorning its surface threaten to draw them into a dizzying, inescapable labyrinth of their own visages. Here, amidst the shattered fragments of their own myriad faces, hundreds of humans, orcs, elves, and dwarves find themselves ensnared in a waltz of shadows and reflections, the air thick with trepidation as if the very atmosphere itself were a living, malignant entity poised to strike. And honestly, at this point, it might be fair to assume that it is.

If nothing else, the Demon King's castle has shown that nothing is to be trusted. Not the stones, not the wood, not the walls, and not the floor. Nothing.

In the center of this chamber, the priestess Revir stands, her matted hair cascading like a midnight waterfall over her tired shoulders, the flickering torchlight casting a halo of gold around her muddied, broken features covered in filth, if only to mockingly illuminate them even more. Her luminous eyes survey the room, penetrating the haze of unease, seeking to pierce the veil of darkness that threatens to suffocate her and her comrades. The silken folds of her ivory robes, embroidered with the intricate sigils of her sacred order, ripple gently as if stirred by an unseen breeze, the hem dancing just above the cold, glassy floor.

In this hall of mirrors, where the boundary between reality and illusion blurs and wanes, the priestess feels the weight of the darkness pressing upon her, a palpable force that seeks to infiltrate her very being and corrupt the purity of her essence. With a resolute breath, she raises her alabaster arms heavenward, her slender fingers outstretched, as if beseeching the gods themselves for their divine intervention. Her voice, clear and melodious, resonates throughout the chamber, its haunting, lilting cadence echoing through the infinite corridors of reflection, the incantations she utters hoping to weave a tapestry of light and hope amidst the suffocating gloom.

But nothing happens.

One, Revir's thoughts, as one can see, verge toward the deeply dramatic. Two, for some reason, her holy magic just isn't working anymore. As Revir's prayer nonetheless reaches a crescendo, the power of her faith ignites within her, if not within anyone else, and . . . nothing happens.

The crusaders, their courage not exactly renewed by the priestess's display of divine grace, simply keep on walking as she stands there in the middle of the room, their eyes alight with the usual determination and fervor, their weapons raised warily in defiance of the darkness that seeks to consume them—even if no monsters have appeared yet.

Revir sighs, clutching her hands together before her chest, watching them all walk. A few of them give her a strange look as they keep moving. She can only assume they too are plagued by some ill from the Demon King's castle and its foul works.

In this hall of mirrors, where the lines between truth and deception are as fluid as the shifting sands of time, the priestess Revir shrugs and marches on with her fellow crusaders, their souls bound together by a shared purpose which surely transcends the strange shadows, even as the malevolent gaze of the Demon King, from his throne of bones and despair, falls upon them, what can only be his laughter acting as a chilling dirge that reverberates through the twisted corridors toward her heart.

"Hey, you good?" asks a man from the side, looking at her questioningly.

Revir nods. "I am well; thank you, Brother," replies the priestess.

A harrowing scream shatters the oppressive silence that had settled upon the chamber. It is the tortured cry of a man ensnared in the clutches of some unspeakable terror, his voice twisted and distorted as if the very sound itself were being ripped apart by unseen claws, which is likely apt, given that the same thing is happening to his body.

Details.

The crusaders whirl about, their eyes wide with shock and horror as they bear witness to a scene that defies comprehension, at least for any-one who hasn't been here for the last few days: a man, his face contorted in an expression of sheer, unadulterated agony, is being dragged, kicking and flailing, into the cold embrace of one of the mirrored walls. It is as if the very surface of the glass has come alive, its silvery tendrils coiling around the man's limbs like serpentine vipers, their grip unyielding, their intent malevolent and insidious.

Revir, her heart pounding like the frenzied beat of a war drum within her breast, leaps into action, her lithe form propelled forward by the des-perate urgency of the moment. With a fluid grace that belies the tempest of fear and adrenaline surging through her veins, she extends her hand toward the doomed man, her fingers outstretched, her voice raised in a fervent incantation, the words spilling forth like a torrent of divine power, seeking to banish the darkness and wrench the man from the clutches of the mirror's deadly embrace.

But nothing happens.

Something grabs her and shoves her out of the way—another priestess of the crusade. Revir falls down, sliding over the slick glass, and looks at the stranger who is casting a spell in her place—one that works.

The other priestess's words resonate within the chamber, a coruscat-ing wave of energy rippling forth from her outstretched hand washing

over the mirrored walls like a radiant tide, its lambent glow casting a kaleidoscope of shimmering reflections across the room that carries from one mirrored surface to the next. For a fleeting moment, the glassy tendrils seem to waver, their grip on the man faltering as if the very fabric of their existence were being torn asunder by the force of what looks like divine intervention.

Alas, it is not enough.

The tendrils, their resolve redoubled by some inscrutable, malevolent will—or perhaps simply offended—tighten their grip on the man, dragging him inexorably toward the mirrored abyss, tearing him in half. Revir watches in helpless despair as the man is swallowed whole by the glassy wall, his final, guttural scream echoing through the chamber until it's muffled as he vanishes, as if pulled beneath a body of water.

Blood floats to the top of the mirror and then runs down its side, dripping through from the other side as if it were fabric.

"Oh . . ." says Revir. "Foobar," mutters the priestess, rising to her feet. "Sister, what was that?" she asks.

The other priestess turns her head, looking at her. "Get it together!" snaps the woman before rolling her eyes and walking off, leaving Revir standing there, somewhat bothered. She supposes it's only right for them to be annoyed by her. What good is a priestess who can't use any magic down in the Demon King's castle?

In the aftermath of this horrifying spectacle, the crusaders march in a tighter formation now, their metal boots clinking over the glassy floors, their eyes wide, and their breaths ragged. The priestess Revir, her shoulders heaving with the weight of her grief and the burden of her responsibility to be useful in any fashion at all, raises her head, her eyes ablaze with a fierce, unwavering determination. If nothing else, she can keep a strong spirit as they march to the throne of the wretched Demon King himself, where they will confront the monstrous architect of the world's suffering and bring his reign of terror to a final, cataclysmic end.

Probably.

Revir walks on, rubbing her face. Maybe she's just out of soul points. Maybe that's why her magic isn't working? It's been a long trek so far; it wouldn't be surprising. But it's not like she's been able to get any good sleep here, for obvious reasons. Plus, she's hungry and really thirsty, but they're not allowed to eat or drink inside of the castle for some reason.

The air within the chamber of mirrored glass suddenly grows thick, the atmosphere charging with a palpable malevolence that seems to seep into the very marrow of the priestess's bones, filling her with a disquietingly familiar sense of impending doom. The whispered echoes of the lost man's final anguished cries still linger in her ears.

Without further warning than that, the mirrored walls begin to shudder and tremble, the glassy surface undulating and writhing like the surface of a storm-tossed sea. The crusaders, their eyes wide with terror and disbelief, watch as the reflections adorning the walls take on a life of their own, their forms twisting and contorting, their faces warped into grotesque parodies of their true counterparts.

It is as if the very essence of the Demon King's malevolence has seeped into the glass, imbuing it with a monstrous, insatiable hunger for the lifeblood of those who dare to trespass within his unhallowed domain. With a sound like the splintering of a thousand panes of glass, the mirror images burst forth from their planes of existence, their claws outstretched and their eyes burning with a fathomless, unholy rage. The chamber erupts into a cacophony of screams and the clash of steel as the crusaders desperately attempt to fend off the relentless onslaught of their twisted doppelgängers.

"FORMATION!" screams a voice at the front of the line as people begin to try to form up, sometimes confusing their contemporaries with their nearly perfect copies. Although, the giant claws and fangs are sort of a giveaway.

The priestess Revir, her heart hammering within her chest like a thunderclap, raises her arms in supplication, her voice rising in a desperate plea to the divine powers that guide her to finally let her cast a useful spell so she can help everyone. The words of her prayer, in her mind's eye, weave a shimmering tapestry of light, the radiant glow suffusing the room, a beacon of hope amidst the relentless tide of darkness that threatens to engulf them all.

In reality, however, nothing happens. She's just standing there with her hands above her head, muttering to herself as people around her scream and fight to the death.

As the battle rages on, the air is thick with the coppery tang of blood and the stench of fear, and the floor is slick with the viscera of the fallen. The screams of the dying and the howls of the mirror-born monstrosities

meld together into a single, discordant symphony of pain and horror, a testament to the unspeakable cruelty of the Demon King and the depths of his depravity as men are torn into the mirrors and as beasts are torn from them.

Amidst the chaos and carnage, the priestess Revir, her robes spattered with the lifeblood of her comrades, stands perfectly still, a very useful, purely metaphorical beacon of light and hope, her unwavering faith a bulwark against the tide of darkness that threatens to engulf them all. With every incantation and every prayer, she battles to turn the tide of the conflict, her every breath a testament to her indomitable spirit and her undying commitment to the cause of righteousness.

It's not like she's actually fighting, since she has no magic. But she's sure that her prayers are very useful. The gods are listening to her, right? So it makes sense that even if she can't fight, she can make herself useful by praying during the fight!

It's a perfect system.

Revir beams with pride, watching as the last of the mirror-born abominations is vanquished, the chamber of mirrored glass falling silent once more, the shattered remnants of the once pristine walls littering the gore-streaked floor like shattered dreams. The priestess Revir, her strength all but spent from her very zealous praying, gazes upon the scene with tear-filled eyes, her heart heavy with the weight of the sacrifices made in the name of their quest.

Soldiers lie, screaming and clutching their eviscerated guts and lost limbs, all over the room, covered in razor-sharp glass, on which many more are impaled.

She did great.

"Hey," says a voice from the side. She turns, looking at the man. He nods his head. "Why don't you stay in the back, huh?" he asks.

Revir smiles, shaking her head. "Don't worry, Brother," she replies. "I'm here for you all," finishes the priestess eagerly, not sure why he rolls his eyes and walks off.

People are kind of grouchy. It's not that she doesn't get it, but it does seem a little unnecessary.

"There's no need to have an attitude!" she calls after him, cupping her hand by her mouth.

Some people are so ungrateful.

With a quiet determination that belies the fresh doubt that threatens to consume her, Revir decides to lead the remnants of the crusade onward, deeper into the heart of darkness, their eyes fixed upon the promise of retribution that awaits them at the end of their harrowing journey. For some reason, nobody stops her from marching out of formation, let alone near the front of the line. But that's fine. Maybe they're all just being supportive of her efforts.

She appreciates that.

The Demon King must pay for the suffering he has wrought upon their world, and it is by their hands, bloodied and battered though they may be, that his reign of terror shall be brought to an end—a final, cataclysmic conclusion that will see the dawn of a new age, free from the shadow of his malevolent tyranny.

Through the twisted corridors of the Demon King's horrific castle, the weary band of crusaders presses onward, their footsteps echoing like the forlorn cries of lost souls. Each step takes them deeper into the heart of darkness, the air growing hotter and more oppressive, as if the very walls themselves sought to smother them beneath the weight of broiling despair. As they navigate the mazelike passages, the specter of loss haunts their every step, the memory of their fallen comrades a constant reminder of the price they have paid to stand against the Demon King. And yet, even in the face of such overwhelming sorrow, the flame of hope refuses to be extinguished, its flickering light casting away the shadows of doubt and fear that threaten to engulf them.

Revir stares smugly at the darkness.

And then, at long last, they stand before the throne room of the Demon King, the massive doors etched with symbols of torment and suffering, a grim testament to the horrors that lie within. With a deep, steadying breath, the priestess Revir places her trembling hand upon the cold iron door, her heart pounding within her chest like the beat of a war drum. As one, the crusaders steel themselves for the final confrontation, their eyes alight with the fire of determination, their souls bound by a shared purpose that transcends the ravages of time and the specter of death.

With a thunderous roar, the doors are flung wide, revealing a chamber bathed in darkness, its air thick with the stench of decay and the palpable aura of malevolence that emanates from the monstrous figure that sits upon a throne of bones and despair. The Demon King, his form wreathed

in shadow, gazes upon the ragged band of crusaders with eyes that burn like the embers of a dying fire, a cruel, mocking smile playing upon his twisted, inhuman visage.

"So you've finally made it," says the beast from his throne.

The priestess Revir, her eyes locked upon the monstrous visage of the Demon King, raises her arms in a final invocation, her voice resounding with the full force of her divine power, a clarion call that echoes through the chamber like the trumpets of judgment. As her words weave a—metaphorical—tapestry of light, the crusaders rally past her, their weapons raised, their hearts filled with the unshakable resolve to bring an end to the Demon King's reign of terror.

As the battle unfolds, the very fabric of reality seems to tremble under the weight of the conflict, with the forces of light and darkness locked in their latest skirmish in their ever-eternal struggle which threatens to rend the world asunder. However, amidst the chaos and the carnage, the priestess Revir stands as a beacon of hope, her unwavering faith a bulwark against the tide of darkness that threatens to engulf them all.

She stands there, holding her hands in the air, as a man flies past her, crashing against the wall and flattening into a paste. Revir winces, closing the one half-squinted eye she had open, and then continues praying as the sounds of metal and bones strike out all around her senses.

And then it's done.

The dust settles and the shadows recede; the Demon King is vanquished, his twisted form cast down upon the cold, unforgiving stone of his once impenetrable fortress. The ground starts to shake. The Demon King's castle trembles as it begins to fail, his foul demons running in panic as their magic wanes and they are hunted down.

The priestess Revir, her robes stained with the blood of her enemies—mostly because of backsplash—raises her eyes to the heavens sealed by the stones above their heads, her heart filled with a mingled sense of triumph and sorrow, knowing that the price of their victory has been steep and the road to redemption long and fraught with peril.

People cheer all around the room.

With the Demon King defeated, the crusaders must return to a world forever changed by their sacrifice, their names etched into the annals of history as champions of light and defenders of the innocent. And though the darkness may rise again, one thing remains certain: the goodness of

life shall never falter, for there will always be those who stand against the encroaching malignancy, their hearts burning with the indomitable spirit of hope as they stand strong against the ever-returning darkness that plagues this good world.

Something feels off.

Revir's smile drops from her blank face as she stands there, staring vacantly for a while, before suddenly, a disorienting sensation washes over her and her fellow crusaders. With a sickening lurch, the illusion that had ensnared them shatters like a pane of glass, revealing the cold, cruel truth: they had never left the chamber of mirrored walls.

"BLUEBERRIES!" yells the priestess, hitting her fists against the glass as she looks around the room they have been teleported back to, or maybe, more aptly, the one they had never left.

Everything that just happened was an illusion, a mind game.

She narrows her eyes, staring around the room as the rest of the crusade comes to the same realization. They've been played. This was just another trick of the castle.

Of course, it wouldn't be that easy.

This is another attempt to break them down and weaken their spirit. But it's not going to work.

The priestess Revir, her breaths ragged and her heart heavy with the bitter sting of betrayal, gazes upon the faces of her comrades, their eyes wide with shock and disbelief as they realize the extent of the Demon King's malevolent deception. The realization dawns upon them too that their battle, their triumph, and their sacrifices were all but an elaborate ruse, a cruel game designed to break their spirits and shatter their resolve.

Though the weight of this revelation threatens to crush them beneath its oppressive burden, the priestess Revir refuses to succumb to the manufactured despair seeking to consume her. With a steely determination that belies the tempest of fear and doubt that rages within her, she raises her head, her violet eyes ablaze with the fire of defiance.

"Let's not worry about it!" she declares, her voice resolute and unwavering as it echoes across the glassy room they're all still trapped in, standing in puddles of blood and gore from their friends' bodies. "The darkness cannot prevail so long as the light of our faith burns brightly!" she says, clasping her hands together and holding them over her heart.

People look her way before turning away, many of them mumbling and muttering. She's not really sure what their problem is, honestly. People have gotten so sour lately. If only they could find another safe room, like the one just after floor ten, so that everyone could rest in peace. But that's a long way back from down here, where they are now.

The crusade returns to its formation, somewhat more disorganized than a moment ago.

Revir can nonetheless only imagine that everyone's hearts are filled with a renewed sense of hope and determination after her prior statement.

United in their shared purpose of getting the hell out of here one way or another, the ragged band of crusaders presses onward, their eyes fixed upon the promise of redemption that lies just beyond the veil of deception. Though the shadows may gather, and the darkness may threaten to engulf them, they know they are not alone, for they carry within them the light of hope and the indomitable spirit of their shared resolve—just like Revir does. Together, they will face the Demon King and his legions of darkness, and they will stand as champions of the light, their hearts bound together by the unbreakable bonds of faith and camaraderie!

What else is there to do? It's almost a romantic thought, isn't it? All of this doom and gloom really offers a person with a thinking pattern like her a great opportunity to really flex her mental muscles. People always told her she was dramatic, but what's wrong with a little drama?

Their footsteps echo like the hollow beats of a funeral march as they navigate the treacherous confines of the room, their eyes darting between the myriad reflections surrounding them, searching for any hint of an escape as they move through it again a second time.

And yet, despite their best efforts, the chamber seems to defy their attempts to leave, its mirrored walls shifting and undulating with a malevolent intelligence that confounds their every move. It is as if the room itself were alive—its thirst for their suffering insatiable; its hunger for their despair unquenchable—until they once again find a large, grand door at the end of a way.

As they approach the threshold of the chamber, the air is thick with a palpable sense of dread and foreboding, and the illusion begins anew. The mirrored walls tremble and shudder, their glassy surface coming to life as the twisted reflections of the crusaders burst forth once more, their claws outstretched, their eyes filled with a fathomless, unholy rage as the trap

springs a second time, with the catch that those who died the first time are still very much very, *very* dead.

That's the game the room is playing; it's grinding them down not only in body but in spirit at the same time.

With a sinking feeling of despair, the priestess Revir and her fellow crusaders realize that they are trapped within an endless cycle unless they find the real way out, the Demon King's malevolent laughter once again echoing through the chamber like the mocking chimes of a twisted bell. The room seems to revel in their suffering, its mirrored walls reflecting the agony and anguish that fill their hearts, a cruel testament to the depths of the Demon King's depravity.

And yet, even as they face the relentless onslaught of their twisted doppelgängers, the priestess Revir refuses to succumb to the despair that threatens to engulf her. With a fierce determination belying the tempest of fear and doubt that rages within her, she stands there in the middle of the room and prays very loudly, not casting a single spell—because her magic isn't working.

Funnily enough, no doppelgänger ever comes to claim her.

Weird.

The battle rages on, and the crusaders continue their desperate struggle against the mirror-born abominations.

From the depths of the mirrored walls, disembodied whispers begin to slither forth, their susurrant hisses echoing through the room like the rustling of dead leaves in a desolate graveyard. The voices, insidious and malignant, speak of terrifying truths that burrow into the minds of the crusaders like ravenous maggots, gnawing at the fragile strands of their resolve, and threatening to unravel the very fabric of their sanity.

Revir clutches at her head, listening to the words flowing into her like babbling water, their sinister whispers a constant, insistent refrain that threatens to drown out the light of her faith. She prays louder, clenching her eyes and holding her head; the chilling revelations they speak of shake her to the very core, forcing her to confront the darkest corners of her own soul—the most horrifying truths that she had sought to keep hidden, even from herself.

She might be kind of useless.

Revir falls down to the ground, holding her head, and catches sight of her own reflection in one of the mirrored walls, the image staring back at

her with an unblinking, predatory intensity that sends a shiver of primal terror down her spine. The reflection, a twisted doppelganger of herself, seems to be watching her every move, its unblinking gaze a silent, malevolent accusation that pierces her heart like a dagger of ice.

With a gut-wrenching scream, Revir collapses to her knees, her anguished wails echoing through the chamber like the mournful cries of a lost and tortured soul. Her eyes, once filled with the light of hope and determination, are now hollow and haunted, the windows to a spirit shattered by the cruel whims of fate and the unfathomable depths of the Demon King's depravity. Tears streaming down her face, Revir raises her gaze to the one remaining, unbroken mirror, her eyes locking with those of her own reflection.

The reflection, its expression impassive and cold, seems to mock her anguish, a chilling reminder of the terrible secrets she has been forced to confront. With a ragged, desperate voice, Revir screams at her reflection, her words a torrent of rage and despair that reverberates through the chamber like the howls of a damned soul. The mirror remains silent, its empty stare offering no comfort or solace as it bears witness to her torment.

"Why?!" she shrieks, her voice cracking under the strain of her grief.

The chamber echoes with her screams. The reflection, its unblinking gaze never wavering, offers no answers, no reprieve from the terrible burden she must bear.

In the suffocating silence that follows, Revir's sobs gradually subside, together with the sounds of battle and death.

The sound of broken glass crunching beneath Revir's feet fills the air as she rises back up to her feet and looks around herself. The shattered remnants of the once pristine mirrors reflect her tortured visage from countless angles.

As she moves forward, her footfalls echoing through the oppressive silence, Revir casts her gaze around the chamber, her heart seizing with a sudden, gut-wrenching realization: she is utterly, irrevocably alone. The rest of the crusade, the brave souls who had fought alongside her, who had shared in her struggles and her triumphs, have vanished without a trace, leaving her to face the darkness that lies ahead with no one by her side.

A creeping sense of dread begins to envelop the useless priestess Revir, its icy tendrils snaking their way through her mind, sapping her of her

strength and her resolve. The shadows around her seem to grow darker and more menacing, their inky depths teeming with the nameless horrors that lurk just beyond the edge of her perception.

She's the last one left.

She's . . . she's all that there is.

What is she supposed to do? She's not enough. She can't do anything. She's nothing alone.

The priestess stares at her broken reflection, its fathomless gaze filled with the terrible knowledge of what awaits her. The oppressive weight of her isolation bears down upon her, crushing her beneath its suffocating embrace, her spirit buckling beneath the enormity of the task that lies before her.

Her breaths come in ragged gasps, the air heavy and stale as if the very atmosphere of the chamber were conspiring to choke the life from her. The whispers of the damned—the tormented souls who had succumbed to the darkness—seem to echo around her, their voices a cacophony of misery and despair that claws at the tattered remnants of her sanity. And yet, even as the shadows close in, Revir cannot escape the terrible truth that gnaws at the edges of her consciousness, a truth that threatens to consume her whole: she is alone, abandoned by her comrades, her faith, and perhaps even her gods, left to face the darkness and the horrors that await her with nothing but the broken shards of her own reflection for company.

With faltering footsteps, Revir makes her way toward the door that had led to the Demon King's throne room in the last illusion, the broken glass that litters the floor crunching beneath her feet like the many ground bones of the fallen. Her heart pounds with a terrible, suffocating dread, each beat a harbinger of the horrors that await her beyond the door.

Her hand trembles as she reaches for the door, the cold metal of the handle biting into her flesh like sharp teeth. With a ragged breath, she pushes the door open, the hinges groaning in protest as though they, too, sought to warn her of the unspeakable terror that lies within.

As the door swings open, Revir's breath catches in her throat, her eyes widening with a mixture of horror and disbelief at the sight that greets her.

There, seated upon the Demon King's throne, is her own reflection, her missing doppelgänger who had never shown up in any of the fights, her face a twisted mirror of her own torment and despair.

The figure on the throne wears a cruel, mocking smile, its eyes gleaming with a malevolent intelligence that chills Revir to her very core.

As she stares into the eyes of her own twisted reflection, Revir feels her sanity begin to fray, the terrible realization that she has been cast into a nightmare from which there may be no escape clawing at the edges of her consciousness. The whispers of the damned grow louder, their voices a cacophony of suffering that fills her head like a swarm of ravenous insects, each one gnawing at the fragile strands of her resolve. Her knees buckle, and she collapses to the cold stone floor, her breaths coming in ragged, uneven gasps. The doppelgänger on the throne watches her with a cold, unblinking gaze, its smile a cruel parody of her own anguish, as if to mock her for daring to believe that she could . . . well, do anything.

She lies there, broken and alone, the cruel laughter of her dark reflection echoing through the chamber like the peals of a twisted bell. She knows the horrors that await her are far greater, far more terrible than anything she could have ever imagined.

The darkness, it seems, has finally claimed her.

Sharp, clacking footsteps move her way as the beast walks over from the throne—the Demon King, for some inexplicable reason, wearing adventuring boots with a platform heel. She lifts her gaze and looks up as sharp fingers grab the bottom of her head, lifting it.

"You're not real," says Revir, wanting to crawl back but being unable to as she stares into the cold eyes of the thing before her.

Long blue strands of hair fall down past the doppelgänger's face as they look at her from up close, their pupils fractured and spiderwebbed like shattered glass. "Well, one of us isn't," it replies.

"Don't send me back," begs Revir, closing her eyes in fear.

"Why not?" whispers the Demon King, their lips next to her ear.

Revir cries, not wanting to go back again. Not to the mirror room, but back. Back there. Back to where she really is.

"I'm scared," admits Revir. "Don't make me go back alone," pleads the useless priestess who has no holy magic at all because, well, she isn't a priestess, and she doesn't have access to real holy magic to begin with. "I don't want to be alone again."

"Ah . . ." whispers something softly into her ear, a tongue feeling like it's pressing itself in through it and moving toward her brain like a worm. "Well . . ." says the voice. "That's. Too. Bad." The voice changes from that

of a very familiar woman to that of a man she is repulsed by—her father.
"*Ruhr.*"

Ruhr opens her eyes, staring up at the ceiling. Something feels off.

A strand of her own wet hair, soaked from sweat, clings to the inside of her ear as she shoots upright, looking around the room. She immediately feels down next to her for Zacarias.

But he isn't there.

Ruhr stares at the empty spot next to her for a moment before looking back out at the crusade's camp they've set up to heal the wounded and rest for a few hours.

The river sorceress pulls in her legs, pressing the blanket against herself as she wraps her arms around them, staring down at the floor between her knees.

That's right.

Zacarias is dead.

She was dreaming and got to forget for a while.

Ruhr flops over sideways, staring vacantly into the distant crowd, who mostly ignore her, as they have been doing. She seems to have lost her authority, probably because she's spent the hours babbling in derangement. Her arm stretches itself out, a finger tracing over the dusty floor to rewrite the name *Revir* mirrored backward.

River.

CHAPTER 16

MAGGOT UGLY

~ [Guezel Aschk] ~
Human | ♀ | Priestess
Location: The Demon King's Castle, Floor ???
Level: 73

They walk past a few puddles reflecting the visages of the passersby back toward them. Strands of silk line the walls here and there.

Guezel turns her head, looking at the otherwise blank wall to her left. Beautiful things matter more than ugly things.

It's an undeniable truth of the world. People value beautiful clothes more than ugly ones—this is why expensive brands and designers exist. It's not about the robustness of their designs; it's about the look of them and the social story they tell about the person wearing said pieces. People value beautiful stones more than ugly ones; this is why the concept of gemstones as a rare, luxury good exists, despite their limited usages in practical matters. People value beautiful food more than ugly, poorly plated food, even if the nutritional content is one and the same in both dishes—the eyes and mouth eat together. People value beautiful art more than ugly art; this is why children's valueless scribbles do not find themselves in the grand art galleries next to the works of the old masters, as their creations are, strictly speaking of exterior matters, bad.

And people value beautiful people more than they do ugly people.

Sure, there are many voices who would decry this statement if it were to be made in public, wildly aghast that anyone could ever insinuate such a terrible thing, that anyone could make a statement only a socially unfit, soulless monster would make. "Of course everyone matters as much as anyone else." "Of course they would never think that someone who is ugly

is inherently less valuable than someone who is undeniably beautiful." But the truth is, they do.

We know this because beautiful people are treated more kindly, are given more chances upon failure, and more social doors and opportunities are held open to them than their less attractive counterparts. And while beauty is, of course, dependent on a specific time and place within a society, the desired standards of that beauty matter deeply there within. Even if the standards of a city to the west vary from a city to the east, a person who is beautiful within said domain of their living will have an easier, more desirable life on average than someone who isn't.

That's just what it is.

There's no need for anyone to play these games of pretending it isn't the case so they can be seen as virtuous. Everyone knows, but everyone pretends they don't. Everyone acts like they're so great.

But those same people still all called *her* ugly back in school for all of her life.

That's what she hates the most about it all. Back then, everyone tore her apart because she looked different, and now that they're older, everyone is pretending like they're such moral saints, even if they still look at her sideways, if they avoid facing her or being seen talking to her too much. Even if she's always somehow the person who walks in the back of a group of three, trailing after the other two, who seem more than content to talk with one another and to pretend that she simply doesn't exist.

It's always been like this.

People don't really choose to associate with her in their work freely, but if they're assigned to be in a group with her, somehow everyone will find themselves together in one unit plus her, rather than all of them together. It doesn't matter if it's three people, four people, five, or any other number. She's somehow always the odd one out.

When her bootlace comes loose and she needs to stop to tie it, nobody stops to wait for her or looks back her way until after she sprints to catch up. They then turn for a brief second, perhaps afraid they're being rushed, but only seeing her, their bored, disinterested expressions turn away as quickly as if they had seen nothing at all. When she leaves the cathedral after sessions of chores and prayers, and everyone veers off down all possible corridors and streets, heading out in groups of two or more to their destinations, she has no choice but to quickly hustle out of there by

herself on her way to her quarters alone—because it kind of stings to look at everyone else every day.

In a way, one gets used to it, yes. One gets used to being an outcast and alone and, in general, worthless. But to say that one becomes numb isn't entirely correct either. Yes, there is a certain level of numbness that sets into place. But rather than this numbness being a full shut off of feelings and ache, it is rather simply a new lowest baseline of existence. Being numb in this context doesn't mean feeling nothing; it means feeling the same bad feeling for so long—the emptiness—that it becomes the standard.

In adult life, ugly people aren't treated as viciously by their peers as they might have been when they were all young and without inhibitions, but that is not because their peers have learned to better themselves, but rather that they have learned to protect their own social images, and so, the treatment becomes one of total, undeniable disinterest and distance rather than direct attacks, which would make them look bad within their inner and outer social circles.

It's not wrong to want to be beautiful. In essence, it's the same as wanting to be healthy, strong, rich, smart, or any other positive attribute. It serves to make life for the possessor of such things much, much easier, and who doesn't want an easier life?

Guezel adjusts the straps of her expensive rucksack—very out of place for a priestess with a more than meager take-home pay—looking ahead of herself at the others walking there, talking to one another about this and that. Her standard-issue robes, tailored and custom lined with a sleek, comfortable silk, flow against her as she walks, her nice boots— muddied—striking the stones.

She's recently gone through a phase of overcompensation by trying to be as fashionable as possible. People don't like her face, her hair, her body—just about anything that is her, really. So, she's tried to take control of the things she can control. Her bones are what they are, but she can control her hygiene, what she wears, her hair—on which she spends the last of her salary after clothes—the ash lining under her eyes, and the off-red, soft, waxy grease for her lips.

With each of these things, which she became obsessed about after their discovery, she was certain that they would be the healing for her wrongness, that they would "fix" whatever problem she had. Maybe if she dressed

nicer, people would realize she didn't actually have such a weird body. Maybe if she took better care of her face, people wouldn't think it was so ugly. Maybe if she learned to take care of her hair properly, according to its unique needs, people wouldn't look at it like they would at a rat's nest.

But the problem is that, after each and every one of these attempts, people just still wouldn't look at her to begin with.

So she just moved on to the next thing and then the next thing, and one day, she simply ran out of things to try, and that was that.

Everyone laughs up ahead.

Guezel freezes up, stiffening like a board as she stands perfectly still and looks at them. They're laughing at her, right? Sweat pearls on her skin almost immediately, soaking the fabric of her robe even more than it already is in this furnace of a dungeon, a cold chill running up her spine.

But they're not.

They just keep walking, talking about something that isn't her.

She hates when people laugh in public. As soon as she hears it, no matter where or when, her first thought is that it's about her. Again, this hasn't actually happened in a long time, but it happened so often when she was younger that it's simply imprinted into her now. The sound of laughter, without fail, brings her dread.

Guezel looks around herself at the corridor they're in. It's one of a hundred and some. They reached the next room of the Demon King's castle, only to find out it is a labyrinth of sorts. There is a core room lined with dozens and dozens of tunnels, and it's impossible to say which one is the right one, so the crusade sent several scouting parties into each tunnel. This little group of theirs is one such thing. She wasn't chosen by these other members of the crusade so much as they were assigned to be together by the raid leader.

Something clacks against her boot.

As if provoked by her own thoughts, the lace of her boot seems to have come loose and undone, the aglet striking against the leather. She sighs, kneeling down, not bothering to say anything because it wouldn't get her anything other than a sour look at best or vacant disinterest of people who pretend not to hear her at worst. The priestess works for a minute in the dark, fumbling with the lace to try and tie it up right, before rising back up, shaking out the leg to see that the boot is sitting right, and then looks ahead of herself, toward the emptiness.

They didn't just keep on walking—it's almost like they went out of their way to walk faster. She can't even see them anymore.

Guezel lowers her head, staring at a puddle for a second, where some white strings have fallen into, before she realizes that the eyes in it are staring back at her and she breaks contact, quickly shuffling onward to try and catch up with the group.

There's a fork in the path.

Guezel stands there at the end of the tunnel, looking at the diverging branches that break off—one to the left and one to the right.

The rest of the group isn't in sight, and she can't hear them either. The priestess, worried, rubs her arm and looks around the area for any markings, like scuffs on the ground, that could maybe give her a hint. However, she can't see anything. The floors are made up of meticulously lined brickwork, none of which is displaced, and there isn't any layering of disturbed dust or sand or anything of the sort.

Silently, she swears beneath her breath, a cool anxiety building in her again. She doesn't expect them to wait, but the fact they didn't even make some kind of mark to let her know which way they went is really a new blow she hasn't experienced before. They knew she was in their group and walking with them. Surely, they had to notice she wasn't there at the junction.

Should she go back?

Guezel looks back over her shoulder, down the long corridor that leads back to the chamber they started from.

. . . But if she goes back, she might get in trouble.

She might get accused of cowardice or dereliction of duty. Sure, she could say she got separated from her group, but would anyone really believe that? Probably not. They wouldn't really care if it's true. One look, and they'll be sure it is, and she'll be punished. These things have happened before. She's had plenty of extra chores and duties in the cathedral hoisted onto her for things like this.

But that they'd do it in the Demon King's castle, where their lives are actually on the line, is far grimmer than even she had expected. It's heartless. All by herself, she could actually die here.

The priestess looks back toward the two paths, closing her eyes and listening as she tries to make a choice. She has to take one of them. Going

back isn't an option. She'll just quietly move through. If there's anything scary, she can always run back the way she came. At least she'll have proof that she tried her best if some monster is chasing her out toward the rest of the crusade.

As sad as it is, that might be her best bet at this point.

Fumbling with her thumb, which rests trapped beneath the shoulder strap of her bag, Guezel nods and heads left. She's not really sure of any particular reasoning for this choice. It's just a fifty-fifty pick guided by her gut feeling.

There's nobody here.

Guezel looks around herself, staring at the chamber she's arrived in. It's an underground, cavernous space. Water crashes in the distance, coming from a small fall that runs down the wall into a large pool of unnaturally bright blue water that shimmers as if glowing with its own light. Ruins of an ancient white marble temple lie strewn about the area. Collapsed pillars and archways dot the space, hidden, in part, by the fine mist and softly roaring voice of the falls that never dry.

"Hello?" calls Guezel quietly, looking around at the chamber.

Is this the next floor of the castle?

... No, it doesn't seem like it. She didn't ascend or descend. She's still on the same floor.

The wary priestess looks around the area, scanning the ruins as she walks, trying to find her group. There doesn't seem to be much of anything here, actually. There aren't any people. There aren't any monsters. There's just the ruins, the water, and her.

As odd as it is, given that her life is on the line, she's very thankful for this.

Guezel can only imagine what would have happened if she had actually found her party. As always in such situations, she would have gotten some snide remark about finally catching up, or that they thought she had ditched them—the shamelessness of the statement never quite seems to bother them as they make it.

The priestess climbs over a collapsed pillar, brushing the deeply green ferns that grow over it aside, as she steps toward the water, looking at it.

She can't see her reflection. The disturbance from the falls causes too many ripples and too many waves, and the image is distorted and broken

and, for this, she's innately grateful without being able to say or even think of any reason as to why. It's a trained, inner reaction.

When one really hates oneself, one goes out of their way to avoid one's own reflection. This can be as simple as averting one's gaze when entering a washroom so as not to see oneself in the looking glass. It can mean never going outside on rainy days, never staring into the windows of shops upon passing for fear of seeing something too much within the glass.

The turmoil of disturbed water brings her peace.

She rises, looking around the room, and then sits down, leaning with her back against a crumbled pillar as she stares at the water cascading down from above.

How did she get here?

Guezel leans back, resting the back of her head against the stone, and listens to the water as she thinks about, well, vaguely everything.

She's not even sure why she signed up to go on this crusade. Demon King this, Demon King that.

She doesn't actually care.

The world wasn't ever really nice to her, so she's not that worried about it, honestly. And as for herself, well, she's not that worried, honestly. It doesn't matter. Somehow, she just ended up here. Even back then, she became a priestess after her childhood education because she didn't know what else to do with her life, even if she's not exactly pious. Plus, it allowed her to excuse herself from . . . other, more physical matters of body and heart, from which she wouldn't likely be able to partake anyway. She's always just sort of drifted from one thing to the next, not because it's what she wants from life but because it's just . . . what's next.

"Did you get lost too?" asks a voice from the side.

Guezel jumps to her feet, the stones beneath her boots crunching as she turns, looking in surprise at the person sitting behind her atop the broken base of a crumbled pillar, leaning back with legs outstretched, a pad of paper and pen in his hands. He looks her way.

"It's a big place," says the strange man, a laissez-faire tone to his voice.

Instinctively, she lowers her eyes, allowing him to make eye contact with the top of her hood.

"Who're you?!" she asks, not recognizing him. Although, to be fair, it would be more surprising if she did, since she doesn't actually know anybody. But she does know he wasn't a part of her group.

"Lost," replies the man, tapping against his stack of paper. "A few too many lefts and rights here, you know?"

Oh.

He must be with one of the other groups. There's probably a second entrance to this chamber somewhere in the ruins.

"Yeah," says Guezel. "Any idea which way we have to go?"

"Sorry," he replies. "I guess if I knew that, I wouldn't be here thinking it out," says the man.

"Right . . ." Of course. That was a dumb question. She shouldn't always ask dumb questions.

"But it's not a bad place to be lost, right?" he asks as the scratching continues. "Very scenic."

Guezel presses a smile out with pursed lips, like she was trained to do in priestess social training. It's good to smile when people make jokes. It helps social cohesion. It's not that it was a terrible joke and she wouldn't smile at it normally, but these sorts of things just don't really reach her anymore. "Yes," agrees the priestess, her feigned maybe-real-maybe-fake smile not reaching him anyway, since her obscured face is aimed toward the ground.

"Have you been here long?" she asks, turning back to the water. "Why not just go back the way you came?" The woman sits back down on the ground, leaning against the collapsed pillar again, fumbling with the ends of her sleeves as she looks down between her boots at the ground.

"A while, I guess," he answers, scratching coming from his paper as he works. She can only assume he's a scout, making a map for future documentation. "And I tried that, but somehow, I circled back around and ended up here again," says the man. "It's a funny place, the castle."

". . . *Funny* . . ." repeats Guezel. "I'm having the time of my life."

"I bet," he replies. "Hey, weird question," says the stranger. "Can you do me a favor and stand next to that column there?"

"Huh?" Guezel lifts her gaze slightly, looking at him from below the fabric of her hood toward his outstretched pen, which is pointing toward a column by the water.

"Just for a minute," he continues, lifting his sketch pad and showing it to her. "I could really use a person to show scale here."

She looks away and toward the pillar, fumbling with her sleeves.

"Can't you just . . . draw a person without me doing that?" she asks.

"It's not the same thing," he explains. "Having a reference lets me see that the details line up." Guezel frowns, fumbling with her hands and looking at the column covered in ivy and flowers—very out of place in the Demon King's desolate, dry, hot castle.

"I'd rather not . . ." she mutters quietly, feeling paranoid about this. Is this some kind of setup? He's trying to get her to do something stupid, right? Her mind races, trying to go through all the possibilities, given her experience in such manners up until this point.

The first scenario in her head tells her that he's going to calmly sketch as she stands there and then show her some picture of an ugly witch's face.

Maybe the others are here after all?

Guezel looks around the room nervously, expecting half-snickering faces to be barely peeking out of the ruins, watching her and waiting for her to make a fool of herself so that they can justify their usual laughter at her by saying that she's foolish, when in reality, they've once again gone out of their way to make her look so.

But there's nobody there.

"Please?" he asks. "I'll only need a minute. Just to make sure the sizes are all right."

"Can't . . . can't you just stand there yourself?" she mutters.

"I would, but I'd have a very hard time drawing me standing there then," he explains.

Ah. She asked something stupid again.

Of course he can't stand there and draw himself for reference. How would that even work? He wouldn't be able to see himself in the frame of the scene outside of his imagination, which isn't helpful for a detailed sketch.

"It's okay," he says. "Never mind. I'll work it out."

She's not really sure why, but her voice calls out, "Wait." Maybe she still has some innate desire to be useful in the hopes that this might convince people to like her. She had tried this during her years of becoming a priestess, diving deep into industriousness and productivity to compensate for her lack of exterior grace.

It didn't work.

All that happened was that people just unloaded even more work onto her than they would usually do, and she, dumb and desperate enough to want to be accepted, took it on until, eventually, it all came crashing down on her.

Nervously and quietly, she shuffles over to the pillar by the water, looking down at the ground. "Like this?" she asks, watching her boots press into the wet stones below.

"A little to the right, so you're in front of it please," he replies.

". . . Here?"

"Thank you, that's perfect," says the man. "Hold it there for a second. Mind the water."

Guezel stares at the ground, her heart striking in her chest as she stands there, very much akin to a fearful animal. In a way, her life isn't different from that of a mouse's, standing in the middle of the field and always watching for the shadow of a hawk that will come at any second to snatch it away, like it had done so often before. Her life is that of a prey animal in a society that claims to have no such things. She knows it. She's fought against it as best as she can, but nothing's worked.

A mouse can't stop being a mouse.

Ugly can't stop being ugly.

She stands there tensely, listening to the scratching coming from the pillar and the droning of the waterfall as her sweaty fingers nervously rub against one another, her fidgeting boot sliding back and forth over the slick stones.

The priestess turns her head, looking back over the water and staring at it for a time, noticing something familiar.

There are white strings washing down the fall, floating into the pool. She thought it was foam at first, but as she leans down, looking at a few of them floating past toward an unseen drain in the pool, she recognizes them as thin, silky white fibers—the kind she had seen on the way here several times.

Curiously, she looks closer, and then, her very expensive and beautiful but not exactly functional boot loses its traction on the slick stones, and she falls in, not able to let out more than a squeak before she tumbles into the water, immediately tumbling as the current and her momentum cause her fabric-laden body, weighed down by the heavy bag on her back, to spin around, disorienting her.

Fighting against the water, she kicks and tries to swim out, but finds it impossible to do so, despite the surface now being above her. Her bag has gotten caught on some rocks or something below her and, since she's still wearing it, she's also tethered to the submerged underground. Of course,

the obvious thought is to just remove the straps of the bag and swim up, but given the icy coldness of the water and the sudden disorientation, mixed in with the fresh animal panic that she's about to die inside of the Demon King's castle after all, somehow, she just doesn't manage to make this simple thought come into reality.

Guezel flails, trying her best to fight against the current. Not having had the opportunity to hold her breath before falling in, her lungs are already starting to burn, along with the rest of her body, which stings deeply from the icy water.

She exhales, her body instinctively trying to open her airway even if she's underwater by forcing her to let go of her throat muscles, bubbles rising up from her mouth straight toward the hands that reach in and grab hold of her robe, which had cost her a full four months of her monthly salary to have tailored.

A moment later, she's pulled out of the water by a very strong grip that has absolutely no problems removing her and her bag in one yank.

Coughing out water, Guezel crawls to the embankment of the pond, apologizing profusely to the stranger who just saved her for having messed up while she looks down at her hands and the white threads wrapped around them. She shakes them off and looks at him—but only his boots and legs. She doesn't want to lift her head so that he can't see her face.

The wet stones, the white strings, the water—everything rumbles for a second as some disturbance, a vibration, moves through the ground.

"You need to hide," he says, ignoring her out-of-place apologies. "It senses you through the water."

"Huh?" she asks, slowly lifting her gaze—only reaching his chest—before a long, protracted groan comes from the distance, down from the tunnel she herself had come from.

"Ah, hell . . ." he mutters. "I thought it was further away. Get down!" he orders, and a second later, Guezel is yanked back to the pillar she was sitting at before, the fabric of her soaked hood now suffocatingly clinging to her face, together with her wet hair, as they hide.

The stranger shushes her from next to her as she quietly looks, watching as a . . . a thing . . . begins to move into the chamber.

At first, she thought the tunnel she had come from was sealing itself back closed with some soft, white flesh, as if it were a regrowing scar.

However, it's not. Rather, what comes is a large, soft, meaty thing with a white body and a black, round head at its elongated, wormy end that is too large for the tunnel but traverses it anyway. A maggot. No . . . something else . . .

Strands of white, shiny silk are wrapped around its body, torn and cut from the jagged stone walls of the castle it is too large to move through. Its shiny mandibles click and chitter excitedly. From its head emerge several stalklike growths—like thin mushrooms—that rise into the air, pulling free several silk cocoons from the imprisonment of its body that dangle freely in the air like the many broodsacs of a spider.

And inside of them are, what are undeniably, people.

Guezel's instincts are to scream and run, so she proceeds to start wanting to do exactly that.

Before she can even move, a hand that smells of dyes covers her mouth, smearing her face with color, while another one presses her back into hiding, leaving the same marks of touch on her wet robe.

The Thing That Weaves's stalks turn toward them as they hide again. There's a sickly, wet squelching as it begins to move. Its soft, supple, grubby body slides over broken stones and rocks, over debris and rubble, as the mass moves toward them, *squick*ing and *ick*ing like the sound of a fist pressing ground meat over and over until it loses all coherence and becomes an undefinable paste.

The stranger holds her there as a shadow moves over them, the air above their heads filled with nothing but pliant, soft, wet flesh. Her heart threatens to break her ribs with every strike it makes. Hands press against her face and body, holding her still as the maggot crawls over them, over the collapsed pillar, its sagging lower half sliding only inches over their heads, close enough to touch with a tongue with only a little exertion.

The screaming voices of her party members, the people she had lost contact with on their way down the tunnel, come to her ears as she lies there against the man and the column, coming from the cocoons it holds on its long stalks. A slick, slimy ooze leaks down from the stone pillar they're against as it scrapes against the maggot, the lubricating jelly protecting its soft body from its movements in the tight passages of this region glooping downward in abundance—a thick, colorless mucus that runs over his shoulder and between them.

It passes by, crawling into the water, its massive body filling the pool entirely as it feels around, and then, finding nothing, crawls up the side of the fall, simply arching its massive body over the overhang and pulling the rest up with little effort.

The two of them watch as it, up on the cliff, reaches toward the ceiling, the elongated stalks on its head pressing further and further out, stretching themselves into firm rods that reach the barrier above, pasting them with a sticky substance that then holds the people-filled cocoons in place, impossibly high up above the ground.

And now, for the first time since she got here, Guezel looks up at the ceiling she had failed to notice at all, given that she never looks anywhere but down.

Covering it, all around the stones, are silk cocoons the size of people. Dozens, maybe hundreds—she doesn't know. There's so little light and so much movement above from the squirming, fighting contents of the soft prisons that the ceiling itself, which ought to be stone, looks the same as the supple moving body of the maggot that birthed it.

It ripples.

Her panicked, labored breathing, which still hasn't recovered quite yet from almost drowning, can't quite keep pace with her attempts to sustain her life, given that her mouth is still covered by the man's hand.

"You can't touch the water," he whispers. "It hears you if you do," he explains quietly into her ear, causing her to think back to the many puddles she had seen on the way.

They weren't just puddles of water from a leaky dungeon.

They were alarms. Each and every one of them a signal to the thing, the maggot, that something is coming its way.

A hand slowly retracts itself from her mouth and then from her body. "You should go," he says. "It's going to do a lap. It won't be back the way you came for at least another two hours."

She crawls away, the terror of dying now weighing far less in her heart than the terror of being touched, let alone so closely. Guezel quickly scrambles over the rocks, wiping her face with her dirty hands, looking down at the smears of ink on her fingers as her head buzzes, far too much air reaching her now all at once from her hyperventilation, her vision shaking as she looks away and toward the ceiling.

What the hell is this place?

"I don't want to be here anymore," says Guezel, realizing something. "I don't . . . I don't . . ." She breathes, holding a hand against her heart as if to stop it from breaking free through her aching chest.

"It's not so bad," he says. "You get used to its quirks," explains the stranger. "It has a rough exterior, but when you look past that, there's a real beauty to it."

". . . Beauty?" she mutters, not sure if she's hearing him right.

This is the most horrifying thing she's ever seen. Even the floors until now, with all of their terrors, haven't really hit her quite like this one just now. But maybe that's because this time, rather than being in the back of some defensive line, she's right in the middle of it, by herself, alone.

One gets used to being alone in life and, under normal circumstances of everyday life, that's . . . fine. A person learns to make do, and then, after a while, they even begin to love solitude. However, the danger of this trap only becomes apparent when one is no longer in a normal circumstance.

Being alone, in the wild, can very quickly mean death in all manner of gruesome ways.

So what does one do, when one has no choice but to be alone despite their best efforts? What does one do when one becomes desperate?

Anything.

Survival is paid for with any price.

Her breathing starts to slow as she—her lizard brain hissing for her to come up with a way to not have to go back alone, to not have to be alone after what she just saw, because doing so would mean to die as far as its shrieking voice is concerned—exhales one final time in a slow, controlled breath. "I'm okay," says Guezel. "I'm . . . I'm fine," she lies, running a hand over her shoulder and looking at the thick mucus that's stuck between her fingers. "Let's . . . let's finish that sketch, okay?" she asks, rising back to her feet and then standing next to the pillar.

Now, to a reasonable person in this situation, the idea of a drawing would be beyond absurd. After they both came this close to becoming prey to that monster, after they both came a breath's distance from true horror, the idea of suggesting that they finish something as inconsequential as a sketch of this forgotten, off-branch of a room seems like evidence of a total loss of sanity.

But that's because they aren't thinking with the mindset of a desperate, wounded creature.

In her mind, the drawing mattered to the stranger, so by insisting on its continuing, she's doing him a favor to repay him for saving her just now. This act is a bargaining chip; it's her offer of reciprocity which will allow her to not have to face the future and to sate the hissing voice in her head with the only solution it offers, even if it makes little sense logically.

"Are you sure?" he asks as she leans against the same column as before, making sure that her footing is better this time. "Thank you," says the man. "I appreciate it."

"Just . . . don't . . . I mean, yeah," says Guezel, nodding and looking at him—sort of—through her lowered hood. "Can we go back together after this?" she asks, doing her best not to hear the muffled sounds coming from far above their heads that she is now able to distinguish from the sound of the roaring water.

"Sorry," replies the man, sitting down on the broken pillar where they just hid as he grabs the paper from the side and returns to his work. "I can't. But you'll be fine. Just go straight back down the way you came."

"Huh? Why not?" she asks. "I thought you're lost too?"

"I am," he confirms, the sound of scratching on paper coming to her ears. "But I have to go another way," explains the man.

Guezel, now meekly lifting her gaze past her lowered hood, looks at him for the first time—at his face, which is gray and ashen, and his eyes, which are yellow and unnatural in their tinge.

He isn't human.

"What are you?!" she yells in surprise, her soaked rucksack pressing against the pillar as she watches him work, indifferent to her sudden surprised reaction. He sits there, his hair hanging down over the paper as he draws, finishing his strokes with ink that doesn't quite stay where it should on the page—as if it were a living shadow rather than pigment.

The man holds his drawing out in front of him, tilting first it and then his head as he examines it, an unnatural shadow coming from behind him and covering one of his eyes as he tilts his head, the two of them looking at the sketch, before then turning her way.

"Lost," says the gallu, a demon of the Demon King's creation, as he rises to his feet and moves toward her. Guezel's instincts tell her to run, but she doesn't because . . . she doesn't. Her legs just don't really listen to the voice in her head as the man approaches her, standing before her and towering over her.

She looks up in terror at his face staring down her way, his yellow eyes cutting into her as he stands far too uncomfortably close, which in the context of her social understanding, is anywhere near her at all, let alone a breath away, which is terrifyingly close—demon or not.

He lifts his hands, and she flinches, not because of that but because she suddenly realizes that he's been looking at her face for seconds now from this close.

"What do you think?" asks the demon. Her terrified eyes slowly turn, looking at the paper he holds out to her; at the drawing. "I'm never sure about pieces like this. I always think they're a little . . . I don't know . . ." He sighs. "I feel like I need the edge to my work, and in things like this, I feel like people just won't like it because it's missing the grit," explains the artist. "But then, I also worry they won't like my other pieces because maybe they're too gritty," he finishes.

Depicted there is a woman—her—standing by the water in the room; this room they're in. But rather than the column of stone being behind her, the column is depicted as a cocoon like those on the ceiling—except this one is broken and ripped apart and from it, she emerges, radiant.

"You see, the problem is that, well, beauty is in the eye of the beholder," he explains. "So, what do you do when your best work isn't appreciated by the masses?" asks the demon artist. "The largest collection of eyes?"

Guezel looks at him, deeply confused and terrified and also confused in many other ways that are hard to explain. Nobody has ever drawn her before; not like this in detail, and not in a way that is flattering in any sense at all.

"I . . . I—!"

A finger touches the bottom of her chin, lifting her head which has already started lowering again to instinctively hide her face.

"You realize it doesn't matter what they think." The man shakes his head as he looks at her from up close. "They're animals. Mindless. They can't see it."

"See . . . see . . ." She gulps, accepting her death. "See what?" mumbles Guezel.

"What matters most," he replies. "Real beauty," finishes the demon painter, Abydos, as he swipes a finger over the drawing in his hands, bringing it to life, the woman on the paper moving and flying around the scene, the living shadows causing the scene to dance with joyful colors that all stem from black.

And now, she's as good as dead, metaphorically pierced through the heart.

"I can't go with you," repeats the man, pulling away, which causes her a strange mix of terror in ways she can't grasp due to her inexperience. He looks over his shoulder, back at her, the shadow that sprouts from him reaching out a hand. "But I need a model," he says. "If you want to come with me," asks the demon, his voice surrounded by droning water and the muffled screams of people who are "on her side."

Her outstretched hand reaches out before her mind can form any other thoughts, immediately grabbing hold of the shadow's grasp without so much as a moment's hesitation.

A soul isn't easily corruptible if it is molded within a solid firmament of compassion, understanding, and nourishing wholeness. However, in the total absence of such things, an intrusion into the sanctity of the spirit is very easy, as it will latch on to literally any spark of that which the human soul innately craves and has been deprived of for so long; that for which it always hungers and, in those who are void of its presence, starve for: the evidence and truth that such a thing as unwarranted, indiscriminate kindness is able to exist somewhere in this world. It is a beauty that surpasses anything else in the material world, and it is perhaps the most wicked weapon fielded by the Demon King to date.

The perhaps naive priestess goes with the demon, throwing away a lifetime of training, lifestyle, and other such investments, shedding them off as if they had never really mattered at all, much as if throwing off threads of a broken cocoon.

The Demon King's castle claims a soul for itself to make use of in the coming skirmishes, taking it for itself not through death or resurrection, but just by asking.

THE RETCHING DARKNESS

~ [Peribsen] ~
Gallu | ♂ | Craftsman {Reengineer}
Location: The Demon King's Castle, Floor Thirty-One
Level: 100

Perennial shadows surround the man as he stands there, his silhouette framed within the empty halls of the Demon King's castle. His presence—the only disturbance inside of a massive, square, empty chamber—stands out, as if he himself were the first nail struck into an otherwise motionless board. His hands are held out at his sides, as if he were holding something aloft and had yet to decide what to do with it. His body is stiff, marking his indecision, as he stares blankly toward the ground. His matted hair, greased into long, thin strands that hang over his neck in bundles, waves in the underground winds that push through the depths of the Demon King's wretched castle.

Air pressure inside an open-mouthed cave system will, generally, always balance itself out to be equal to the pressure outside on the surface. However, the load placed on the surrounding material increases with depth, as does the makeup of the stone and soil. With varying compositions comes varying properties in relation to structural integrity and so on.

Of course, there is a bit of leeway here, given that the castle is more of a magical, artificial construct rather than a naturally occurring cave system. Different rules apply.

His hair blows as the castle exhales, the hot winds that stem from the heat source at its deepest pit, the Demon Core, pressing outward, as the pressure inside the tunnel system is greater than that of the world outside.

In turn, after this purge and the pressure equilibrium, the air pressure outside of the castle will be greater than the inside, leading to an influx of air as it is drawn through the gate and down into the bowels of the underground. In. Out. In. Out.

He stands there, his hair moving in just that same motion—back and then forth.

It's as if the castle as a whole were a living, breathing thing. And, really, who is to say. Maybe it is?

The properties of the Demon King's magic are, in and of themselves, unique.

The once man, Peribsen, who is now a gallu under the Demon King's employ, lifts his gaze, following the underworld's exhalation toward the door leading to the upper reaches of the castle.

There, off in the distance, comes the counterforce.

It's not the wind; it's the crusade. It is the destructive force that comes to destroy this unique construction—just the same as people had come to destroy his bridge.

The world is full of so many unique things, some of nature and some of nurture, such as this place—or such as his own precious bridge. And just as with it, there will always be those who desire to destroy its incredible, unique beauty.

The engineer watches the lights come from a distance.

Humans as a whole aren't capable of really appreciating beauty—neither natural nor that which they themselves make. Yes, there are those who cherish it deeply. However, there are also those who would tear it down, who would cut it flat and lay roads over it; those who would destroy amazing works of wonder only for the sake of logical sense and rationality, robbing the future world of such amazing gifts for the sake of their own gray pragmatism.

Just like humans make their own cities more droll, more pragmatic, more gray, functional, and inorganic with every passing generation—robbing them of their unique characteristics and charm—so, too, will they do to the world as a whole.

He's decided.

Something roars in the distance, the drone of a marching stampede with weary, grim faces led by a speck of azure blue.

Peribsen turns his head.

The color reminds him of the bluebirds that used to fly over his bridge.

He lifts his hands, the ground shaking and rumbling as if the stone floors were attached to strings wrapped tightly around his fingers, pulling them this way and that within sight of the encroachers, changing the world, changing the bones of the Demon King's castle, as if he were reshaping a body by cracking its solids. Deep water presses out from the moving surfaces like leaking marrow, hissing as it touches the hot surfaces.

He begins to shape and make floor thirty-one of the castle himself as his first grand project in his new employ.

Great, twisting organic spires begin to move and grow out of the soil and rock. Things grow from the surfaces—a combination of organic and inorganic matter, symbolizing the communion of the two worlds in which they all live. The square chamber, now blank, changes. The entire room, as massive as it is, fills and tightens unnaturally like a compressed intestine full of biomatter, squished by a hand that has reached into someone's gut to clench it shut. Fluids of the world and those born of the magics of the Demon King's power begin to leak and drip all around them as the chamber turns from a square into a long, sideways cylinder—a tubelike tunnel. He stands on one end, and the encroaching crusade comes from the other.

Peribsen moves, the castle moving with him, as decreed by His Majesty, the king. Rough edges and perforations begin to form in the cylinder on all sides on the inside of the shape. The stone fractures and tears as if it were being perforated. Organic, soft, living growths begin to fill the rips, pressing into the damp inside from beyond, at first like roots but then like worms.

The tunnel begins to break further, twisting into ups and downs as if its overall shape as a whole was that of the inside of a parasite-riddled snake ascending a ledge.

Movement fills the crooked space—not from people but from things.

The Demon King's castle, as a whole, is a beautiful architectural marvel. However, it has only represented the inorganic nature of the world—construction, building, rigid shapes, and ideas of the physical and metaphysical planes.

What it has been missing is organics.

Organic shapes. Organic smells. Organic movements.

Architecture moves. It lives and breathes.

It is the creation of organic beauty from inorganic substances.

~ [Dungeon] ~
[Section Four - Wrath]
Floor {31}: Crush
A sensitive space, the thirty-first floor of the Demon King's castle is made out of a confused mixture of meat and grime. It pulsates, writhing in and out, moving those who tread through it by itself, pressing them past difficult ridges and clusters of parasites to wear them down.
The walls undulate in and out, compressing repeatedly at different intervals to facilitate this process.
It smells unpleasant.
Room Effects: Living Bowels - The room is alive. The things in the room are alive.
Every death results in a direct feeding of the room, allowing the room to grow stronger as it takes the bodies to use them to grow.

~ [Cartouche] ~
Gallu | ♀ | Dancer
Location: The Demon King's Castle, Floor Nine
Level: 100

What was wrong with it?

Cartouche stands on the platform, looking around the heavy, perfume-filled room on floor nine of the Demon King's castle. It is a floor that not only the first incursion party but also the second—the crusade—fought their way through. It didn't stand up to the challenge.

Demons bound by the spiritual realm of lust—succubi and incubi—wander the room, having returned to life after a sufficient period of death. They are restored by the magics of the Demon King's castle. However, with the crusade being now far deeper down below in the dungeon, they have nothing to do, and so, they mill about their own lives, like performers hustling around in the back of a staging area between shows.

The dancer watches them move about.

This floor was a failure, clearly. It is, regarding the audience, provocative and engaging, but it failed to captivate the souls of many for . . . extended periods of time.

Several members of both incursion parties fell to the room's charms, letting their spirits be corrupted by its magics. Their bodies having broken and changed, they shifted from their prior shapes to those of the demon inhabitants of the floor.

But just a small segment of the total number of intruders.

The dancer sways on her feet as she thinks, not dancing to any particular tune but just keeping herself busy and in motion as she observes the space—the failed act of her performance. *Failed* not in that it was an entirely pointless endeavor, but rather in that it didn't reach the mark she had hoped it would have.

The same can be said of many other floors.

Once is a mistake; twice is a failure. It would be a shame to repeat this pattern a third time for any future entries into the castle, which are sure to come shortly. The world is large, after all, and there are many more outsiders who would seek to stop the Demon King's great work.

As such, there are so many more members of the audience to come to the stages of her performances, of which this is one.

An artist of any nature creates failures over and over again, as if constantly birthing out of a dead womb, creating only silent, still things. However, one day, the thing they create will be different. It will be different not only in the eyes of the creator but also in the eyes of the audience; in the vision of the world as a whole, it might be perceived as something beautiful.

However, the process to get there is . . . messy.

Cartouche waves over a demon, looking at it and holding out a hand for a dance. Assuming something else, the succubus takes her palm as the dancer starts to move.

A ripple moves up along the succubus's arm, the monster screaming in fear and pain as the movement separates its flesh from its bones. Its sinews rip, its joints falling loose. Its limp body falls apart into a screaming, powerless rag doll of disjointed meat that she swings around as her dancing partner.

Screams fill the room from all sides as the stage is reset for a new dance, something different that uses the lessons of the past to move the great act on toward a place of ascendancy.

~ [Abydos] ~
Gallu | ♂ | Demon Painter
Location: The Demon King's Castle, Floor Sixteen
Level: 100

Change.

The woman breathes, her chest heaving and sweat pouring down her face as she stands there, rigidly in pose, the sweltering heat of the Demon King's castle enveloping her body.

Life is ever moving and ever changing. It isn't a rigid, static thing. It's soft and malleable. It has a give when one presses against it, just the same as it moves against oneself, forcing a person to give in some manner. Life as a concept itself is alive in that manner.

This is the weakness of the art of depiction—painting, drawing, and such things. It is the attempt to capture movement in something that is very much still. It's trying to capture a river in a jar without also losing the flow of the water. There's an impossibility to the challenge that is beyond the human state, locked in its innate shackles of physicality.

His thumb presses into the priestess's cheek, his upper palm resting on her chin as he turns her head to the side, hot, living breath flowing over the edge of his index finger that seals her lip.

"Don't move your face," says the demon painter, stepping back and looking at her—a woman undergoing change, as is natural in life. "I need it like this."

Life never stagnates. It always warps and flows, moving in some way or another as it advances toward a state that it defines as perfect. This state is entropy.

The living condition differs in this way from life, as those with a passionate soul do not seek entropy, but rather the opposite. The full, total manifestation of everything brought into frame and reference; an ushering in of the vastness of life's many experiences, made whole through the process of manifestation.

Abydos, the demon painter, frames her with his fingers, stepping backward and forward again, his fingers sinking into the flesh of her torso and legs as he turns her this way and that way, mechanically adjusting her pose like one would a doll before placing it on a shelf.

". . . Like this?" she asks, her hand on her shoulder, holding on to the fabric of her priestess's robe as if it were meant to stop her from falling down somehow, her eyes scanning the dark room they're in on the upper part of the Demon King's castle. It's a room the crusade has already moved through, herself included. It's a room that has been . . . insufficient.

It wasn't a good piece.

Or, well, maybe it wasn't bad. However, it failed to achieve what had been hoped for. It was one painting of the ten thousand needed to make up the staircase to the glory of perfection. But that's fine. He has an eternity to get this right. It was just the first real attempt, but there will be another now, this time with new tools and mechanisms. A painter has so much more to employ than just a brush and their imagination.

Their eyes meet, but she doesn't move her face, as instructed. His hand rests on top of hers, both of them moving at the same time in the same direction to pull the already loosened fabric of the sweat-soaked robe gently down off her shoulder, exposing her.

"No," replies the painter as the stained, white robe drapes down over both of their arms near her midriff. "Like this," says the demon to the corrupted priestess Guezel, as both of their hands move back up again over her stomach and chest, placing her hand back where it was a moment before. "Don't move your face," he repeats, letting go of her hands and body with his and letting go of her changing expression with his own as he turns to return to his easel.

Living shadow leaks from the canvas, running down the easel's spread legs as heavy condensation. It pools down at its stiff feet like spilled ink that he steps into. Abydos looks at the blank surface as he considers the changes to make before then taking his brush and setting to the task. Living, moving lines of shadow crawl out from the puddle, creeping toward the room, toward the priestess, like fresh, scratchy pencil sketches on paper—marks of changes to come.

~ [**Ruhr, the River Sorceress**] ~
Half Elf | ♀ | Sorceress
Rank: SSS
Location: The Demon King's Castle, Floor Thirty-One
Level: 100

The room rumbles, changing before her, the Demon King's castle once again making itself seen for what it really is.

Malignant.

Ruhr lifts her hands, staring blankly ahead of herself as she stands at the head of the crusade. Softly glowing water, imbued with holy magics that intensify in their radiance to a level that hadn't been present before, drips from her fingers as a surge of magic presses up through her core. The water rises from the base of her inner body, welling to the surface like the burst of a sudden realization. It comes forward, escaping from her, as she fully intends to not only flood this new floor before they step foot on it but to flood it so much that it bursts like an overfilled intestine—so that it ruptures, so that the Demon King and every other wretched, disgusting, foul thing below drowns a thousand times.

For her, this was all just a fun game before.

Then it was about survival.

And then it was about . . . something else—Zac.

And now . . .

The stones beneath her boots crack as her arms hold themselves out, as if holding the weight of the ocean itself aloft. A flood of violent, holy enchanted water blasts out of her hands and into the now changed room beyond it, which she refuses to even entertain.

One thousand demons and monsters are washed away by the rising tide, their bodies burning in the holy water as if it were acid.

The sorceress and the crusade march on forward, not stopping, as their boots crush over the melting bodies of the freshly dying and flooded.

Wash it away.

She's going to wash it all away.

All of it.

Ruhr stares blankly ahead as she walks straight through the tunnel and its horrors—now pacified—on the way to it, to the beast, to the rot that started all of this.

It's a gangrenous wound that needs to be cleansed.

The Demon King.

~ [**The Demon King**] ~

Souls Collected: 750,001/1,000,000

WARNING—THE DEMON CORE IS REACHING CRITICAL MASS.

Screams fill the world, stretching from every shadow born of the weak glows of candlelight that remain lit in the towers of civilization. A sea of flickering flames fights against the howl that never stops—the roaring of the Demon Core—as its radiating power makes itself heard throughout the world as a constant, never-ending drone.

The wretched Demon King sits on his throne, watching the waltz of souls trapeze through the superheated air of his court. The stone walls around him crack and crumble as even they begin to falter under the immense pressure that releases from his body. The paper he writes on no longer remains whole, instead burning to ash in his presence, requiring him to switch to more unconventional canvases for his work, his long, heavy claw cutting into the "paper" held out for him.

A cut, flayed, rolled out soul, stretched thin and wide, is held there by the demon Byblos, who sits on his lap, watching as he carves black magic words into the thing that screams but has no mobility of its own anymore.

His claw, radiating with supernatural heat, carves into the meat of the trapped thing, screaming with a hiss as he drags it along, writing a word that he, in all of his horrific maliciousness, simply doesn't understand the nature of. It's out of place.

But something, somewhere in his black heart, tells him to write it, and as an artist, he knows to listen to such inclinations, such musings, as they lead one to ideas and places one would have otherwise never gone toward. Such things are often very . . . unusual.

The lesser demon leans back against him, looking at the word that he cuts into the flayed being, her hair resting against his chest.

Goose.

~ [Shaushka] ~
Elf| ♀ | Classless
Location: The Wildlands
Level: 4

The elf stares at the demon general standing there. His body is covered in fur and bones.

Muffled voices fill the clearing; thousands of crying, screaming people, gathered into a mass of prisoners, stand bound and captured, surrounded by swarms of monsters of horrific shapes and compositions. Armies of the Vildt and the corrupted of many legions. The death march toward the Demon King's castle has come to a pause.

Others come too. Six figures more move out of the shadows, and all seven demon generals collect in the clearing, together with two more demon knights.

"... Ah ..." mutters Shaushka quietly, staring.

And then, all nine of the demons turn toward the north and begin moving, marching as a great horde that trails in the wake of the Demon King's castle toward the human capital that is now closer than ever. Thousands of bodies move as monsters usher the prisoners onward, the ground below them rumbling. The ashen, trodden, and dead landscape quakes as the demon army makes its way toward the final battlefield, which is not much further over the now still distant horizon.

There, she feels something calling to her, but she isn't quite sure what.

ABOUT THE AUTHOR

D. M. Rhodes is a rising star author in the fantasy and LitRPG space, crushing the top rankings with popular series such as Demon Core, Dungeon Item Shop, Sunflower: The LitRPG, and Reborn as the Black Knight. Find out more at www.DMRhodes.com!

DISCOVER
STORIES UNBOUND

PodiumAudio.com